STONE

COLD

A Chance and Choices Adventure

Book Seven

Lisa Gay

Chance and Choices

This book is a work of fiction. The names, characters, places, and incidents either are the product of the author's imagination or used factitiously. Any resemblance to an actual person, living or dead, business establishment, or event is entirely coincidental.

ISBN-13: 978-1-945858-15-4

In loving memory of Oliver.
I'll miss you, Dad.

Those Involved in these incidents:

Place of Origin – Dardanelle

Big Lou – Tavern owner and sponsor or the rock climbing contest

Fabienne- barmaid

Basil – rock climbing contestant

John Henry – rock climbing contestant

Bruce - rock climbing contestant pressed by his wife to continue

Frank - rock climbing contestant

Ross- rock climbing contestant

Pierre Lafayette– Frenchman and friend of Basil

Millie- purchaser of John Henry tickets and original owner of the coin with a hole

Place of Origin – Harmony

Ann Williams – oldest sister – Noah's wife

Stephanie Yates – middle sister – Eli's wife

Sally Williams – youngest sister

Eli Yates – Stephanie's husband

Tom Yates - Eli's father/owner of Yates Mercantile

Hattie Yates – Eli's dead mother

Smithfield Wyman –livery owner/ blacksmith/ sheriff (Smitty)

Mara Wyman- Smitty's wife

Earl Carpenter– a man, temporarily running Yates Mercantile

Clara Carpenter– Earl's wife

Joseph Pinckney – saloon owner (Joe)

Zachariah Eggleston – previous travel companion

Clyde Eggleston - Zachariah's father

Patty Eggleston – Zachariah's mother

Horace Devine– a friend, shot while tracking the

Butterfield Gang
Betsy Devine– Horace's wife
Eyanosa – Noah's stallion

Place of Origin – Indian Territory
Quapaw Land:
Noah Swift Hawk – Ann's husband (Tahatankohana)
Chetan – Noah's father
Bethany – Noah's mother
Luyu – Chetan's mother
Hanataywee – Noah's oldest sister
Ehawee – Noah's next oldest sister
Ke – Noah's brother
Chumani – Noah's youngest sister
James Williams –Ann, Stephanie, and Sally's uncle
Algoma Williams – James' wife
Dowanhowee – James' oldest daughter
Mache - James' second daughter
Mi - James' youngest daughter
Te – James' oldest son
Nanpanta – James' youngest son
Ppahiska – the village chief
Mikoishe – Ppahiska's wife
Chaska – Ppahiska's oldest son
Mikakh - Ppahiska's oldest daughter
Kanizhika - Ppahiska's second son
Eyota - Ppahiska's second daughter
Wakanda – village mystery man
Weayaya - Wakanda's daughter
Nikiata – mystery man-in-training
Enapay – Nikiata's father
Anpaytoo- Nikiata's mother
Mina – Nikiata's wife
Tatonga – a man of Noah's village
Metea - wife of Tatonga

Zitkala - Tatonga's daughter
Kimimela – Tatonga's second daughter
Capa – a man of Noah's village
Wichahpi – Capa's wife
Awinita – Capa's daughter
Paytah – a man of Noah's village
Mantu - a man of Noah's village
Nahimana – Mantu's wife
Wesa – chief of another Quapaw village

Cherokee Nation:
Waya- warrior of the Cherokee
Dustu – grandson of Waya and twin of Adahy/ Hanataywee's husband
Adahy - grandson of Waya and twin of Dustu/ Ehawee's husband
Tizhu – Weayaya's husband
Petang- Zitkala's husband
Leotie- chief of her village
Salali- chief of her village

Place of Origin – Kuhn Bayou
Minnie – Zachariah's wife

Place of Origin – Pine Bluff
Roscoe Bacon – owner Bacon's Trading Post
James Bacon – Eli's alias as Roscoe's nephew
Nancy Bacon – Sally's alias as Roscoe's niece

Place of Origin – Philadelphia
Reginald Canfield –guest in Lucy's house with Roy's ghost / pain doctor
Fabia Canfield – guest in Lucy's house with Roy's ghost / Reginald's wife

Abbott Doggett - guest in Lucy's house with Roy's ghost

Ophelia Doggett - guest in Lucy's house with Roy's ghost / Abbott's wife

Place of Origin – Unknown
Butterfield Gang – Gus, Ben, Roy, and others
Russell French – Traveling Resupply Business co-owner
Arnold Buzmann-Traveling Resupply Business co-owner
Beauty –mule, severely injured in winter storm
Dollie – mule, eye injured in winter storm
BlackJack – Edwin Snow's horse
Fred – a traveler who helped Joe
Hazel – Fred's wife

Place of Origin – Little Rock
Daniel Hall – Judge of State of Arkansas
Luke Smith –Noah's alias / doctor
Isabelle Smith –Ann's alias / Luke's wife
Marie - Stephanie's alias
Thaddeus Pratt - preacher
Martin Harrow – livery owner
Dollie Harrow – Martin's wife
Edwin Snow – original stable hand at Harrow's Livery and friend of Noah
S.R. Snow– Edwin's father
Mary Snow - Edwin's father
Robert Teal– Edwin's friend
Bertha Teal– Robert's wife
Phebe Teal – Robert and Bertha's baby daughter
David Thomas - Bertha's father
Louise Thomas – Bertha's mother

Simon Teal - Robert's father
Ruth Teal - Robert's mother
Clark – the owner of the general store
Candace Daniels – mugged woman\husband killed
Joe Smith – an assassin hired by Judge Hall
Zane Stone – alias of Joe Smith
Boots – Robert Teal's horse

Place of Origin – Fletcher Creek
Katie – Underground Railroad guide
Morris - Katie's husband / one of the people who
stopped the mugger Roy Butterfield
George - Katie and Morris's oldest son
Carmen - Katie and Morris's oldest daughter
Lewis –Morris's brother
Matt – one of the people who stopped Roy, the footpad
Sarah - Matt's wife
Elizabeth - Matt and Sarah's oldest daughter
Justin - Matt's oldest son
Will - Matt's brother
Andrew – Sarah's brother
Theodore – Roscoe's alternate identity (Theo)
Abraham – Noah's second alias
Lily – Ann's second alias

Place of Origin – Maumelle
Lucy – the owner of Lucy's Boarding House
Horatio Knapp– Man mugged in an alley
Esther Knapp– mugged in alley / Horatio's wife
Murray Strong – Esther Knapp's brother

Place of Origin – Perryville
Adeline – Innkeeper
Raymond Pence – a local farmer

Sebastian De La Cruz – town resident
Lola De La Cruz– town local resident
Chester – stable owner
Doctor Higgins – village doctor

Place of Origin – Fort Gibson
Colonel Stephen Howland – Commander
Sergeant Matthew McCormick - Master of Supplies
Sergeant Timothy Anders (Tim)
Private Ezra Knuckles
Private Ham Blanders
Private Morgan Finch
Private Dennis
Lieutenant Jackson
Lieutenant Olson

Place of Origin – New York
Woodrow Yates
Helen Yates

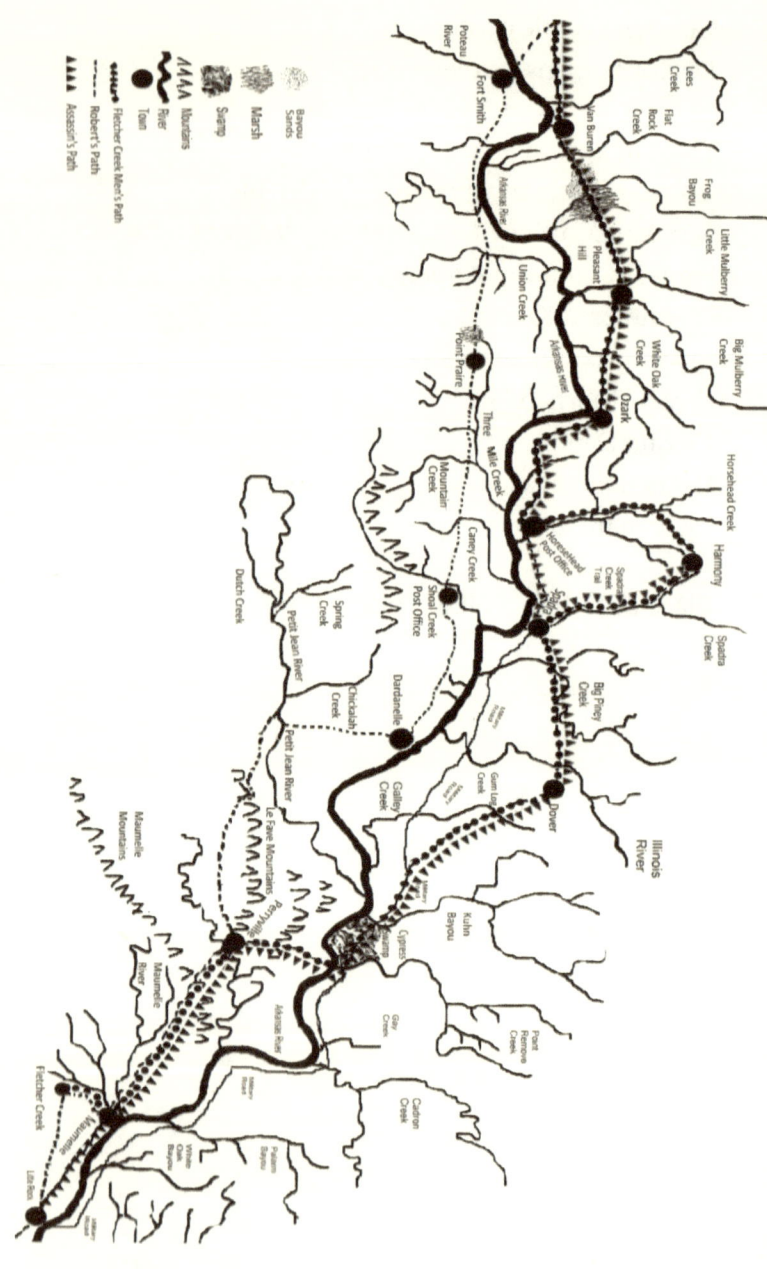

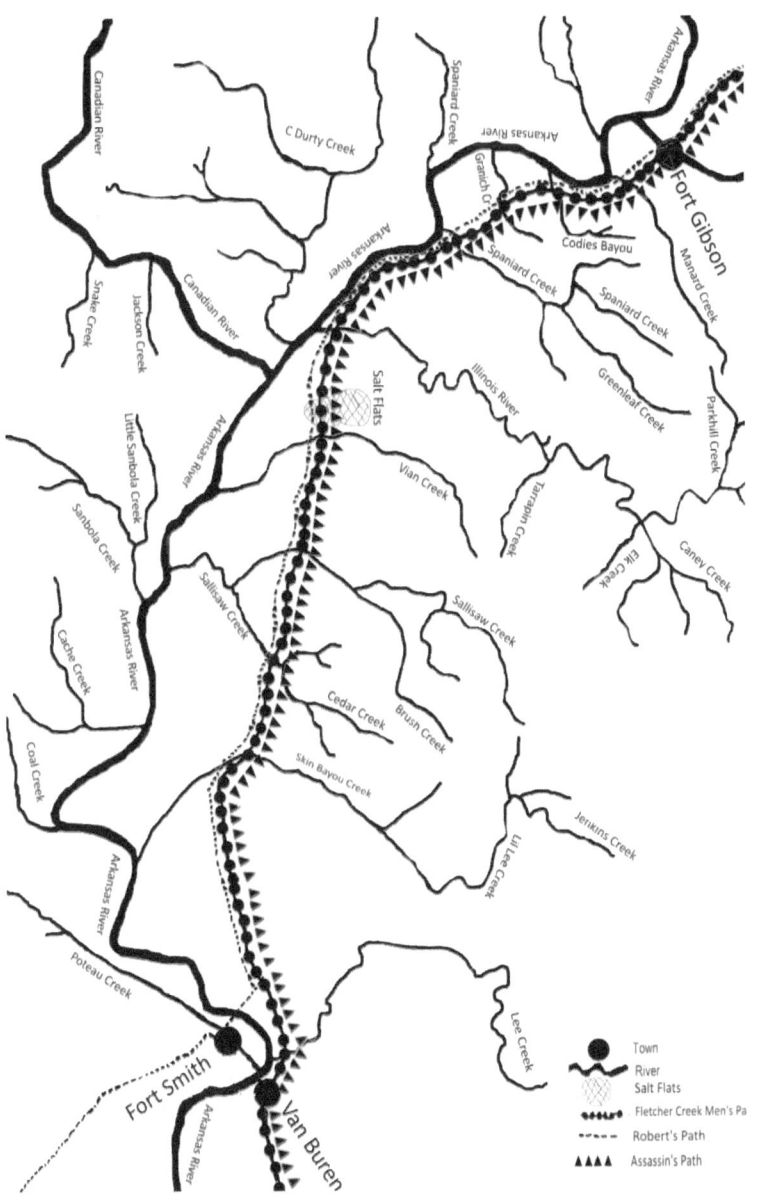

Canadian River

C Durty Creek

Spaniard Creek

Arkansas River

Arkansas River

Granich Cr

Codies Bayou

Fort Gibson

Spaniard Creek

Spaniard Creek

Greenleaf Creek

Manard Creek

Parkhill Creek

Snake Creek

Jackson Creek

Canadian River

Arkansas River

Salt Flats

Illinois River

Vian Creek

Tarraten Creek

Elk Creek

Caney Creek

Little Sanbola Creek

Sanbola Creek

Cache Creek

Arkansas River

Sallisaw Creek

Sallisaw Creek

Coal Creek

Cedar Creek

Brush Creek

Skin Bayou Creek

Jenkins Creek

Lil Lee Creek

Arkansas River

Poteau Creek

Fort Smith

Van Buren

Lee Creek

● Town

～～ River

Salt Flats

▲▲▲▲ Fletcher Creek Men's Pa

– – – Robert's Path

▲▲▲▲ Assassin's Path

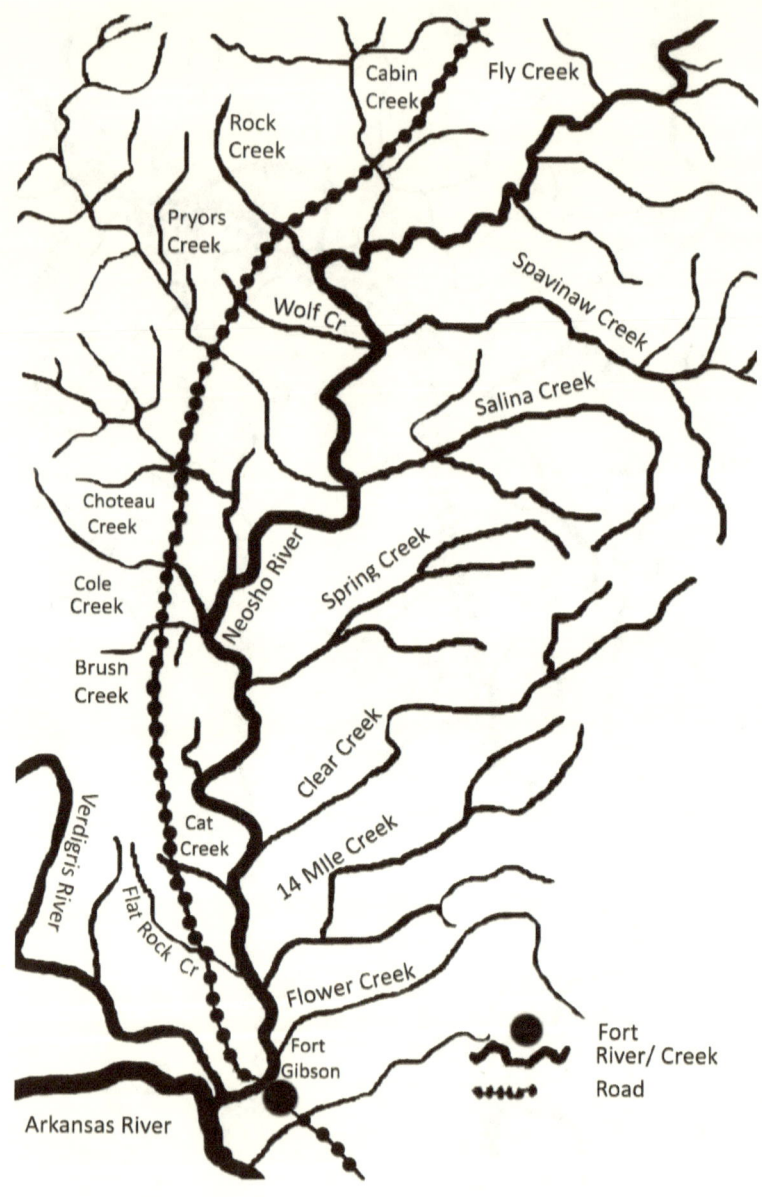

Cabin Creek

Fly Creek

Rock Creek

Pryors Creek

Spavinaw Creek

Wolf Cr

Salina Creek

Choteau Creek

Neosho River

Spring Creek

Cole Creek

Brush Creek

Clear Creek

Cat Creek

14 Mile Creek

Verdigris River

Flat Rock Cr

Flower Creek

Fort Gibson

Fort River/ Creek Road

Arkansas River

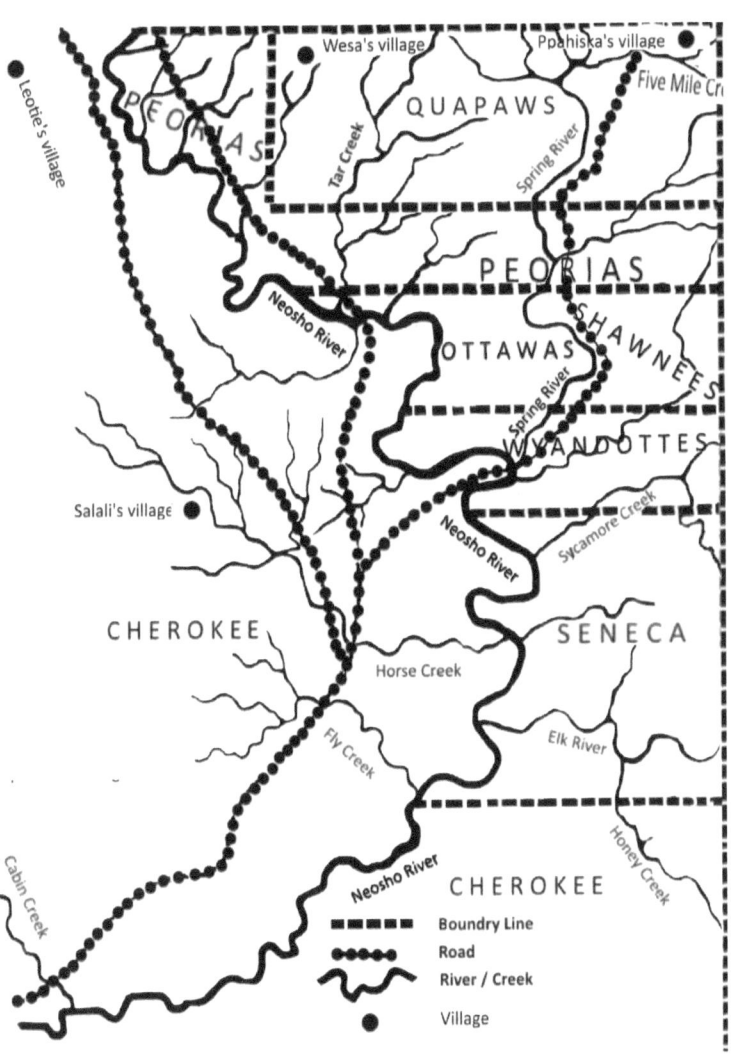

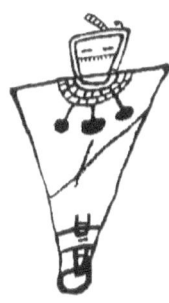

ONE

Eli would have told you he had a good reason to be in Harmony, Arkansas, and he did, at least in the beginning. His father, Tom Yates, had not been there in the spring of 1840 when Eli had returned home. Everybody agreed that his father's absence had forced Eli to stay behind when the others had left.

However, it wasn't really his father's fault. Eli had been gone nine long months. That had been seven longer than it should have taken him to go to Little Rock and back. His father had come to believe that his son had passed; another person Tom had allowed to slip into Hell. Nineteen years earlier, when he had left the eastern shore of New York, Tom had stepped onto the path of losing people he had loved beyond everything. He had believed that his love would conquer Hattie's refusal to accept God and his parents' disapproval of the non-believing woman. He had eventually given up on his parents and had gone west to begin his life with Hattie.

Five years after Eli's birth, Hattie had died. As far as Tom knew, she was still an unbeliever and,

1

therefore, spending every second in torment. Tom had failed to lead his wife to God. Thus, he had failed her.

Mad at God for allowing his wife to die, Tom had walked away from his faith. He had raised Eli into a young man who had never heard a single word about the Creator of everything. Now, Tom feared that Eli was in Hell with Hattie, and Tom believed he was the one to blame. He had to go back to the place where things had been right; back to his parents.

When Eli had finally gotten home, his father was in New York. That would have made it Tom's fault that Eli and his wife, Stephanie, were not with her older and younger sisters, Ann and Sally Williams.

Eli knew he had only himself to accuse for Stephanie's unhappiness. Tom had eventually brought his mother, Helen, back to Harmony. The four of them could have packed up Yates Mercantile and gone deeper into the west—into Indian Territory— where Stephanie's sisters were hiding with Ann's husband.

Eli wanted his wife to be with her sisters. However, since she was pregnant with their first child, he was afraid to drag her into the wilds where he might lose her if the child was born far away from Harmony's doctor.

Compounding the problem was the need for Ann and her husband, Noah Swift Hawk, to get as far away from Little Rock, Arkansas as possible. They might not even be able to stay in Noah's village. If Noah and Ann were forced to flee from his Quapaw village, Eli and Stephanie would never be able to find them.

Therefore, Eli had left his wife, father, and grandmother in Harmony. His previous arrangement with his brother-in-law was for Noah to go to Fort Gibson on the first of every month to look for them. Noah had been true to his word. On the first day of September in the year of our Lord 1840, Eli had met with and then begged Noah to send Sally back to Harmony to be with Stephanie when she had the baby. Eli and Noah had returned to their separate homes, neither knowing if Sally would do so.

More than a month later, Sally rode into Harmony with her uncle, James Williams. James had indirectly been the reason Eli was married to Stephanie, and Noah was married to Ann. When the Quapaws had been forced into Indian Territory, James had left his farm to whoever in his family would take it and had gone with his Indian wife. Two decades later, he had sent Noah to Harmony to see what had happened with the farm.

It had been James's brother, Chris, who had taken the land and house close to Harmony. He and his wife, Emma, had raised Ann, Stephanie, and Sally on that farm. The great sadness of the sisters was the deaths of their parents that had occurred two years prior to Noah's arrival.

Eli was there because Tom ran the store in Harmony that he had started with Hattie. Thus, Noah, Eli, Ann, Stephanie, and Sally's lives had intertwined.

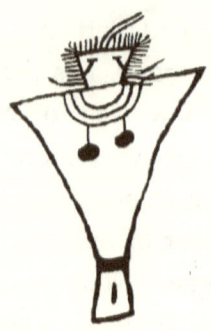

TWO

Sally convinced Eli to leave Harmony. Two weeks after she had returned to her hometown, the family packed two covered wagons full of supplies from Yates Mercantile and then traveled south beside Spadra Creek toward the Arkansas River. They wanted to do everything they could to make themselves invisible to anybody sent by the man who had forced Noah and Ann to hide. They were sure Judge Daniel Hall's assassin would kill them if he discovered their location.

Daniel Hall not only hated interracial marriages, he especially hated Ann. She had broken the law, but what had really riled him up was that she had told him she would fill the world with Noah's babies. She had even insisted that she would be right before God, but he would not be. She had flaunted her relationship with the Indian. It didn't matter to Judge Hall that Noah was as much a white man as an Indian man. He didn't admit it festered under his skin that a beautiful woman, who he would have liked to lie with, would rather have been in the arms of Noah. Instead, he desired to see her dead, and the heathen too.

4

As they traveled, Stephanie picked up small, green, pumpkin-shaped Shagbark Hickory nuts and dropped them into one of the leather pouches hanging on the wagon. "We need to cast away everything, so we can't be followed. I think we should travel under new names."

Since his father and grandmother had left Harmony with him, Eli asked his grandmother, "Who would you like to be, Grams?"

"I once knew a woman named Blanche Kennedy. When I was young, I wanted to be her."

"Then, we'll be the Kennedys." Tom told her, "I'll be your son, Phillip."

Remembering his friends, the people of Fletcher Creek, Eli informed his family, "I'll be Fletcher."

"Call me Royal," said James.

Sally laughed. "Sure, Your Highness. I'm Prudence."

Stephanie stated her choice. "How about Sarah for me? But let's keep all the family relationships the same."

That night in Spadra, they secured rooms as the Kennedy family.

They were almost at the town of Horsehead Post Office the following day when they saw a wagon train heading their way. Through her spyglass, Sally examined the people approaching. "It's Russell French!"

"Can we hide?" Eli asked.

"It's too late." Sally waved at Russell, who looked

back at them with his own spyglass. "He's already seen us, and I'm sure he would recognize Beauty anyway."

Eli quickly reminded his family, "I'm James Bacon. Sally is Nancy Bacon, my sister, and Roscoe Bacon is our uncle." When they came together, Eli asked, "How goes the trading business, Russell?"

"It's going well, James, but Arnold was some trader. I miss him."

Sally asked, "How are Arnold and the trading post he bought from Uncle Roscoe?"

"Arnold is doing very well. He married the woman who caused him to want to buy your uncle's trading post. He's settled down. It seems to agree with him."

What about the other mules he let get injured in the blizzard. Sally asked, "How are the mules Arnold kept?"

"All his mules are doing fine. Is that Mule 17?"

Sally straightened Russell out. "Her name is Beauty."

Russell was surprised. "When I gave her to you, I was sure she would be dead before the end of the day."

"Lots of Nancy's care and love saved her," Eli informed him.

"What about the rest of them?" Russell inquired.

Sally reported the condition of the other mules they owned that had been injured in the blizzard. "All the mules we have are fine, except Dollie. She still doesn't see well with her right eye."

When they heard that Mule 17 was alive, Russell's

men walked to the front of their wagon train to look. They gathered around the mule. Will, the man who had attempted to have his way with Sally earlier that spring, rubbed the mule's neck and side. "She feels lumpy." *Nancy is a remarkably beautiful woman.* Will glanced at her brother, the man he knew as James.

Eli put his hand on the gun that was strapped to his hip. "Hello, Will."

"I see you. Don't worry. I'm not a complete idiot." Will approached the woman he knew as Nancy. "I'm glad she didn't die. I hope you're doing well too."

"I'm well, and you?"

"I'm fine." *I don't want James to think he needs to protect his sister with that gun.* "I'll just be going back to my wagon." He walked away

"How is Roscoe? Is he close to here? I would love to visit if he's not too far."

Sally reported, "He's fine, but he is far away."

Russell asked, "What are you doing here?"

Tom came up with a plausible excuse that he believed could only be satisfied by going west. "I'm going to Fort Smith to get fruit for my store. They're helping me."

"I have apples and limes," Russell informed him.

Tom was astounded. *I wish I had known of this trader years ago.* "How many?"

"Four barrels of apples and ten bushels of limes."

"How much? I'll buy all of them."

"Eight dollars for the apples out of the barrels and twenty dollars for the limes out of the baskets."

Our store didn't have some of the things we'll need, and the cost of the goods at Fort Gibson was ridiculously high. Eli inquired, "How about tin dinner sets and green goggles?"

Before Russell answered, Sally asked, "Do you have garlic?"

"Why don't you make a list of everything you want? I'll see if I have it and give you a fair price."

Tom said, "Be right back." At the back of one of their wagons, Tom and his family made their list. Twelve india rubber canteens, twelve tin dinnerware sets, one sheet metal stove, ten green goggles for adults and two for children, ten adult india rubber ponchos, one child's india rubber poncho, five ground clothes, nine tarps, two water mattresses, apples, limes, garlic, paper binders, paper, pencils, and erasers.

"I have all of this. How much garlic, paper, pencils, and erasers?"

Sally replied, "Ten binders, ten reams of paper, two gross of pencils, and ten dozen erasers. We want all the apples and limes as well as their barrels and baskets."

"All ten bushels?" Russell had refunded people's money and accepted back the limes that storeowners had not been able to sell. He never thought he would resell them. "I also have dried cranberries, currants, peaches, and apricots."

"We only have so much room. The fruit is going to take up a lot of space."

Russell offered a suggestion that would allow him

to sell more items. "You could put the limes in ten-gallon washtubs that wouldn't break and attach them under the wagons."

"How?" Stephanie asked.

Helen suggested, "Tie a rope through the handles."

Tom told his mother, "They'll tip over or bounce out."

Uncle James suggested, "What if you attach a net under the wagons, then put a wagon cover inside, and pour in the limes?"

Eli asked, "Do you have any india rubber wagon covers?"

Russell replied, "I do, but you don't want to put something that expensive under the wagons."

Sally spoke up, "Give me all the limes, eight ten-gallon washtubs, two cargo nets, two india rubber wagon covers, twenty pounds of garlic, ten sets of snowshoes for adults, and one for a child. We'll take the dried fruit too." She turned to Tom. "Do we need anything else for the store?"

"Not unless you have powder horns, ammunition, and wadding. If you have everything I need, I won't have to go all the way to Fort Smith. Would you be interested in buying two four-horse harnesses?"

I didn't have a very good year. If I don't have to buy anything and sell everything James and Nancy want, I'll have enough to recover all my expenses, pay the men, and have a small profit. "I'm only selling this time of year." Russell calculated the cost. "Three hundred and seventy-three dollars."

Lisa Gay

Eli handed over the money, "It's safer to carry supplies."

"I have fireproof steel boxes."

Sally wanted a safe place to protect her paper of ownership of her ruby necklace and the red silk dress. "I'll take one."

"Two dollars and fifty cents," Russell told her. Sally gave him the money. "It's been a pleasure seeing you again and meeting the rest of you. Give Roscoe my regards."

"It's been nice to see you too, Russell. We'll tell Uncle Roscoe," Eli replied.

Russell called out, "Forward ho," then left Sally, Eli, the real James, Tom, Stephanie, and Helen to figure out how to get everything loaded.

Everything fit into the back or on the wagon seats and floorboards except the fruit, so Eli and Stephanie waited with the limes and the wagons.

Helen sang "Amazing Grace" as she, Sally, James, and Tom rolled the barrels of apples down the road and then into town. Several people living in the town of Horsehead Post Office observed the spectacle. Tom rented rooms on the ground level. They rolled the barrels down the hall, where they dumped the apples onto the floor in their rooms.

They took the barrels back out of town with some of the townsfolk following. They joined Helen as she sang "The Old Rugged Cross". Once back at the wagons, they filled the empty barrels with the limes. The second set of fruit was brought behind the

10

wagons. All the townsfolk watched the group come into their town.

The travelers, who had again made themselves easy to follow, secured the wagons, barrels of limes, mules, and horses in the barn. They ate supper before sleeping in rooms filled with the pleasant aroma of apples.

Before leaving town the next day, they installed the india rubber covers over the canvas wagon covers, tied the nets under the wagons, and then loaded into the nets those items that wouldn't go through the webbing or be damaged under the wagon. To minimize damage from bouncing, they carefully packed the fruit and then loaded the barrels and baskets into the wagons.

The sun shone through the yellow, red, and orange leaves of the hickory and oak trees as Stephanie walked beside the wagons. "God really took care of us."

Sally said, "I agree. What was the chance that would happen? I can't believe Russell had everything."

Eli pointed out the negative side of the encounter. "Except now, if anybody asks, Russell will know we were here this fall. Somebody could put it all together."

"What are the chances of that? Two things so unlikely won't happen." Helen sang her feelings.

God is so good. God is so good. God is so good. He's so good to me!

God answers prayer. God answers prayer. God answers prayer. He's so good to me!

He cares for me. He cares for me. He cares for me. He's so good to me!

I love Him so. I love Him so. I love Him so. He's so good to me!

I'll do His will. I'll do His will. I'll do His will. He's so good to me!

I praise His name. I praise His name. I praise His name. He's so good to me!

Daily, they traveled to the sound of hymns sung by Helen. Every mid-day, they let the animals rest long enough to roast the hickory nuts they had collected the previous day. Every night, they stayed at an inn or boarding house in the towns spaced just far enough apart to reach the next in one day.

After leaving Pleasant Hill, Sally suggested they cut the mid-day stop short. "We need to hurry. So far, we've been very blessed with good weather, but Frog Bayou could hold us up for days. Stephanie shouldn't spend more than one night away from a town."

The others agreed. After only an hour, they journeyed on until Helen stood beside Frog Bayou. "I'm glad we got here before dark."

Eli squatted by the ford. "It doesn't look too deep."

James frowned. "It's a lot deeper than when we crossed going to Harmony."

Sally told of what had happened when she had been with Ann, Noah, and Roscoe. "We crossed when the water was much higher than this. We rode the ferry. Even so, Ann and Noah barely survived the final

12

ride across. You know we've now learned: if you can, always cross the waterways when you first get there."

"She's right," James agreed.

"Let me drive the first wagon alone," Eli requested.

Helen pointed out the problem. "We can't fit five people in the second wagon."

Because he wanted to be assured of Stephanie's safety, Eli said, "Then the men will go first."

Helen started hyperventilating. "If all of you die, the three of us women will be alone. Sally, Stephanie, and I have no ability to survive in the wilds!"

"Sally and Stephanie do." James had an idea. "Still, Tom and I could ride across on the first wagon. Eli, if we get across all right, you ride that big mule at the front of your team with the three women on the wagon seat."

"You mean for me to ride Glory?" Eli asked.

"Yes."

"All right. Try it out."

Stephanie stopped them. "First, we pray. Heavenly Father, You parted the Red Sea, and You made Balaam's donkey talk. We know You can control both water and animals, so control them and get us safely across this stream of water."

They all ended with Amen.

The six horses managed to pull the wagon carrying Tom and James across the ford of Frog Bayou.

Eli sat where he didn't press the harness into Glory's back. "Mules are stronger than horses. We shouldn't encounter any problems." He called out, "Forward ho," and squeezed his legs.

Their wagon was lighter than the first. It floated at the deepest part of the river. The thick layers of pitch on the outside and inside kept it watertight for the few minutes it was a boat, pulled by six mules with their feet firmly on the riverbed. As soon as they came out of the water, they set up camp. They slept on cedar boughs they had cut from the forest.

After the first night Helen had ever slept on the ground, she told her family, "The cedar branches made the ground soft, and they smell so nice." Before Tom had come home, Helen had spent her life being a respectable city woman married to Tom's father. She thought her new life in the wild, western frontier sleeping on cedar branches was exciting. She had loved her husband very much. She was sad that he had died, and she missed him deeply, but Helen was glad she was free to go with her family. She would never have been able to do anything like this if he had still been alive. It made his passing more bearable.

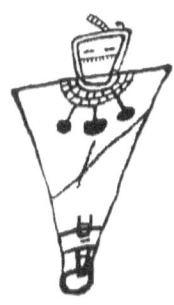

THREE

Seven days after leaving Harmony, while Helen sang Charles Wesley's hymn, "Jesus, Lover of my Soul", a soldier stationed at Fort Gibson inspected the family's wagons. Just before nightfall, he told them, "Go on in."

They parked their wagons where instructed and set up the tent Tom had brought from his store. Luckily, the soldier at the gate hadn't recognized Sally. Inside the fort, she stayed crammed in the wagon until the tent was erected then quickly moved inside and out of view. She hoped she would not encounter the young officer, Lieutenant Jackson, who had wanted to take her ruby necklace and give it back to its previous owner. Nor did she want to see either of the privates who had spent two days carrying heavy sacks of rocks because they had touched her and Ann.

As they set up camp, the smell of baking bread beckoned them, but the bakery was where she and Ann had been accosted when they had ventured in alone. Sally also didn't want to affiliate James with anybody but his village. She spoke up. "James should stay in the tent with me, Stephanie, and Helen. Eli, you and Tom go to the bakery. Get bread, éclairs, and danishes."

While the two men went to the bakery and checked out the store, the women set out a meal of food they didn't need to cook.

Tom joined his family back in the tent. "Stephanie, they were selling peach seeds. We bought some to plant when we get to the western sea."

To their meal, Eli added a loaf of barley bread, along with apple cider and the danishes he had bought. "The prices here are so high. It was really good that we ran into Russell."

The next day, they took down the tent, packed it into the wagon, and then headed to the Neosho River crossing. On the far side, they traveled the road through the land assigned to the Cherokee. They shot prairie chickens, jackrabbits, prairie dogs, and even an antelope. When close to the river they fished. James showed them where and how to gather useful plants and how to prepare them. When they got to the field where they had killed the buffalo, Sally took them to the very place where the yellow buffalo had fallen, slain by her rifle.

Eli commented, "I hope I can get one someday,"

Tom agreed with the sentiment. "I do too."

"And me," Stephanie added.

They were all surprised when Helen said, "Don't leave me out."

James assured them, "You'll come across plenty of buffalo when you cross the plains."

When they arrived at the second crossing of the

Neosho River, Helen asked, "Why are we going back to the east side? If we should be on the other side, why did we come over here?"

James explained, "The land on the east is Cherokee land. They have not given permission for other people to travel there. If we had a hunting talisman, we could, but we don't have one. Anybody can travel this road, and hunt and gather what's close to the road. Also, it's easier to travel on the road."

The weather had been beautiful so far. Eli knew that could change in a hurry. "Let's cross and then camp."

James told his family, "This is where the soldiers and our people stayed while they tried to prepare the buffalo we didn't have permission to kill."

That night, Sally lay beside the fire. "Tomorrow, we'll be home." It struck her that she had thought of the village as home. She had not felt that way when back in Harmony.

"I can't wait to see Ann's big belly." Stephanie closed her eyes.

On guard duty, the chief's oldest son, Chaska, saw Sally through the spyglass. He couldn't believe it. *I thought she would be in Harmony until spring.* He ran into the village. "Tahatankohana, Sally comes with two women, two men, and James."

Noah responded to his Indian name. He put down the cradleboard he was making. "She does?" He picked up his own spyglass and went with Chaska to the lookout. "It is them."

Chaska asked, "Did you think I would not recognize Sally?"

That comment pointed out to Noah that he needed to keep an eye on Chaska. They went back into the village. "Let's get ready to celebrate."

"I need to wait for them at the creek," Ann told him.

Noah replied, "We have time to start getting ready."

Chaska offered, "I will watch and tell you when it is time to go to the creek."

When he came back, the whole village was ready to go to the creek. As they got near, James looked through his looking tube. He saw the crowd on the far side of the creek. "Looks like everybody."

Ann stood on the village side of the creek, "Get over here!"

As soon as he had crossed, James jumped off the wagon. He immediately hugged his wife, Algoma, and their children. When Stephanie and Sally crossed in the second wagon, Ann hugged them as close as she could with her belly in the way. "I've missed you two so much." Ann told the rest of her family, "Get over here." Eli, Tom, and Helen joined the group hug. "You too." Ann requested the rest of them, who had not realized they were included in the request. Roscoe, Noah, and all the rest of Noah's family came into the hug. "Now, we have everybody, and everything is perfect."

Sally then hugged her friends and Chaska, who

stepped over to get a hug as well. She blushed when he gave her more than a very brief hug.

"Welcome home. I am glad you are back," Chaska whispered into her ear.

Noah said, "Let's introduce everybody." Each person told their name as they started across the field: Luyu Noah's grandmother, her new husband Waya, Bethany his mother, and Chetan his father, Noah's sisters Hanataywee and Ehawee, and Dustu and Adahy the Cherokee twins they had married. Bethany named her two youngest children: three-year-old daughter, Chumani, and seven-year-old son, Ke.

They put the wagons beside the lodge, unharnessed the mules and horses, and then led them into the field where they joined the other animals. Even after the long separation, the mules returned to their established places in the herd. The six new horses joined the ever-increasing herd to sort out their relationships on their own.

The wagons remained packed as they went to look at the basket elevator. Petang, another of the Cherokee men who had recently married into the Quapaw tribe, demonstrated how to raise the basket. He pulled himself up only a short way before he lowered the basket back to the ground.

"Very nice," Tom commented in English. Chetan translated into Quapaw.

Noah's young sister, Chumani, hadn't been allowed to go into the basket with her Quapaw-speaking family members. She thought this new person might let her go. She spoke her first English words, "Take me." She had heard so much English that she had learned that language as well. Nobody realized it until she spoke to Tom.

"Chumani, I didn't know you understand English!" Bethany exclaimed.

"May Eli and I take her?" Stephanie asked.

"Yes, but be very careful to keep her away from the opening."

Chumani clapped as she climbed into the basket. She clapped all the way to the top and all the way back down.

The others, who had just arrived, rode in the basket before everybody gathered in the community lodge to listen to the story of the trip to Harmony. Sally told most of it. When she couldn't think of the Quapaw words, James helped. Ann understood most of the story. Eli, Tom, Stephanie, and Helen would have understood none of it, so Noah, Bethany, Luyu, and Chetan each sat beside one of them and translated. At the end of the day, everybody knew the story. They all went to their lodges happy.

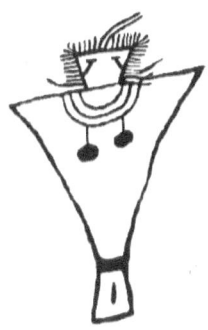

FOUR

In Little Rock, Russell French drove into Martin Harrow's Livery. "You will never guess who I saw."

"You're right. I'll never guess, so just tell me," replied Martin.

"Nancy and James Bacon."

Not far from the two men, Robert, Mr. Harrow's new stable hand, pitched hay as he eavesdropped.

Martin didn't want Russell to give out one drop of information about these specific people to anybody, and he surely didn't want to know. "I never cared for them."

"Really? Well, you might want to know she saved Mule 17. That's the one she calls Beauty. It was all lumpy under its fur, but it was alive and doing well."

Martin derailed the conversation. "I'm always glad when an animal is healthy. I need to get going. Have a good stay in Little Rock." Then he called out to Robert, "Get Mr. French's mules put in and fed before you go home!" Martin made a hasty exit. *I got away in time. I don't know anything.*

Robert helped Mr. French park the wagons inside

where they could lock them up for the night then talked with him as he helped unharness the mules. "Dr. Smith helped me with my father-in-law's pig. That's why Bertha's father let us get married. Did you see him too?"

"No, I only saw James and Nancy. They bought a lot of supplies. If I didn't know better, I'd think they were planning a long trip for ten or twelve people."

"Maybe they are. Where and when did you see them?"

Russell was glad to talk about the family of his old friend Roscoe Bacon. "It was two weeks ago, just west of Spadra. They bought close to four hundred dollars of supplies and all my fruit. That sale made this a good year. I wonder how they got so much money, and James said something odd. He said carrying supplies was safer than carrying money, and then his sister bought a strong box. They were traveling with two older men, a young pregnant woman, and an older woman." Russell chatted on about other people he had met while traveling until they had all the mules in stalls, watered, and fed. "Have them fed again early. Everybody wants to get home before the end of October. We'll be moving out at sunup."

Robert assured him, "Yes, sir. They'll be ready, Mr. French." Robert locked the barn door. *I've finally found out. Now, I can get my money.*

Robert knocked on the judge's door. A servant opened it. "Mrs. Hall gives out scraps to the needy at the back door."

"I'm not one of the needy. I work for my money. Judge Hall will want to talk with me. Tell him the newsboy has arrived."

The butler locked the door — ensuring that the foul-smelling person stayed outside — then went to the library. "The newsboy is here, sir."

"He is! Thank you." A smile spread across Daniel Hall's face. *I'm going to win this one.* He opened the door and stepped onto the veranda. "What did you hear?"

"Give me the money first." Robert held out his hand.

The judge fished coins from his moneybag but held them tightly in his hand. "I have the money right here. Speak, then I'll give it to you."

"Russell French saw the sisters and the brother-in-law at Spadra just two weeks ago."

"Still so close to home." He dropped the payment into Robert's hands. "There's more if you find out anything else significant."

"I'll see what I can find out in the morning." Robert went home to his wife with five silver dollars.

Judge Hall stepped back into his house, possessing the knowledge he needed to finalize his plans against the Indian, Noah Swift Hawk, and the white woman, Ann Williams.

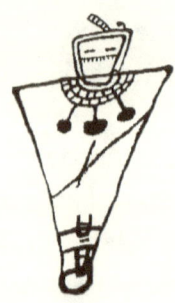

FIVE

In Noah's village, James walked to Chetan's lodge the following morning. "James is at your door."

Ke dashed over to let in the man the family had recently discovered was a relative. "Welcome to our lodge, Uncle James."

"Thank you, Ke." James looked at the grownups. "When are you going to empty your wagons? I want to get the loom and spinning wheel without anybody knowing about it."

Tom remarked, "It's just pieces of wood. You should be able to carry it to your lodge without anybody knowing what it is."

"You brought a loom?" Noah inquired.

"Yes. I want to give one to the village as a gift."

"Petang is building two looms because that was his bride price. I don't think you ever knew about that. Now, several of us are building looms. You might wait to decide if you still want to give it to them."

"I'll reevaluate. I'd still like to get them now."

Chetan told James their plan. "We're going to rearrange today. We'll put them aside for you."

"We can help you," James offered.

The eighteen people of Luyu's family were clearing out a temporary staging area. Luyu replied, "We're already getting in each others' way. We have enough people."

Except for the dynamite, everything from the cave was back in their lodge with the explanation that they were making room for others to use the cave.

"All right, I'll come over later and get them." James dragged his feet as he left.

Roscoe stated the obvious, "Most likely, we'll have to keep some of this stored in the wagons."

Having already independently come to the same conclusion, Eli, Chetan, and Noah spoke together, "Agreed."

Helen started to sing Martin Luther's hymn, "A Mighty Fortress Is Our God".

Roscoe told her, "You have a beautiful voice. May I work beside you and listen?"

Helen smiled, "You may."

Adahy, the man married to Noah's sister, Ehawee, carried more and more into the lodge. "You are very rich!" When Adahy, his twin Dustu, and great grandfather Waya, had decided they wanted to have Ehawee, Hanataywee, and Luyu as their wives, they'd had no idea the family was so wealthy. Chetan made sure they did not know until after they were married. He wanted to be sure the men were joining the family because they loved his mother and daughters.

"Does that upset you?" Chetan inquired.

"No. It is just that I planned to hunt and work hard to get food for Ehawee to show her how much I love her."

As they rearranged everything in the one large room that was their lodge, the man Adahay knew as Tahatankohana replied, "There are many ways to show her your love. Besides, this food will not last forever. We will still have to do plenty of hunting. We should keep as much of the preserved foods as we can. It will not be easy when we cross the prairie."

Sally and Stephanie made sure to place the white deerskin pants, moccasins, beads, and sinew with the items they could easily access. However, they used the crates of supplies they wouldn't need to get into before they started west and built walls to make separate areas, which were just large enough for sleeping pallets. Across the front of each space, they wedged a branch and hung a sheet of the cloth they had brought from Bacon's Trading Post or Yates Mercantile. They put down ground cloths, then a water mattress, with a feather one on top. Bethany and Chetan put a second set in their larger area for Chumani and Ke to share.

As soon as Chetan had laid it out, Chumani tested the waves of the water inside. She pushed down with her hands as she knelt on it. Then she lay on top and pretended to snore for five seconds, after which she decided to jump on the mattress to experience the waves again.

Chetan scooped her off the bed. "Enough. You'll pop it."

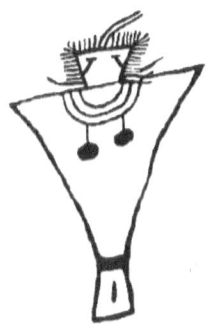

SIX

That morning in Little Rock, Robert didn't have a problem getting to the stable early. He wanted five more dollars and hadn't slept a wink. He had thought and thought about the best way to get more information. He wanted his source happy and willing to talk. He brushed, fed, and watered Mr. French's mules.

When Russell French arrived, Robert probed for information. "I sure hope James, Nancy, and Roscoe also get safely home before the end of October. How far do you think they were going?"

"You don't have to worry about them. One of the men said he runs a store somewhere around there. They were probably home in just a few days."

"Good. I wonder if they know where I can find Dr. Smith. My father-in-law has another sick animal."

"I have no idea if they know anything about Dr. Smith, but they wanted large quantities of different things; bushels of apples and limes, and pounds of garlic and dried fruit. They didn't even have enough space and had to buy rubber wagon covers, cargo nets, and ten-gallon washtubs to carry everything."

"Really? How many wagons did they have?"

"Two and they were packed full. That's why they had to carry the fruit in nets under the wagons."

"How many people had to sleep out in the rain?"

"Well, there was James and Nancy, a pregnant blonde-haired girl, the man who said he owned the store, another man, and an old lady. They wanted me to buy two four-horse harnesses, so they wouldn't have to go to Fort Smith. If I were a betting man, I would say they're planning a long trip with twelve people. If you need to find Dr. Smith, you'd better find them soon."

"Find who?" Martin asked as he entered the stable.

Russell told him what the young man had wanted. "Robert has a sick animal and wants to find Dr. Smith."

"Does he?" Martin knew Robert didn't have a sick animal. "Robert, you did such a good job getting everything done early. Why don't you take a few hours off?" As soon as Robert had left the barn, Martin told Russell, "Two dollars. See you in the spring," then left him to get himself out of the barn. He tailed Robert.

Martin hid around the side of Judge Hall's house. He listened intently as Robert told the judge, "They're definitely going to be traveling, and they have other people going with them. Russell said there was a blonde-haired girl who was pregnant, two other men, and an older woman. James had a blonde with him just before he left Little Rock. Mr. French said they bought a bunch of traveling supplies. They're going to be leaving from around Spadra. I would guess in the spring. It's too late to be traveling this year."

"Thank you, Robert." The judge gave Robert five more dollars. *Stephanie Williams is a blonde. Eli Yates was probably with the Williams family for her. His father wasn't there this spring when Captain Cornish's men went to get that worthless AWOL soldier, Melvin Hatcher. Eli must have kept her with him in Harmony because he was sleeping with her. Now she's pregnant. Thomas Yates probably came home. They'll be joining up with Noah and Ann with enough supplies to cross the country. Those people in Harmony probably know where they are, since Sally went back to Harmony to get the others. That other man must have been somebody who went with her from wherever Noah and Ann are hiding, and I have somebody who can make them give up the location of Ann Williams.*

Martin slipped away. *I should tell Dollie that the judge is still after Luke and Isabelle, or Noah and Ann, as he called them when he tried to kill them in my house. I should wring Robert's neck for secretly spying in my stable. I'm going over there and tell him to never come back. No, then he'll know that I know, and he'll warn the judge. I guess I shouldn't tell Dollie either.* He went into his house and lied to his wife. "I need some herbs. I have somebody who needs something specific. I didn't realize I was out. I bet Edwin has some. Would you like to go with me and visit with the Snows in Maumelle?"

"I would, and the fall trees will be beautiful." Dollie packed while Martin went to talk with Robert.

Robert promised, "I'll take very good care of the place. Where are you going?"

"Visiting friends. We'll leave in the morning and be back in a week."

"Enjoy your visit." Robert returned to shoveling manure.

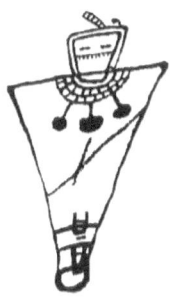

SEVEN

In the Indian Village, Waya found the tied-together bundles of wood and sent Ke to get James.

James walked beside Ke. "Did you get everything into your lodge?"

"Yes, except the dynamite. My brother told me what that stuff does. We don't want it with us."

"I wouldn't either." James stepped into Luyu's home and looked at the walls of crates stacked to the roof. "This is a good idea." He picked up the bundles that were his. "Ke, would you roll those spinning wheels to my lodge?"

Ke balanced one on its edge and pushed it toward the door.

Chumani was sure she could do the same. "Me do it!"

"You're a baby. You can't help." Ke informed his little sister.

"Me do it!" Chumani struggled to get out of her mother's arms.

Chetan instructed Ke, "Son, go on and get them both out the door."

"All right, father." Ke gladly kept his sister from being involved. He put both wheels outside and then closed the door. *It is fun rolling this wheel, and I get to roll both of them all the way across the village. Besides that, father and Uncle James both think I can do it.* Ke loved them both for believing in him. After the mid-day meal of corn, butternut squash, fresh beans, bread, honey, and smoked ham, Chetan sent Ke on another mission. "Tell each family, you know the proper order, to come and get apples if they want any."

Eli put the especially tasty apples from Mara out of view. They set out the apples from Russell.

The village chief's wife, Mikoishe, and their daughters Mikakh and Eyota arrived first.

Chetan explained in Quapaw, "Mr. Yates offers you apples. As you know, he brought them. He wants to offer them to all the people here. We will keep the baskets. Do you accept the gift?"

Ppahiska's wife, Mikoishe, knew how to say a few words in English. "I do. Thank you, Mr. Yates."

"You are welcome, and please call me Tom."

Mikoishe stood between two baskets. She took one handle of each. Her daughters took the outer handles of the baskets. They carried away two bushels of apples. Ke ate an apple as he followed to retrieve the baskets. He carried them to the home of Mystery man Wakanda. With his wife Onida, daughter Weayaya, son-in-law Tizhu, and Ke, Wakanda went to Luyu's lodge. The baskets were filled again.

Ke helped himself to another of the delicious fruit.

Being the Mystery man-in-Training, Nikiata, as well as his wife Mina and mother Anpaytoo, expected to receive two baskets full, which they did.

Ke ate an apple every time he left the lodge to get the baskets. The women of Tatonga's family came. They expected to receive only one bushel of apples. They were given two. Kimimela whispered to her friend, Sally. "I stood just inside the opening of the cave. You want to come with me later and try it?"

Both girls had been badly scared in pitch-black caves. Sally was pretty sure she didn't want to try it. "Maybe."

Last, Uncle James's wife, Algoma, and daughters Dowanhowee and Mache came for their apples. Dowanhowee asked Helen, "How do you know the song you sang earlier?"

"I have a hymn book."

"What is that?"

Helen went to the area that was her place then came back with a book. She opened it to the hymn. "These marks tell you how the melody goes." She hummed the melody of a hymn. "The words are under the notes, so you know what to say using the same melody." She sang the words.

Dowanhowee told Helen, "This is beautiful. I would love to learn how to do that."

"I will teach you what I can while I'm here."

"Thank you," Dowanhowee replied as she, her sister, and mother carried two baskets of apples out the door.

Ke came home with the baskets. "My belly hurts."

Bethany wasn't surprised. "It is no wonder. You ate eight apples. Go on and lie down."

Ke lay on his soft bed. Meanwhile, his family cut apples into thin slices.

Sally looked in the barrel. It still held apples. Beside it stood two more, full to the brim. They also still had all the apples from Mara. "I was hoping we would give away more of them."

Adahy decided cutting apples was one of the other things he could do to let Ehawee know he loved her. "I will help you cut them."

"I'll bake pies." Ann got out goose fat, flour, and eggs.

"I remember baking pies with Mama. I'll help." Stephanie went for sugar, cinnamon, and cloves.

"Me too." Sally retrieved the pie pans that had been full of rhubarb pies when she had earned them back in Little Rock. She cut apples into wedges for the pies. "I wonder if we could get rhubarb plants."

EIGHT

At that moment in Little Rock, Robert finished his chores at Harrows' Livery. He didn't want to look like a needy person, so he hurried home, cleaned, and redressed. Once presentable, he stealthily slipped along the back way, hoping he would not be seen.

Judge Hall's servant opened the front door. "I'll tell him you're here again." Even clean, the butler didn't find Robert acceptable. He bolted the door with Robert outside.

While he waited for the judge, Robert prepared to up his take. Bertha deserved better than what he had been able to give her. When Judge Hall arrived, Robert informed him, "I can tell you how to go right to them, but it'll cost more."

Judge Hall didn't like the change to their agreement. "How much?"

Robert decided to be greedy. "Twenty dollars."

The judge thought the young man should be reasonable. "That's high, don't you think?"

Robert, however, thought he should wisely

explain why the judge should give him the money. "I could tell Mrs. Hall that you're still searching for Dr. and Mrs. Smith."

In Judge Hall's mind, Robert had pointed out something different. *Robert knows too much. If he thinks he's going to blackmail me for twenty dollars, it won't stop there. I hate to waste Joe's time on the ratbag, but I see that he needs to have a talk with Robert.* "All right, let me get it." As Robert stood on the front porch, Daniel Hall deployed his assassin out the back, "I have a second job for you. Follow the man at my front door. When you're done, your pay will be in his pocket."

"Yes, sir." The man slipped into the darkness.

To give his assassin plenty of time to get into position, Judge Hall slowly retrieved the money for Robert, who was waiting for his reward. Darkness congealed in his mind as he stepped onto the front porch. "I have the money, Robert. What do you know?"

"Follow Martin Harrow. He will take you to Edwin Snow. Then follow Edwin. He will take you to Noah Swift Hawk."

"Thank you, Robert." Judge Hall put the dual-purpose payment into Robert's hand. "You should be more careful about what kind of deals you make."

"I will, Judge. Nice doing business with you." Robert stepped off the porch.

Judge Daniel Hall should have listened to his own advice.

NINE

In Indian Territory, Chetan told his family, "As soon as we harvest the last of the crops, we'll take the rest of the shells to Fort Gibson."

Bethany sat beside her husband, slicing beets. "We can harvest the three sisters tomorrow."

"You can't harvest us!" Stephanie exclaimed.

Luyu explained, "The three sisters are corn, beans, and squash. They must grow together, like sisters."

"Oh! Why?" Helen was curious about this technique.

Luyu described how the plants help each other. "First, you plant corn and give it a few weeks to start growing. Then you plant the beans. The beans need the corn to climb, and the corn grows better when beans are around them. Animals try to eat the beans and corn, so we plant the squash. The stems are prickly. Animals don't want to walk through them. The leaves are big and cover the ground, so the sun does not dry it out. The smell of the pumpkin or butternut leaves drives away the insects. All three plants do well when together. If you plant them separately, none of them grow as well."

Sally looked up from the pants of white leather she was beading. "How clever! I looked at them yesterday. They're healthier than ours ever were. They seemed ready to pick."

"Who's going to pick vegetables, and who will go to Fort Gibson?" Ann asked.

Noah reminded his wife, "You know I should avoid the place."

"Me too," Roscoe replied.

Eli also hoped to decline. "Pop and I were just there. It might raise suspicion if we were back so soon."

Waya bored a needle hole into a bone sliver. "I would like to stay with Luyu, but I'll go if you want me to."

"I guess it is me again." Chetan asked the twins, "Either of you want to come?"

As twins, Dustu knew what he and his brother felt and replied for both of them. "If you want us to go, we will, but we would rather not leave our wives. We have already had to leave them once."

Stephanie didn't even look up as she sewed a red bead to a moccasin that matched the white pants. "Probably none of you has to go."

Bethany, however, was proud of her husband. "Chetan should go. Our people need him to translate, and this time, they're going to divide the money between everybody. He should be there to make sure we get an equal share."

Tom gave his opinion of the store operator.

"Chetan, keep your eye on Sergeant McCormick. He's charging way too much."

"That's what I said!" Roscoe agreed. "I even told him his prices are too high. He said to buy at his price or leave it."

Helen again cut apples into thin slices. "Maybe you shouldn't stop there. Maybe you should go to Fort Smith. If he's selling the shells to them, they have to be buying for more than he gave you."

"You're right. We might as well get as much as we can. I'll suggest going to Fort Smith." Chetan went to speak with Ppahiska. He came back quite a bit later. "We will all work to finish the harvest tomorrow. Since we're taking the shells to Fort Smith, we'll need to leave the very next day."

Eli scraped out a buffalo horn, "Why don't you nine men go? The rest of us can harvest the vegetables."

Chetan returned to making arrows. "Everybody wants to be here to get their share of the food, and they all want to go to Fort Smith to get their share of money and buy everything they need for the winter."

Waya picked up a buffalo horn. "I thought everybody had plenty to survive the winter when we picked the summer squash, pole beans, parsnips, and turnips."

"I thought the same thing during the carrot, radish, and onion gathering, but when we harvested the broccoli, beets, and okra, I heard Capa telling Tatonga that this family is at the bottom, so they don't have to leave us very much." Adahy shaved a buffalo leg bone to make it into a spear.

Luyu also sliced apples for sun drying. "And remember how we had to argue to get our share of the early tomatoes? That's one reason why we should leave with Tahatankohana."

"Who is Tahatankohana?" Tom asked.

Noah spoke up, "That's how you say my name, Swift Hawk, in Quapaw." He returned to the previous topic. "We've always known what they think of us, but they really made it obvious during the green corn harvest celebration, and Capa didn't even help us harvest the hay we stored in the cave. He told me, 'None of those animals are mine,' but he's eaten plenty of the eggs, and I'm sure he'll want wool in the spring."

Bethany agreed, "And he complained a lot about our share of sunflower heads and every other crop we divided by the size of the family."

Dustu worked on a second bone spear beside his brother. "He was too happy when Wakanda said to divide the flax, tobacco, and cotton equally between the families."

"The cotton harvest should not have been divided equally." Chetan balanced the arrow shaft across his finger. "Those sharp husks sliced up every person in Wakanda's family before they dressed properly for harvesting cotton. Most of the others wouldn't even help after only a few scratches. Wakanda's family and ours should have gotten more for our injuries and the amount of work we did compared to the others."

Ann beaded the white deerskin shirt. "The others in the village could easily have been more helpful. All anybody had to do was wear long-sleeved buckskin shirts, pants, and gloves like we did. The husks didn't cut us very much."

Chetan added, "At least they have all the seeds they'll need for next year's planting stored in jars in the cave. They're safe from fire, so that won't happen again."

Tom sliced fruit with Luyu. "Except the corn, October beans, butternut squash, pumpkins, and tomatoes still in the field."

Luyu cored another apple. "Capa will probably argue about them too."

Roscoe picked seeds from the apple cores. "I'm glad Wakanda insisted they first repay you for the original seeds you gave them before they divided anything."

Bethany folded paper packages holding twenty apple seeds each. "I only care that we have enough."

Ann switched to making apple turnovers. "You're right. We do have enough, but it was good for the sake of integrity. Wakanda is a good man."

Since the pie pans made her think about the original pies, Sally requested a favor from Chetan. "Since you're going to Fort Smith, would you see if you can get Rhubarb plants?"

Chetan agreed. "I'll try, but I don't even know what they look like."

Throughout the village, everybody ate or cored

and sliced apples for drying. Every family kept the seeds to plant in the spring. When the day ended, Chetan's large family had prepared an entire barrel of apples.

They lay on their comfortable beds in their newly created sleeping areas, ready for the next day when they would harvest the crops that Chetan's family had been assigned to plant and tend. Chetan thought about the people around him. *Everybody thought I would never be able to have children. Look at my family now. In my quiver, I have many fine arrows ready to go into the world.* He kissed Bethany. "You are the most wonderful thing God ever gave me. I love you and our family. Life is very good. I hope we make another child."

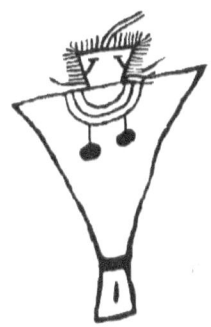

TEN

Night approached as Robert walked home from Judge Hall's house. *That was a strange thing for the judge to say.* He tried to put the idea out of his mind, but it nagged at him. Then, he noticed the shadow following him. *I need to stay in the light and go directly to Hillcrest Inn.* He sat at the bar and watched the door out of the corner of his eye. A man slid into the darkest corner. *I'm so stupid. If he'll hunt one man, he'll take down another. I guess he didn't take kindly to my threat to tell his wife what he's doing. How am I going to get out of this?*

Robert's brain started churning. *I bet the twenty dollars the judge gave me is that man's pay to eliminate me. He'll kill me when I leave. But what if he only cares about the money? I can give it to him. Maybe he'll take it and let me go. But maybe he wants the money, and he likes killing. Then he'll take the money and kill me anyway.*

Clark, the owner of Little Rock's general store, rose to leave the Inn. He had to walk right past Robert's house to get home. Robert quickly walked to the corner and put the two ten-dollar gold coins in front of the man who had kept his face under the hood of his cloak. "Say you did it. I'll never be seen in Little Rock again to prove otherwise." Robert followed Clark to the door. He started a conversation. "How are things going at the store?" They left together.

The man from the shadowy corner picked up the money. He slipped out of the inn and slinked along behind them.

Robert looked over his shoulder. *We're being followed. I hate to leave Mr. Harrow's livery unattended, but there's no other way. I should never have gotten involved in this.* At his house, he told Clark, "Come in and have another drink."

To Robert's dismay, Clark declined. "No, I'm going home."

Robert stepped into his abode, where Bertha sat in the rocking chair, cuddling their daughter. "Grab your coat and the heavy blankets." He darted across the room, yanked open the dresser drawer, and grabbed the ten dollars he already owned.

"What's going on?" Bertha got her coat.

"I'll tell you later." Robert grabbed the blankets from the bed. "I'm sorry. Take this. Wrap up with Phebe good and warm."

He retrieved the bridle he kept inside where he could protect it, threw it over his shoulder, and then grabbed the saddle. He then immediately dropped the saddle. *I probably don't have time to get it on her. Then again, if he's going to do it, I'm not getting away anyway. I don't want Bertha or Phebe involved. If I can put the saddle on Boots, he's going to let me go.* He picked the saddle up again. "Lock the door behind me. If I'm not back in five minutes, I'm not coming back. Don't open the door until the bright light of the middle of the day. I love you. I'm sorry."

"Robert, what's happening?" Bertha demanded to know.

Robert kissed her. "I'm sorry." His heart pounded. Breathing hard and rapidly, he opened the door. He didn't see the man. He took a chance and stepped out of their home. He put the bridle on his horse, white from its knees down on all four legs. *I can't believe I'm not dead.* Expecting to feel a knife or a bullet, he threw the saddle over the horse's back. He cinched and buckled the girth strap. He was still unharmed. He squinted into the darkness. *Nobody. Maybe the man is going to let me go.* He walked back to his door. "It's me. Robert."

Bertha opened the door. "Robert!" She threw her arms around her husband. "I'm scared."

"I'm sorry. Let's go." He kept Bertha behind him then held Phebe while his wife got on Boots. He quickly kissed his daughter and then handed Bertha their baby. She slipped the child into the shawl she had tied across her chest and over her shoulder. Robert swung up on the horse behind them. *I can't believe I'm still alive.* He urged the horse. "Run!"

Bertha knew something was terribly wrong. "Don't ride in a straight line!"

Robert pulled the reins to the side. Something very sharp slid into his back. He slumped forward. "I'm sorry. I love you."

Bertha felt Robert's body bump hers. She didn't want to think about what it meant. Robert's hands went limp. Bertha grabbed the reins. As sure as the night was black, she wasn't stopping.

From the shadows, Joe Smith saw Robert's head drop. Joe was sure, one way or the other; the man would never again be seen in Little Rock. Before Joe left on his second mission, he would tell the judge he had put a knife in Robert's back. He had the twenty dollars in his pocket to back up his claim that he had completed assignment one. He had killed the first of the three on his list. Only one man and one woman to go.

Bertha had to decide. Should she involve her parents or Robert's? She was sure Robert needed medical help fast, but he was involved in something deadly, and she did not want their families drawn in. Probably they would never be able to see them again. She didn't want to ride away without telling anybody anything, but she knew Robert's life was on the line.

Faintly she heard, "Get help."

The decision was too heavy for her alone. Bertha needed God's help. She turned back and rode toward the only man of God she knew. At the back of Reverend Thaddeus Pratt's home, she rode into the shed, slid off Boots with Phebe still strapped to her chest, and then leaned Robert forward over their horse's neck. Just as she suspected, there was a knife in his back. *I shouldn't remove it.* "I'll be right back. Don't move." Bertha quickly made her way to the reverend's door and knocked.

Thaddeus opened the door. A young woman with a baby strapped to her chest stood outside. "How may I help you?"

"My husband has a knife in his back. He's in your shed. We need help."

"Come along." Thaddeus shut the door and walked to his shed. A man lay slumped over his horse. A knife protruded from his body. "It's not good to move him with the knife in there. I'm going to pull it out then carry him over my shoulder. You walk behind and hold that blanket over the wound. Stop the bleeding as much as possible. Are you ready?"

Poised so she could quickly press the blanket against the hole in Robert's back, Bertha replied, "I'm ready."

Reverend Pratt removed the knife, threw it on the ground, and quickly pulled Robert onto his shoulder. Bertha followed, pressing the blanket against her husband's back. Reverend Pratt carried Robert into his home. He laid him on the bed, then removed Robert's coat and shirt. The hole was just to the left of his spine. "Luckily for your husband, whoever threw the knife has bad aim. It's too high to hit his lung or heart. I think he'll recover."

"Thank You, God. All I could think was that I need God to help me because I don't know what to do. I don't know what's he's gotten into. I don't want to get anybody else hurt. I probably put your life in danger by coming here, but I was afraid he would die."

"It's going to be all right. I'm guessing you need to get out of Little Rock right now, and unseen."

"I'm afraid we do. I don't know what happened. I don't want to leave our families, especially without them even knowing what happened to us. I don't know what to do."

"How big is your family?"

"My parents and his. Robert is an only child, but I have seven sisters and brothers. I'm the oldest."

"Are they married?"

"No."

"What are their names? What do you and they own here?"

"Robert and I don't own anything. We were staying in the home of the Snows while they're gone. Robert's parents are Simon and Ruth Teal. They live in one of the little tenant farmer houses the Peters give to the families who farm their land. Robert's folks only have some personal things. My folks are David and Louise Thomas. They have a Reynolds' tenant house full of furniture my father made."

Thaddeus finished stitching the hole in Robert's back. "I'm going to take you someplace where Robert can recover enough to travel. By that time, I'll know if your families want to leave with you. If they don't, they'll at least know why you're gone. All right?"

"Thank you."

"I'm going to blindfold you to take you." To make a bandage, Thaddeus wrapped Robert's body with long cloth strips. "Clean up all this blood. Be very thorough. There's water and rags over there. I'll clean up outside. Don't leave the house." Bertha made sure she did not leave a drop of blood anywhere before she wrapped all the bloody clothes and blankets together with the clean side out. She fed Phebe and then waited.

When Thaddeus came back an hour later, he inspected the house. "Good work. Put the baby back into the sling. We're going." Reverend Pratt picked up Robert. In the shed, Bertha got on the horse. Thaddeus laid Robert over the horse in front of Bertha and then handed her a cloth. "Tie this around your eyes." Bertha did as she was told. Thaddeus led the horse away from his house. He picked up the mule he had packed with everything the couple would need for a week. The reverend took them in circles and wrong directions but eventually arrived at a large cave. Inside were an animal corral, hay, a freshwater spring, and a pile of wood that would be more than enough for a week. "You can take off the blindfold."

"Oh, my. I see God did send me to the right place. This is a well-planned escape route." They set up a soft clean pallet for Robert, then brought him over and laid his still unconscious body on the bed. Thaddeus explained the rules, showed Bertha where to have the fire, and helped her to start one. After they unpacked all the supplies, Thaddeus carefully instructed Bertha on how to brew a concoction to help stop internal and external bleeding and reduce pain. It was well into the night when Thaddeus lay in his bed, wondering what was happening in the town that was his home.

In the cave, Robert woke with an awful pain in his back and chest. A teapot of the concoction sat beside the fire, staying warm. Bertha saw Robert was awake. She poured out a cup of medicine. "Drink this. It will help you heal and reduce the pain." She didn't tell him it would put him back to sleep.

Robert didn't see the baby. "Where is Phebe?"

"She's right here." Bertha pointed to the sleeping baby on her other side.

Robert took the tea. "I should tell you what's happening."

"Tell me tomorrow. Tonight, we're safe. So rest and heal."

"How do you know we're safe?"

"I'll tell you tomorrow, but I'm completely sure."

Robert put down the empty cup. "Thank God we're all alive." Twenty minutes later, Robert, Bertha, and Phebe were all asleep.

When the sun came up, Bertha prepared a breakfast of boiled oats and coffee.

With perfect weather, the Harrows started toward Maumelle under the different shades of orange, yellow, and red leaves of the oak and hickory trees that surrounded them. The assassin followed, always out of view of the two people who didn't know to look for anybody.

Bertha stepped out of the cave, looked around, saw the same beautiful fall forest, and then went back into the cave with Robert.

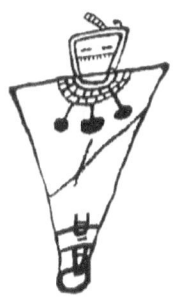

ELEVEN

The sun barely lit the world when Chief Ppahiska and Mystery man Wakanda, along with Enapay, Mantu, Capa, Tatonga, Paytah, Chetan, and James, the other men of the village, left for Fort Smith. They had scarcely left when Chief Wesa of one of the other three Quapaw villages, and his hunting party joined them.

At Spring River, a group of Cherokee dragged a net to the west side of the river. Wesa waved at the woman to whom he had given a stone impregnated with cubic galena crystals, his talisman that validated her permission to harvest mussels.

"What did you hunt on their land?" Ppahiska asked Wesa.

"In the north of her section, there were thousands of antelope. We took many. We are going back for more. Since we are not allowed to keep hunting in the same place, we will run them into another section. Can I use your talisman to give permission to gather mussels?"

Ppahiska told him, "Absolutely not. We are not to overharvest. We need ours for our village. You will have to go to the same section and trade the other items. I see you have no pottery. Before you hunt, ask them if they will trade for seeds."

"Since you will not help us, I will have to do it that way."

"How have we not helped you? What do you call the seeds we gave your village and the trade agreement we made for you and the talisman we gave you?"

"You are right. You have done much to help." Wesa waded into the river. Leotie came from the other side. The fast-moving water stopped them both from crossing all the way. Wesa hollered, "We do not have any pottery made yet! We will trade seeds to hunt again on your land."

Leotie screamed over the roar of the water. "What seeds do you have?"

"Cotton, flax, tobacco, and corn but not with us."

"We will be done here very soon, but we will wait here for the seeds and give you back your stone."

"Some of us will stay and gather mussels on this side. Our women will come and get them while we hunt." Wesa waded out of the water. He gave instructions to one of his men before the man ran off.

Ppahiska and his men left Wesa by the river and crossed to the western shore at the ford.

Capa said, "Let us continue on."

James spoke up. "That is not a good plan."

Chetan agreed with James, but the rest decided to keep going, so they traveled five more miles. Shortly before nightfall, they stopped for the night.

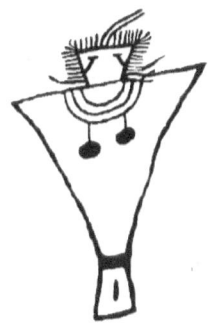

TWELVE

Not many miles away, thinking they were safe, Tom told his mother, "Don't overwork yourself. I don't want to be without you again."

"I won't, but I am going to help harvest the three sisters," Helen replied.

Noah followed the comment with a protective statement of his own. "Ann, I'd like it if you wouldn't work in the fields at all."

Since she was still worried about the baby growing inside her, Ann agreed. "You can leave Chumani here with me. We will listen to our hearts with your stethoscope."

Chumani begged, "Me stay. Chumani listen."

"All right," Bethany agreed.

Ann and Chumani lay on the mattress together. The others went to the large field. As predicted, all the families in the village came to help and get their share of the fall harvest of tomatoes, butternut squash, pumpkins, corn, and October beans.

After listening to her own heart and Ann's heart, Chumani pointed at Ann's belly. "Listen."

Ann wasn't sure if Chumani heard anything until Chumani said, "Whoosh whoosh!"

"That is Wambleeska's heart," Ann told her niece.

Chumani put the stethoscope against her heart again. "No whoosh whoosh. No heart."

"You have a heart. Yours sounds different, like mine." Ann found Chumani's heartbeat again and then put the earpiece to Chumani's ear. "That's yours." Ann found her own heart and then put the earpiece back to Chumani's ear. "My heart sounds like yours."

"Chumani heart like you heart." With the stethoscope earpiece in her ear, Chumani snuggled against her aunt and fell asleep. Ann put the medical equipment aside and then decided to also take a nap so as not to disturb her niece. They were both asleep when Tahatankohana came into the lodge to be sure Chumani wasn't a problem for Ann. He saw they were fine and went back to help with the harvest.

"I'm going to get the cart Stephanie made at Fletcher Creek." Eli went back to the village, climbed into the wagon, and got out the cart.

Everybody came over to examine it. Petang said, "I think I can build one of these."

Noah told Eli what Petang had said.

"Tell him I'd be happy to show him how."

Noah not only explained that Eli would show him how to build one but also told Petang that Eli had built the carts they had used to travel a hundred miles from Cadron Creek to Pine Bluff. He also told him that the man who had bought the trading post at Pine Bluff had insisted on owning all four of them because they were so well made.

Across the field, Helen sang "Amazing Grace" while she picked pumpkins.

Dowanhowee worked beside her. "Can we try it together?"

Helen started at the beginning. Dowanhowee joined. Roscoe thought Helen sounded like an angel. He joined the song the third time around.

Helen told him, "I'm so glad you joined. The bass tones of your voice are perfect with ours. Shall we sing it together again? Amazing grace, how sweet the sound…." More than the three of them joined in.

Petang used the cart to haul some of his family's share of corn to their lodge. He became convinced he should make at least one. Every family tried out Eli's cart then squabbled over who would use it next.

Finally, Noah told them, "My family owns it. We are using it for the rest of the day," and then tried to ease the irritation. "Anybody who wants to can make one. I'll translate the instructions."

Every family decided to do so.

By the time all the produce had been picked, everybody knew "Amazing Grace". Although, most of them did not understand what they were saying.

Tom offered, "I want to give each family a portion of the limes and another basket of apples."

Luyu's family divided out five bushels of limes and half a barrel of unprepared apples to the other eight families.

THIRTEEN

Hundreds of miles away, Edwin Snow, the young teenager who months earlier had helped Noah, Ann, her sisters, and Eli escape Judge Daniel Hall, bundled up the plants he purchased. Edwin was one of the few people who knew how to find the Fletcher Creek community. For two months, the fugitives, Noah and Ann, had lived with the rest of their family in that hidden portion of the Underground Railroad. While there, Noah had arranged a business deal between the people of Fletcher Creek and Martin Harrow of Little Rock.

Many of the plants Martin needed to treat ill animals grew in the forest beside Fletcher Creek. Edwin had worked as a stable hand at Marin's Livery when Noah, as Dr. Luke Smith, and Sally, as Nancy, had worked with Martin Harrow as veterinarians for a few days. At Mrs. Harrow's dinner party, Judge Hall had come across Noah and Ann still together as husband and wife. Guilty of violating the prohibition against interracial marriage, Ann and Noah had to run for their lives. Edwin got them into the Underground Railroad going out of Little Rock.

Noah had brought the folks of Fletcher Creek, Edwin, and Martin together as supplier, deliverer, and purchaser of medicinal plants.

This day, Edwin prepared to take the latest batch of plants to Maumelle, his current place of residence. Before he left Fletcher Creek, he secretly kissed Elizabeth. "I probably won't be able to come back before spring." This was the longest amount of time Edwin had ever stayed with his friends. He could barely drag himself away, but he knew he had to return home.

Elizabeth kept her arms around Edwin. "I hate for you to go. I'll be thinking about you all winter and counting the days until you return."

Edwin kissed the girl one more time and then got on BlackJack, the horse that had belonged to Roy Butterfield before the outlaw had been killed. Edwin cantered away through the woods.

Elizabeth walked the short distance to the cabin where she lived with her parents, Matt and Sarah.

FOURTEEN

In Maumelle, Martin knocked on the door of Murray Strong. Horatio Knapp, Murray's brother-in-law, answered. "Martin. Dollie. Please come in. Edwin is out right now. He should be back today. He went to get this year's last harvest of plants."

Martin didn't want to impose. "We'll go to Lucy's boarding house and wait."

Murray joined Horatio at the door. "I insist you stay here. Nobody can sleep at Lucy's boarding house on the days Roy's ghost is in the parlor."

Horatio replied, "True, but nobody goes there to sleep anyway. They go to see the ghost."

"You must tell us about that, but first tell me how Esther and Candace are doing." Dollie did want to hear about the ghost, so she would have a good story to tell back in Little Rock. However, more than that, she cared about the friends Roy Butterfield had brought into her life.

Candace Daniels and Esther Knapp entered the library. "What a nice surprise!"

Murray brought the women up to date. "Martin and Dollie just arrived. They came to get the plants, but Edwin hasn't returned. Dollie was just inquiring about the two of you."

Esther related her condition. "I'm healing. Horatio tells me that Abraham did an excellent job sewing me together, but I hurt a lot, and I'm tired all the time. Edwin fixes me a tea that helps. I'm sure I'll continue to get better."

"And how is your shoulder?" Martin asked Candy.

She pulled her shirt slightly to the side and showed the scar on her shoulder. "Actually, I think it's quite nice. It's like a decoration. Doesn't it look like a moon with stars?" Candy looked at Murray and smiled. "Murray helps me do my exercises. I can move my arm all the way around if I do it slowly." She demonstrated.

Horatio stated his opinion of Abraham, the man who, in reality, was Noah when he had dyed himself black with walnut husks to hide at Fletcher Creek. "That slave friend of Edwin's was such a blessing, but it's strange that we've never seen him before or after. The Snows refuse to talk about him. I almost believe he was an angel."

Martin thought about telling them that the man they were praising needed help. He decided against involving them. Instead, they shared the latest news about Little Rock and Maumelle. Mary and S.R. Snow, Edwin's parents, returned from the market. They carried their purchases into the kitchen. Mary started washing vegetables. S.R. walked into the library.

Murray told S.R. what he could already see. "Martin and Dollie have come to visit. Join us."

"I'll get Mary." S.R. departed but quickly returned with his wife.

Mary's skin glowed, her hair gleamed, and her eyes looked bright. Dollie hugged her neck. "You look wonderful!"

"That's what I tell her. I say, 'Mary, you are looking very beautiful these days.' " S.R. quickly added, "Not that you haven't always been beautiful. I mean, it's just that you're looking even more beautiful than ever."

Mary saved her husband. "Thank you for the compliment."

Since he didn't know if the Harrows were staying for dinner, S.R. asked Murray, "Should I go back to the market?"

"The Harrows will be staying until Edwin returns. Sit and visit for a while. Go and buy more when Mary starts preparing supper."

"Of course," S.R. replied. The Snows sat in the library. After many minutes of pleasant conversation, S.R. informed the others, "I'll be running off to the market now."

"And I'd best be starting supper." Mary left the study with her husband.

Martin and Dollie continued to talk and enjoy their visit while they waited for Edwin to return.

Joe Smith, the assassin, settled down in the bushes outside the window and listened.

Mary put supper on the table. She handed Murray the basket of biscuits she had just taken from the oven. Then she sat with her employer, Candy, Esther, Horatio, Martin, Dollie, and S.R., "Do you want to hear the story of Roy Butterfield's ghost?"

Before anybody foiled her chance to hear the story, Dollie answered, "I do!"

"Lucy swears this is true. On the twenty-fifth day of every month at exactly 4:47 in the afternoon, Roy Butterfield's ghost appears in Lucy's parlor. The overwhelming smell of soiled clothes permeates the room. It seeps out the windows and doors and gags anybody in the room. The top of the shiv gleams in his boot as he stands with a Lefaucheux twenty shot revolver clutched in his hands. Lucy says, 'Your heart will stop if his evil, glowing red eyes look into yours.' Anybody who goes there had better be sure the ghost doesn't do it.

"Then, at 4:50 to the second, his body is flung to the ground. A flash comes from the barrel of the revolver. The revolver flies out of his hand, skids across the floor, and then disappears. Some people who have stayed at Lucy's boarding house say that a single shot woke them from sleep.

"With a wild look in his eyes, Roy gets to his knees. Just like he's praying, he puts his hands together in front of him and begs, 'I didn't mean to do it. It's their fault. Don't kill me.' At 4:51, another shot rings out, his body jerks as if from an impact, and then blood actually drains from his heart through the new hole in his vest pocket." Mary pointed to her chest. "Right here where the bullet hit him. His eyes start to dim. You hear another shot and then his body falls over. His eyes go black. An unstoppable stream of blood flows from his belly."

Dollie put her hand to her mouth in suspense.

"Blam! Another shot rings out. His body jerks as the bullet hits him. Blood sprays out. It spatters the furniture, everything, and every person in there.

"Blam! Blam! Blam! Shot after shot slams into his body then another and another. Seventeen shots make seventeen new places for the blood to leave his body. He lies in the blood as it covers the floor. The next two days, the ghost makes unearthly sounds, sits up, and lies down. At the second day's end, his feet break, and his boots disappear."

Candace stated her opinion, "That's absolutely ridiculous. Why would his feet break or his boots disappear?"

Horatio told them, "The whole story is a lie. He didn't even die in Lucy's parlor."

Esther refuted her husband's statement about the situation. "It's not completely wrong. He did beg for his life. I did shoot him in the heart. He did stay on his knees until I shot him again, and I did shoot him nineteen times."

Murray still didn't believe there was any such thing as a ghost. "Everybody knows those facts. Lucy probably made it up to get more people to stay at her boarding house. And now, she charges more as well."

Dollie said, "Tonight is the twenty-seventh. He'll be losing his boots tonight. We could go and find out."

"Esther has already been through too much. I'm not dragging her into that," Horatio replied.

Esther shifted in her chair. "One way or the other, I'd like to put that ghost story away. It bothers me that he will forever be in Lucy's parlor."

"We can go home and be rid of him," Horatio offered.

Esther pointed out, "But I'll know he's here with my brother and Candy. We need to get rid of him."

"Who do we need to get rid of?" Edwin sauntered into the dining room.

Candy said, "Clean up, then come eat. We'll tell you."

"Hello, Mr. and Mrs. Harrow. I'll be right back." Edwin knew Mrs. Daniels always wanted him to be squeaky clean, but he wanted to get back as soon as possible, so he washed quickly. He hoped he was clean enough for Candy. He hurried back to the dining room. "Am I good?"

Candy wanted to make Edwin into a man who would fit into the upper crust of society. He, S.R., and Mary all received lessons as to how to present themselves as well-refined people. At this moment, Candy decided Edwin was clean enough. "Come in, Edwin."

Edwin knew it was his turn to go to Little Rock to

deliver the plants. "Is everything all right in Little Rock?"

Martin told the story he wanted everybody to believe. "We're doing fine. We just wanted to get out of Little Rock and visit with our friends here in Maumelle."

"Well, I'm glad you came. So, who are we getting rid of?" Edwin spooned corn onto his plate.

Murray explained, "Your mother told us the Roy Butterfield ghost story."

Edwin looked at his mother with irritation. He had asked her not to pass on the stories about Roy's ghost. "She did?"

With an obvious dedication to the task, Esther stated, "Edwin, maybe you can help. I need to make that ghost leave."

Candy asked the question on all their minds. "How can we make a ghost leave?"

Dollie offered her thoughts. "I've always heard that ghosts are here to resolve some life issue. Usually, about their death."

Murray was flabbergasted. "We have to help Roy Butterfields's ghost resolve his issues? I would never have imagined I would have to help a shade."

As if somebody in the room would know, Esther inquired, "How can we find out what he's trying to resolve?"

Dollie fancied herself an expert on the subject. She believed she had grown up with the ghost of her grandfather, who she had found dead in the hayfield. "We ask him just like we asked my grandfather."

"But if he looks you in your eyes, your heart will stop," Mary reminded them.

S.R. spoke up. "That part probably isn't true."

Esther looked at Dollie. "So, what do we have to do to get prepared?"

Horatio didn't want his wife to undergo any more trauma. "Are you sure you want to do this? You're still healing."

"I need to, Horatio," Esther told her husband.

Mary prodded them on. "Let's make our best guess about what we think he's trying to do."

Edwin stated what he thought. "If I was Roy, I would be upset that I died begging and didn't go out in a blaze of glory."

"He would never have had glory," Candy replied.

"I mean with lots of panache." Edwin used a word he had recently learned.

"That may be it," Martin contemplated, "With his warped reasoning he probably feels that he didn't deserve to die. He thinks he accidentally shot Esther. Even though we all know he planned to get around to it."

Murray added his guess as to the issue. "The strange part of the story is about his feet breaking and his boots disappearing. I wonder what that's about."

Edwin confessed, "I know."

"You do?" his father asked.

"I think Abraham is a good man, and that was the only time I ever saw him act this way. He hated Roy Butterfield something awful. He said he wanted him

65

deprived of all dignity. He told me the clothes and boots belonged to somebody else, and he didn't want Roy to have them. I helped Abraham take off the boots. That's when Roy's feet broke."

Horatio said, "I knew there was something personal about it when he sewed Esther's back together."

Murray added, "Roy's stolen items contained a music box that Abraham said belonged to his family."

Martin decided to ask, "If Abraham needed help, would you help him?"

"What's wrong?" Edwin assumed that must be why Martin was in Maumelle.

Martin informed them, "Judge Hall got information as to his whereabouts."

"Oh, no!" S.R. exclaimed.

"What's going on?" Murray asked.

Martin tried to give out as little information as possible. "It's better for you if you don't know anything. I just want Edwin to take the warning to Abraham and then come home before winter sets in. If he can't get to him quickly, he may have to be gone until spring."

Candy said, "But Judge Hall issued the warrant for Roy Butterfield when he killed Jasper."

Dollie explained, "He has a problem with one particular topic. Trust me when I say, he wants to kill Abraham and especially his wife." She turned to her husband. "You should have told me."

"What topic?" Esther could not fathom what

would make an honorable man like a judge want to kill people.

Martin resisted. "He will stop at nothing to get information out of you if he thinks you know anything. It would be better if you don't know anything."

Mary asked her son, "Edwin, can you and BlackJack travel alone to wherever you need to go, and do you want to go?"

"I can do it, and I absolutely want to help. But first, I want to help Mrs. Knapp get rid of Roy's ghost."

"Can we get the boots back?" Horatio wondered.

Edwin replied, "Maybe if I find Abraham, but that will be months."

Murray tapped his finger against his chin. "Maybe we can trick him into thinking we have his boots."

"How?" Esther asked.

Murray told them his idea. "The thing about those boots was the shiv in the seam. We can put a shiv into some similar boots."

Mary believed that very night would be the best night to try. "Since he wants his boots tonight, we should try that. This will be the safest day. His eyes won't be open, so he can't look into ours. I like my heart beating. I think we all do."

Murray stood up. "I'll get my old boots."

"I'll go to the blacksmith and see if I can get something that will pass for a shiv." Horatio left the house.

When Horatio left the house, the Harrows' shadow lay flat behind the thickest part of the bush and tried to remain unseen. *How can people believe that kind of rubbish?*

"I'm going to finish my supper if that's all right." Edwin stuck his fork into a roasted potato cube.

Esther turned to Mary, "I'm going to give Edwin enough money to rent rooms and buy food for six months, but I want you to make Edwin plenty of nonperishable rations for emergencies. Fill up his saddlebags."

S.R. instructed his son. "Be sure to take the revolver, ammo belts, and plenty of extra ammunition."

His mother added, "Don't try to be brave and loyal. If you get caught, just tell them where to find him. Abraham is a very resourceful man, and he would not want any harm to come to you."

Edwin chewed a piece of meat. *I can't say anything. I have no idea where to find Dr. Smith, but I will take the revolver and bullets.* "I promise to do both of those." He then thought, *even when I do figure it out, I won't tell that murderous man a thing.*

Horatio returned with a shiny shiv and reservations at Lucy's haunted boarding house. With the thin leather of a moneybag, Mary sewed a pocket inside Murray's boot.

While they made the boots, Judge Hall's hitman sat outside, feeling hungry.

Edwin believed what the man he had known mostly as Dr. Smith had told him: that Edwin worked for God. "We need to pray about this."

"Go on, son. Pray." Mary joined hands with Edwin.

"God, Roy Butterfield hurt the people in this room in many ways. He hurt many others we don't even know about. His ghost is still hurting the people here by remaining in Lucy's parlor. We ask that you will be with us and cause his ghost to leave the Earth forever. Give peace and healing to the people gathered here. I ask you for this blessing in the name of Jesus Christ."

Everybody ended the prayer together with "Amen." The seven people in the house were ready. With the boots, which they hoped would exorcize Roy Butterfield's ghost, they went to Lucy's boarding house.

The man in the bushes knew he could find Lucy's place, the food inside smelled delicious, and he was very hungry. He sneaked inside to eat the leftovers Mary had carried into the kitchen and left on the counter. He told himself, *don't eat so much they notice anything is missing.* He ate a few bites from all the plates, wiped his mouth, folded the napkin, and put it inside the plate. He looked out the window. Nobody was around. He slipped out of the house.

FIFTEEN

Joe easily found Lucy's haunted house, which was full of people. That was good. They wouldn't think it strange for another unknown man to take a room. "I hear this place has a ghost. I came to see it. Is this the night?"

Lucy told the truth. "One of them. The best was two days ago."

The man, seemingly innocently, informed the woman, "I'm here today. I'll see what I see."

"Two bits for the night and breakfast in the morning."

The newly arrived ghost hunter handed the innkeeper two quarters.

"Sign here." Lucy pushed the registry toward the man and then got the key to the last available room.

The man signed the book, Joe Smith.

Lucy showed him to his room, unlocked the door, and handed him the key. "Settle in quickly. You have to get into the parlor in time, or you'll be locked out."

Five minutes later, Joe joined Edwin and the other people loitering in the parlor. Murray held the satchel with the boots.

Lucy stood outside the room. "I have to lock you in, or he won't come." She turned the key then immediately left the house.

One of the women gripped her husband's hand. "No matter what, don't let go of my hand," she laughed nervously.

Edwin was not afraid at all. He had been there with Roy's real but dead body. Nothing could be worse than what he had already experienced.

A portly man with a slender, very attractive woman introduced himself and his lady. "Abbott Doggett and my lovely wife, Ophelia."

The other woman in town to see a real ghost stated her name, "I am Fabia. Pleased to meet you."

"Doctor Reginald Canfield here," Fabia's husband informed the others.

Joe and those who were there hoping to dispatch Roy's ghost from Lucy's parlor also introduced themselves.

Abbott asked, "I wonder where the body was?" His wife slipped her hand into his just as Fabia had taken her husband's hand.

"I'd hate to have him appear right where I'm standing," Reginald remarked.

"He was over there," Edwin told them.

"How do you know?" Fabia asked.

Murray stood behind the two couples. He put his finger to his lips. Edwin replied, "I've heard people talking."

Like the night when Edwin, Elizabeth's father

Matt, and another man of Fletcher Creek named Morris had sat locked in the room with Roy's body, the pale orange light of the setting sun added an eerie aura to the haunted room. Reginald loosened his wife's fingers around his hand. "Honey, ease up."

"I don't want to do this. I need to get out." Fabia called out for release. "Lucy, I've changed my mind!" Lucy did not appear to unlock the door. The woman hollered, "Lucy, let me out!"

"She's not here. Stop screaming!" Joe commanded her.

Edwin also reminded the woman that Lucy was not in the house. "She left. I'm sure she won't be back until morning."

Fabia continued to scream in fear, "Let me out!"

Joe Smith was going to make another ghost to haunt Lucy's parlor if the hysterical woman did not shut up. "Stop it!"

Reginald saw the look on the man's face. "Honey, calm down. I'm here. I won't let anything happen. There's probably not any ghost here anyway." He put his arms around Fabia and held her close. She stopped screaming but quivered in his arms.

The last ray of sunlight disappeared from the room. Together and resolute that they would face whatever was going to happen, Esther and Candy held hands in companionship against the man who had shot them both. Horatio and Murray stood protectively beside the two women. Edwin, who had told himself he was not afraid, backed into the corner with a handful of the same plants he had taken into the room five months earlier. They waited, and they waited, and they waited some more. "You see, honey? There isn't any ghost. It's just a story."

As if summoned by the denial of its existence, a vague shape shimmered on the floor exactly were Edwin had told them the ghost would arrive. The petrified woman whispered, "It's happening!"

The body slowly coalesced into the shape and features of Roy Butterfield. The day he had died, Roy was still a dark-haired, six-foot-tall man with a square, sad face. However, he had no longer been the muscular man who had nearly killed Noah with one blow of a rifle butt to the head. The image of his ghost looked as withered and haggard as Roy had been when he had begged Esther to spare him. An overwhelming stench emanated from the ghost. Edwin remembered the horrible smell after the body had fouled itself as decomposition progressed.

Unexpectedly, the body sat up. Screams ripped from the people locked in the room. Joe looked to see if the others had realized he had screamed with them. Nobody was paying him one iota of attention. With their eyes riveted on the ghost of Roy Butterfield, every one of them had pressed him or herself into the farthest corner.

Murray wanted to be ready to deploy at a moment's notice. He opened his satchel and got a good grip on the boots. An hour passed. Their hearts pounded, and their stomachs turned sour.

"Does he look different to you?" Joe asked no particular person.

Edwin stated what he remembered the body had done as it lay on a tarp on the floor. "His body is starting to lie down again." Another hour passed. They watched the body slowly lie back until Roy was again almost horizontal.

"Crack." The sound of breaking bones sounded across the room.

Every person crammed in the corner jumped. Almost knocking everybody down, Reginald careened into Horatio. As he tried to regain his balance, he accidentally stomped Fabia's foot. She screamed with pain and terror.

Joe had never felt fear before this night. *I'm not afraid. I'm just concerned,* he told himself.

One of Roy's boots pulled away and revealed the foot that dangled broken inside its sock. Murray pulled the substitute boots part of the way out of his satchel. The women clung to their husbands and attempted to prepare their minds for the next sound. "Crack."

Fabia, terrified since the beginning of the night, let out a mind-rattling screech of terror then passed out into her husband's arms. He dragged his heavy wife along the floor and then sat with her away from the feet of those pressed into the farthest corner of the room.

The second boot disengaged from the other leg and exposed a mangled foot inside a drooping sock. Exactly as previous people had reported, they could barely breathe due to the stench. Horatio unsuccessfully tried to open the window. The nights when Roy's ghost occupied the room, the windows would never budge. Edwin got the letter opener. He inserted it into the groove they had made on the night they had pried the window open. He pulled up. The window slid open.

Fresh air flowed into the room. Unlike all the previous nights when Roy's ghost had occupied Lucy's parlor, the reverent abruptly sat straight up. It swung its head and scanned the window area with open eyes. The poltergeist's partially rotted brain recognized the one who had opened the window the night it had died. The one holding the letter opener was the one who had knocked him down and made the gun discharge. The ghost believed Edwin was the guilty one, the one who should be dead.

With eyes glowing intensely red, it jetted toward Edwin. Edwin closed his eyes and turned his face away. With both hands, Edwin brought the letter opener up directly in front of him. The ghost slammed him into the wall. Edwin shrieked. Screams filled the room and rolled out the open window into the night. The apparition had wanted to crush the culpable and stop the guilty heart from beating. Instead, the letter opener had knifed into Roy's ghostly heart. It vaporized. Immediately, the manifestation reformed.

The smell of the urine of the terrified people joined the other foul odors in the room. Edwin cowered among the others in the corner. The ghost believed it should not be a shade. Its beady eyes blazed as it scanned the window. This time, it saw nothing. Its head slowly rotated as the specter's focus moved.

"Don't look it in the eyes!" Mary warned.

Ethereal eyeballs considered those gathered. Roy Butterfield's shade recognized someone else. A woman he had shot. No, two of the women he had shot cowered in the corner with the man who was with the woman who had slain him.

Keeping her eyes tightly closed and her son behind her, Mary whispered, "This isn't how it happens. Don't look into its eyes."

So he didn't draw unwanted attention from the poltergeist, Abbott barely breathed the question. "What?"

"Do it now," Esther ordered Murray.

"Do NOT make it mad! Tell me what you're doing!" Abbott demanded.

Murray took a tentative step forward. The one advancing reeked with the aura of the woman Roy had shot in Little Rock, but he wasn't the one he had killed in Little Rock. The shade still deemed the one approaching as an adversary. Roy's arms stretched toward the man. Murray retreated into the corner, but Roy's icy arms still advanced. They encircled the aggressor and then tightened. The ghost attempted to collapse Murray's lungs and deprive him of air. Murray's feet left the floor.

Mary shrieked, Joe shrieked, Edwin shrieked, all the others shrieked. They scurried out of the corner where the ghost was trying to kill the man who had dared to approach him.

Murray needed to breathe. He dropped the bag and tried to pry the supernatural arms from his body. Edwin heard the boots clatter as they slid out of the satchel when it hit the floor. The others, too afraid to help, watched in horror. Murray's struggling stopped. His eyes closed. His body hung limp.

Candace resolved to herself that Roy was not taking another man from her. She took a deep breath, steeled herself, then walked to the ghost and slapped the back of its head. "You tried to kill me once. Let him go and try it again."

Roy's ghost removed its death grip to finish the task Roy had started during life. Murray dropped to the ground. His almost lifeless body involuntarily drew precious air into his lungs. Making most of its form incorporeal to protect itself from further assault, the thing locked into the shape and consciousness of Roy Butterfield. Completely focused on Candace, it reached for the throat of its next victim.

Edwin grappled for the boots.

Esther hollered, "I've stood at the gate of the spirit world! I know where you belong! You are not going to escape your damnation by staying in this room! I'm dragging you into Hell!" She pulled a dagger from her skirt and plunged the blade toward her heart.

Roy let out a blood-curdling sound so loud and shrill that the windows exploded. The whites of the living eyes in the room turned blood red as capillaries popped.

Horatio swung hard to deflect the knife. "I won't let you give your life!"

Its trajectory altered; the dagger missed her chest. As the blade sliced her arm, Esther's hand lost its grip. The knife dropped to the ground.

Their ears rang from the concussion of the high-pitched screech that had been heard by all the citizens of Maumelle and shattered objects across the entire town.

Edwin came to a decision. *I helped remove the boots from Roy's body. I'm putting them back. It's just that I don't see how I'll be able to get the boots on him. There's no way I can get them on like I'd put on mine.* The feet of Roy's ghost didn't touch the floor as they dangled limply from the bottoms of his legs. *Maybe I don't need to.* Edwin slid across the floor with the boots.

With each hand, Roy's ghost held the throat of a person who had attacked it. As the women struggled for air, Murray revived. He saw that Roy had his sister and Candy. Horatio was desperately trying to disengage Esther from the grip of Roy's shade. He pulled her with all his might and yelled fruitlessly, "Let her go, you demon!"

Murray jumped to his feet and dashed across the room. Just as Horatio attempted to free Esther, Murray tried to pull Candace out of the otherworldly hands.

"God, save Candy. Save Esther," Murray begged.

Seeing the bravery of the four locked in battle with the evil remains of Roy Butterfield, Mary and S.R. overcame their fear and grabbed for the ghost. There was no substance to hold. The remaining five people cowered as far away as they could and screamed in abject fear. Edwin, however, took advantage of the distraction and made it to the back of the poltergeist undetected.

Candy thrashed as she tried to break free. Her foot kicked one of the boots out of Edwin's hand. It slid into the corner with the living.

Abbott looked down. He saw the gleam of the shiv in the boot. "Don't you dare! Don't draw its attention."

Joe locked eyes with Edwin. "God, free us all." He gave the boot a hard shove. It slid across the floor into Edwin's hand. Edwin stood both boots up on the floor behind Roy's apparition. He pushed the boots onto the legs of whatever was the ghost of Roy.

The demon looked at its feet, saw the gleam of the shiv, and uttered, "You little thief. You brought back my boots." The ghost of Roy Butterfield vanished. Esther fell into the arms of Horatio. Murray caught Candy, who had completely collapsed from the longer oxygen deprivation and the removal of the support of the ghost, who no longer had her by the throat.

"We did it." Edwin jumped up off the floor.

The husband of the still unconscious woman stated, "I hope it's gone for good." He frantically surveyed the room for a reforming ghoul. "I don't know why I ever wanted to see a ghost. I didn't know they were so evil and hated so much."

Candy regained her breath, "He was a truly evil man when he was alive."

"Who are you people?" Abbott asked.

"Roy Butterfield shot me here and killed my husband." Candy exposed the scar on her shoulder.

Esther raised the back of her shirt and displayed the bright red patchwork of scars. "He shot half my body away. I'm the one who killed him."

Edwin declared, "And I'm the one to blame."

Esther immediately corrected him, "No, Edwin. You are not to blame. He would have shot Horatio and me straight through our hearts if you and your friends hadn't knocked him down. You are a hero."

"Exactly," Horatio affirmed.

Ophelia felt astounded. "You are the actual people of this story?"

Joe told the truth. "I would never have been as brave as you."

"You just were," Edwin reminded him.

Esther testified, "It wasn't bravery on my part. It was pain and justice. I hurt all the time. I would have been free of the pain, and Roy would have been in Hell where he belongs."

Horatio held his wife. "My love, I'm so sorry. I didn't realize it was that bad. We'll go back east and find somebody who can help."

"You don't have to go east. I happen to be a doctor who specializes in pain relief." Reginald Canfield still sat on the floor with his unconscious wife.

Murray decided to invite the people who had shared the terrifying ordeal. "You must all come to my house when Lucy lets us out."

Joe thought; *this will work out perfectly. Now I can go with Edwin openly.*

So, they would not soil the sofas or chairs with the sweat and other bodily fluids and substances on their clothes, none of them sat on the furniture. As they talked and waited for morning and their release from Lucy's parlor, they diligently watched for any evidence that Roy was reforming.

Joe thought about his own fate. *I'm a murderer. The first one deserved it. Now I've killed a man with a wife and child, and I'll have to kill at least two more before this is over.* He didn't want the fate of Roy Butterfield. *Judge Hall will send somebody else after them, and me too if I don't.* He shoved all thoughts of ultimate consequences out of his mind.

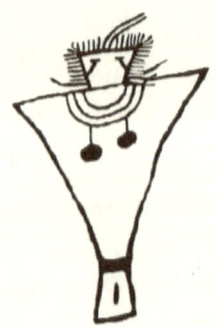

SIXTEEN

That same night, in the dark of the cave, Robert and Bertha heard. "Have you made the item?"

Robert spoke the words Bertha had told him to say. "Look in the wooden box."

Thaddeus came into the light. He had already accomplished what he had promised Bertha. "How are you, Robert?"

"Stupid, but alive," Robert replied.

"That's not what he meant, son." Simon Teal stepped into the light with his wife, Ruth, right behind.

"Father! Mother! You came."

Robert's mother gently wrapped her arms around him. "Of course, it wasn't even a choice." She hugged Bertha. "What do we have in Little Rock? Nothing. We only have you, Bertha," she reached out for her granddaughter, "and Phebe."

Bertha burst into tears. "My family didn't come! They don't want me!"

"I'll bring them tomorrow. If they don't deliver the cotton in the morning, they'll lose a year's pay and draw too much attention to their absence. Your father says he always told the Reynolds he was going to move when he got enough money. He thinks he'll be first in with the cotton this year. After he sells it, he's going to let everybody know he's leaving. Nobody will wonder why they're gone."

Bertha said, "Still, it will be obvious when Robert, me, and both our families are gone."

Thaddeus explained, "It would only be logical if you all leave at the same time. You're one family now." He added, "Robert, you might want to know that two wagons and four mules were stolen from the Harrow's livery along with a wagon full of hay."

"Oh no! I didn't want anything bad to happen to Mr. Harrow! I don't know why I ever thought it would be good to give people over to Judge Hall."

Reverend Pratt had thought the judge was back on the path of sanity. "Him again?! What did you tell him?"

"I told him he could follow Mr. Harrow to Edwin Snow. Then follow Edwin to Doctor Smith, his wife, Nancy, and James."

The Reverend asked, "He saved your father-in-law's pig, so you could marry Bertha. Why would you want to turn him over for destruction?"

Robert explained, "Judge Hall said they broke the law, and he just wanted to bring them to justice. I wanted Bertha to have more than I've been giving her, and he paid me for the information."

"The law he's worried about is the one that says

whites can't marry non-whites. Judge Hall is fanatic about keeping interracial couples apart. Didn't Mr. Harrow tell you what happened in his house?"

"Only that Mrs. Hall told the judge to shoot her if he was going to go after Dr. Smith and Isabelle, but they're both white."

"If he wasn't doing the wrong thing, why would his own wife do that? Dr. Smith is half-Indian, but what made Judge Hall really mad happened in the courtroom. In front of everybody, Isabelle told the judge he was a horrible man, and she was going to fill the world with Dr. Smith's babies, and they would be right before God, but Judge Hall would be wrong. Judge Hall sentenced then to rebuild the Cadron Crossing dock and the ferry. He told them never to go around each other again, and then he found them together at the Harrow's home. He wanted to give them lashes, especially Isabelle. When they escaped, he wanted to kill them."

"I didn't know that, but I believe you. All I said to him was that he had to pay me twenty dollars for the information. I told him if he didn't, I would tell his wife he was still hunting the Smith family. I know it was Judge Hall who tried to have me killed. He told me I should be more careful about the kind of deals I make. I wish there is something I could do. I've probably gotten them both killed."

"Then travel north from Spadra and go to Harmony. Tell the people there. They may be able to direct you or get a message to them."

Robert looked at his family. "Do you want to do

this? I can go alone. I don't want to drag you into a deadly situation."

Robert's father told him, "You already have, but let's fix this together. That's what a family does."

"Bertha, tell them the rules. I'll be back tomorrow with your family." Thaddeus slipped into the night and secretly made his way home.

"I'll bring in the wagons, hay, and mules that we took from Mr. Harrow."

"Father! You stole them? You have to give them back!"

"I saw people ransacking the place. If I didn't take them, somebody else would have. Besides, I took my pay for the year and your mother's and paid off our account and yours at Clark's store and then put the remaining fifteen dollars as a credit on Mr. Harrow's account. I sold our farm wagon. It wasn't good enough to go very far. I only got twenty dollars, but I put it to Mr. Harrow's account too. I know it doesn't come close to buying two wagons, four mules, and a load of hay, but it was the best I could do. We brought all the food and everything that was ours from our home."

Robert's mother said, "I went over to your house and got yours too."

"Did you get the cradle Robert made for Phebe?" asked Bertha. "I hope we don't have to leave it behind."

Robert's father withdrew the cradle from the wagon. His mother laid the baby in the cradle and rocked her to sleep. Soon, Robert, Bertha, Simon, and Ruth slept as well.

SEVENTEEN

The first thing the next morning, Capa started pressuring. "We should do the same as yesterday. Not stop very long at mid-day and travel longer before we stop for the night."

That's a very bad plan. James disputed heatedly. "The animals need plenty of time to eat all the grass they need."

Chetan pointed out, "It is just like when you wanted to run the mules into the ground when we killed the buffalo."

"They were fine. These will be too," Capa told him.

Ppahiska overruled James and Chetan. "Winter is coming. We should get this trip over."

In the village, the young men climbed the crevasse in the cliff wall and then hunted.

Sally avoided Kimimela's suggestion to stand at the edge of the cave by insisting that they needed to search for fall plants. She and the other women rode the basket to the plateau. They found, documented the locations, and then gathered persimmons, fox grapes, pine nuts, the tiny black seeds of amaranth, and hackberry tree fruit. Before they dried the fox grapes into raisins, they removed the seeds. They toasted bars of ground grape and hackberry seed paste, along with most of the pine nuts.

Once again assigned the job, Ke wrapped seeds to plant when they arrived at their final destination and to trade along their way.

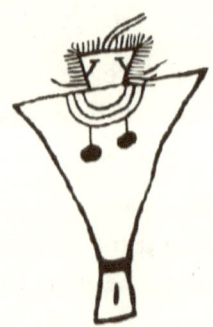

EIGHTEEN

In Maumelle, Lucy forced herself to go home. She had heard people scream on previous nights but never like the night that had just passed. The entire town had heard the sound that had broken windows, mirrors, glass jars, and china all across the town. Lucy expected to find her parlor full of bodies.

She opened the front door and cautiously peeked into the parlor. As if her clients had slept through a peaceful night, the people in the room sat on the floor chatting. Before she unlocked the door, Lucy inquired, "What happened last night?"

As if it was nothing significant, Joe Smith stated, "They put boots on Roy's ghost."

"Who is going to pay for everything that broke because you put boots on him?" Lucy asked.

The pain doctor clarified the facts. "It wasn't when Edwin put the boots on the ghost that the glass broke."

Horatio pushed past Lucy to get out of the parlor. "Regardless of when, I'll pay for the damages. It will be worth every penny if he's where he belongs and gone for good."

The day before, they had paid Lucy for breakfast. Even so, they left without eating. All of those who had encountered the demon went to Murray Strong's home. Mary went into the kitchen to prepare the morning repast for everybody. She picked up the plates. *That's curious. Nobody put a napkin on their plate like that. Candy would never allow such inappropriate behavior.* Mary looked closely at the plates and bowls. Food was gone. She never would have noticed if it hadn't been for the napkin. She finished cleaning up while she made an egg soufflé. She cut slices of bread, which she put on a tray with honey, butter, jam, cheese, prepared mustard, and cold cut meats. She poured French Roast coffee into a silver carafe and then placed it on its silver serving tray along with cream and sugar, also in silver containers. Then, every person who had spent the evening with Roy Butterfield's ghost enjoyed the wonderful breakfast together.

Joe Smith had a marvelous time. After eating, he wiped his mouth, folded his napkin, and put it on his plate. Mary's mouth almost dropped open. *There isn't a chance that somebody other than Joe folded his napkin just so and put it in a plate. Joe was in this house while we were gone. He showed up at Lucy's right after we sat in this very room and talked about going there. Joe wasn't here or at Lucy's for no reason. Martin came here with a message to warn Dr. Smith that Judge Hall was on to his location. What a perfect way to find Dr. Smith. Follow Martin and then follow my Edwin. He'll probably even protect Edwin until he has no further use for him, but then he'll kill him for sure.*

I'm not going to let that happen. "Husband, I need your help."

Mary had never asked for help with dishes. S.R. knew something was wrong. He stood up, picked up a stack of dishes, and followed his wife into the kitchen. Mary closed the door.

Always in tune with what happened around him, Murray stood up. "Would you excuse me for a moment? Candace, would you serve the coffee?"

"Of course."

When Murray opened the kitchen door, Mary almost jumped out of her skin. He crossed the room, whispering, "What's this about?"

Mary explained what she suspected.

S.R. agreed, "I think she's right. We can't let our son go with a murderer on his tail."

Murray said, "Maybe Joe should accompany Edwin. Joe will protect him and help him because Edwin is the key to his success. In addition, Joe would know he would be a suspect if anything happened to him. If Edwin knows who Joe really is, he can misdirect him and escape at the end."

Mary rejected that plan. "I don't know if Edwin would be able to do that. It's a very big risk. I don't want to do that."

"He is going to follow Edwin one way or the other," Murray pointed out.

Mary's heart beat wildly in her chest. "Not Edwin!"

"Then we don't send anybody to warn Abraham," S.R. stated the only logical solution.

"What about one of the men from Fletcher Creek? Joe wouldn't know about them because Judge Hall doesn't. We send Edwin on a trip to Perryville. Joe would think Edwin was unaware that he was being followed. Edwin could stay in Perryville for however long it takes to appear that he tried very hard but wasn't able to figure out where Abraham went. If Joe was listening earlier, he already knows we don't know where he is. He'll let Edwin come home and try some other way to find Abraham."

Mary liked the plan. "Agreed, but only if S.R. goes with him."

"Does anybody but Edwin know how to get to Fletcher Creek?" Murray asked.

S.R. answered, "Edwin has learned how to make good maps."

The three in the kitchen returned to the dining room with fresh fruit. Softly enough that it appeared Murray was trying not to correct Mary in front of others but loudly enough for Joe to hear, Murray chastised Mary, "Next time, pay attention. I've told you not to forget to put out the fruit." They hoped Joe would believe Murray had gone into the kitchen for disciplinary action.

After coffee and fruit, Murray asked, "Doctor, would you take a look at Esther?"

The meal was over, and the pain doctor would soon be examining his patient. Mrs. Doggett thought that was their cue to leave. "Thank you so much for your hospitality," Ophelia told their host.

Murray maneuvered to get Joe into a position to be

under his control. "Won't you stay and get some sleep before you leave? It's the least we can do after what we put you through last night."

Joe stood up. "Thank you for the fine breakfast and a very exciting night. I'd go back to Lucy's to sleep, but after last night, I'm sure I'd never be able to sleep in that house. I'll take you up on your offer if you show me where." Joe couldn't believe Murray had offered to let him stay. He was exhausted, and he had actually told the truth when he said he wouldn't be able to sleep in Lucy's house.

Fabia said, "Thank you, but we did have some things we've planned to do today. Let's see what my husband says about Esther and decide what to do after."

Abbott declined the invitation. "We have a steamboat to catch."

The Doggetts exchanged goodbyes with the people they would never forget. Murray walked with them to the door. "I wish you the best."

Martin, Dollie, S.R., Mary, and Edwin went off to get some rest after the harrowing night. Before he went to his room, Edwin joined his parents for a few minutes. They were all asleep when the doctor came back to the dining room with Esther and Horatio.

Horatio gave the others the news. "The damage is severe. Esther needs surgery. The doctor thinks she needs to go east. Esther and I have decided to take the steamboat to the hospital in Philadelphia. We're going to see if we can get on the steamboat leaving today." Horatio left with the doctor and the doctor's wife.

Murray was dismayed. Candace would have no reason to stay without Esther. That meant she would leave. He wouldn't need Mary, S.R, and Edwin with only himself in his home again. He didn't want to return to his previous lonely life. Murray showed Joe to his assigned room and then went to speak with his sister. "I don't want you to go, Esther. I'll hire a doctor who can do the surgery here."

Esther knew her brother well. "Oh, for pity's sake, Murray, just ask her. I need to go. It's not just the doctor; it's the hospital and the equipment too."

"We've only known each other for a few months, and her husband just died. I don't know how she feels about me. I don't want to be too forward."

"She loves you too."

"She told you that?"

Esther ushered her brother out of her room. "Ask her. Now, go on. I have to pack."

Murray was tired. Candace was tired. Both of them had just gone through a mental, spiritual, and emotional wringer. *This isn't a good time to talk about such an important matter.* Murray glanced out the upstairs window. Candace had not yet retired to her room. She stood in the garden alone. *Candy is a beautiful flower that belongs in my garden.* He joined her outside.

Joe secretly watched through the window of his room. Murray gently took Candy's hand. He led her to a bench and then sat facing her. "Candace, I know this isn't the best time, but I don't want you to go. I've come to love hearing your voice at the breakfast table. I love seeing your beauty before me. I look forward to our conversations. Even in the face of the tragedy you've suffered, you have a beautiful and pleasant nature. I know you love Jasper, and you miss him terribly. I don't want to diminish the love you have for him, but I've come to love you. Is it too soon for you to be able to love again? Would you want my love, even if it was years from now? I want to love you for the rest of our lives. Will you marry me?"

Joe couldn't hear Murray's words. He clearly saw the love on his face.

"Love doesn't have a timetable, Murray. When Jasper died, I couldn't imagine I would ever love again, nor did I want to, but then I met you. Your generosity, gentleness, and kindness have helped heal not just my shoulder but also my heart. I find you intelligent and interesting. I look forward to talking with you as much as I know you enjoy speaking with me. I've sat at the breakfast table and walked here in the garden with you and almost called you 'darling' because you feel like you should be my darling. I want you to be. I say yes, Murray. I love you too, and I'll marry you."

Murray drew Candace into his arms and promised, "I'll do everything I can to be a good husband and to make you happy."

Joe watched Murray kiss Candace. He was glad she had said yes. He wished his father had asked his mother to marry him. Instead, he had her and all his other women. Joe's life could have been so different. He lay on the bed and dropped into the sleep of the troubled.

Candace went to tell Esther the news. "I'm staying here. Murray asked me to marry him. I love him. I said, yes. I love you too, Esther. Nobody can duplicate the bond I have with you. I want you to come back as soon as you're better."

Esther hugged Candy. "I love you too, and I'm very glad you're going to be my sister-in-law. We will come back, but I don't know when. I can't live with this much pain. I have to try to make it better."

Candy supported Esther's decision. "I understand. I want you to get the help you need."

Horatio came back from the dock. "We booked passage. I convinced the captain to fix all the broken glass in his boat before he leaves, by paying for it, of course. The glass won't be installed until this evening, so let's all get some sleep." When they returned from their previously planned activities for the day, Murray showed the doctor and his wife to their room then went to his own.

NINETEEN

In Little Rock, David Thomas, Bertha's father and the overseer of Mr. Reynolds' farm, led a wagon train past the competition still in their fields picking cotton. David and the tenant farmers he oversaw arrived at the receiving dock then waited to be first in.

Every year, the storeowner, Clark, gave a bonus to the first to bring in the harvest. That way, Clark got the whole harvest in quickly. He paid for only one shipment of the goods back to the east, thus saving drastically on freight expenses. David and the other Reynolds' men were happy. They all believed they would get their full pay.

David, Clark, and Mr. Reynolds had an arrangement. Mr. Reynolds received the first six hundred dollars. David would get the next one hundred and fifty dollars for the year's salary as the overseer and then pay all the other workers. If any money remained, the man who had made Mr. Reynolds rich would receive it on top of his regular pay. This year, all the farms had a very good yield. As Mr. Reynolds' overseer, David expected to get bonus money.

David had known for the last two days that his son-in-law would not be harvesting the field of Mr. Snow. Therefore, he, his wife, and all their children had worked both nights and harvested Mr. Snow's small field. Clark weighed the first wagon, which was filled with Mr. Snow's cotton. David jotted the figure on an individual sheet of paper and slid it into his pocket. In Mr. Reynolds' farm ledger, David wrote the total weight of all the cotton he had delivered, minus the amount on the paper in his pocket.

Clark calculated the payment. It was much more than six hundred. He kept Mr. Reynolds' money to give to him directly and then handed the remainder to David. The bonus for the first delivery was a percentage of the entire weight. David calculated and separated out Mr. Snow's share, including its added bonus amount, and crammed it into his pocket. Next, David counted out his own pay. The workers from the Reynolds' plantation waited in line. He handed out the annual pay, including one hundred dollars to his oldest son. Money remained in his hand. *Wonderful, I do get extra money.* "Clark, how much do I owe?"

Clark kept the records of what was owed, which almost always happened to be almost everything anybody earned for the year and sometimes even more. This year, David still had one hundred and seven dollars after settling his account. He knew Robert's father, Simon, wanted to pay for the wagons and mules he had taken from Mr. Harrow. He also knew that Simon, after squaring with Clark, had left his remaining thirty-five dollars as a credit to Mr. Harrow.

"This is the harvest that will do it. I'm selling out, Clark."

"Bring me what you want to sell. I'll take a look at it."

At home, David loaded nine beds with their ropes and mattress, nine chests of drawers, two trunks, a large dining table with ten chairs, two overstuffed chairs, one stuffed sofa, and a floor mirror. He hauled it to Clark's store in Mr. Reynolds' wagons.

Clark went out and looked. Everything was very well made. "Not bad." Clark didn't want to sound too impressed, even though he was. He calculated in his head. He could probably sell it for over two hundred dollars.

David puffed out his chest. "Made it all myself."

Clark had discovered if he gave an odd amount, people tended to believe he had calculated an actual value by item. Most of the time, folks agreed to the amount. "I'll give you one hundred, forty-nine dollars, and three cents."

"Since I'm going to spend it all right here right now, make it one hundred and seventy-five dollars."

Clark hadn't realized that. "All right, if you unload the furniture into the storage room."

"Done." Mr. Thomas handed over Thaddeus's list of the things he should buy in order of priority. "Put one hundred dollars toward Mr. Harrow's account and then start at the top. Go until I've spent the seventy-five."

"Why are you putting money on Harrow's account? He doesn't owe me money."

"I bought some things from him. He's out of town right now, and I'll be gone before he gets back."

"All right. Take the wagons to the back of the store and get started." Clark called out, "Leave the wagons back there. We can load what you're buying when they're empty."

Clark brought lard to the wagon. Mr. Thomas stopped him. "Wait, I don't need to buy that." Clark tried to pack soap. David stopped him again. When Thaddeus had told him the news, David had been much too busy trying to get the harvest in fast. He had only stuck the list in his pocket. "I should have read Louise's list."

"Why don't you read your wife's list now and tell me what you don't need."

David went down the list. He marked off lard, soap, candles, water keg, and vinegar keg. He and his oldest son put the last sacks of flour into the wagon.

Clark said, "That's everything on your list. It took all your money."

"It's not a good idea to travel with no money at all. What about my hogs?" David asked.

Clark didn't want to give out money. He needed it all to buy the cotton from the other farmers. "I don't usually trade livestock. Do you owe Mr. Harrow more?"

"I do."

"How many hogs?"

"I got my three-year-old sow and her five piglets that were born this spring."

"I think Harrow will take them. Twenty dollars each."

"How much would it run for two wagons with covers, four mules, and a load of hay?"

"I'd say two hundred eighty dollars. That would only give you two hundred and twenty toward it."

"Put it all on Mr. Harrow's account. You better keep them hogs here."

"What about my banjo, Pa?" his son suggested.

"No, son. I want you to keep it." It was one thing to sell things they couldn't carry. It was another to sell something his son loved. He turned to Clark. "I'm going home to pack the rest. I'll come back if I think of something else."

They left the store with the supplies they would need to get far away from the town where a judge could try to kill a man and get away with it. They went to the sharecropper's house where they had lived for the last twenty years. They loaded their cooking utensils, eating utensils, weapons, ammunition, all their clothes, blankets, pillows, food, soap, shoes, lantern oil, linseed oil, washboards, washtubs, tallow, matches, candles, fishing gear, lanterns, ropes, gun powder, axes, handheld farming tools, the tools he used to build furniture, and the banjo.

He slipped a buckskin moneybag with his one hundred and seven dollars into his pocket. In addition, his son had the money he had earned as one of Mr. Reynolds' sharecroppers.

As instructed by Reverend Pratt, David Thomas and his family packed everything in the wagon that belonged to Mr. Reynolds. After several hours of waiting, Thaddeus Pratt arrived at the Reynolds farm.

He blindfolded the entire family then drove the wagon south out of town. Not far out, he turned up a dry wash. They were taken, still blindfolded, through the beautiful fall forest they could not see. They turned this way and that way, backtracked, and then went across a wide expanse of flat bedrock. They turned and circled for a couple of hours until Thaddeus thought he had sufficiently confused the travelers.

When they finally arrived at the cave, the Thomas family thought they were far away from Little Rock, instead of the thirty minutes they really were. Thaddeus called out, "Have you made the item?"

The wagons that had belonged to Mr. Harrow already had good brakes. Thaddeus had not told them to put brakes on the wagon. Therefore, the saying made no sense to Robert. However, he once again stated the required words. "Look in the wooden box."

Thaddeus led Bertha's family through the low, narrow opening into the cave. They moved David's supplies into the two wagons Simon Teal had taken from Mr. Harrow's livery during the looting.

Three families became one. Bertha's mother, Louise, held two dutch ovens. "We don't need all this cookware. It just adds weight." She handed the best one to her daughter to load.

David took the smaller pot. "We probably should

have given Mr. Harrow twenty-five more dollars, but I can't take anything back there now."

"Like Robert and Bertha, sometimes people come here without things they need. I'll keep these for the future and give the money directly to Martin when he gets home."

"Wonderful. That's good all the way around. Bertha, you finish." Bertha's mother went in search of her youngest children, who were hiding somewhere in the very large cave.

"I'll be back after dark. Be ready to go." Thaddeus drove the wagon back to Mr. Reynolds' farm and let the horses into their field. He hid all the discarded items he had brought back from the cave. Later, he would take them home a little at a time. In Little Rock, Thaddeus bought meat, bread, and vegetables for supper, in order to make sure many people saw him in town. *I do not want to have another incident like what happened to Eli when we couldn't slow the wagon. Even with good brakes, two horses won't be enough. I've got to keep the wheels from rolling. Oh, I know...*

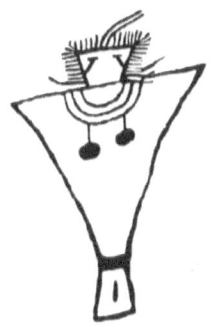

TWENTY

By the time Thaddeus had decided what to do, everybody in Murray's home was awake. Esther's tears flowed. "I'm going to miss you all terribly. Edwin, you must continue with your studies." Esther knew with her injury that she would never have a child. She had placed Edwin in that position in her heart.

"I will. I'm going to miss you too. I hope they help you feel better. Do you have the plants to make the tea?"

"I do. Thank you."

Everybody went to the dock. The Doggetts, who had thought they would leave much earlier, saw them from the deck of the steamboat and joined them. They were pleased that the six of them would travel together.

Joe told the three couples leaving, "It was nice to meet you." He had truly enjoyed them. They cared about each other. They were brave and interesting. He had always been a solitary person, never really knowing anyone and thinking the worst of everybody.

He felt he knew these people, and he liked them. Joe stood on the dock with those staying and waved goodbye. *Maybe I won't have to kill any of these people.* Joe started thinking about how he could find the two lawbreakers who deserved to die without these people knowing he was a murderer. Then, maybe one day, he could live in Maumelle and have friends.

Murray offered lodgings to Martin, Dollie, and Joe, "It's too late to leave tonight. Stay with me until the morning." They all gratefully agreed. Before they went back to bed, they shared a wonderful dinner prepared by Mary.

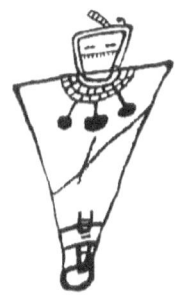

TWENTY ONE

At the cave, Thaddeus again called out the greeting. He got the proper reply, so he went in and found them ready. The way between the trees was precise. One mistake would trap the wagons. Thaddeus needed to see his marks to find the way and night would soon be upon them. Without even taking the time to blindfold anybody, Thaddeus led them away from the cave. They wound through the trees until they arrived at the extremely steep hill that was the secret to Thaddeus' escape route.

Any sane person would have sworn it was not possible to descend in a wagon. Everybody except Thaddeus assumed they had taken a wrong turn. David's young son looked at the long slope, not much wider than a wagon. He asked for confirmation that they weren't taking the very scary route before them. "We're not going that way, are we, Pa?"

Louise assured her child. "No, son. We aren't."

Thaddeus went to the back wagon where Robert rode. "You need to walk. You can't take the roughness of this descent in a wagon."

Robert walked to the edge of the precipice and looked at the hill covered with a thick layer of leaves. "Surely, you're joking."

Thaddeus once again encouraged reluctant travelers. "It can be done. Even though none of them thought they could when they stood here, many people have gone down this hill."

After much persuading, David stepped back from the precipice. "Thaddeus, we'll try it if you drive the first wagon all the way to the bottom. You can use all four mules and put the poles you brought in the wheels. If you don't die, bring the poles and mules back up here. We'll use them to get the other wagon down."

"I won't be able to get the mules back up the hill, but I'll go before you. Wait until I'm all the way down, so you can see how it's done." He drove to the very edge and then stuck a pole into the rear wheels. He urged the two mules in the harness to pull. As soon as the wheels went over the edge, he called out, "I'm not even applying the brakes, but I have my foot on it just in case."

The wagon slowly slid to the bottom then made the easiest transition from the sharp slope to the horizontal ground of the valley Thaddeus had ever made. It was a long hill. The people above couldn't see the bottom clearly, but they could perceive that the wagon was still in one piece.

David shoved the other pole into the wheel spokes and then started the second wagon down. Simon helped Robert navigate the steep incline. Bertha, not taking a chance that she would fall and hurt her baby, put Phebe in the sling, sat on her bottom, and then scooted through the leaves. Everybody else attempted to walk.

The forest ground cover crunched under their feet as people and mules tried not to slip. Robert stepped on a stick hidden under the leaf litter. His foot shot out from under him. Simon's arm around his son kept Robert from going down immediately. That was not a good thing. The sound of ripping filled their ears. Robert knew it wasn't cloth. As gravity pulled him to the ground, and his father tried to prevent it, Robert yelped in pain. The thin beginnings of his new skin had torn apart. Blood flowed. The cloth wrappings around his body, and then his clothes, quickly saturated.

"I'm so sorry," Simon told his son.

"It's not your fault. Help me get in the wagon. It's too hard to walk."

Behind her husband, Bertha saw Robert fall. She watched Simon help him get into the wagon. *That had to be bad.*

Simon felt terrible. He got into the wagon with Robert and searched for the first aid kit. When they were at the bottom, Simon got Thaddeus. "Robert needs help."

"What happened?" Thaddeus asked.

"He slipped. I tried to keep him from falling. That ripped the wound open. I found the first aid kit."

Thaddeus instructed Simon, "Get him out here. The sun is almost down. Very soon, it will be too dark to see, and we can't light a lantern. I need to get started."

Simon helped Robert lay on his blood-soaked clothes. "This needs to be sewn together again. This time you're awake, and we can't make a sedative. It's going to hurt."

"I deserve it. I might feel less guilty if I suffer." Even so, he clenched his teeth to keep from calling out each time the needle jabbed through his skin. Bertha finally arrived at the level ground. She took Phebe out of the sling, handed her to Louise, and then lay in the leaves beside Robert. She laid her hand over Robert's clenched fist. "You are very brave, and I love you."

Thaddeus made as few stitches as would hold the wound together. "I know you don't want to waste clothes, but blood will attract coyotes. These woods are full of them. You need to leave everything with blood behind and completely wash all the blood off Robert."

Bertha took control. "Simon, get me the ten-gallon tub and a canteen of water. Mother, give father some of Robert's clean clothes, a washcloth, and soap, then take all the children to the other side of the wagon." Bertha started removing Robert's clothes. Simon returned with the washtub and water.

"Get in," Bertha told Robert. In the dark, she poured water over her husband. She told nobody in particular, "Get another canteen of water," then soaped Robert up. To be sure she had rinsed off all the soap and blood, she poured the second batch of water over him very slowly. "Step out."

As soon as he was out, she threw the bloody clothes in the water with the soap. "You two take this to Ma. Ask her to wash them and then pour out the water. Ask Thaddeus if that will work." David and Simon carried away the washtub as Bertha helped Robert dress. When they got back into the wagon, they discovered the bloody blanket. Robert said, "It's too big to wash in the little bit of water in the washtub."

"We won't have enough blankets if we don't keep this."

"It's not that much blood, besides I already feel blood on my back, so it won't matter anyway. Maybe I should go in this wagon, and the rest of you should travel far away in the other."

Simon came back around the wagon. "You can't fight coyotes on your own. Give me the blanket. Ruth and Louise can at least try to wash it." He carried the blanket to the women and told Thaddeus that Robert was still bleeding.

David wanted to protect his other children. "Maybe we should separate."

Thaddeus advised them, "The more people and guns you have, the better off all of you will be against coyotes. You should stay together."

Ruth suggested a plan, "If dirt masks the blood, maybe we can put a tarp in the wagon, then a lot of dirt, then the clean clothes, then the blanket with Robert inside, and then lots more dirt."

"Too much weight," Simon informed them. "If it's about the smell, what do we have with an overpowering smell?"

Louise said, "Nothing."

Simon changed his mind. "Then, we need to not use too much dirt. Let's move some things to the other wagon."

They rearranged and then buried the clothes, the blanket, and Robert in the wagon. With only Robert's head visible, they finished the trip to the gap. The night was very dark. They could barely see a few feet in front of them. Even so, Thaddeus got out his spyglass and carefully looked up into the city of Little Rock. He was confident nobody would see them, so he led them across the gap.

When they were safely on the other side, Thaddeus told them, "Stay between these two ridges. You'll come to a creek you can't cross. Your next escort will say. 'It's a foolish person who waits here.' You should say, 'Fools find fools that find the foolish way.' It may be a while before your next contact arrives. Just keep waiting." Thaddeus asked, "You see that star?" He pointed at a particular star.

"Yes," everybody replied.

"That's the north star. I don't know what comes next, but if you keep it on your right, you'll be going west."

"Thank you so very much for your help, Reverend Pratt." Bertha hugged his neck. She remembered the night she had shown up at his door. "There is no way to know everything that would have happened if I hadn't gone to you, but Robert would surely be dead, and that would be completely terrible."

"You're welcome. As you all know, you must never tell anybody about me or any of the people who help you or any place they take you."

All assured Thaddeus that they would never give up any information. They parted ways. Thaddeus took the short route home. He prayed that God would protect them and make them invisible to the coyotes. Robert, Bertha, and their families traveled through the very dark night.

Several times, they heard coyotes howling. Not even one approached. Just before dawn, they arrived at a creek too wide, deep, and fast to cross. Wrapped in a bloody blanket and buried in dirt, Robert slept. Beside him, most of the others slept as they waited. David and Simon, however, stayed awake to protect their family.

TWENTY TWO

After another excellent breakfast, Joe asked S.R., "May I join you to Perryville?"

S.R. needed to monitor Joe's actions, and he wanted him to leave town, so Martin could go to Fletcher Creek without Joe knowing. "Of course. We might as well go together if you're going that way."

"Great." Joe went to get ready.

Mary packed for her husband and son while Martin spoke with Edwin. "I chose to come to Maumelle. It wouldn't be fair to take away your pay." He pressed two silver eagles into Edwin's hand. "Here's your fee for collecting the plants, as well as the fee you would have earned for bringing them to Little Rock."

Martin and Dollie prepared to head home with the plants he had purchased. In his pocket, Martin had Edwin's map for the secret detour.

Joe, S.R., and Edwin were well on their way to Perryville when Martin and Dollie went to the store with Candy and Murray. As promised to the people of

Fletcher Creek who had saved their lives from the mugger Roy Butterfield, Esther and Horatio had left money for arithmetic and reading books, paper, pencils, both rubber and chalkboard erasers, chalkboards, and chalk. Candy bought oil paints, canvases, brushes, a violin, a flute, and several music and painting books to send for the upcoming school year. They also procured pack mules and packsaddles to carry the supplies and a tent to protect everything if it rained.

Martin and Dollie set off on their part of the mission. The couple followed along the east side of Fletcher Creek, hoping they would not miss the obscure cutoff to the small community in the forest. The cool early November day got colder as night approached. Dollie feared. "We might not get to the warm cabins before dark." Ahead they saw two wagons. Dollie commented, "That's strange. Surely they wouldn't leave wagons beside the creek."

"Let's sneak closer." Martin led Dollie into the woods before he looked through his spyglass. "If I didn't know better, I'd say those are my wagons and mules."

"What do you see?"

"Those are our wagons and mules, along with Robert, Bertha, and their folks."

"What would they be doing out here? Let me see." Dollie took the small telescope. After she looked, she added, "I see Phebe, too, and it's much too cold for her."

David saw people approaching. "That looks like the Harrows. What would they be doing in the forest so far from home? And here we are with their wagons and mules."

The reason why all of them were there called out, "Mr. Harrow. It's Robert."

Mr. Harrow did not speak the proper words. "Why are you here?"

"Is that what you're supposed to say?" Robert asked.

Everything became clear. *Robert told the judge about Doctor Smith. Judge Hall must have turned on Robert too. Now, his whole family is out here in the Underground Railroad. I don't want to compromise the people of Fletcher Creek.* "What would you expect me to say when I come across you with my wagons and mules in the middle of the wilderness?"

"Let me explain what happened." Robert turned, raised his shirt, and showed Martin and Dollie the blood-soaked bandage. "Bertha and I ran for our lives. Bertha, being the very smart person she is, took me exactly to the right place to get help. We escaped with your wagons and mules, but we put two hundred and fifty-five dollars on an account for you at Clark's Store."

"Even though you didn't have permission to buy them, at least you paid for them. I also understand that your life was in jeopardy, but really, Robert, what did you think was going to happen? And why would you turn over a man who helped you and a lot of other people as well?"

114

"I thought Dr. Smith is smart enough to not get caught, and I was trying to make a better life for Bertha. I almost had thirty dollars, but I paid the assassin twenty not to kill me. The dirty good-for-nothing took the money and tried to kill me anyway."

"Robert, don't talk like that in front of the children." Louise held her hands over the ears of her youngest child. "Besides, if he was an assassin and he wanted you dead, you would be. I think he was trying to create the illusion that he killed you."

Simon confessed, "It wasn't Robert who took the wagons and mules. I'm the one who did it. We left you twenty-five dollars more with Reverend Pratt. However, you should know, after two days of not seeing anybody there, people were looting the livery. I knew the wagons and mules were going to be taken one way or the other, and at least I'd pay you something for them."

Dollie was upset. "Are you saying the people in Little Rock took everything? Animals, wagons, hay, and oats?"

"I'm afraid so. Even the watering troughs, buckets, bridles, saddles, and hoof picks. I even saw a couple of men taking down the big sliding door."

"What will we do, Martin?" Dollie asked. "We've lost so much. We'll be destitute."

Martin assured Dollie. "It's not the end. We'll be all right. We only lost things out of the stable. The stable itself is still there. Our home is safe. Robert's family paid for the two wagons, four mules, and a wagon full of hay. We have our horses with us. I don't like what happened, and I am going to try to find out who took our things, but even if we don't, we can recover."

Robert told Martin, "I'm so very sorry about what I did. If I had just been happy with what I had, you wouldn't have been robbed, and I wouldn't have a hole in my back or be running for my life. I uprooted both our families. I feel horrible."

"I hope you learned your lesson," Martin told him.

Robert hung his head. "I have."

"Follow me. I missed the cutoff to Fletcher Creek." Martin turned back the way he had come.

Robert informed his employer about his plan. "Martin, I want to fix what I did wrong and warn Dr. Smith. I know where to go."

Martin quickly stopped him. "Don't tell me. It's dangerous for you, me, or anybody to know that information, especially for Dr. Smith and his family."

David came back from scouting ahead. "I found the cutoff."

Under her coat and with both of them wrapped in a blanket, Bertha clutched her daughter tightly to her chest. "Good. It's gotten very cold. I'm afraid for Phebe to be out here much longer."

David stopped at a wide, shallow loop of the creek. "I think this is it."

They turned in and found the cabins. Martin knocked. "Martin Harrow and company."

Blessedly, Martin had knocked on the cabin door

of one of the few people there who knew him. Matt joined them outside in the twilight. "Martin, what brings you here, and how did you find us?"

Martin asked for all of them, "We have women, children, and a baby. Can we spend the night in your homes and explain in the morning?"

"I'll go ask." Matt went to speak with the others.

Lewis, Will, Andrew, and Morris came out. They helped unload the supplies from Maumelle. Lewis showed David and Simon where to put their mules and Martin's horses. Everybody settled in for the night and told their hosts their own version of why they were there.

TWENTY THREE

In the cold morning air, the Fletcher Creek community gathered outside and ate breakfast. Martin Harrow first related the easy information. "Esther and Horatio went back east to get help for Esther's pain. Candace and Murray are getting married. She's going to live in Maumelle."

Elizabeth raised her hand, "Are the Snows still going to live in Maumelle? Is Edwin still going to buy our plants?"

Martin explained, "I buy the plants. Edwin only helps me get them from you. While we're talking about the plants, thank you for gathering plenty of plants and for finding so many of the plants I need."

Elizabeth pressed the subject. "But is Edwin still going to be helping you? He isn't moving away, is he?"

"Edwin is on a very important mission right now, and that's the other reason I'm here."

Martin still didn't answer the question Elizabeth had asked. "But is Edwin gone, or is he still going to be coming here?"

Dollie said, "We hope he will continue to come here. We hope nothing will go wrong."

"Oh, no!" Elizabeth exclaimed.

Her father, Matt, asked, "Do you want to tell me what this is about, Elizabeth?"

"No." Elizabeth folded her arms across her chest and stared at the ground.

Sarah touched her husband's hand and whispered. "I think this is something you should leave to me."

Robert explained what had happened with as little detail as possible.

"What does this have to do with Edwin?" Elizabeth was not giving up until she had the information she wanted.

"The people the man is trying to find are folks Edwin knows and cares about. We discovered the identity of the assassin. Edwin is trying to lead him astray."

Elizabeth grew more upset by the moment. "Oh, no! Edwin shouldn't try to deceive a murderer! He may be killed if he gets involved with this!"

Dollie Harrow remarked, "Strangely, the man seems to be a very pleasant and likable person."

"A murderer would have to appear that way to do his job." Robert squirmed in his seat.

Martin returned to the primary topic. "S.R. is with Edwin and a man who goes by the name of Joe Smith. They led him to Perryville, so we could come here without him knowing."

"What does this have to do with us?" Morris inquired.

"You know them too. It's Abraham and his family."

Red-faced and eyes blazing fury, Matt's son Justin jetted to his feet. "Somebody is after Nancy?!"

Morris's daughter, Carmen, didn't like the strong defensive reaction from Matt's son. Even though Justin had chosen to stay in Fletcher Creek with her and let the girl leave without him, he obviously still had feelings for the fifteen-year-old they had known as Nancy.

Dollie had seen real hatred and a desire to inflict pain upon the people she had known as Dr. Luke Smith and his wife, Isabelle. She knew the folks of Fletcher Creek had known the fugitives as slaves named Abraham and Lily. "Judge Hall wanted to shoot Abraham and Lily in my living room. He was even willing to let Abraham go but not Lily."

Katie remarked, "But Lily is a wonderful woman. She's compassionate, and she understands how I feel about my daughter's death. I can't believe anybody would want to hurt her."

Dollie remembered what Judge Hall had said when he had confronted Isabelle and Dr. Smith. "She also stands by those she loves beautifully. That's what put her at odds with Judge Hall. He wants her to suffer. Actually, he wants to whip her and then kill her. I had the feeling he wants to do other things too."

"Aren't they long gone?" Will, Matt's brother, asked.

Robert stated the alias he knew Sally, Eli, and Stephanie had used. "For some reason, Nancy, James, and Marie were up at Spadra only a few weeks ago. I told the judge to follow Martin to Edwin and then Edwin to Lily and Abraham."

Elizabeth criticized Robert, "That was a rotten thing to do. Not only against people who saved our lives but now you've involved Edwin too."

"I know. I'm stupid. I should be punished."

Martin directed the conversation back to the issue at hand. "It comes down to this. Edwin and S.R. are misdirecting Joe, so somebody else can find Abraham and Lily and warn them. We hope one of you will take on the mission. Because of winter, we assume it will be at least a six-month excursion."

Justin wasn't going to let any harm come to any of them, but especially not Nancy. "I'll go."

"Me too," George, Morris's son, offered.

Matt knew Justin needed his father to acknowledge him as a capable man, but this involved a known murderer. Matt saw only one solution. "I'll go."

Morris also decided that was the best way. "I'll make it four."

Robert felt desperate to make amends. "I will, as well."

Morris, however, nixed his addition, "You wouldn't be helping. You're injured, and Joe will recognize you. I don't want you with us."

Martin turned to Robert. "He's right. You'll have to live with what you did without this form of penance." Martin then instructed the others, "Those going on this mission should go to Murray and Candace in Maumelle to get provisions."

Matt had an idea. His community had talked about something after Abraham's family had left. "God sent Nancy, James, Marie, Theo, Abraham, and Lily to save us, and we provided a safe place for them to stay while James healed. All of us were greatly blessed by helping each other. God put us in this remote little community to be a safe haven. God will continue to bless us if we continue to provide this service. Your four mules won't be able to pull those wagons far. It's already October. You wouldn't get far before winter would overcome you. Since you have enough provisions for yourselves for several months, and since people don't know about this place, why don't you hide here until spring?"

"In the spring, we'd no longer have provision to move on," Simon replied.

To which David answered, "What good will provisions do us if we're frozen? I don't want to risk my family, and your son needs time to heal."

Simon didn't want to spend a whole winter crammed into the cabins of the people already living at Fletcher Creek. "I wonder if we'd be able to build a cabin before winter."

Will offered, "We'll help. We'll keep at it until the cabin is built."

Simon looked at David, who nodded. "We'll stay. Thank you."

The four leaving Fletcher Creek loaded clothes into the packsaddles that had been used to bring the school supplies. Martin decided it would be best if he and Dollie went back to Maumelle with Matt, Morris,

Justin, and George and would then leave early the next morning. That way, he and Dollie could go from Maumelle to Little Rock in the light of day.

David called Martin aside, "Robert was supposed to harvest Mr. Snow's cotton. When I found out Robert couldn't, my family did it. I sold it with Mr. Reynolds' cotton. I was the first to deliver. A hundred dollars is S.R.'s share. Since you're going to see them, would you give Mrs. Snow their money?"

Martin took the money. "That was a very thoughtful thing to do. I'll give it to her."

Meanwhile, Robert spoke with Morris. "Martin says the less information anybody knows, the safer everybody will be, but I know some things I think you need to know."

"Come with me." They went into Morris's cabin. "I'll write everything down. After I memorize it, I'll destroy the note."

Robert related his knowledge. "The middle of October, James and Nancy were seen by Spadra. Their homes are a day's ride north from there in a little town named Harmony. You'll have to figure out how to get the right people to understand that you're there to help and not harm them. Abraham and Lily also go by the names Dr. Luke and Isabelle Smith. Their real names are Noah Swift Hawk and Ann Williams.

"For sure, the older man, Theo, is really Roscoe Bacon. James and Nancy claimed they were his niece and nephew. James said he met that blonde-haired woman in Little Rock. She went by Marie when they were there. She's really Stephanie Williams. They're all one family. Ann, Stephanie, and Sally Williams are all white. Ann married Noah, who is half Quapaw Indian. Stephanie married Eli Yates. Roscoe Bacon is traveling with them."

"Thank you. I do need to know this information."

After they left, those remaining at Fletcher Creek went into the woods with mules, saws, axes, harnesses, and sleds to start the work of building a cabin large enough for thirteen people and a baby.

Robert held Phebe and watched Bertha put her back into sawing down trees to build their family a home. *I can't even help build the house. I'm worthless. All I wanted was for Bertha to have a better life. Instead, both our families are in a forest, struggling to build a house before winter. Instead of bringing two people to justice, six innocent people will probably be murdered. I can't stand myself.*

Phebe felt the tension. She cried, even though her father rocked her. Robert called out, "Bertha, Phebe is hungry." Bertha sat beside Robert and nursed their baby. Robert told his wife, "I have to go. I'll never be able to live with myself if I sit here and don't even try to save that family. I won't interfere with the others."

"A saddlebag is already packed."

"It is?!"

"You are a good man, Robert. I knew you would fix what you did."

With tears glittering in his eyes, he looked into hers. "Thank you. A man couldn't have a better wife. Tell the others after I'm gone." Robert kissed his wife and then the top of his daughter's head. He stood up and walked away. Five hours after the first group had ridden out of Fletcher Creek, Robert left the little group of cabins in the woods. In his pocket, he had the ten dollars he had earned betraying the man who had made it possible for him to marry Bertha.

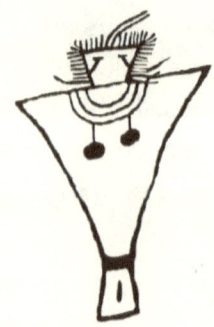

TWENTY FOUR

Unaware of the approaching threat, Noah lay beside Ann in Luyu's lodge. Before the sun came up, he heard a sound he had heard every spring. "Geese are coming."

Everybody hurried to dress. Like a ferocious storm, a mass of grey approached. When he heard the raucous honking, Chaska joined the people looking into the northern sky. "Canada geese."

In Quapaw, Sally informed him, "I am getting my bow and arrows."

Chaska thought, *she cannot be good with a bow and arrow. Those are our weapons.*

Every villager old enough to do so held his or her weapon of choice and looked into the sky. To prevent accidentally shooting each other, they agreed to spread out in a line across the field and shoot only to the north. As soon as the birds were in range, the slaughter started.

Birds dropped from the sky, victims of either an arrow or a bullet. The loud honking of the geese prevented the people and the other geese from hearing the report of the rifles or the zing of flying arrows. The gigantic flock filled the entire sky and kept on coming.

Roscoe helped Helen practice shooting a rifle. They were so thick that Helen hit a flying bird. "I got one!" She hugged Roscoe in her excitement.

Roscoe hugged her back then let her go. "Good shooting. Keep at it. I'm sure you'll get more." He continued to give her suggestions. Tom noticed how often his mother and Roscoe were together. He didn't mind.

At the other end of the line, Sally skewered bird after bird with arrows.

Chaska stopped his slaughter of geese and looked at Sally. "I did not know you could shoot an arrow so well."

"My brother-in-law is a good teacher."

"You can do many things. You could survive all alone."

"I do not want to."

"I would want a capable wife like you."

Sally blushed at Chaska's comment that she would be the kind of wife he would want. "Thank you for the compliment." Side-by-side, they continued to take down geese with arrows.

Ke planned to determine if his brother or Dustu could shoot faster. The two men shot geese so fast and accurately that Ke couldn't decide. He stopped trying to figure it out and shot birds himself.

As soon as everybody was empty, they retrieved the arrows in dead birds and those that had fallen to the ground after missing their mark. Not caring whose arrow was whose, once all the easily found arrows were back in quivers, they reformed the line and fired another barrage of arrows and bullets at the geese that continued to fill the sky in what seemed like a never-ending stream.

The flock still swarmed over them when they had again gathered arrows. They returned to formation and repeated the procedure many times.

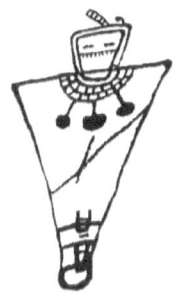

TWENTY FIVE

As the sun went down, the geese became a gray blanket lying across Indian Territory. Far away, S.R, Edwin, and Joe arrived in Perryville. They went to Adeline's Inn, opened the main door that always remained unlocked, and walked into the large dining area filled with tables. Over the bar at the back of the room hung a large sign that read, 'Knock on the door under the stairs'. A large arrow pointed to a door with a big white X painted across it. Sounds of pots and pans clanging and somebody walking came from an open door in the back left beyond the bar. Stairs leading to the rooms upstairs ran along the right side of the room over the door with the X.

S.R dinged the bell on the bar. An attractive woman in her late twenties with light brown hair and matching eyes took their money and gave S.R. a key. The two men deposited their bags in the room. Joe not only wanted to follow Edwin to Ann and Noah Swift Hawk, but he also enjoyed being with friends. He wanted to remain with S.R. and Edwin. He checked in too.

Edwin and his father pretended to have business as they alternately acted as if they were secretly gathering intelligence about Noah. Joe let S.R. and Edwin do the work. He shadowed them, believing they didn't realize he was there. Edwin and S.R. discovered Noah's skin had still been dyed brown with black walnut husks when he had been in Perryville. At that time, Noah had been pretending to be a slave named Abraham. At the end of May, he and his family had bought medical equipment at the store then left town headed north toward the Arkansas River Crossing.

TWENTY SIX

Far away, by the light of the moon, the man Joe Smith was tracking and the other people in Noah's village peacefully gathered dead birds. Since they didn't want a single goose to go bad, they spent the night opening and disemboweling carcasses. They fried and ate goose livers as they worked. When the sun finally rose, every goose had been cleaned.

The people continued their work long after the sun had risen. They ate roast goose while they proceeded to the next step of processing. To kill lice and dissolve the oils, traces of flesh, blood, and dirt, they placed the soft down needed to make comfortable pillows and the tiny feathers used to make mattresses into tubs of white lime soil and water.

Ann plucked the chests of the gray geese and also dropped intact wings into other tubs of limewater. She planned to make the wings into a garment large enough to cover an entire person and then wear it with the collar she had already made with the white wings of the snow geese.

Just like everybody else, after many hours, Ann's fingers ached. "I propose we take turns plucking and butchering. Half of us can start butchering. After whatever amount of time you want, we can trade jobs."

Knowing they needed to compact what they would carry across the plains, they cut the breasts and legs off the plucked birds and threw the meat into the big pile of salt they had put on a tarp. They tossed the carcasses into a different pile. When the sun went down for the second time after the geese had arrived, they were still plucking and butchering.

Ann's fingers barely gripped the feathers. "I know the birds have already been dead a long time, but I have to quit."

Eli said, "Remember how much down we used when we made the pillows at Fletcher Creek? We need to pluck eight hundred geese to make eleven more."

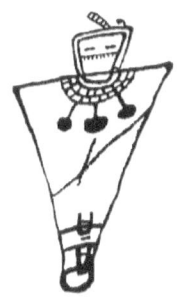

TWENTY SEVEN

In Maumelle, Martin knocked on Murray Strong's front door. His new housekeeper, Mary, expected to see the men from Fletcher Creek, not the Harrows. "Dollie! Martin! Why are you back?"

"We would rather not travel at night. We hope we can spend the night here then leave early in the morning." Martin whispered, "The men for the mission are at your other door."

"I'm sure Mr. Strong will be very happy to see you again. Please come in. Dollie, go into the sitting room. I'm sure you know what to do. I'll slip out the back and run to the bread store. "

As secretly instructed, Dollie went to close curtains. Martin followed Mary down the long hall that ran from the front to the rear door. "David Thomas harvested your fields for you. He sold your cotton with Mr. Reynolds' harvest. He asked me to give this to you." Martin handed a bag to Mary.

Mary dropped it into her pocket. She held the rear door open longer than it should have taken her to go out.

Later that night, four men ate a hot, delicious meal, hidden in the warm sitting room. The Harrows ate with Mr. Strong and his normal guests in the dining room with the curtains open.

As she prepared for bed that night, Mary gave the moneybag to S.R. He counted what was inside. *So much!*

Outside, squirreled away in the hay to which Boots helped himself, Robert slept in the very cold stables behind Mr. Strong's house.

TWENTY EIGHT

Very early in the morning, Robert ate dry hardtack. He drank from the pump that brought cold water into the stable. He and his horse slipped away before anybody realized he had been there.

Those who had arrived from Fletcher Creek ate a fantastic breakfast prepared by Mary. Murray reminded the men in the sitting room, "We're giving you the money you need, but remember, we don't want anybody to know we or yourselves have anything to do with this mission." Murray sent them out the back door to buy four riding horses with bridles and saddles.

While the day was still young, Morris, Matt, and their sons started west to Perryville with new horses, the two pack mules, plenty of supplies, and more than enough money for a six-month journey.

Robert watched the men take the west road out of town. He waited until they were out of view before he went in the same direction.

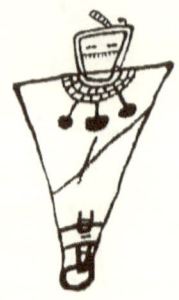

TWENTY NINE

By the middle of the third day after the goose slaughter, Ann, Noah, and family had an immense pile of down, sixteen hundred goose breasts and legs covered in salt or smoking on racks, smashed carcasses in a large cauldron becoming soup, and mounds of fat to render.

Finally done processing the birds, they returned to their earlier activities from before the geese had swarmed them on their way south. They dried their produce, gathered, boiled, dried, and ground acorns into flour, toasted hackberry and grape seed paste into bars, and started anti-parasite medicine with walnut husks and alcohol. In addition, they cleaned the goose down, feathers, and wings. Mounds of acorns and walnuts sat beside their lodge awaiting processing.

Zitkala, one of the new wives of the village, went up to the plateau. She reached for an acorn but saw something much better. *How wonderful!* When she knelt to harvest the roots of the black cohosh plant, she saw the four dead and folded-down branches of ginseng.

Since the plants were almost completely hidden under the forest litter, she jammed a stick into the ground beside them and then carefully scavenged through the leaves.

After an hour of crawling and marking the locations of ginger, ginseng, and black cohosh plants, she went down to the village and got her friends. "These sticks mark the plants I found. They are mine. There are probably more."

THIRTY

It was Edwin, Joe, and S.R.'s third day in Perryville. As if he didn't already know that Joe wouldn't go anywhere until they did, S.R. asked him, "We have more business here. Will you be moving on?"

Joe tried to think of an excuse to stay. Luckily, he didn't have to give an answer. Just then, they found out why there were so many empty rooms at Adeline's Inn.

The door marked with the X opened. A man stepped into the dining room and saw three people sitting at a table with nothing except cups of coffee.

The man bellowed, "Adeline!" as he headed toward the open kitchen door. As if it would keep anybody from hearing, he slammed the door shut behind him. He screamed, "I don't know how you ever ran this place! I've told you a thousand times to have food on the table before guests come down in the morning!"

Adeline cringed. She squeaked out, "My customers like warm, freshly cooked food."

The three in the dining room heard the sound of a fist hitting flesh and then crashing pots. "They are our customers, and I've told you not to talk back to me!"

Joe, Edwin, and S.R. stormed into the kitchen as the furious man yanked Adeline off the floor by her hair. His face turned beet red as he ordered, "Get food out there now!"

"Let her go!" S.R. grabbed the man.

Adeline begged, "Don't hurt Raymond. He just wants me to serve you well. Please, just leave the kitchen."

S.R. did not. He jerked the man toward him and drove his fist into Raymond's right eye. "Does that feel good to you?"

Raymond tried to return a punch.

S.R. blocked and leaned out of the way. "You think it's all right to hit somebody who can't defend herself?" His left hand slammed into Ray's jaw.

Ray tried to kick S.R., "Get out of my inn!"

"It's not your inn, and the owner hasn't asked me to leave." S.R. bobbed around Ray with his hands in front of his face.

Scared of retaliation, Adeline took the side of Raymond. "Please, get your things and leave."

Edwin immediately went to their room to pack.

S.R. backed away from Raymond. "Woman, throw this worthless man out of your life. If you don't get rid of him now, he'll kill you one day."

Joe stood just inside the kitchen door and watched.

***

He remembered very well this kind of man, and he remembered that his mother, Regina Stone, had always thought it was her fault when his father had beaten her.

Until he was thirteen, he had gone by his given name, Zane Stone. Joe Smith, Zane's sorry excuse for a father, had beaten his mother to death. Zane had come home and found her mangled body. He had taken a butcher knife from the kitchen drawer and gone to the saloon. His father sat at a table with his friends. In his hand, Joe held a bottle of whiskey. As if he had not a care in the world, and hadn't just murdered a woman, he let out a belly laugh.

Zane had walked to the table with the knife behind his back. "You didn't even cry over her, did you?" In a room full of people, he had driven the knife into the side of his father's neck. The whiskey bottle crashed to the floor. Every eye turned. There stood Zane, hand on the knife in his father's neck as Joe's blood drained out.

A man called out, "That's Joe Jr! His son just put a knife in his neck!"

The men who frequented the groggery knew Joe's name. Joe had never told his drinking companions his son's name. Zane knew he would spend the rest of his life in prison. He didn't see any reason to correct them. He didn't bother to tell the judge his real name either. They had put him in prison as Joe Smith. He still went by the name of the father he had killed ten years earlier when Judge Hall had freed him.

***

S.R. and Edwin came down the stairs with their bags. S.R. put thirty-seventy cents on the bar. "One room for one night."

Joe hadn't been asked to leave, so he didn't. He hadn't been able to save his mother, but he was older now. Zane had learned a lot from the hard men around him the previous ten years. *I'm finding a way to save this one.* Joe didn't bother to follow S.R. and Edwin, but Raymond did. Joe stayed in the kitchen and helped Adeline pick up the pots from the floor.

Tears streamed from Adeline's eyes. "It was my fault." She put a damaged pot into the washtub.

Joe carried two more pots to the water. "It was not your fault. You were serving us perfectly, and there was never a reason for the man to hit you. Do you understand that?"

"I don't know what happened to Raymond. He isn't the man I loved. The person who came back after chasing Lola and Sebastian is mean and violent."

"Who are Lola and Sebastian?" Joe placed a shelf back into position.

"Lola is a woman Raymond wanted to marry, but she loved Sebastian. Lola and Sebastian tried to leave town, but Raymond shot Sebastian and took Lola to his farm. Raymond thinks a family that was here drugged him somehow and helped her escape. He thinks they saved Sebastian too. He tried to chase them down. He came home saying alligators had tried to eat him in a swamp but that God had saved him. He said God had drowned Lola and all the people with her in Gum Log Creek."

"When was that?"

Adeline remembered it well. "It was the end of May."

"What do you think?"

"Those people may have helped Sebastian, but I don't see how they could have drugged Ray. They were gone before Lola disappeared. They may have drowned. Ray said he saw the wagons tracks go into the flooded creek, but none came out the far side."

"What did they look like? Would you want me to find them?"

Adeline answered, "I only saw the old man and the one girl. She was very pretty. She had perfect heart-shaped lips and long thick eyelashes. I'm sure her eyes would knock the socks off any man. I don't want to find them. I don't care what happened to them. I just wish Ray had come back as the same man who left here looking for them. I hate the man who came home."

"S.R. was right. You have to get rid of Raymond. He will kill you. I've seen it happen."

"I don't know how."

"Would he leave if he thought he could find those people?"

"I don't know. Maybe. He's not happy with anything I do, but he would probably come back. He thinks he owns this place with me."

"Do you want him gone?"

"I don't want you to hurt him."

"What if he left willingly and unharmed? Except for the harm already given by S.R."

142

"Yes. I would want him to go." Adeline made the best breakfast she could for the only one still at the inn.

After eating, Joe left Adeline's with an idea. Maybe he could send Raymond after Noah Swift Hawk and Ann Williams. Maybe they actually were the people who had helped Lola, but Raymond wouldn't know if they weren't. Raymond could complete the mission, take the heads to Judge Hall, and get the final payment.

If Raymond would, Joe wouldn't have to kill anybody else. What nagged at him as he went looking for Raymond was that he had killed a man in Little Rock who had been trying to flee with his wife and their child.

Even though everybody had told Joe he was a murderer, during all the years he had been in prison, he had never felt like one. Killing his father had felt like justice to him. Joe knew killing the man in Little Rock had been murder. If he didn't kill the woman or her Indian husband but got Raymond to do it, he would still be an accessory to their murder. Still, he couldn't imagine himself cutting off the heads of anybody to take them to the judge. *Maybe this is the way I can get out of it. I owe the judge the payment for my freedom. If the judge hadn't gotten me out of prison, I would still be there.*

THIRTY ONE

Edwin and his father talked with the man who operated the stable. "I remember a group like that coming through here this spring. There was a young man, an older man, and two girls traveling with a couple of servants as black as the ace of spades. They smuggled a Spaniard named Sebastian out of town. Sebastian was injured. One of the women had to help him into their wagon. She took the backboards off the wagon. I remember how much easier it was. I fixed one of mine like that." Chester showed them his wagon.

Edwin and S.R. knew about the wagon with the removable backboards. They were sure the people had been Dr. Smith's family. "A few days later, I found out a woman named Lola was also missing. I'm sure they didn't take Lola when they left. I've always thought Raymond killed her. I think Ray tried to kill Sebastian, but he was able to escape. I know both their families. Ever since they disappeared, I've been looking for a way to prove what Raymond did."

Raymond had followed S.R., looking for a chance to retaliate. Hiding outside the barn, he heard every word Chester had said. He was scared. *I need to get out of here. If Chester keeps looking, he'll find out what happened.* He forgot about S.R. and raced back to the inn.

Joe saw Raymond running toward the inn. He followed. He planned to protect Adeline if needed. Raymond stopped at the door, peeked in, and whispered, "Adeline." He heard no reply. He headed to their room.

Adeline had heard Raymond. She quickly hid in the secret, tiny space behind the closet in her bedroom.

Joe waited a minute before he went to the open door. "Would you want to know the location of people who may have disrespected you in the past?" he asked.

"If you mean that man who was here this morning, no," Raymond replied.

"Not him, he's nothing. I'm talking about somebody who helped steal a woman."

Raymond's eyes narrowed. "What woman would that be?"

"The one who left here alive with a living Spaniard and some other folks. I can tell you where they went and how to get paid for taking them to justice."

Raymond wasn't confessing to having anything to do with Lola or Sebastian. "I'm not saying I know any woman or Spaniard, but you can tell me what you know."

The man Raymond knew as Joe Smith explained the deal. "Judge Daniel Hall in Little Rock will pay you one hundred dollars for two of the people who helped Lola and Sebastian leave town. He'll take them dead or alive. In the process of finding them, you'll find Lola and Sebastian. If you sell your farm to me, never come back here, and stay away from Adeline, then I'll tell you how to find them. I'll also give you a name you can use when you leave."

"You can have Adeline. She's a hussy. She sleeps with me, and I didn't even marry her. I'll sell the land to you, but not my horse or personals, and only if I think what you have to say means anything to me." Raymond didn't mention he had previously made up his mind to leave forever.

"There are three sisters named Ann, Stephanie, and Sally Williams. The oldest one, Ann, married an Indian man named Noah Swift Hawk. That's why the judge wants them. He knows they are still together. Noah Swift Hawk might be going under the name Noah Williams or Dr. Luke Smith. Ann might be calling herself Isabelle Smith. Stephanie also goes by Marie Bacon, and Sally calls herself Nancy Bacon. She pretends to be the sister of a man whose real name is Eli Yates but who calls himself James Bacon. Eli actually married Steph…"

"Hold on. This is too confusing. Write all the names out for me. Where are they?"

"Except the Indian, their home was around Spadra. He's a Quapaw, so they're probably all in Indian Territory. Somebody who knows them as Nancy and James Bacon saw those two with some other people up by Spadra just a few weeks ago."

"You are sure about all this?" Raymond asked.

"Straight from Judge Hall's mouth," Joe assured him.

"You want nothing but Adeline and the farm?"

"I want you to stay away from Adeline. She decides for herself what she thinks about me. I want the farm signed over to me legally."

Everything Ray owned, except the farm, he rolled together in Adeline's blankets on Adeline's bed. "I agree. Let's go see the town clerk." Raymond opened the closet to get his rifle and to search for the inn's moneybox that he knew was somewhere in the closet. Adeline stood in the hidden space right beside every cent she owned. *He's going to find me.* Her heart beat so wildly she was sure her chest was moving the clothes hanging in front of her. "Found it." Ray closed the door. Adeline heard the sound of her money jingling as Ray dumped it on the bed. "I'm taking my share. I guess I should leave Adeline a dollar. She was a good whore."

Adeline almost flung open the secret door to slap him, but she knew it would be the second stupidest thing she ever did. The first was letting Ray into her life in the first place. *He can have the money. Good riddance to bad rubbish.* After she hadn't heard anybody for several minutes, Adeline carefully opened the secret door. The coast was clear. She hurried to the kitchen. *Joe must be a bounty hunter. I hope he got rid of Raymond. I'm glad he doesn't think just because he made Ray leave that I'm going to be his. I really hope Lola will be safe.*

An hour later, Raymond left Perryville. With him, he had the twenty dollars he had taken from Adeline, the fifty dollars Joe had paid him for the farm, and the name Joe Smith.

The new owner of the farm went back into the clerk's office. "Now you can write my name on the deed. It's Zane Stone." He walked back to Adeline's with the deed to fifty acres, a house, and a barn.

As Joe Smith, Zane stepped through the unlocked door into Adeline's Inn. He heard her humming in the kitchen. For a moment, he watched her putting together a beef roast. "Adeline, may I come in and speak with you?"

She turned toward him. He saw the joy and peace of a woman just freed. She was beautiful. Adeline invited him to join her. "You may."

He walked in. "It's nice to hear you humming."

"It's nice to feel like it." Adeline knew she had been blind. She hoped her eyes were now seeing properly.

"Raymond is gone. He's not coming back. He sold me his farm. He stole money from you, so he could leave. I'm the person who convinced him to go, so I want to give it back to you. " Joe handed Adeline twenty of the expense dollars Judge Hall had given him to find Noah and Ann. "Last, may I go tell S.R. and Edwin to come back?"

"Please do, and thank you, Joe."

Zane left Adeline in her kitchen and went in search of Edwin and S.R. He walked into the stable.

Edwin was still there with his father and Chester. "Here you are! I've been looking for you. Go back to Adeline's after you've finished your business. Raymond has left town."

Chester said, "He left? Why?"

"I bought his farm, and he wanted to go."

Chester grunted, "So he got away with it."

THIRTY TWO

S.R. and Edwin sat in Adeline's dining hall eating pot roast when Morris, Matt, Justin, and George checked in. The four new arrivals ordered a meal and then sat at the common table with S.R., Edwin, and another man who they assumed was the murderer, Joe Smith. They ignored their friends completely, who ignored them back, thereby proving to each other that they all knew the situation.

After the meal, Edwin watched to see which room had been assigned to his friends before he joined his father in his room, "I wished we knew how to write. We would have been able to give Morris a note and tell them what we've learned. But then again, if we slide a note under their door and Joe is watching, he'll know they're involved."

Zane had noticed how carefully S.R, Edwin, and the men who arrived the night before had gone out of their way not to acknowledge each other. Zane had an idea. As he did every day, he carefully watched S.R. and Edwin leave the inn to do more reconnaissance.

He saw Justin in the dining room. Joe made sure Justin did not see him as he used the lock picking skills he had picked up in prison. He let himself into S.R. and Edwin's room.

Zane left a note on the table with every bit of information he knew about Noah and Ann. He rigged a key, so somebody could sneak into and then back out of the room. When his setup was in place, making a lot of noise, Zane left the inn.

Once Justin saw the suspected killer leave, he tried Edwin's door. *Locked.* He lay on the floor and looked under the door. *What's that? The edge of a string?* Justin fished it with his knife and then pulled. At the end of the string was a key. He tried it in the lock. The tumblers turned.

Justin went into the room and saw a letter on the table. He folded it up and put it in his pocket. In place of the letter, Justin left a root of sassafras. After he locked the door, he shoved the key at the end of the string back into position.

In his room, Justin pulled out the letter. "Look how well Edwin or S.R. has learned to write." He handed the letter to Morris.

Morris read the letter. "They sure learned a lot. Says here to go to Harmony, explains how to get there, and lists all the names of Abraham and his family. This letter also says they might be in the land assigned to the Quapaws but to first go to Harmony and warn two people named Lola and Sebastian that Raymond is

151

coming. It says to leave immediately and go to Harmony with all haste because Raymond, who is going under the name Joe Smith, is a day ahead of us. The man has a black right eye and a bruise on his left jaw. The letter says he is stone cold murderous, so we should be careful." Morris refolded the letter. "S.R. must have gotten somebody to write the letter."

After Zane saw the four men leave Perryville in the direction he had instructed in the letter, he went back to Edwin's room, pulled the string with the key, unlocked the door, and went inside. The note was gone. A root of some kind lay on the table.

Zane had spent all but a few of the dollars Judge Hall had given him to fund the search for Ann Williams and Noah Swift Hawk. He knew Raymond would look harder for the two of them than he himself would have. Zane felt he had honored the deal with Judge Hall. He had his freedom. In exchange, an exhaustive search for Ann and Noah was in progress. However, he had also arranged it so good people, who were better provisioned then he was and would look harder, knew all his information about how to find Ann, Noah, Lola, and Sebastian, and he had sent them to warn them.

Zane had sent equal forces on both sides. The outcome would not be his doing. He believed he was completely out of it. Now he could be Zane Stone, and maybe Adeline would love him. He could have the life he had always wanted, except he had killed a man in Little Rock. *Maybe I don't deserve to have a good life*, he thought.

THIRTY THREE

Ppahiska and the men from his village crossed the Neosho River at Fort Gibson. James told them, "If you are going to push our animals hard, we should buy hay at the fort. There isn't very much grass this time of year."

Capa countered, "Stop pestering. The horses are fine. We would waste our money buying food that the animals can eat for free."

Tatonga joined James. "We should take care of Petang's horses. I will buy the food from my share."

"The others do not want to be gone from home so long," Capa added.

Chetan said, "I think we should give the horses more time to eat."

"They are not your horses." Capa reminded him.

For some reason, Wakanda felt compelled to agree with Capa. "Half of the horses are mine. They eat all night. We will not break apart. We will all go."

They rode past Fort Gibson without stopping. James prayed, "God, do something to protect these animals."

As they went on, Wakanda remembered that he had given permission to Tizhu to marry Weayaya for the horses they were pushing hard. He was treating them as if they meant nothing. He spoke up, "Tonight, we will stop early."

Capa, however, pressed his agenda. "They'll be fine. We will be gone for a whole month. The others do not want to be gone so long either."

They were not far past the fort when the horses slugged along with drooping heads. Wakanda's mind cleared. He knew they had made a mistake. He ran to the front of the wagons and blocked the way. "We stop now." They could easily have gone around him, but Wakanda was their mystery man.

They stopped and unharnessed the horses as a front of black clouds gobbled away the blue sky. They quickly climbed into the wagons and sat on top of the shells as the storm raged. Wakanda wondered, *why did everybody agree with Capa? We all know to take good care of our horses.*

THIRTY FOUR

In the village, the people heard the storm screaming toward their lodges nestled close to the cliff wall. Noah's family barely got the platted cattail-leaves, filled with partially dried food, safely propped against the wall before the rain and wind whipped horizontally across the village. It slammed into the mountain and then swirled in a vortex beside the cliff.

To give the animals as much protection from the wind and biting rain as possible, the young men in the village moved them to a ridge high above the creek that flowed at the bottom of the ravine. They returned to their lodges rain-soaked and windblown. Once safely inside, the villagers hunkered down while the wind howled.

A hammering started at Luyu's door. "Let me in!"

Noah opened the door. Lightning flashed behind a dark silhouette. "I cannot find Kimimela!"

"Come in, Metea." Noah stepped aside.

Sally remembered that Kimimela had told her she went to the cave and walked in a little farther every day. Sally's young friend had been trying to get her to

155

go with her for days. Kimimela had been very upset earlier that day when Sally had again refused to go. "I think I know where she is. This is my fault. You can stay here while I get her." Sally put on her poncho and tightened the drawstring around her face.

"That is my daughter out there in this storm. I am not waiting safely in a house. I am coming with you."

Ann handed Metea one of their waterproof ponchos. Stephanie gave her another. "For Kimimela, when you find her."

Noah put on his. "Let's go." The winds drove him, Metea, and Sally toward the mountain. The rain beat on their backs.

Metea called out, "Kimimela!"

If only I had been willing to try to overcome my fear. I hope Kimimela was able to do it and went far enough into the cave to get out of the storm. "I think she is in the cave!" Sally screamed above the howling wind.

"My daughter would never go into a cave! You are wasting time!"

Sally stood outside the opening. "Kimimela!" She heard nothing.

Metea ordered, "She is not there. We need to go."

Sally put her head inside the entrance and called out as loudly as she could. "Kimimela!"

If Sally put her head in the cave, she truly believes Kimimela is in there. Noah yelled with her.

They got no reply. Metea pulled on Sally. Sally knocked her hand away. "She is here!" She stepped inside the edge of the cave. "Kimimela!" Still nothing. *I can't leave Kimimela in a dark cave.* She went in farther.

Noah joined Sally in the cave. "I will go in and look." He called out the girl's name as he walked into the darkness with Metea behind him. Noah found the lantern stored in the cave. He opened the bottle of matches he had brought and lit it. Holding the light high, he moved deeper into the cave. Sally's heart pounded. Paralyzed with fear, she stood not far from the entrance.

The light grew fainter as her brother moved farther away. Sally absolutely was not remaining in the darkness alone. She swallowed hard then hurried to join the others.

Metea called, "Kimimela, are you in here?"

"Here I am!" Kimimela ran out of the darkness.

Metea held her daughter close before handing her the poncho. "Put this on."

Kimimela took the waterproof cover but stepped over to Sally. She hugged her tightly. "You came into a cave for me! I knew you could do it."

"Did you come in here to make me do it?!" Sally asked incredulously.

"I came to make ME go in. When the storm came, I went in farther to get away from the lightning. I got lost, but I remembered what happened when Takoda and I kept wandering in the cave all those years ago. I knew I could not be far in, so I sat down and waited."

Sally looked into Kimimela's eyes. "Now, we both know we can do it."

Kimimela put on the poncho. "How can we get out?"

"We follow the water I caught in my poncho to leave a trail." Noah led them out.

THIRTY FIVE

The men in the wagons out on Military Road had planned to hunt. Therefore, they had no food. Hungry, they sat inside the wagon on sharp, uncomfortable shells while the horses crowded together with their rumps into the wind and ate the lush grass.

Wakanda thought, *The God of the universe listens to those who believe. James asked God to protect our horses. God commanded the skies, and the clouds gathered. He commanded the grass, and it grew high right here at the place He knew we would stop.* Wakanda had another thought he believed came from God. *The God who controls everything says, 'Go back to Fort Gibson and buy food.'* Wakanda got out and started walking.

A moment after, with two large shoulder bags, James struggled against the wind beside him. The rain beat against their faces.

"Help us, God!" James called out over the howling. The wind turned and pushed from behind. Just before nightfall, James saw the fort ahead. "Act exhausted, like you cannot go on."

"That will not be an act," Wakanda replied.

James carried Wakanda over his shoulder. He informed the soldiers, "I need to get into the fort."

"You can't bring that Indian in here. It's almost time to close the gates."

James growled out, "Then you will explain to the spirit of our mystery man why you let him die in this storm."

Private Dennis didn't believe Indian mystery men had supernatural powers, but he wasn't really sure. He was, however, completely certain he didn't want to call over the anger of the entire Indian Nation. "We'll go see the commander right now." He escorted them straight to Colonel Howland's office.

The soldier reported, "Colonel Howland, there's a man who wants to bring an Indian in here tonight."

"Who are they?" the colonel asked.

"They're here."

"Send them in." James and Wakanda walked into the colonel's office. Colonel Howland recognized the two men. He told the young soldier, "Leave us, but stay outside the door." After the door closed, he asked James and Wakanda, "What are you two doing outside in a storm like this?"

James told him the truth. "We were traveling. We didn't let our horses rest or eat enough. They became too weak to go on and then this storm came. All we could think to do was to come here."

"I can't let you stay inside the fort."

James suggested what he and Wakanda had already planned. "Lock us up for attempting to get inside. When the storm is over, let us buy supplies and then leave."

"You agree?" the colonel asked Wakanda in Quapaw.

Wakanda smiled. "Yes."

The colonel opened the heavy wooden door. "Private Dennis, these men attempted to stay in our fort after dark illegally. Throw them in the stockade."

The private gloated as he escorted the lawbreakers to the place they wanted to be. "I told you he wouldn't let you stay, and now you're going to the stockade for trying."

God had already prepared. Wakanda saw the shock in the eyes of the guard on duty at the stockade. The private who took them to the jail informed the officer-in-charge why he was receiving prisoners. "They were trying to get inside the fort for the night. The colonel ordered them into the stockade for trying."

Sergeant Timothy Anders took possession of the prisoners. Private Dennis smirked as he left. Tim locked his friends into their cells. "I guess this is your plan to get out of the storm."

James said, "The private was right. We were trying to get into the fort for the night, and the colonel did sentence us to the stockade until the storm has passed."

"Be back shortly." Tim left. Ten minutes later, he returned with a large duffle bag and a tray.

"This will help." He passed each man a covered plate. "I'm going off duty, but I'll be back in the morning." He gave James the items in the bag.

The prisoners got out of their wet clothes, put on the dry clothes from the bag, and then lay the extra blankets on the steel beds.

Wakanda ate salted pork and hardtack as he drank hot black coffee. "Not the best meal, but it is hot."

"Better to be in here dry and warm than out in that storm, eating nothing." James dipped his hardtack into his coffee.

The night guard came on duty. Sergeant Anders transferred control. He informed the new guard of the state of affairs. "Two prisoners in custody. They shouldn't give you any problems. Have a good evening. I have the morning shift. I'll see you then." The night guard never went to see who was in the cells.

Wakanda whispered to James. "What do you think of Capa? Why did we do what he wanted?"

"I've asked myself many times why everybody agreed with him," James replied.

"Last year, he never would have left a man in a dangerous situation. This year he did, and he has been very greedy. Now, he almost killed sixteen horses."

James pointed out, "He's been different since the sweat lodge ceremony."

Wakanda put into plain words what he had concluded. "We did not keep all the demons out of our world. There were so many, and they tried so many ways to get past. Sally found one that got into our world and threw it back. I think we missed one. I think it found a home in Capa."

"I have no idea how to get a demon out of a person. What can we do?"

"I will meet with the mystery men in the other villages."

In the morning, Sergeant Tim Anders came with eggs, bread, and coffee. Tim gave his prisoners some of his own sugar and milk rations. "Morgan, Ezra, Ham, and I got double pay and double rations for bringing the buffalo meat and making arrangements to trade for vegetables."

"I'm glad something good happened for you," James replied. "I guess you don't know what happened after you left us with the Cherokee."

"Did they find out about the other buffalo?"

James replied, "No. Our daughters got married!"

"What? I didn't expect that answer."

I need to keep Noah's name hidden. James picked up a strip of bacon. "My two oldest daughters, Chetan's mother and his two oldest daughters, Wakanda's youngest daughter, and Tatonga's oldest daughter, were noticed by some of the Cherokee men. Before we left, they wanted to marry our women, and later they did."

Tim knew Chetan's son only by his Indian name. "I didn't know Tahatankohana has so many people in his family. I thought he only had his wife and parents."

"His family is the biggest in the village." James tipped up his coffee cup.

Sergeant Anders asked, "Are you happy about your women marrying Cherokee men?"

"Yes. I like my new sons."

162

"So it worked out well. That's good."

James divulged more information. "It worked out extremely well. Chetan told the men who wanted to marry his daughters that they had to get permission for us to hunt on Cherokee land."

The Sergeant was again surprised. "They did it?"

James scooped eggs onto his fork. "They are very intelligent young men and managed to arrange a negotiation. A few of our people and a couple of Cherokee came to an agreement." James failed to mention they were all women. "Now we can hunt but only as agreed."

Very excited, Sergeant Anders asked, "May I hunt with you?"

James swallowed coffee. "The agreement is for the Quapaw people to hunt, but we can have seventeen people in a hunting party." *Today, we have the talisman and only nine men, but it would not be good to have very many others, especially people I am not sure will behave properly. I do know four soldiers I would take.* "Maybe."

"What would I have to do to make that a 'yes'?"

James translated the request to Wakanda. The thought came to Wakanda; *Ask for everything.* "We would have to go now. In your wagons, you will have to bring hay for your horses and ours. You also have to supply food for you and for us all the way to Fort Smith and back to here. We have sixteen horses and nine men, and I have to approve the men coming." James passed on the requirements.

"Get back into these clothes." He handed them the

clothes he had dried for them the night before. "Wrap the clothes I lent you and the blankets together with the sheets on the outside. I'll be back soon!" Tim dashed out of the jail.

The sergeant came back with Colonel Howland. "Sergeant Anders said we could hunt with you on Cherokee land if we provide our own wagons, rations for everybody, and hay. Is this correct?"

James answered, "Not too many men. We approve of the men who will come and probably only this once. You will have to provide your own trade items."

The colonel asked, "What are the trade items?"

James explained, "Depending on what you kill, either mussels in brine, empty mussel shells, pottery, crop seeds, or permission to gather live mussels in Spring River."

The colonel stated the provisions he had to offer. "We have plenty of seeds and mussel shells. We can't give permission to gather mussels, and we don't have any pottery or mussels in brine."

James told Wakanda what the colonel said. Again, the thought came into Wakanda's mind; *ask for everything*. "We brought pottery and mussels in brine, and we could give permission to gather mussels. Depending on what you need to trade, we will sell you what we don't need to use for ourselves."

James relayed the message.

"Do you have enough extra?" the colonel asked.

Wakanda understood the question. *I will make sure we do.* In English, he said, "Yes."

The colonel counted on his fingers as he named the men, "I will be going, Lieutenant Jackson, Lieutenant Olson, Sergeant Tim Anders, Sergeant Matthew McCormick, and five privates to do the butchering."

Wakanda watched the counting. *That is almost as many as us.*

He was about to say 'too many' when James said, "Only three privates. We can only have seventeen. Every one of you has to dress in Indian clothing. When we go to the village to give them the trade items, all of you will stay in the wagons and say nothing, especially Sergeant McCormick with his red hair. Your wagons must have waterproof covers to protect the supplies. The privates must be Ezra Knuckles, Morgan Finch, and Ham Blanders. We already know them, and they already know how to butcher buffalo."

"Agreed. We'll prepare to go immediately." Colonel Howland opened the door. He saw a soldier in the yard. "Private Henderson, you are now on stockade duty. These prisoners are released."

"Yes, sir." The soldier entered the building.

Sergeant Anders unlocked the cells. He picked up the bedding and clothes. "Probably have lice in them now." He carried away the spare clothing and extra blankets without anybody knowing he had given them.

James and Wakanda walked out of the cell. The colonel issued orders. "Complete your business quickly and then meet us on the south road."

165

They didn't have any more business. They had just accomplished their objective with the Colonel. They walked to the gate. James said, "Very good work, Mystery man. Éclairs are on me." James, being a very generous man, bought three dozen of them. He held one pastry and passed one to Wakanda. He smiled. "Only so we will have exactly the right amount to give everybody two later."

After loading all the shells from the shed and the other agreed-upon supplies, three wagons left the fort. Wakanda and James jumped on a wagon when the soldiers caught up. At the Indian wagons, Wakanda explained. His people agreed it was a good arrangement.

Chetan asked the colonel, "Did you successfully blow up whatever you wanted to destroy?"

"Yes. Thank you for arranging for us to purchase the dynamite. We opened a road to Fort Leavenworth."

"Are more soldiers coming here?" Chetan asked.

"I don't think so. We've been able to do what we're supposed to do."

The horses were refreshed after they had rested and filled up on wet grass. The soldiers and the Indians traveled on.

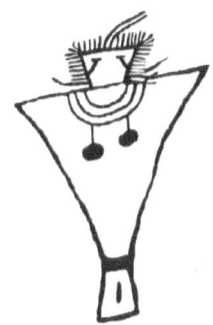

THIRTY SIX

When the sun rose, the young men of the village led the animals out of the ravine. On the way to the large field that was their usual home, Petang looked at his lift. "Oh, no! Look at the basket!"

Noah's brother-in-law, Dustu, walked over. "Probably the wind smashed it against the cliff."

"We will ask the women if we need to make another. We must tie down the next one." Nikiata noticed a branch with a cleanly sawed end. "I think this is from the tree we used for the lift. The storm must have blown the cutoff branches over the edge."

"I will get Luyu." Noah went home. The others took the animals to the field.

Luyu tipped the basket onto its side. "We will have to make another. We need more vines."

Algoma picked up the cut end of the large branch Nikiata had examined. "If we tie the broken parts together, it might be good enough to take us up while we make another?"

Behind Algoma, Helen pulled two smaller tree limbs into the village. "Why try?"

"There are acorns up there," replied Algoma.

Petang pulled at the broken part of the basket, "It would be easier to get up there to get more vines if we can use the basket."

"I'll get some rope." Noah again started toward his home.

"Probably only one person should be in the basket." Ann rubbed her belly. "Calm down, Wambleeska! This child is trying to run before he even gets out!"

When they got the broken part sufficiently roped up, the women, men, and children took their gathering sacks, saws, machetes, and other tools to the plateau. They harvested acorns, vines, cedar trees to make another lift frame, and ironwood to make spinning wheels and carts. Algoma and Bethany worked together. They sent down and then also unloaded everybody's baskets of acorns. The men raised the broken lift basket back up and out of the way before they pushed the newly collected vines and trees over the edge.

At the end of the day, the women had enough acorns to boil for days and everything they needed to build another basket.

However, since Stephanie had discovered a walnut grove, they decided to keep the broken basket in service. Those who were not assigned to build the new lift were to collect walnuts until they had every one they could find. Then, they would divide the total harvest by the number of people in each family, no matter who had done what.

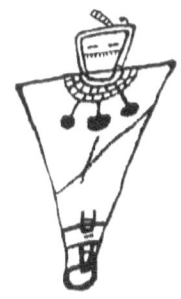

THIRTY SEVEN

That same day, a delirious man rode into Perryville. His horse went where hunger told it to go. It stopped and helped itself to stacked hay. When Chester walked into his barn to feed his animals, he saw the man slumped over his horse. Blood ran out of the man's back and dripped off the belly of the horse onto the barn floor. Chester ran for the doctor. They hurried back.

The doctor quickly assessed the situation. "We need to get him to my office."

Dr. Higgins was old. Chester knew he couldn't help carry a grown man. He stepped out of the barn and saw a man walking down the street. "You there! We need you to help carry an injured man to Doc's place."

For the first time in his life, the man wanted to be somebody people were happy to see. "I'm glad to help. Name's Zane. Zane Stone."

Chester and Zane pulled the man from the horse. He fell into Zane's arms. The delirious man's eyes looked directly into Zane's, but he was barely holding on. He couldn't understand what the face meant.

Zane barely believed it. *What are the chances I would be able to help save the life I thought I had already taken? This didn't happen by chance. If the doctor saves this man, I won't be a murderer. Maybe I won't end up like Roy Butterfield. Maybe God will even let me have a good life.* Zane and Chester laid Robert Teal on the doctor's bed.

Dr. Higgins removed the man's shirt and the bandage wound around his body. He probed the deep, badly infected wound in the man's back. "This is too close to his heart. He's not going to live."

Zane did not want the hope he had just received to be ripped away. He needed to talk to somebody, and he knew of only one person who might listen. He went to Adeline's Inn.

Adeline's sweet voice floated across the room when she saw Zane. "Hello, Joe."

"Adeline, a man rode into town in bad shape. He's somebody who HAS to get better, but I don't think he's going to make it."

"Do you need to bring him here?"

"He's with the doctor."

Adeline told Zane, the man she knew as Joe, her opinion. "Doc won't try if he thinks he's a drifter. Do you think he can pay?"

"I saw a moneybag. It looked like it had something in it."

Adeline walked to the door. "Come on. Let's go talk to Doc Higgins."

S.R. and Edwin returned as Joe and Adeline were leaving the inn. "Where are you two going?" Edwin asked.

Adeline told him, "A very sick man came into town. We're going to see if we can help."

Edwin was curious. "Do you mind if we tag along?"

Adeline kept walking. "Come if you want to." They opened the door and stepped into Dr. Higgin's office. "We've come to see if we can help."

"Nothing to do but dig a hole and bury him," the doctor replied from the back room.

The four went toward the sound of the doctor's voice. Adeline stepped into the room where a man lay on his stomach. The others followed her. Dr. Higgins looked toward the door. "Hello, Zane. This kind man helped Chester carry this poor sot over from the stable."

Adeline, S.R., and Edwin looked at Joe.

"I'll explain later," Joe told them.

Edwin looked at the man. "He's Robert!" He immediately went to the bed. "It's all right, Robert. We're here now. We're going to take care of you." Robert looked at the young man talking. He should have known him, but his mind was cooking with a high fever.

S.R. told the doctor sternly, "You will do more than just dig him a hole. You will do everything humanly possible to save him!"

"There's nothing humanly possible to do. He's already delirious from the infection," replied the doctor.

Adeline said, "We'll take him to my place."

"If he dies, it's on you." Dr. Higgins left the room.

Zane, Edwin, S.R., and Adeline carried Robert away. As soon as Robert lay in a bed at Adeline's, Edwin went to collect the maggots he had seen.

Over the last ten years, Zane had seen many wounds treated by prisoners. If they died, nobody cared, and the guards had never tried to help them. The prisoners had learned to help themselves. Zane did what he remembered. He started scraping the pus and infected flesh out of the hole he himself had made when he had flung his knife into Robert's back.

Adeline and S.R. returned with warm water to wash the wound and cool water for Robert to drink. Adeline also brought a soup that Robert could swallow in his current mental state. When Edwin returned with the maggots, Robert's wound was as clean as they could make it with the tools they had. S.R. poured whiskey over the injury. Edwin took the bottle, poured some into the empty soup bowl, and then swished the maggots in the whiskey.

Adeline cautioned him, "Don't drown them."

"Or get them drunk," his father joked.

Edwin had seen the small, squirmy, white creatures used before. He had developed a big appreciation for the services they provided. He thought the maggots looked clean enough. He carefully positioned the insects in the places he thought their small mouths needed to be to remove the remaining infection. "These are very smart," he informed the others, "They know exactly what to eat. They leave the good flesh alone."

At the end of the day, Adeline, S.R., Zane, and Edwin had done what they could. Robert had plenty of water and soup in him, most of the infection had been removed, and the maggots were working on what was still there. Adeline prayed. "God, when Raymond hit me yesterday, I prayed for You to deliver me from him. In mere seconds, these servants of Yours did what I had asked. I never knew You before, but I know You now. I'm asking You to perform a miracle again. Use the four of us as Your instruments to save Robert."

"Amen," concluded S.R. and Edwin.

Zane thought about Adeline's words. *Did God really use me to answer a prayer? Why would God do that if He plans to send me to Hell? Murderers don't go to Heaven.* Finally, Zane added, "Amen. I know Robert's going to live." Zane wanted to explain everything, but he was afraid.

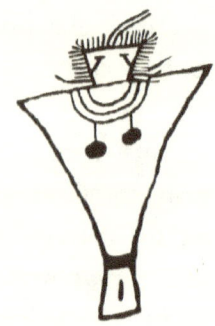

THIRTY EIGHT

Due to hunkering down during the storm, Raymond was not as far west as he wanted to be. He paid to cross the bridge over Kuhn Bayou. He didn't want anybody tracking him as Raymond. Therefore, he made sure the ferryman would remember him as Joe Smith. The gap between him and Matt, Morris, Justin, and George narrowed when the four crossed the Arkansas River.

Oblivious to the approaching danger, Ann and the other women hung meat in billows of smoke. They placed fruit and vegetables in the sun to dry, boiled or roasted nuts, and built the replacement basket. Noah and the other young Quapaw men searched for game with the new Cherokee members of their village.

A day's travel south of Fort Gibson, Ppahiska and his men camped with Colonel Howland and his soldiers. Chetan and James translated the many conversations as the two groups of men spoke with each other.

Robert's body had lain buried in dirt to keep him from drawing coyotes, and then in a stable to hide. In

Perryville, his body fought to survive the invisible attackers he had not avoided.

Zane's desire to confess grew stronger. *I wonder if I can trust them. I don't want my past to ruin the life I may be able to build here.* He looked at Robert. He turned to Edwin, then S.R., and then Adeline. *Probably not.* He remained silent with his mind and heart in turmoil.

Robert burned up with fever while the people he had put into jeopardy peacefully slept in their lodge in Indian Territory. Zane spent the night using wet washcloths to keep him as cool as possible. Edwin never allowed the man he knew as Joe Smith to be alone with his friend. S.R. never left his son alone with the man he believed was an assassin.

A spider web glittered in the morning light. Zane remembered the old man in prison who had daily put a fresh spider web in a cut on his arm. The wound had never become infected.

"I'll be back." Zane walked the inn. He collected every web he could find, then went back and started to shove them into Robert's infected wound.

Edwin knocked his hand to the side. "What are you doing? Joe or Zane or whoever you are, I'm not going to let you kill him. I know you're the one who put this hole in Robert's back."

Zane was speechless. He had no idea Edwin knew what he had done, but Zane's first concern was to stop the infection in Robert's back. *If Robert dies, I'll end up a tormented ghost like Roy Butterfield. If I go back to prison for attempted murder, I'll do it, but I am saving Robert if there is any way I can.* "You're right. I am the one who threw a knife into Robert's back, but I don't want Robert to die. I'll explain, but first, get these into the wound. They'll help get rid of the infection."

"No," S.R. refused to give permission.

"Then let me get Adeline, so I can tell you together."

"You'll run away." S.R. instructed his son, "Edwin, get her."

When Adeline and Edwin were back, Zane told his story. "My mother named me Zane. Her last name was Stone. My father was Joe Smith. He never married my mother." Water glittered in his eyes. "I found my mother beaten to death. She was so mangled I couldn't even understand how my father kept hitting her for so long after she must have already been dead."

Anger flowed with his words. "He wasn't sad or upset when I found him. He was laughing. He was happy. In a room full of people, I walked up to him and stuck a knife into the side of his neck. All I could think was he was not getting away with what he had done. None of his friends knew my name, but they knew I was Joe's son. They called me Joe Smith Junior when they sentenced me to life in prison."

Zane told the story of ten years in prison from the time he was thirteen. He told them about the man using spider webs on his arm. Then he told them, "I thought I would live my whole life in prison. Then, out of nowhere, Judge Hall showed up and gave me a chance to have my life back.

"Judge Hall kept me locked in his cellar until the night I threw the knife into Robert's back. When he set me free, I was already a murderer. I had killed my father. That was why I had been in prison. I didn't feel like a killer, but I knew if I didn't do what Judge Hall asked, I would go back to prison.

"Even though I had plenty of chances, I couldn't make myself tackle Robert and drive the knife into his heart. He even had the courage to walk over to me, put twenty dollars on the table, and ask me to spare him. I followed him anyway. Then, I saw the man's wife and baby. He tried to protect them and keep them with him. I saw that he was somebody who knew how to love, so I let him ride away. I struggled inside. I didn't want to hurt him, but I couldn't go back to that cesspool of a prison. When I threw the knife, part of me hoped Robert was far enough away to survive.

"When I saw Robert here in the barn, I thought God was giving me a chance. I thought, maybe I'm not a murderer. I don't want to be a killer. Don't you see? Robert has to live, or I will be.

"I also know, to remain free, I have to honor my word to the judge. What Judge Hall really paid for is a search for the woman Ann Williams and her Indian husband, Noah Swift Hawk. Raymond has gone to look for them. He'll look harder than I would have, so I think Judge Hall is getting what he requested for my freedom.

"I saw those men come into Adeline's. I thought you knew them, so I left them a note telling them everything I know about how to find and warn Lola and Sebastian and everything I know about Ann and Noah. I set it up, so they could break into your room. They did, and they took the note. In its place, they left a root of some kind. I took the root and relocked the door. Now, those men are on their way to warn those in danger.

"If the judge tries to find out about Joe Smith's search for the people he hates, he'll discover that Joe Smith was here but continued on. Because Raymond wants to make sure Raymond Pence isn't found, he'll use the name Joe Smith for the rest of his life. Judge Hall won't care that a person named Zane Stone bought the farm of Raymond Pence. Those names mean nothing to him. Now I can be the person I want to be, but only if Robert lives."

Edwin told Zane, "Go on. Put the webs in the wound."

Zane looked at Adeline. "Do you understand?"

"I do." She left the room. She wasn't saying anything about the man or his life except that she understood what he had told them. Time would tell what would happen between them, if anything ever did.

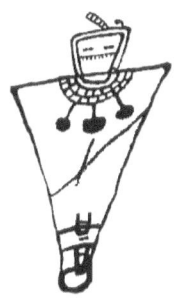

THIRTY NINE

The older Indian women made a basket better than the first. They used thinner vines to make the weave tighter to better protect against arrows. After many rows of vines, they started the opening for the door. Several layers up from that, they dropped the first three rings around the heavy, ironwood stick that was the side of the door and the other that was the edge of the basket. The middle ring would rotate between the upper and lower rings so that it wouldn't cut the vines.

Leaving only the door area open, they wove rows of vines about a third of the way up before they added the next three rings. Afterward, they wove the basket two-thirds of the way up. They put on the last set of rings then added several more rows.

From there, they wove the vines all the way around the basket cage. They made each ring smaller until they completely enclosed the top like a dome. They wove the door to the stick joined by the rings. Last, they added tie-down ropes so that they could secure it at the top of the cliff or the floor of the valley.

FORTY

In Arkansas, south of Dover, Matt, Morris, and their sons arrived at Gum Log Creek in the dark. Matt called out, "Hello in the camp!"

The man at the fire answered, "Have some coffee."

"Thank you. I'm cold. Hot coffee would be wonderful." Justin got out his cup. He attempted to get the man to state his name. "Name is Justin."

"Nice to meet you, Justin. Sit by the fire and get warm." The man poured a small amount of coffee into all their cups, then pulled out his bag of ground coffee.

"It's late. Don't start more. We'll set up our camp here if that won't bother you." Morris hoped this man was the one they wanted to overtake.

"Suit yourself."

They wanted to wake up without a knife in their hearts. They set up camp beside the man, but then followed their prearranged sleeping and keeping watch schedule.

The man didn't know the people who had just joined him, and there was only one of him. He didn't sleep. He already had a big pot of coffee brewing when the other men woke. "Coffee for anybody?"

In the morning light, they held out their cups and saw the black eye. They were with Raymond, now known as Joe Smith. They sat the coffee on the rocks beside the fire while they got the food they planned to cook for breakfast. When they saw the maker of the coffee pour some from the same pot into his own cup and then drink it, they started on their own coffee.

George probed, "Where are you heading?"

"Why do you want to know?" the man asked.

George felt brave, invincible, and determined to outsmart Raymond. "I thought you might like to travel with us. We're going to Fort Smith."

"I'm not going that far, and I'm waiting for somebody to meet me, but thanks for the offer."

Morris saw the man didn't have many provisions. He knew very well the feeling of hunger. He had lost a daughter to starvation. He didn't want any person to go without food. He cooked food for all of them. "Have some, as thanks for the coffee."

Raymond held out his plate, and Morris filled it full. The five men ate the large breakfast as they talked about nothing in particular. Morris, Matt, George, and Justin tried to glean every bit of useful information they could. After finishing every bite of food, George and Justin cleaned while Morris and Matt packed up.

"Much obliged for the coffee, Mr. …" Justin shook the hand of a man he believed was a murderer.

"Think nothing of it." Raymond was kinder to strangers than he had ever been to Lola or Adeline. Morris, Matt, and their sons rode through the shallow water of the creek. Raymond stayed in camp, sulking over Lola's rejection and her escape.

In the spring of the year, he had seen the tracks from Lola's wagon go into but not come out the far side of Gum Log Creek. He didn't see how it could be possible, but it wouldn't be long before he would find out if Lola and the others were alive. He thought about the man she thought was better than him. He thought about the people who had drugged him, taken two horses, and helped Lola and Sebastian leave town. The more he thought about it, the angrier and more irritated he felt. Because of them, he no longer owned the farm. Because of them, he couldn't live in Perryville anymore. Because of them, he was outside in the cold with nothing to his name but a horse and a few personal things. He didn't think about the fact that he carried a bag of money. He wanted to hate all of them. As he fell asleep after the sleepless night, he did.

"I wonder if Raymond knows exactly where to go?" Justin asked after they were far away.

Morris gave his opinion, "I have no idea what he knows, but we should move quickly and increase our lead, in case he does."

"You're right, Pa." George flicked his reins.

Matt suggested caution in the future. "People like Raymond may seem very nice, but you need to be careful. They can turn on you like a mad dog. It's not wise to stay around them. Let's not suggest something like traveling together again."

"I guess it doesn't matter now that we've left him behind," replied George.

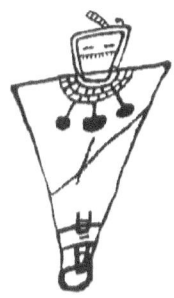

FORTY ONE

Wasting no time, they arrived at Dover that night. They planned to stay in rented rooms and eat meals prepared by others as often as possible. Therefore, as directed by the storeowner, they went just north of town to the Butterfield Boarding House.

Clarabelle Butterfield showed them to their rooms. A steep set of stairs rose to a landing where a person could turn either right or left to enter the rooms over the two just below. When she had inherited the house, she had sealed the secret doors inside the closets and used the long, narrow hidden compartments between the lower rooms for the stairwell. The space below the stairs was now a linen and storage closet. Clarabelle had converted the other end of the house the same way. Her boarding house now had eight bedrooms, a large central sitting room, a dining room, and the kitchen. She opened the doors into the two upper rooms at the south end of the house.

Clarabelle had been making a good living providing rooms and meals to the people traveling the road that ran through Dover. She held her one-year-old son on her hip as she handed the men the keys. "I'm Clarabelle. This is Hank. If you need anything, call me. I have chicken pot pie if you want it tonight."

Justin answered quickly, "We would love it. Anything else come with that?"

"I have plenty of bread and cheese and a cherry pie. I can make a pot of coffee or tea. I have ale too."

Matt ordered dinner. "Chicken pie, bread, cheese, pie, and ale for all of us."

Clarabelle went off to the kitchen. Morris and George went to one room. Since each room had only two single beds, Matt and Justin went to the other room. They put their packsaddles in their rooms then went downstairs to the dining room.

Clarabelle placed the food on the table. George swallowed his first-ever taste of ale. "You have a strange configuration for your rooms."

"It's a long story."

George wanted to hear the details, but mostly he wanted to talk to a woman as a man who could drink ale. "I'd love to hear it."

Clarabelle sat. While the men ate, she told her story. "I married a man I had known since childhood. His name was Hank Butterfield. A few months after we married, some friends of his came to visit. He started acting like a different person. Before long, I realized he had many personalities. He built this house to accommodate those different personalities. It had secret rooms where he hid parts of himself from the other parts. Different manifestations of Hank knew about different rooms. The upper rooms and the staircases were those rooms. I put in the stairs and divided both of the large upper rooms at each end of the house."

Matt wanted to know more. "What happened to your husband?"

"He was shot by the sheriff of Harmony."

"What?" all four men exclaimed.

"Supposedly, Hank picked a fight with an Indian and then broke a chair and tried to attack the sheriff with part of it. The sheriff and the other men in the town shot and killed my husband."

"I'm so sorry. Were you there?" Morris asked.

"No, I've never been there."

"Why was Hank in Harmony?"

"I had run away from him. I think he was trying to find me. I guess it's my fault he got himself killed."

Matt told her, "Don't believe that. You didn't make him pick a fight or break a chair or try to attack a sheriff."

"As it turned out, the man he wanted to fight got entangled with the rest of Hank's gang. They attacked some girls living on a farm. A posse went after them, and there was a fight. The very one Hank had tried to fight, the one who started the whole mess, killed one of the other men in the gang. They had a trial with all kinds of charges about all kinds of crimes against Hank's gang and several of the people in Harmony.

"My brother-in-law found everybody innocent of everything. He let every one of them go and told them to leave each other alone. Hank's stupid brother Roy had to keep going after those Williams girls and that Indian Noah Swift Hawk. He burned down their entire farm. Every one of Hank's gang eventually got himself killed. Except maybe one."

"How did you get this place?"

"It's just so strange how things work out. When Roy was killed, he had letters to my husband with him. Those girls and that Indian found the letters then found this house and everything here. They took some things out of this house and sent them to me by the sheriff of Harmony. They wrote a letter telling me the whole story from their point-of-view. They explained that Hank and Roy were both dead, and the house should be mine. My brother-in-law helped me inherit this house." Clarabelle sat at the table with the men and bounced her child on her knee.

"So, who do you think was right or wrong?" Justin, of course, knew exactly who she was talking about. He wondered how her opinion would compare to his opinion of the people.

"Hank was wrong. When he was the outlaw, he was mean. He tried to start a fight with a man who was only sitting at a bar minding his own business and eating a meal. Hank could have left him alone and never started the whole chain of events. However, if he hadn't, he might have found me and made me his prisoner again. Then I wouldn't have this house, and our son wouldn't have any chance of being a decent man when he grows up."

"Did you love him after you found out he was a bandit?" George asked.

"When the man I knew and married was there or when the boy I grew up with was there I did, and also one of his personalities that was very passionate and loved me desperately. When he was there, I did. I loved Hank when he was one of those men right to the very end."

The men finished eating and then stood up. "Wonderful meal. Thank you. Too bad Hank didn't realize what a lucky man he was."

Clarabelle picked up the dishes. "Breakfast starts at six."

The four boarders went first to the same room. "We need to stop Clarabelle from telling this story to anybody else," Morris told the others.

George plopped into an overstuffed chair. "Everybody must notice the unusual configuration of the house and ask about it. We don't know how many times she's already told that story."

"We could just ask her not to talk about it and explain why," Justin suggested.

"But then she would have even more information she could spread. She may crack under pressure and spill the beans," George replied.

Matt sat on the edge of one of the beds and raised a foot. "If that woman was able to handle a man like Hank Butterfield, she's not going to crack under pressure. I bet she knows just how to read a man and knows when to keep her information to herself."

Justin pulled off his father's boot. "We can feed her a little and see what happens."

Morris walked to the door. "All right. See you in the morning."

Coffee, milk, sugar, and sweet rolls already sat on the table when the men walked into the dining area in the early morning. "Good morning, Clarabelle," George called out.

She replied from the kitchen, "Good morning! Be right out with the rest," then brought omelets made with eggs, green peppers, onions, and cheese. She also brought biscuits, sausage gravy, and grapes.

"I think we might have met those girls you were talking about last night." Morris spooned gravy over a biscuit.

"Really? I always wondered what happened to them. My husband and his gang took everything from them. I hope things worked out for them."

"One of them married that Indian and one of them married a man from Harmony. The youngest hasn't married. At least not before we last heard about them." Justin wondered if the girl he had known as Nancy had married since then. She hadn't been gone long, but she was so beautiful he knew other men would want her just as he had.

"Where were they?" Clarabelle asked.

George said, "They came to our community when we were starving. They gave us all their food."

"They saved our lives. I think they're good people." Morris savored a bite of cheesy omelet.

"I've thought so since Sheriff Wyman brought me

188

the letters. I wish I could do something to repay what my husband took from them."

Matt saw the other three men signal to go ahead. "There is something you can do." He watched her reaction.

"Really? What could I possibly do?"

Matt started the explanation. "There's a man coming behind us, and there may be others hunting them too. It could be soon or a long time from now."

"Hunting them? Why?"

Matt spread knowledge of Judge Hall further. "Supposedly because Ann married Noah, but really because Ann affronted Judge Hall in Little Rock."

"There's more to it than just the hunt instigated by the judge. The man coming now is also after them because they helped a woman escape him," Morris added.

"What?" Clarabelle was very much on the side of anybody who would help a captive escape. Even more, she was against a man who held somebody, especially a woman, who wanted to leave.

"He goes by the name Joe Smith, but his real name is Raymond Pence. He shot a man named Sebastian De La Cruz when he and the woman they both loved rode away from Perryville. Raymond took the woman, Lola, to his home and kept her prisoner. Somehow, Noah's family rescued her, saved Sebastian's life, and got both of them away. Now Raymond wants to find all of them for retaliation."

"How can I help?" Clarabelle asked.

Matt told her their request. "Stop telling your

story. You will end up directing Raymond or any other person the judge sends right to them."

"That's simple. Only you and a few others have ever asked me anything. If anybody asks in the future, I can just say the house was built this way when I got it. Forevermore, names, places, and details are locked behind these lips."

"Thank you, Clarabelle," George hugged her. He believed no clues would be discovered at the Butterfield Boarding House ever again.

Clarabelle knew beyond any doubt that she would protect Lola and the rest of them. *I could poison him if he stops here* then immediately thought, *No! I won't let Hank Butterfield or Raymond Pence turn me into a murderer!*

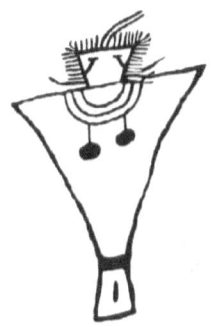

FORTY TWO

Raymond wasn't in any hurry, and he had the money to fund a long search. He trekked along, not pushing hard but determined to move forward to find the people responsible for his unhappiness. He imagined Lola with Sebastian. He told himself Sebastian had prevented Lola from loving him. Every minute of every day, he focused on their cruelty, except when he was trying to figure out how they had knocked him out. Raymond fed a daily heaping helping of thoughts and imaginations to the hatred in his heart. His anger and resentment grew as he traveled toward Spadra.

As Morris, Matt, Justin, and George left Dover, a man walked into Clarabelle's Boarding House and signed the registry, Joe Smith. *It's him, Raymond!* She steeled her heart and politely doubled her prices for everything. "It's seventy cents for a room and fifty cents for each meal."

"I'll take a room, supper, and breakfast." Ray handed Clarabelle two dollars. She gave him back thirty cents before she retrieved the key to one of the lower rooms. She pointed. "Number 3 is your room for the night. Supper will be on the table in ten minutes."

She handed him the key and quickly walked away. She could barely stand the man being in her house and even less in her presence. She served a large supper, so Raymond would feel there was a reason for the high price. She almost spit on the buns but restrained herself and served him good food. However, she absolutely could not bring herself to serve him any pie. "Anything else I can get you tonight?" Clarabelle asked.

"Whiskey, if you have it."

"I do."

"I'll take a whole bottle."

"Ten cents." She held out her hand.

The man gave her the dime. She left but quickly returned with the whiskey. "Breakfast is at six. Mr. Pe–" Clarabelle stopped before she said the wrong name. "Smith."

Raymond looked at Clarabelle. She thought she was in trouble. He took another slice of buttered bread from the table. "Is there any way it could be later?"

"If you want me to fix cold food that can sit until you get up, I can."

"That will work fine. Just put out the food. I'll eat it when I get up."

"I'll put a small table beside your door and leave your breakfast on the table."

"It's nice to meet a woman who will do what I ask." Raymond walked out of the dining area.

Suddenly, Clarabelle felt afraid. All night, she lay awake and worried about what she could do if he tried to attack or capture her. In the morning, Clarabelle prepared boiled eggs, cold sliced ham, cheese, bread, butter, honey, jam, and an apple. She put them on the table with a saltshaker, black peppercorn grinder, and a large glass of cider. She heard Raymond snoring inside the room as she set the food on the table.

During the night, she had decided it would be best to avoid the man and stay completely out of sight. He had already paid for everything, so Clarabelle left a note on the table. 'Gone out. Thank you for your patronage.' She took Hank back to her room and locked the door.

Much later in the day, she heard Raymond open the door. He found the tray of food. He thought it was a wonderful breakfast and ate every bite before he packed up and walked to the dining hall. "Mrs. Butterfield?" he called out.

Clarabelle didn't move. She prayed Hank Jr. would be quiet. For the first time since she had started running the boarding house, she didn't feel safe. She stayed locked inside her room for a long time after the departure of Raymond Pence, also known as Joe Smith.

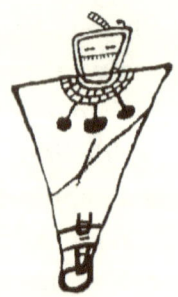

FORTY THREE

In Adeline's Inn, Robert's eyes focused. "Edwin, where did you come from?"

"It's a long story. The good news is you know who I am. You haven't for the last five days."

"I haven't? What happened to me?"

"Infection set in to your stab wound."

"The last thing I remember is leaving Maumelle."

"You were delirious when your horse brought you into town."

"I need to warn Doctor Smith."

"You need to stay right where you are. The others are way ahead of you. You leaving now wouldn't do any good."

Adeline opened the door to the room. "Did I hear talking?"

"Yes. Robert is awake."

Since Robert was coherent, Adeline asked, "May I come in?"

"Yes."

Adeline carried in a tray of food.

"That sure smells good." Robert tried to inhale deeply. He coughed painfully.

194

"It's for you." She handed Robert the tray. "The doctor didn't think there was any hope for you. Edwin, his father, and I also weren't very confident you were going to survive, but Zane always said you were going to be fine."

"Who are you, and who is Zane?" Robert took a big bite of mashed potatoes smothered in gravy.

"I'm the owner of this inn. I'll let Edwin or S.R. explain who Zane is."

Robert shoved steak into his mouth. "I can see why you started an inn. You're a great cook."

Adeline informed him, "It's just because your body needs real food. That's what makes it seem so good," but she appreciated the compliment.

"So, who is Zane?" Robert asked as he enjoyed his meal.

Edwin started the explanation by telling how Zane had carried Robert to the doctor and to the inn. He described everything Zane had done to care for Robert. After that, he told Robert the story of Zane's life.

When he started to explain about how Zane was released from prison, Robert stopped him. "This isn't going where I think it is. Is it?"

"Yes. It is."

"How could you let the man who tried to murder me get anywhere close to me? Where is he? I'm gonna kill HIM!"

"Calm down, Robert. He worked harder to save you than any of us, and besides that, we never left him alone with you."

Zane came into the room. "I want to say I'm very sorry about throwing a knife into your back. I feel horrible about it. You have no idea how happy I was to find you alive. You don't have to forgive me. I just want to tell you how sorry I am for what I did."

Robert had no intention of forgiving the man. "So now you've told me. Go away."

Zane walked to the bedroom door. "I'm very glad you're going to be all right. For your sake and for mine. I don't want to be a murderer." He stepped out and closed the door.

"What do I feel on my back?" Robert asked.

S.R. replied, "Probably the maggots and spider webs."

"Get them off," Robert demanded.

"The maggots and spider webs are what saved your life," S.R. informed him.

Edwin gave the credit where he thought it belonged. "It was God. The maggots and spider webs only helped."

"Can I see my back?" Robert asked.

"I think I can rig up some mirrors." Adeline went off to get what she needed.

When Robert saw his flaming red back with the hole filled with spider webs and maggots, he passed out again.

"I guess that would be an upsetting image." Edwin casually commented.

As they ate breakfast the next morning, Robert asked Edwin, "Am I well enough to travel home?"

"I think you can go home if you're very careful, so you don't open up the injury again. Stay very clean, eat right, and drink plenty of water."

Robert informed his friends and the man Zane, whom he barely tolerated, "I want to leave today."

"Father, I should go with Robert. You can go home and tell mother I want to be sure he gets home safely."

"All right," S.R. agreed.

After eating a delicious meal, they got ready to leave. Zane wished they weren't breaking up. It occurred to him that he was feeling exactly how Murray had when Esther and Horatio had left. There wasn't a reason for Candy to be there anymore. This time, however, Zane was the one who would have to leave, but at least he would still be close to Adeline. S.R. paid the room and board for Robert, Edwin, and himself. Zane tried to pay too, but Adeline told him, "You gave me back the twenty dollars Raymond stole. You don't owe me anything." Adeline hugged Robert gently. "Take care of yourself."

After only a few minutes, they had said their goodbyes and stood in the street. Zane conveyed his feeling to Robert again. "I really am glad you're well, Robert, and I'm sorry about what I did." Robert ignored him, so Zane rode off to his farm.

Robert had a plan. "Mr. Snow, I thought Edwin and I could take the south road out of town. We can ride through the gap in the Maumelle Mountain then follow the valley to Fletcher Creek. Once I'm there, Edwin can go home. I'll go to the store here in town and get enough supplies for both of us."

"Be careful. Have a safe trip home." S. R. hugged his son. "Love you. I'll tell your Ma what you're doing." S.R. rode east to Maumelle.

Edwin and Robert went to the store. Robert still had his ten dollars, so he bought everything he thought they would need. Edwin thought it was much more than they needed for a few days. They packed everything into their saddlebags and mounted up.

"Edwin, you can come with me or not. I hope you do because I need you."

"I already told you I was coming with you."

"I'm not going home. I'm going to warn Noah and Ann. I guess I do understand Zane. I have to make amends for what I did. Judge Hall used both of us. Zane is not after them now, but Raymond is. According to Adeline, Raymond won't even try to take them alive. He'll kill them for sure. I have to do everything I can to prevent that."

Edwin knew Robert needed him. He knew Noah did too, but he thought Robert would die for sure if he didn't go straight home. "Don't you think the others will be able to warn him?"

"First, they're going to Harmony to warn Sebastian and Lola. They might get caught up in that for a long time. I'm going straight to Fort Gibson and find out where the Quapaws are."

Edwin said, "My mother will be worried sick. Let me leave a message for Adeline to send to her."

"Can you write one?" Robert asked.

"I've learned a lot, but I'll get her to help."

They went back to Adeline's place.

"Why are you back?" she asked when Robert and Edwin walked through her door.

Edwin explained, "We've changed our plans. I want to send a note home. Have you got some paper and something I can use to write?" Adeline got paper and a pencil. Edwin wrote the note. "Will you see if I did it right?" Edwin handed her the note.

Adeline read it over. "I don't think you should do this, but I understand. Let me give you some things to help keep the wound from getting infected again." She came back with two flasks of whiskey, several rolls of bandages, surgical thread, a scalpel, and a ball of spider webs. "Let me fix you up again before you go. Then you can take the rest." Adeline washed the injury with whiskey, matted some of the webs over it, and then wrapped the bandages around Robert several times. "This whiskey is only for keeping this wound clean. It's not for drinking."

"All right. Thank you. You've taken very good care of me, Adeline. You're a good woman."

"Wait a week before sending the note to my folks," Edwin instructed Adeline.

Robert and Edwin rode west out of town past the oak and blackjack trees blown completely bare by the wind that swept down the road. As they cantered over the hilly terrain toward the Le Fave Mountains, Robert felt as empty in his soul as the lifeless trees. To the north, they could see the peaks of Petit Jean Mountain. Seventeen miles from Perryville, they stopped where the range swung south. The gap through the mountains lay just ahead.

The next day, they made the difficult climb up the mountain. It was cold on the ridge, but Edwin found plenty of wood. Their meal bubbled over the fire while Edwin checked Robert's wound. "It doesn't look any worse." He wrapped Robert back up. They kept the fire going to stay warm that cold November night.

FORTY FOUR

During the week since they had left Fort Gibson, James and the colonel had told each other stories their parents had passed down. They discovered both of their grandparents had lived in Plymouth, Massachusetts in the year of 1790. Both of their grandfathers had told the same story about a small, beached whale. The whole community had worked together to tie its tail to a rowboat. They had pulled it into the deep water before they let it go. It had joined a larger whale before it swam away.

The two men knew their grandparents must have at least known each other and were probably even friends. James Williams and Stephen Howland no longer felt they were people who simply knew of each other; they became friends.

People buying at the Fort Gibson store mostly dealt with the supply master. Chetan wanted to get to know the man, so he could decide if he was trustworthy, and he wanted Matthew to see him as a friend. Therefore, Chetan spent most of his time with Sergeant McCormick.

However, all the men talked to each other, mostly in English, since all the Indian men knew at least a tiny amount of English and of the soldiers, only Colonel Howland knew any Quapaw.

When the seventeen men arrived at Fort Smith, Sergeant McCormick offered, "Let me sell your shells together with ours. The military gets a better price than anybody else."

Ppahiska called the nine people from his village aside. "Tom and Roscoe both told us not to trust this man. What do you think? Should we let Sergeant McCormick sell our shells with theirs?"

Chetan offered his opinion. "I don't think he will agree to sell his shells for less than what he thinks is the best possible price."

Wakanda agreed, "It will only work well for him or for us if we sell everything together."

Chetan went to Sergeant McCormick. "All right. Thank you for helping us."

"You're welcome." The sergeant also knew he would get a better price if there weren't two groups selling shells. In addition, he had come to like the men he had traveled with and was glad he could help.

While Colonel Howland spoke with the commander of Fort Smith about military concerns, Sergeant McCormick sold their five wagons full of shells for one hundred dollars each. They kept only enough shells to trade for the animals they hoped to kill on the way home. However, as part of the trade, they had to unload the shells onto the boat that would take them down the Arkansas River. Sergeant McCormick secretly gave Ppahiska two hundred dollars.

Since they had gotten a much better price than they had expected, Ppahiska brought up the topic his people had asked him to discuss with the sergeant. He spoke the words Chetan had helped him learn. "Would you sell our pearls too?"

Sergeant McCormick was surprised they trusted him. "Let me see them." He held out his hand.

Ppahiska gave him the pearls. Each family had their own sack with the name of the owner. They were purposely all very similar in size and shape to make it easier.

"Same price for all of them?"

Ppahiska talked it over with his men then went back to the Sergeant and said the word James told him to say. "Agreed."

"All right. I'll sell them for you." First, Sergeant McCormick sold the pearls as one lot. Then, he and the other soldiers drove all five wagons of shells toward the dock.

"Should we help?" Ppahiska wondered aloud.

"No, but we will not drink lemonade under a shade tree in front of them while they work." Wakanda held out his hand for his twenty-two dollars and twenty-two cents for the shells.

"We have these left that we cannot divide." Ppahiska still held two cents.

While they waited for Sergeant McCormick to

return with the money for the pearls, the village men discussed what would be the fair thing to do with the pennies. They decided to see if they could buy nine dill pickles from the barrel. When the Sergeant returned, he gave each man four dollars for their pearls. Since the day was drawing to the end, the Indians immediately went to buy their supplies.

James looked in the pickle barrel. "How much are pickles?"

"Two cents per pound."

James placed a large pickle on the scale. He put it back and tried another until he knew about the size to get. As James searched for the right pickles, the others bought the supplies they wanted.

With his family's share of the money from the shells and pearls and the money he had brought with him, Chetan bought what his family had decided to purchase, if possible. Two large round tents like the one from Roscoe Bacon's Trading Post that they had made into an animal tent, two bolts of heavy duck cloth, four large spools of heavy cotton thread, and ten horse blankets.

James had nine similar pickles on the scale. It was a skoosh over one pound. He was about to put them back and start over. The shop owner, however, was selling quite a bit of merchandise and decided to be generous. On top of that, he thought James had already handled more than enough of the pickles. "Two cents." He got out a sheet of butcher paper.

James handed the man the pennies. "I don't need

them wrapped." In Quapaw, he told his friends, "Come get them."

As they crunched on the pickles, the soldiers from Fort Gibson arrived with the five empty wagons. The sergeant smelled the pickles and heard the crisp snap of the bites. He handed the army's list to one of the workers the shopkeeper had called in to help. "Eight large dill pickles for me too."

"Fish them out." The worker handed him a long fork to spear the pickles floating in the barrel. He stabbed the biggest he could find and put them on the scale. When all of Sergeant McCormick's purchases were in the wagons, it was past sunset.

The Indians had been told to leave Fort Smith immediately after their purchases but had waited outside. Even though it was after sundown, the gate was opened to allow the soldiers from Fort Gibson to leave. The soldiers remaining inside closed and locked the gates right behind them before taking the message from Colonel Josiah Habersham to the storekeeper. "We had to open the gate after dark because of you. The Colonel said you have to move your business to the town outside the fort."

The seventeen men finished their pickles in the cold. They set up camp just beyond the view of the Fort Smith sentries.

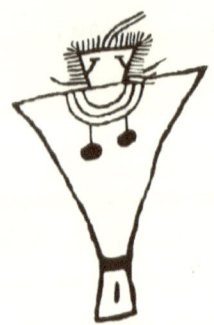

FORTY FIVE

The third day after Robert and Edwin had left Perryville they went down the far side of the Le Fave Mountains then spent several hours in a grassy field letting their horses eat. Edwin felt compelled to finally ask, "Robert, why did you turn against Dr. Smith?"

"I've been thinking about that. It wasn't about him. It was about me. I'm not good enough. I barely earn enough to buy food for Bertha and me. I don't want to be somebody Bertha probably wishes she hadn't married. I thought I could get a lot of money and hardly even do anything. I almost earned half a year's wages in two days. I didn't realize how far the judge planned to go. I didn't know he was like that until I was running for my own life. Now everybody hates me. I'm even more worthless than I first thought."

"You're not worthless, and I know something you can do for God when you get back to Little Rock."

"I can't go back there! Judge Hall will have me killed, and I won't put Bertha and Phebe through that again."

"It's just that God had me doing something that needed to be done, and now I'm not there to do it. I don't want to let God down."

"What were you doing?"

Robert probably can't be trusted anyway. "Never mind." *I used to think I wasn't even a real person. Now, I know that's not true. How can I help Robert know that too?*

FORTY SIX

The day after Colonel Howland, his soldiers, Ppahiska, and his men had left Fort Smith, Paytah took his turn with the spyglass. He saw black fuzz on the horizon. "I see many buffalo." He passed the spyglass to his chief.

Ppahiska looked. "You are right."

Colonel Howland also looked. He didn't like the location of the herd. "This isn't good. We're still six days from Fort Gibson."

Lieutenant Jackson stated an idea. "We can herd them toward the fort."

Chetan heard the suggestion. "The people in this section wouldn't like us running them out of their area and not giving them the trade. The people by the fort wouldn't like us not trading with them if we kill them there. We need to kill them in this section and trade with this village."

James remembered what had happened when his village had tried to move ten buffalo. He pointed out another thing to consider. "Five buffalo will be too much weight for our animals to haul that far."

"We all want to shoot one." Colonel Howland stated his orders gently, "We have to kill more than five. We can ride north to the end of the herd and kill them in the farthest section. We wouldn't have forced them anyplace they weren't already at."

Sergeant Anders took himself out of the problem. "I don't need to shoot one."

Ezra said, "We're just privates."

Chetan proposed, "So take only four. I promise it will be more than enough. Since the treaty didn't say we have to take them the second we see them, we should do as you suggest and follow them north."

Knowing they would have to stay in one place for a least half a day after killing the buffalo, they stayed on the road far to the east of the herd and hurried north. Lieutenant Jackson said, "I want the head and hide of the one I kill, but I don't know how to tan a hide or preserve the head."

Chetan offered, "My family could tan one or more if nobody else wants to help, but it takes time. Winter will be here before they are ready. We wouldn't be able to bring them to you until spring."

"What would you want to prepare them for us?" the colonel asked.

In Quapaw, Chetan explained what the soldiers wanted. "Do any of you want to tan a hide and a head for them?"

"My women can do one," Tatonga replied.

"Mine too," Mantu offered.

James waited to see if anybody else would offer before he said, "Mine will too. Let us discuss what we want."

The four men talked. Chetan suggested, "My woman will do the work. I want to get what she would want, but I don't know what that would be. I will ask for a five-dollar credit at the store. That's how much Sergeant McCormick charges for a hide."

Wakanda spoke up, "Five is not enough. What about the head? Five more for the head."

Tatonga said, "I'm sure the colonel would honor the agreement in the spring, but I want to take chickens now."

James stated what he wanted. "If he trusts us, he might let us have them before doing the work. I also want chickens now."

Wakanda thought Chetan's plan was the best. "I will ask for the credit. I can't be robbed of a credit, and a credit won't die."

Ppahiska thought for the village. "And twenty dollars of credits at the store for the trade items the village will want for the four buffalo."

They all approved. James told the colonel the offer.

The colonel quickly replied, "Agreed."

At the end of the day, Ppahiska spoke with all his men but sent his white man. James told the colonel. "Ppahiska thinks the herd will go farther north during the night. We should wait to move on until the morning."

They set up camp. The buffalo behaved as if they had followed orders. Most of the herd was again north of them and much closer to the road as well. They again traveled at quick time. At mid-day, when the herd started to turn west, the colonel estimated they were only two days from the fort.

James instructed the soldiers, "Get your rifles ready, but don't shoot until we get them close to the wagons. Remember how we did it the last time?"

Ezra said, "We run them southeast and then turn them north and force them over to the wagons. We shoot them by the wagons."

Sergeant Anders rubbed his back and said with a smile, "And stay out of the way of sliding buffalo."

"Let's do it!" the colonel commanded.

They did what Ezra said. The officers fired into the small group of giant plains bison they drove close to the wagons. The animals thundered past. "Got one!" Lieutenant Jackson was so jubilant Chetan would have been happy for him, except that he knew the man was the one who had tried to take Sally's necklace. When the buffalo had stampeded away, four carcasses lay close to the wagons.

Ppahiska spoke to James. James passed the message to the soldiers, "You start butchering. We will go to the village with the trade items."

Even though Ppahiska was a village chief, the colonel informed him, "I'm going with you."

In English, Ppahiska issued orders of his own. "Come. Do not talk."

Chetan, Enapay, Paytah, Tatonga, Wakanda, the three privates, Sergeant Tim Anders, and Sergeant Matthew McCormick stayed with the buffalo. The colonel and the two lieutenants went with Ppahiska and the rest of the Quapaw.

Morgan, Ezra, Ham, and Tim cut open the buffalos. Ham drew out and then threw the insides on the ground. Wakanda immediately ordered, "Stop!"

Bewildered, Ezra looked at the mystery man.

Chetan reminded him, "You never saw us throw anything on the ground."

"I didn't know that was important," Ham replied.

Wakanda instructed by showing. He plucked out an eye and then scooped brains out through the hole. He held up a small jar and spoke in English. "Put in." He started the intestines into a separate jar. "New jar." Wakanda waved his hand over all the other innards and handed Ezra a third jar. "In this jar." Wakanda then demonstrated how to remove the skin.

Tim continued to remove brains. Morgan, Ezra, and Ham slid intestines into jars. Sergeant McCormick skinned a buffalo. He repeatedly nicked the skin.

"The skin won't be good enough to tan." Chetan held out a saw. "Cut off the hooves." He, Wakanda, and Tatonga took over skinning.

Once the jars were full, Enapay showed how to cut the meat away from the neck while leaving the skin on the head and neck intact. Three more heads lay on the ground, so Ezra, Ham, and Morgan started in.

The soldiers and Indian men skinned all four animals. To keep the carcasses out of the dirt, the skinless animals lay on their hides. All the men worked together to cut up the meat.

Ppahiska, James, the colonel, and lieutenants returned from the village. Whether they understood his words or not, Colonel Howland informed those who had remained behind, "We paid eighty mussel shells and forty seeds each of corn, tobacco, cotton, flax, yellow squash, pumpkins, butternut, pole beans, October beans, turnips, parsnips, okra, tomatoes, radishes, and carrots." The colonel owed nobody anything more since he hadn't needed any items that he hadn't already owned.

Wakanda took Ppahiska aside. "I thought we would get the twenty-dollar credit. The first trade should be to gather mussels."

Ppahiska told them what had happened. "They said it was too far to get the mussels. They said they wanted seeds. I could have insisted they follow the agreement, but the colonel knows Cherokee, and I know he wanted to trade the seeds. I didn't want him to speak, so I agreed."

Wakanda had made the deal with the colonel. "Still, it was good to let them join us. We ate their food, and our horses ate their hay. We had a military escort, even if they were in disguise. We also still have our talisman and all our trade goods. We can hunt for ourselves after we separate from the soldiers. We also made good relationships with these soldiers. I think we are friends now."

Ppahiska affirmed his mystery man. "You also did a good thing."

Chetan spoke up. "I want to move all the supplies to our wagons with the heads and skins that we will take home to prepare. We should load all this meat into

Colonel Howland's wagons. That way, we won't have to move it when we get to the fort."

The colonel said his currently favorite word, "Agreed."

They put the brainless buffalo heads together in one wagon and moved all the supplies to the other wagon going to the Indian village. The rest of the carcasses went into the three military wagons.

The colonel said, "Let's camp here tonight. We can keep working on the buffalo by moonlight."

Chetan translated the colonel's suggestion. Ppahiska decided for them. Chetan passed on the offer. "If you give us all the insides, we will help you butcher."

The colonel didn't want any of the innards anyway. "Agreed." He gagged as he watched Ppahiska slurp down what had been in a stomach.

"You want any of this?" James pulled long strings of sinew from one of the back muscles.

Since he was the one James was helping, Lieutenant Olson replied, "If you cut off the silver skin, you can have it."

James passed on the good news. "We can have all the sinew." They would make sure they got it all.

"What should we do with all this?" Lieutenant Olson held a glob of milky white tissue.

James spoke the request in Quapaw. "He wants to know what to do with the fat."

As if it was inconceivable that a person would not want it, Capa asked, "You do not want?"

"Do you?" the lieutenant asked.

"Yes!" Capa replied emphatically as he thought about all the pemmican his wife could make.

The lieutenant passed him a handful of white goo. "Have all of it."

Capa stood up. "What about the rest of you?"

Chetan repeated the question in English.

Colonel Howland said, "We have lots of fat in the salt horse. Take however much you want."

The Indian men put the fat in the jars they had brought to trade and squirreled them into the wagon with the heads, hides, and jars of internal organs. Halfway into the night, they stopped working and slept.

The next two days, they took turns driving the wagons, removing the sinew, and cutting the meat into strips to smoke at the fort. To get them out of the way, they threw the bones into the wagon with the heads.

At the fort, the colonel said, "You keep everything in your two wagons."

James wanted to be sure the colonel understood. "The last of the hay you bought at Fort Smith is in our wagon, and we haven't eaten all of your rations either."

"I appreciate you allowing us to hunt with you. You keep what's left. We just want the meat for now. Bring the tanned hides and heads to us in the spring."

"We will. Thank you."

Colonel Howland walked into Fort Gibson, doling out orders. "Build fires. Finish processing the meat. Get it all smoked and stored. James and Tatonga, go into the fort and get those chickens. Sergeant McCormick, write the credits. While you're at it, write an order for the ferryman to let them cross free of charge."

It wasn't long before Ppahiska and his men continued home with the skins and heads to prepare for the soldiers, as well as the fat, hooves, sinew, bones, jars of innards, chickens, store credits, and the supplies they had bought at Fort Smith. Most importantly, men stationed at Fort Gibson considered them friends.

Capa asked, "I wonder if we can find that herd of antelope Wesa was hunting?"

"I thought you were in a hurry to get home." Mantu reminded him.

Capa pointed out, "It will only add a few extra days, and we are ahead of schedule. It won't take as much time to butcher antelope as buffalo."

Mantu replied, "Its fine with me. I just thought you were in a hurry."

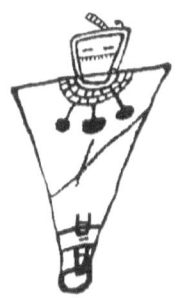

FORTY SEVEN

Matt, Morris, George, and Justin checked into their room in Spadra. Matt felt relieved they had completed the task without any problems. He told his son, "We're almost there. Just one more day before we'll be able to go home."

"It's not over until it's over. We haven't done anything yet," Justin replied.

They looked around once the sun came up, but found no evidence of a road going north. They thought Raymond might know more than they did, but in case not, they didn't ask the townsfolk how to get to Harmony. They feared they might accidentally leave him a clue.

Justin and George came up with a plan. They went to the store. "We heard there are some very friendly women somewhere north of here."

"The only place north of here is Harmony, but there aren't any women like that up there or any place else around here. You would have to go to Little Rock, I would guess."

"How would we get to that place up north if we wanted to check it out and make sure? We'd hate to miss out after coming all this way." Justin knew Nancy wasn't like that. However, he did hope he would find her there.

"Just ride north on the west side of Spadra Creek. It's not a real road, but you can drive a wagon all the way."

"Thanks, Mister." George hurried away as if they couldn't wait to get there.

Morris stood beside the creek. "Surely this isn't the way."

George repeated what the man in the store had told him. "He said it's not a road, but if you ride right beside the creek, you can get a wagon all the way."

"Well, let's get a move on." Matt decided to do what told to do.

Not much before nightfall, they saw the town. George said, "I told you."

Above the door of the first building hung a wooden plaque with the carved word, 'Joe's'.

"We would like rooms for the night," Morris informed the man behind the bar.

"Thirty-seven cents for each room. Fifty cents if you want two servings of supper tonight and breakfast in the morning. Twenty-five cents more if you want a hot bath. You take them in the room back there."

Morris felt like celebrating. "We'll take the top of the line. Two rooms, all the meals, and four hot, fresh-water baths." He put two dollars on the counter. "And four shots of whiskey." He put another bit piece on the counter.

"That will buy you a whole bottle of whiskey."

Matt told the man with a scar on his cheek. "Bring it, barkeep."

"Name's Joe. Here are your keys. Go up those stairs. The numbers are on the doors."

Each key had a wooden disk with a carved number attached with a rawhide strip. They went upstairs to find the rooms. Joe went to prepare the baths.

"Are you going to let me have whiskey?" Justin asked his father in their room.

Matt didn't even have to think about his answer. "You've been man enough to ride for two weeks to help people you don't even know. I think you're man enough to have a drink of whiskey." He added, "Just don't tell your mother."

"I won't." They went back downstairs and sat at a table with the bottle and four small glasses. Two other men sat at a nearby table playing checkers.

Matt poured a swallow of whiskey into each glass. "We should find them right away and warn them. We don't really know how much time there is before Raymond gets here."

One of the men playing checkers bolted out of his seat. "Raymond is coming here?! Who are you?!" The man ordered, "Start talking!" as the other man ran out of the saloon.

Morris was shocked. "We're friends of Noah Swift Hawk, Ann Williams, Eli Yates, Stephanie Yates, Sally Williams, and Roscoe Bacon, but we knew them by different names."

The man was clearly upset. "What names?"

"Abraham, Lily, James, Marie, Nancy, and Theo."

"Where are you from?"

"Fletcher Creek."

They must be Morris, Matt, Justin, and George. The man walked to the saloon register. As they had studied how to read and write, the people of Fletcher Creek had learned how to write their names. They were proud they were now able. Each of them had done so when checking in. The names written in the register were right.

"I'm Sebastian. Tell me what's going on."

"Thank God we found you so quickly," Morris replied. "We were told to come here first and warn you and Lola that Raymond is coming this way."

"How did he find us?"

Justin said, "An assassin told him."

"How would an assassin know where we are?"

Matt explained, "Because Judge Daniel Hall told him to look for the others. Somebody overheard that conversation and then set things into motion to warn them. Then he found out about you and put it together."

George said, "We don't know much about Raymond or why we are supposed to warn you, but the note said he is murderous and to be careful. He's stone cold. A stone-cold killer."

"Thank you. Are you going to go on and warn Abraham and the rest of them?"

Morris informed him, "We don't have any idea

where to go from here except to Indian Territory. From what I've been told, that is a very big place."

"Let me go and start packing. After you finish your bath and supper, come to the last house on this side." Sebastian hurried from the room.

Joe brought a tray with four plates of food to the table as the sheriff walked into the saloon.

"Earl tells me you're here to warn us that Raymond is coming."

"Who are you?" Morris asked.

"He's the sheriff," Joe informed them.

The man introduced himself. "Sheriff Smithfield Wyman." He shook hands with the four men then sat at the table. "Eat while we talk."

Matt told the sheriff their mission. "… the assassin is going under the name of Joe Smith, but his real name is Raymond Pence."

"Why does he think Ann and Noah are here? He sent people before, and they weren't here."

"Some traveling trader recognized Nancy and James down by Spadra and told a man named Robert at Harrow's Livery in Little Rock about seeing them. Robert told Judge Hall. The judge lined up an assassin to find the Williams girl and her family. When Robert tried to blackmail the judge, the judge sent his hired murderer to kill Robert too. He thinks he did, but he wasn't successful."

"How long do we have before Raymond gets here?" the sheriff asked.

Morris said, "We passed him at Gum Log Creek

on the way here. We haven't seen him again since. We don't know if he's right behind or days behind, or even if he knows anything more than 'around Spadra'."

"Eat up whatever you've ordered from Joe. Be ready to go at any moment."

"Can we take our baths or spend the night?" George asked.

The Sheriff issued orders. "Take your baths quick. You may not be able to spend the night. I'm going to go see what I can find out."

Joe said, "If you don't want them real hot, they can be ready when you're done eating."

"As long as they feel warm and the water is fresh, that will be fine," Morris agreed.

They ate quickly and then got into the relaxing water without having shots of whiskey. "What do you think, Pa? These people seem to be really concerned about this man." George sat in a separate tub in the same room and soaped up.

Morris said, "I don't think he's right behind us, but let's keep everything packed. Leave the packs on the mules and the horses saddled. We should sleep in our clean clothes and boots. We'll only have to jump on our horses and ride away."

Matt soaped his underarms. "I agree," he said just before he went under.

When they finished bathing and had dressed in clean clothes, they walked back into the saloon. They found the whole town sitting at the tables. The sheriff directed them, "We've been talking about this, and we have a plan. Sit down, and I'll explain."

Outside, they heard, "I don't want to talk about this! We have to leave now!"

"We all need to know the plan." Sebastian tried to talk rationally to his pregnant wife.

"I know everything I need to know, and that is to leave!" The woman spoke with panic in her voice.

Sebastian pulled Lola into the saloon. "Make it quick," he told Smitty.

"Lola and Sebastian go to Rock House Cave. As you know, everything you need is already there for this very reason. We don't want a house that is clearly being lived in empty. Clyde and Patty, you won't be stumbling around in a house you don't know, so move back into your old home. Zachariah and Minnie stay where you are in the new house.

"Nobody denies that Lola and Sebastian were here. Admit that Lola and Sebastian came here with Eli and the others to get Eli's father, Tom. Eli and Stephanie stayed here to wait for Tom to come home. The rest of them left because Noah and Ann were being hunted.

"Later, Sally came with her Uncle James Williams to get Eli, Stephanie, Tom, and Helen. They went to live with James. We don't know where he lives, other than it's west. Every word of that is true. We don't mention that Lola and Sebastian didn't go with them. The closer everybody stays to the truth, the better."

"Perfect." Lola said, "Let's go, Sebastian."

Sebastian wanted the latest group of people who had saved them to get away safely and travel quickly. He wanted to make sure they avoided the main cause for delays. "One thing we learned traveling here is something you may already know, but I want to be sure you know that creeks and rivers should always be crossed as soon as you get to them if they are not already impassable."

The sheriff told Sebastian, "Go on. Take her where she'll be safe."

"All right, Smitty. Let us know when it's safe to come home." Sebastian helped Lola up from the chair.

Betsy whispered to Clara, "It's going to be hard on poor Lola being six months pregnant and living in a cave."

"Come on, honey. We need to move our clothes." Clyde left with Patty.

"I'm going to go and see what I can find out about Raymond's location. Everybody go home and behave like you would any other day." Smitty then turned to Morris, George, Matt, and Justin. "I'd hold off on drinking that whiskey. I see your mules are still packed, and the horses saddled. Leave them that way. Try to get some sleep while you can."

Matt stood. "I'll just put these dirty clothes with the rest of our things."

Joe spoke up, "Let me wash them tonight. You can always take them wet if you need to." He handed Morris back his money. "Everything is on me. Thank you for coming to warn us."

"We can pay." Morris refused the money.

Joe picked up the clothes and left to wash them in the still slightly warm tub water.

Morris picked up the whiskey bottle and glasses.

In his room, he poured four shots. "To the successful completion of mission one." He drank down a shot.

"You're men now." Matt passed George and Justin their glasses. The two young men choked and then tried to breathe when the whiskey burned their throats.

"Let's try to get some sleep. We need to move on to our second mission tomorrow."

When they woke, it was morning. Smitty was standing at the bar talking with Joe. Joe heard the sound of the men walking in the rooms above them. He felt the clean clothes that hung by the fire. He was glad they had dried during the night. He folded them neatly and stacked them in a pile. When his four guests came down the stairs, he told them, "Your clothes are ready. Have a seat. I'll get your breakfast." Joe went to the kitchen.

"I went halfway to Spadra last night." Smitty sat at the table. "Raymond's not going to get here until this evening at the earliest. Are you planning to go on to warn the Yates and the Williams family?"

Matt told him what he wanted. "We hoped somebody here would know how to find them and go warn them. We would like to get home before winter sets in."

"Here's the thing. Earl's leg is bad. Zachariah and I have to be here to keep things going because we have small babies. Horace or Clyde could go, but neither is the kind of person for this mission. Most of all, our town is under a threat, so we need everybody here. It would be best if you continue."

Even though they had hoped they could get out of it, the four men from Fletcher Creek had known the night before that it was still going to be up to them. "All right. I guess we'll be heading out this morning. The only thing is, we might run into Raymond when we go back to Spadra."

Smitty wanted to help as much as he could without neglecting his own family, "I'll take you the back way to Horsehead Creek. You can follow it down to the road. I'll be back before Raymond gets here. Let me go home, tell my wife, and pack some things for the trip. I'll come back here."

When Smitty got to his house, he told Mara, "I'm going to take them through the woods to Horsehead Creek, then I'll come home."

"I remember what Sally said when she was telling us about what happened over there. She said they went back and forth between their village and Fort Gibson on a road. It took about a week to make the trip. The village is north of Fort Gibson. When they got to some other big river that joined from the east, they had to cross back over to the east before they continued north. There was another creek just before the village."

"She explained all that to you about how to get there? That was very stupid."

"No, she didn't say it that way. When she was talking about different things, she said they were coming home and saw some buffalo close to the road. Once she said, 'The men were secretly trying to get some buffalo they had killed off Cherokee land.' She said, 'Most of them were safely back on the other side of the river, but not all of the people were over there yet.' She also said, 'The men went down to the Fort.' "

"Very good, my observant wife. I'll give them the information, and I'll tell them to explain to Sally how to be more careful when she talks with people."

Mara handed Smitty a bag with food and clothes for him in case he got wet. "I love you. Be careful."

"I will. I love you and Junior." Smitty kissed them both then left with his pistol, a rifle, ammo, a knife, and his bedroll. He went into his barn to get his quarter horse, Bliss.

The men from Fletcher Creek were already at the barn. Earl was on his horse, ready to travel. "I'm guessing you were going to take them to Horsehead Creek. I'm not good for much with this leg, but I can ride there and back. You should be here, in case Raymond gets here sooner than you think. I told Clara to go immediately to your house if he shows up."

"Thank you, Earl. I agree. I'll keep Clara as safe as I keep my own wife." Smitty passed on the information from Mara and told them to warn Sally to be more careful about what she said.

FORTY EIGHT

Far to the south, Edwin and Robert rode into the Petit Jean River. In the deep, they let go of the reins, slid off, and then held to their horses' tails, so the animals could swim. Edwin's wet packsaddle strap started to slip. He saw his possessions headed toward the water and grabbed at them. That jerked the tie-down loose. The thing hung under BlackJack's belly. "Wouldn't you know it?! Now everything I own is underwater!"

"Pull it up."

Edwin informed his friend, "It's too late. Why bother?" BlackJack started to thrash. Edwin ducked under and saw his horses' legs banging the pouches. Just as the flap started to open, Edwin got his hand on it and squeezed it shut. He needed air, so he pulled the bag up with him. Without the packsaddle fouling his ability to swim, the horse calmed, but Edwin had to stay beside BlackJack to hold the packsaddle up. It was very tiring.

"That sounds bad," Robert turned his head but

228

couldn't see beyond the bend. "We should have asked about possible hazards before we left Perryville. I hope it's only rapids and not a waterfall!" Being practically in the middle of the river, they couldn't go back, nor could they get to the other bank before they would round the bend. "I hope my back doesn't rip open again!"

The current picked up speed as they approached the curve. Around they went. Not far ahead, deep water jetted through a long, narrow gap between two huge boulders. The river flowed slower to either side, but they were sure to be shredded on sharp stones. The river disappeared beyond the rocky ledge. "We'll have to shoot the gap!" Edwin turned BlackJack toward the dangerous but only way through. "Swim fast, boy!"

As the fast channel grabbed Boots' front legs, Robert screamed, "I hope it's not a high waterfall!"

Swoosh!

The horse was sucked into the gap. Its tail jerked from Robert's hands. Edwin saw Robert's head go under just as BlackJack entered the vortex. *God, help us!*

The pressure in the narrow waterway swept the horses and men into the deep center. The extreme momentum would have crushed them if that had not been so. Robert had no idea if he was up, down, or sideways, but he knew he needed air soon. *God, I deserve to drown, but if You can forgive me, let me get my head above the water and Boots too.*

He was spit from the passageway.

Splash. He barely missed Boots, came back up,

saw a large dark shape in the gap, and then desperately tried to get out of the way.

BlackJack flew through the air.

SPLASH!

I never thought I'd see a flying horse, thought Robert as Edwin soared into view. *Or people!*

Edwin surfaced. After he sucked in a lungful of air, he told his friend. "That was terrifying but exciting!"

Robert looked up at the river cascading over the ledge eight feet up. "We sure are lucky that was only a short drop!" He swam to his horse. "You all right, buddy?"

It looked at him and then started toward the far shore as fast as it could swim. Robert grabbed its tail. BlackJack and Edwin followed right behind.

They sloshed out of the river five miles back toward the east, but farther north and very close to the road to Fort Smith. It was none too soon. The horses were too tired to go farther. All of them were extremely cold, and since everything they owned was soaking wet, they set up camp.

Edwin expected the worst. He looked at Robert's back. "Thank you, God! The wound hasn't opened." He cleaned it with the whiskey anyway. Since the bandages were wet, like everything else, he didn't rewrap his friend. Instead, he took a swig from the bottle. "I know Adeline said it's not for drinking, but I need a swallow or two." He passed the whiskey to Robert.

The two of them found a dead oak. Edwin chopped off branches with the axe they had bought in Perryville. Robert pulled them to their camp. Together they made them into a rack where they hung their clothes and blankets to dry by their fire.

FORTY NINE

Earl took the men from Fletcher Creek into the forest. Most of the leaves from the trees lay on the hidden trail Earl followed as he led his charges west. The bare trees allowed them to clearly see the high cliffs of the Boston Mountains on their right. On the crisp fall day, Earl led them over flat, easily traveled land.

In the forest, Justin rode beside Earl. "What happened to your leg?"

"We were trying to capture some outlaws. I came around a corner on the trail and saw a gun pointing my way. I tried to stop my horse. It fell on me and crushed my leg. It's not too bad, just not real good either."

"When was that?" George asked.

"We were trying to catch the Butterfield Gang after they shot up the Williams house last March."

"Sounds like they were terrible men," Justin commented.

"They were stupid. As far as I can tell, everything

they did made no sense and was done out of pure meanness."

Morris wanted to make a point for his son. "They sound just like this Raymond fellow who shot a man and held a woman against her will. Then, he thinks THEY are the ones doing wrong."

"There's no understanding the logic of a reprobate mind," Matt agreed.

Earl informed the men he was escorting, "It was Noah who saved my life. I want you to get to him. I want to tell you everything I know, in case it might help you. They are trying to make it hard for anybody to find them. Most people who know them love them and aren't going to give out even the tiniest bit of information. Please try very hard to figure it out and help them."

Morris assured Earl their intentions were honorable. "They saved us from starvation."

Matt added, "He saved me doubly because he gave me the medicine I needed to get rid of a parasite. We want to help him as much as you do."

Earl spent the rest to the ride to Horsehead Creek passing on every detail he knew from the time the outlaws came through town the winter of 1838 and bought two horses from the Williams after their parents had died. He told the story all the way to the day Tom Yates had left Harmony with his family. Earl also told the men everything he knew about the events involving Raymond, Lola, and Sebastian.

When they got to the creek, they stopped to eat

dinner before parting. Earl pulled out the dinner his wife had packed for him. Morris retrieved the food Joe had prepared. The five men sat on a fallen tree as a chilling breeze blew along the cold water of the creek.

FIFTY

At the headwaters of Horsehead Creek, Morris laid their dinner package on his lap. "Fall has set in good." He unwrapped the large paper around the four individually wrapped meals. He handed the top package to George, the next to Justin, then one to Matt, and kept the last for himself.

"I've got something here," Justin took a bite of the sandwich, set it on the paper on the log beside him, and opened the other wrapped object. Inside were four ten dollar gold coins and a note. Justin tried to read. "Thank …you for … coming … to warn us. Please … let us … repay … your…" He held the note in front of Morris. "What's this word?"

"Expenses."

Justin picked up again. "Expenses to get here. May …God bless you … and grant you… suc ..cess …. as you … con..tin..ue. Lola and Se…bas…tian." Justin looked up at his friends and smiled. "I read it!"

"Very good, son. Let me see it." Matt tried to read it to himself silently. "I think I can read it too."

Justin switched back to the topic. "We didn't come here to get money from anybody." He tried to hand the coins to Earl.

"You keep it. You probably saved their lives. Let them thank you the only way they can."

"This is a lot of money," Matt stated.

"Not for them."

"All right. We'll keep it." His father instructed, "Divide it, Justin."

Justin knew what to do. They had already divided their other money between them, believing it was safer that way. Each one of them had hidden money in several different places among their belongings. Justin slid a coin into his own pocket and then passed out the rest.

George drank the last of the lemonade then handed the empty leather canteen to Earl.

"Keep that too. The water in this creek is clean up here, but it gets muddy after the waterfall. Fill up everything you have before you go.

"Cross the creek here where it's small, then you can follow it all the way south to the road. Some places you'll have to climb down slippery rocks, so be careful.

"When you get to the road, you'll have to go another mile or so west to get to Horsehead Post Office. Stay on the road going west and then go north at Van Buren. You'll get to Fort Gibson in about a week. Go north from the fort about another week, then cross the river back to the east side and follow that river north. Thank you for what you've done for us and for continuing on to warn our friends." Earl shook the hand of each of them, got back on his horse, and headed back to Harmony at a canter.

"We have a long way to go. Let's move out." Justin urged his horse to follow his father and friends.

While Matt prayed that somehow they could go home instead of further west, Edwin and Robert prayed their blankets would be dry enough to keep them warm when the day ended.

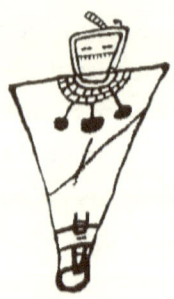

FIFTY ONE

Raymond rode into Spadra, not praying at all. He went into the boarding house to secure a room before trying to find out about a town to the north. He stood at the bar with his saddlebag over his shoulder and tapped the bell on the counter. A woman came out of the side door, wiping her hands on her apron. Right there at the boarding house, Raymond started looking for information. "Is there a town around here where some people named Williams live?"

"No place is near any place around here." To the woman that was true because she couldn't ride anywhere, visit, and get home in one day.

"Any wagons come through here with some people named Williams about a month ago?"

If there was one thing any decent boarding house operator knew about running a boarding house, it was to keep your mouth shut about other patrons, and this man was poking around too much. "I don't think so."

"They're friends of mine. I was hoping to catch up with them." Raymond scanned the ledger as he slowly wrote the name, Joe Smith. The signatures of everybody who had been there for over a month were visible. Raymond didn't see the names Williams, Smith, Swift Hawk, Yates, or Bacon. "What time is supper?"

"Six. Be sharp. I have other people here today." The woman wanted to serve the food hot. People who came late always complained about cooling food.

Raymond fidgeted as the woman searched through her keys for the one she wanted. "How do I get to the store?"

"Go out the front door and turn right. At the second street, go left. You'll see the sign." The woman handed over the key to room 3.

Raymond walked down the hall, inserted the key, opened the door, dropped the saddlebag to the floor, then stepped back out of the room, and locked the door. The woman was in the kitchen cooking.

He followed her directions. He turned the corner and saw the sign, 'Spadra General Store'. At the end of the street, he saw another sign that read, 'Spadra Stables'. He tied Sergeant to the hitching post and went into the store. "Howdy, partner. Just looking to see if you have anything I need." Raymond wanted to have a reason to be there while he asked questions, but he didn't want to spend money he didn't need to spend. "Things are rather dusty. You get many customers?"

The shopkeeper knew there wasn't any dust. He knew people wouldn't buy dusty products. His warning nerves tingled. "I get enough to make a good living. Anything particular you're looking for?"

Raymond spoke a true statement. "I'm mostly

stocked, but I like to look around in stores to see if there is something I think I should get. You have nice things. Do people from towns around here come to your store?"

"Mostly just people passing through. I don't know many people from other towns."

"I guess all the towns out here are far away."

"At least a day."

"I thought I'd move here since Arkansas is now a state. I'm deciding where I want to settle."

"Any direction you go, you'll get to the next town in a day. We're all pretty much the same, except we have the only mail depot this side of the river."

Raymond thought about asking about the specific sisters but decided to be vaguer. "Any town around here with beautiful, available women?"

This was the second man in only two days who had asked about loose women. He hoped nobody had opened a cathouse. *I don't want the kind of people that would attract. Sure, they would be customers but usually drunk and busting things up.* The last young men asked about a place to the north. Just in case there was a brothel up north, he decided to misdirect the man. He hoped the man would go back to wherever these rumors had started and put an end to it. "Maybe west of Horsehead. Never heard of any loose women around here, though." *Tomorrow I'm going up to Harmony and close down anything up there.*

Raymond wasn't learning anything that would help him. "Thank you for telling me about the area." He left without buying anything.

He kicked the post as he untied his horse. He led Sergeant to the stable and started the process over. "Doesn't look like you've had a single horse in here as clean as it is in here."

The man opened a stall door. "Mister, your horse will not get anything but the cleanest conditions and the finest care while he's here. If you want, I can scrub him down outside, but I'll bring him in here to dry where it's warm."

Sergeant always loved him, and Raymond thought his horse would like it. "How much to keep him overnight, feed him some good oats, and wash him?"

"Forty cents will cover it."

"Very many of your customers get their horses washed?"

"Quite a few actually. Most people know how much the animals enjoy it. Especially in the summer."

"Any families come through lately with women who pay for horse washing?" Raymond got out his moneybag.

"Why do you ask?"

"Just wondering if women worry about getting wet if their horses aren't dry enough." Raymond still fished around in his bag for the correct coins.

"Mostly the men bring the horses over, and the women don't come in here. I don't know what any of their women think about it. I guess the men know how their women will like it. To tell you the truth, I've seen plenty of men who treat their animals better than they treat their wives."

Raymond felt irritated. *Does this man know about me? How could he?* He gave the man the forty cents and then hurried away. He didn't know where else he could ask anything. Filled with frustration, Joe Smith ordered a bottle of whiskey and went to his room. *They're all trying to block me and protect them.* Raymond drank a gulp from the bottle.

FIFTY TWO

After a few hours of easy riding, Matt called out, "This must be the slippery rocks Earl told us about."

"He could have mentioned the cliff," Justin commented.

"This is not a cliff." Matt looked at the narrow, steep grade of wet, moss-covered rocks between the creek and the sheer drop off to their right.

Morris looked across the creek at the vertical drop over which the water flowed. "I see why Earl told us to come over to this side."

"Everything else is a cliff," George stated.

Matt got off his horse. "Other than walking, I don't think there is any being careful that's going to help."

"Let's take off the bridles, so they can move their heads freely going down." Morris unbuckled the bridle of his horse. "The mules will be the best at this. We'll let them find the way down with the horses behind them. We can watch and see the best way to go."

They took the bridles off all the horses and the halters off the mules. After much encouragement, they got all six animals over the edge onto the rocky slope. They were committed and continued down.

"Be very sure of every step." Matt took the first step. His foot slipped on the wet moss and wedged into the space between the rocks. He tried to raise his foot. It didn't move. "See what I mean?"

"Can you get your foot out of the boot?" Justin suggested.

Matt tried. "No. You need to get a branch to move the rocks."

Ten minutes later, Morris and George came back with a stick they thought would be strong enough. Morris worked one end in behind Matt's foot then pushed down. Nothing happened. "Help me push."

George got on the other side of the stick and pushed down too. Nothing happened. "Try putting the stick here." Matt pointed to a spot in front of his foot. He sat on the wet ground behind him.

Justin got his hands on the branch. "I think I can pull the end down in this position. You two get on both sides again."

Morris called out, "One, two, three." The three of them pushed or pulled down as hard as they could. Matt felt the pressure against his foot release slightly. He pulled up on his foot and pushed against the ground with his hands. His foot slid out of the boot. The branch snapped. Justin hit the ground with the branch, George, and Morris on top of him. The rocks clacked back together.

"We did it!" Matt reported as Justin rolled on the

ground in pain. Matt crawled to his son. "What happened?"

"Everything came down in the worst place possible." He writhed as he spoke.

"Is it serious or just hurting?" George asked.

Justin felt. "Seems like things are just hurting." Matt tried to get his boot. With his foot out, he pulled it out from between the rocks. The leather was scratched but otherwise all right. He slid it back onto his foot.

Morris looked at the rocks. Their animals waited at the bottom. He had no idea which way they had gone. "It's going to be hard for Justin. Maybe we should do what Bertha said she did and slide on our butts."

"That might hurt too, but at least you'll be more stable." Matt told his son, "I'm sorry about this."

"It's not your fault, Pa. I should have realized I wasn't in a good position. The main thing is we got you out, and I'll recover, eventually."

After several minutes, Justin was able to get up. Matt sat on the wet mossy rocks. "Stay right behind me. All right?"

"All right." Justin sat on the same rock after his father moved down. George followed behind Justin. Morris brought up the rear.

"Everybody all right?" Matt called out over the roar of the waterfall. The other three waved their affirmation that they were following along fine. After eleven minutes of carefully sliding from rock to rock, the four men arrived at the bottom of the treacherous moss and leaf-covered rocky slope.

Morris put the bridle back on his horse. He saw the rears of the others as they did the same. "I don't think the green will ever come out of these breeches."

Justin slipped the bridle onto his horse. "I'm going to have to walk. There is no way I'll be able to get on, let alone ride."

George told his friend compassionately, "No problem. We can walk."

The trip below the waterfalls was as easy as it had been above the falls. Still, they traveled much slower and stopped often. Even in pain, Justin soaked in the beauty of the fall forest full of sparrows and warblers that had come for the winter. The green pines complemented the orange, yellow, and red leaves of the oaks and hickories. They often heard rustling in the leaves and frequently saw squirrel acrobats with their cheeks full of nuts chasing each other around the trees and jumping from branch to branch above them.

"Look!' George pointed at what he was sure would make Justin very happy.

Through the trees, Justin saw the bright yellow leaves of a large cottonwood. "Wonderful! Let's get some."

At the tree, Matt and Morris chopped squares of bark. George searched for dry wood and started a fire. He filled up their coffee pot with water and put it over the fire. Justin scraped the layer of reddish fibers from the back of the pieces of bark and off the trees where the bark had been removed. He gathered it in one of the bags they always had on hand to collect useful plants.

A yellow-bellied sapsucker came to peck at the tree where they had removed the bark. When the water boiled, George took the pot off the fire, put plenty of the red inner bark into the water, and then set it aside to brew. When the tea was ready, Justin gratefully drank a large cupful.

They had spent over an hour collecting the pain-killing inner bark of the cottonwood tree, cooking, and then waiting for the tea to cool enough to drink. They poured the rest of the tea into the leather pouch Joe had sent full of lemonade. The pain subsided greatly as the other men poured pail after pail of water over the fire and then buried it. The trip became much easier for all of them, but especially for Justin. He was able to get onto the horse and ride from there. The sunlight was failing when Matt pulled his spyglass from his pocket for the hundredth time to look ahead. "I think I see the road."

That made Justin happy. "Good. Earl said it was only a short way to town once we got to the road."

A few minutes later, they were on the road. Twenty minutes after that, they arrived at the town of Horsehead Post Office.

Justin didn't think he had ever been happier to be anywhere. They booked rooms at the saloon, ate meat pie, mashed potatoes, green peas, and several pieces of cornbread. Justin drank another cup of cottonwood bark tea with his meal.

Soon after supper, Matt, Morris, Justin, and George slept in warm, soft beds.

FIFTY THREE

Robert and Edwin slept soundly in slightly damp blankets by a fire large enough to keep them warm and finish drying what still hung on the makeshift branch racks in their camp.

Murray, Candy, S.R., and Mary slept unaware that Edwin was not delivering Robert back to Fletcher Creek, nor coming home any day soon.

Ppahiska and his men camped two days north of Fort Gibson with nine more large blocks of salt they had just chopped out of the salt flats.

After a day of gathering, grinding, roasting, and drying, the people in the village slept peacefully.

The Fletcher Creek folks slept soundly after a hard day of house building for the newest members of their community.

FIFTY FOUR

Raymond, however, was not sleeping. Halfway through the night and all the way through the bottle, a male voice came from the hall outside his room. "You hear about a cathouse up in Harmony?"

"I doubt that would ever happen up there. What makes you think that?" a voice answered.

The first voice explained, "I heard Jesse say somebody asked about loose women around here today and yesterday too."

"We should go up there tomorrow and see that it gets closed down. The men they will attract will tear down that town and all the rest of us around here too."

"First, we better test the fare. Then we can close them down." Raymond heard both men laugh and then the sound of a door closing.

Raymond gathered up his things and left the boarding house. *They think they're so loyal, but I'll show them.* By the light of the lantern he had brought from his room, Raymond saddled Sergeant then led him out of the stable. The lantern in his hand lit his way to the northern edge of town. He swung up onto his horse.

"Nobody is going to deceive me!" He threw the lantern against the side of the flour mill.

Not yet very far away, he heard people screaming, "Form a bucket brigade!" Even after he was too far to hear what was happening in town, Raymond could see the light of the fire consuming the mill house, the mill's waterwheel, and the sacks of flour inside.

With a horrible headache and feeling very surly, Ray followed Spadra Creek north.

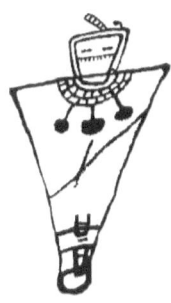

FIFTY FIVE

The following day, Justin was very swollen, and he hurt badly. Matt decided they should go to the town doctor. Justin was even more concerned than his father was. He agreed to go.

Justin told the doctor why he was there. "I had a branch and two men fall on me with a lot of force. It's embarrassing, Doc, but I'm pretty swollen down there."

"It will be two dollars for a consultation."

Matt handed the man two Seated Liberty silver dollars.

The doctor held open the door to his examination room. "Let me take a look." Justin squirmed. "I've got the same parts, son, and I'm a doctor. I've seen plenty of other people too."

"All right." Justin let the doctor examine him.

"Nothing is broken. You just need to take it easy and give things time to heal. Use washrags as cold as you can get them. That will help to bring down the swelling. I have something to help with the pain."

"I sure am glad I'll be all right. I don't need the

painkiller. I already have something." Justin and the doctor went to talk with his father.

The doctor gave his diagnosis. "Your son will be fine. Washrags as cold as you can get them for a few days and nothing strenuous."

Matt replied, "Thank you," then left with Justin.

Back at the saloon, Matt told Morris and George, "I guess we'll have to stay in town for a while," then went for cold water and washcloths.

George got a sheet of paper and a pencil from his bag. "Since this is the postal office town, and we are going to be here for a few days, we should write a letter to Ma."

"Nobody knows where Fletcher Creek is located, and we want it to stay that way," Morris told his son.

Justin waited with George and Morris while his father was gone. "We could write to Mr. Strong. Will might go there to find out if there is any news."

"All right. If nobody goes, at least Mr. Strong and Mrs. Daniels will know the first step of their mission was successful."

George handed his father and Justin a sheet of paper and a pencil then put some on the table for Matt if he wanted to write a letter when he got back. As George and Justin wrote, they asked Morris how to spell words when they came to one they wanted to write but didn't know how to spell and couldn't figure out. Morris wrote a letter to his wife, one to his children, another to all the folks at Fletcher Creek, and a fourth to Mr. Strong and Mrs. Daniels.

Matt knocked on the door. Justin took the water and cloth. He went to his room. "Pa, you can write a letter to Ma if you want. We're going to mail them to Mr. Strong from here."

Matt hesitated. "There are things I would say to her that I don't know how to spell."

"I can tell you, or you can write them the best you can," Morris offered.

Matt missed his wife, Sarah. He thought about her and their children all the time. He sat down and wrote. He asked Morris about some words, but Matt was a man writing to the woman he loved. He tried to write certain words on his own. Morris let him. He didn't want anybody but his wife to read the letter he had written to her. When Matt finished the letter, he stood up. "Let's go to the post office, get some envelopes, and send this off."

At the post office, they labeled seven small envelopes so that each letter would go only to the intended recipient. On the outside of Matt's letter to his wife, he also wrote, "Don't get anybody to help you read this." They put all the individual letters into one large envelope and addressed it to Mr. Murray Strong of Maumelle, Arkansas. They paid the postage and then explored the town.

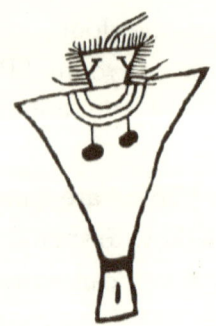

FIFTY SIX

Robert and Edwin made their way to Dardanelle, the Quapaw men continued north toward home, and Adeline rode to Maumelle with Edwin's letter. At the end of the day, Mary heard a knock at the door. She left the kitchen and opened the door. The attractive woman at the door asked, "Is this the home of Murray Strong?"

"Yes. What can I do for you?"

"I'm looking for Mary and S.R. Snow."

"I'm Mary Snow."

"I have a letter from your son." Adeline didn't want to be there when Mary found out what the letter said, and she knew the woman didn't know how to read. She turned to get away quickly.

S.R. joined his wife at the door. "Adeline. What brings you here?"

Mary's voice trembled, "She has a letter from Edwin,"

"Come in and read it to us," S.R. ordered Adeline.

"First, I want to say: I had nothing to do with this. I'm just bringing the letter."

"Oh Lord, please help me!" exclaimed Mary.

Adeline took the letter back just as Murray and Candy joined them because they had heard talking at the door. Adeline read, "Ma and Pa, don't be mad. I went with Robert. He needs me in case he gets sick. We both have good horses. I have my gun and lots of bullets. Martin paid me, and Robert has ten dollars. We got what we need. I want to warn Nancy, Doc Smith, and the family in time. Be back this spring. Tell Mr. Strong and Mrs. Daniels to get married without me. Love, Edwin."

Mary cried. "I know I said he should go, but I'm so afraid!"

S.R. held her. "He's a very smart young man. He'll be fine. I'm sure of it." He believed what he said, sort of.

"Go after him," Mary ordered her husband.

"It won't do any good. They're much too far ahead."

"I'm going to string Robert up when I get my hands on him," Mary stated angrily.

"I'm sorry," Adeline told her.

Mary scolded Adeline, "You should have brought this here immediately."

Maybe I should have, but Edwin asked me to wait a week. I think he can take care of himself. I saw how well he cared for Robert. Robert has to complete this task, or he will never be whole again. "Maybe," she stated.

"Come in." Murray invited Adeline into his home.

Mary tried to behave the way she knew Mrs.

Daniels would want, but she couldn't. *Edwin is my son, and Adeline allowed him to go into danger. Adeline should be punished.* She walked away, went into her room, and shut the door.

FIFTY SEVEN

Just after nightfall, Smitty saw a man crawling up the gully toward his livery. He was glad every animal in town was safely secured inside his barn with the doors locked. In his window facing the street that ran between the two rows of building, Smitty pulled both curtains to the right.

Within a minute, everybody in town knew Raymond had arrived and pulled their front curtains over to acknowledge they had seen the warning.

Raymond crept around the town, trying to determine whether or not Lola was there with Sebastian.

Each family had barred their doors and windows. Some of the women and children tried to sleep, but all the men watched. Raymond spent a cold night not discovering anything.

The next day, it rained all day. Nobody left their home. He couldn't determine anything about who lived where, which got him even more upset. He ate soggy hardtack and beef jerky in the shack behind the store.

When Earl had shown the other people in town

the peepholes in his new home, everybody in town had decided that was a great idea. The small holes that then existed in the outside walls of every home were unplugged and then replugged as they watched their unwanted visitor's movements around their town.

Raymond didn't want to leave town for any amount of time, but he knew he had to move Sergeant to a fresh crop of grass. In town, they thought Raymond had left. Just before dark, Earl saw the man in his storage shed again. He signaled that Raymond was by his house by moving the right curtain to the other side.

During the early evening, Earl burned the lantern in his living room to make things seem normal. He lit one in the bedroom briefly. The rest of the night, so he could better see what was outside, he had no light inside the house. The townsfolk took turns sleeping and watching.

Shortly after nightfall, Raymond lay wrapped in his blankets, asleep behind a stack of boxes in the shed.

The second day Raymond slinked around Harmony, the weather cleared. People came out of their houses and did the things they would normally have done during the day. As they interacted with each other, they secretly passed on the news about where they had seen Raymond.

By the end of the day, Raymond knew that every home had occupants who were not Lola or Sebastian. He didn't know what the Williams, the Yates, or the Indian looked like, but none of the people in town seemed to fit what he knew about them. However, since the sign 'Yates Mercantile' hung above the store, Raymond was sure he was in the right town. He feared all the people he was trying to find had moved on.

FIFTY EIGHT

Edwin squeezed through the crowd in Dardanelle Tavern. He sat in a small wooden booth across from Robert. "I've never seen so many steamboats in all my born days."

"I don't care beans about them. They're all going the wrong way. If even one was going to Fort Smith, we'd be walking in high cotton. But are they? No!"

"That's a crying shame for sure. I'm just saying, even living in Little Rock, I never saw this many all at the same time. Something must be going on."

Robert leaned toward his friend and whispered. "Don't say another word. Let's listen while we wait for supper."

They scooted toward the outer edge of their seats. Behind Edwin, a man twirled the end of his long thin mustache. "You shouldn't try it."

His drinking companion lowered his mug of ale and wiped the foam from his upper lip with the back of his hand. "There ain't no man can climb that rock faster than I can. Besides that, you know I've been study'n that rock with our spyglass. I'm the one who's gonna know which way to go."

The other man's French accent was strong. "You'll never come out of it alive. What good will the money do you then? Not even one of you will ever make it to the top."

"I can! I've got strong hands!" The short, skinny man crushed his now-empty pewter mug and then stormed off.

"What was that sound?" Edwin asked when their food was placed on their table.

The woman with a low-cut blouse raised a mug of ale from the tray she carried. "That man just crushed one of these. Big Lou is signing people up at the corner table."

"What's this about?" Robert took the fork and knife the woman offered.

"Big Lou said he ain't making enough and came up with this contest. He's gonna give a hundred dollars to the first person to climb to the top of Dardanelle Rock. The only gear a person can have is their clothes, a pair of gloves, and chalk. And no practicing."

"Sounds like he's given away money, not making any," Edwin remarked.

"He's already earned more than that from all the people who came for this." The woman hurried off to serve another customer.

Edwin stroked his still hairless chin and gazed at the small man who had just crushed a mug. "I've got an idea. Let's start a bet. One dollar to enter. Whoever picks the winner splits seventy-five percent of the pot, and we keep twenty-five percent for running the game. We don't even have to guess who wins."

If there was one thing Robert had learned from the knife hole in his back, it was not to be greedy. "Make it ninety to ten. As soon as I'm done eating, I'll run to the store, buy paper and pencils, and come right back. You figure out how we keep track of all the bets."

It worked! When Robert left, the Frenchman remained in his seat as he spoke to the young man in the booth behind him. "My name is Pierre Lafayette. Just as it was with you and your companion, I could not help but overhear. I will tell you how to run the betting for five percent."

"Edwin Snow here. Ninety percent to the winners, eight percent for me and Robert, and two percent for you."

"Agreed, but you can't tell my friend I'm involved. Meet me in room twelve when Robert returns."

This might be an ambush. "I might have been born at night, but it wasn't last night."

"If Basil finds out I took advantage of his stupidity, it won't go well for me."

"So, how about the kitchen?"

"That will work." Pierre and his narrow, pointy-toed shoes disappeared into the crowd.

Edwin considered. *What if we're being set up? But how would offering to help us do this be bad? I'll ask Robert what he thinks.*

Robert plopped the papers on the table. "Since we can't write, I don't know how we'll do this."

"I met somebody who offered to help us for two percent of the money we collect. We're supposed to meet him in the kitchen. He doesn't want the man he was drinking with to know it. You think he's trying to take advantage of us? Maybe we shouldn't."

"Of course, he's taking advantage of us, just like we're planning to take advantage of all the folks here."

"It's not really taking advantage of them. We're giving them a chance to win big."

"Did the man look shifty? Did he have beady eyes?"

"He was dressed like a dandy, but his eyes looked straight at me."

"We need him. Let's go." Robert picked up the stack of papers and went into the kitchen. Edwin followed.

As the barmaid scooped stew from the large pot, her rich voice filled the room. On the other side of the door that closed behind Edwin, the raucous crowd didn't hear the melody. Pierre, Edwin, and Robert listened until she turned with several filled bowls on a tray. "Oh!! What are you doing in here?"

Pierre approached the woman. "We heard an angel singing and had to listen. Please, I must know your name."

"Fabienne."

"That's a French name! I'm Pierre Lafayette." He bowed with a grand sweeping gesture. "I hope I might have the honor of hearing you sing again."

"My grandfather was from France. My grandmother was from England. She taught me that song. I didn't even sing all of it."

"Enchanting! Please sing for us again after you have delivered your stew." Pierre held the door open. Once Fabienne was out of the room, he motioned for Edwin and Robert to follow him. He stopped beside a large butcher table. "This is how we do it …"

As he explained, Fabienne returned multiple times for stew, cheese, sliced beef on bread with horseradish, or other items available for purchase. She listened to the plan. "I wish I could buy a chance, but I won't get paid until after the contest."

Pierre offered. "Dear lady, sing another song for me, and get us the list of names of the contestants, and I will buy you a ticket in whatever name you want."

"You would do that for me? My singing isn't worth anything."

Edwin informed her, "People would pay to listen, I'm sure."

"I'm a nobody. That would never happen."

Pierre took her hand and kissed the back of it. "Robert is going to set up down the road. Go ahead and serve two more rounds and then come outside and sing the first song we heard. You'll see how many people you will draw. Then, Edwin can tell them about our game of chance. We'll sell so many tickets you won't believe it."

Fabienne blushed. "I'll do it, but I doubt anybody will come." She once again hurried off to deliver food and ale.

Robert carefully drew together the strips of paper they had made and then left the kitchen out the back door. Pierre and Edwin carried the butcher table behind him.

Not long after they had set up, Pierre slipped away. Fabienne arrived. "Stand right here on the boardwalk." Edwin led her to the proper position.

Fabienne closed her eyes and sang. Her voice lilted like an angel.

> *"Come all ye maids that live at a distance*
> *Many a miles from off your swain*
> *Come and assist me this very moment*
> *For to pass away some time*
> *Singing sweetly and completely*
> *Songs of pleasure and of love*
> *For my heart is with them all together*
> *Though I live not where I love*
> *When I sleep I dream about you*
> *When I wake I find no rest*
> *For every moment thinking of you*
> *My heart affixed in your breast*
> *Although far distance may be assistance*
> *From my mind his love to remove*
> *Yet my heart is with him all together*
> *Though I live not where I love ..."* *

The drunken banter in the street stopped as the crowd drew near. Tears flowed from the eyes of individuals compelled to think of those not with them. As they silenced, the melody floated into the tavern.

265

Big Lou put down his ink quill and went to the door he had widened to get through. "That can't be!" *How do I not know about this? I didn't even need to have this contest. I'll build a stage, and she'll make me barrels of gold.*

> *"…So farewell lad and farewell lassies*
> *Now I think I've made my choice*
> *I will away to yonder mountain*
> *Where I think I hear his voice*
> *And if he hollows I will follow*
> *Around the world though it is so wide*
> *For young Thomas he did promise*
> *I should be his lawful bride"* *

Fabienne opened her eyes. Before her stood every living soul in Dardanelle, they erupted in applause. "Bravo!"

The singer smiled largely. "Thank you!"

Edwin stepped over next to her. "I wish to announce—"

Big Lou grabbed Fabienne's hand. "There will be another song at the bottom of the hour. Entry into the tavern to listen will be two bits." He drew her down the boardwalk.

Edwin spoke the words taught him by Pierre. "I wish to announce the opening of the Dardanelle Climb Guessing Game! For only one skinny dollar, you may purchase a chance to win happiness! Step right up! Name your choice! If your man is the first to the top and you hold his ticket, you will share a gigantic pot! Not one percent of the kitty, not ten percent, not even fifty percent! No, ladies and gentlemen! You won't have to settle for sixty percent, and you won't share an unheard of seventy-five percent! Not in this game! No, that is not going to happen. A fortune awaits you. You, my friends, will share with all those who hold the winner's ticket, a huge, an enormous, an astounding ninety percent! You heard me correctly! Ninety percent! Step right over and buy a ticket to your perfect future!"

From the back of the crowd, Pierre yelled. "Line up the contestants! We need to see the men!"

The climber named John Henry stomped over and grabbed Edwin by the scruff of his neck. "Listen here, mister! You aren't doing this least us climbers get a percentage! Ain't that right, boys?" He jerked Edwin off his feet.

From a different place in the crowd and with a different voice, Pierre screamed. "One percent to every climber, and I'll agree!"

The others who had signed up to risk their lives joined in. "One percent if we win or not!"

"But there are ten of you. That's all the rest."

John Henry drew Edwin's dangling body close to his face and demanded. "Take it or leave it!"

Edwin squeaked out. "The pot will be a remarkable eighty percent!"

John Henry waved Edwin back and forth like a captured fish. "Let the betting begin!" He put Edwin back on his feet and then straightened his scuffled shirt. As he brushed off Edwin's chest he softly growled, "Don't ever try to take advantage of me again."

"Yes, sir! We won't ever!" Edwin hurried to the butcher table where Robert was already selling colored tickets like hotcakes.

Except for tiny Basil, whose stack was still completely there, half of every man's stack was gone, and John Henry had only a few left. "I'll go make more." Robert hurried back to the tavern.

Pierre stepped up. "Fabienne says she wants one of Basil's. I'll take one as well."

How very convenient that he picked his friend after setting this whole thing in motion, and I think it was him who hollered about the men lining up. Edwin marked the sale of four tickets on his sheet, handed Pierre two green tickets with the name "Basil" inscribed, and slid two into his own pocket.

Robert returned. "Wait a minute!" he told the lady before him. "You've already bought a ticket."

"I want one for each of them."

"Can't be done," Robert informed her.

"I should be able to do whatever I want!"

"That must be all the money you own. Besides that, if everybody did that, you would all end up with what you started out with minus twenty percent. That wouldn't make sense."

"It's my money and my choice!"

Edwin offered, "You can buy more for the same man and get a bigger share."

"It's about time you came to your senses! Give me ten more for John Henry!"

Robert handed her ten of the tickets he had just made before he gave Edwin the rest of the strips. "I'll go make more."

Pierre crouched and screamed, "I can't believe it! They'll let you buy more than one ticket for your man!"

The line packed again.

That night, Robert and Edwin sorted coins. They put eight dollars in one pile and then two in the second. Robert held a gold coin in the direction of the room lantern, squinted one eye, and examined it. "Somebody drilled through this one."

"Let me see it." Edwin studied the hole. "It's small. It would have to be a very thin chain to get through. It would break for sure, and then you'd lose it." He handed it back.

"Still, maybe it would be useful to have a hole. I'll take it." Robert put the coin into the twenty percent pile. They continued the division until they came down to a pile of smaller change. "How do we divide these?" Robert asked.

"Separate out the types. Then, we'll divide those eight to two for each kind." That worked until they had five bit-pieces, seven dimes, nine nickels, and three pennies. "Robert, you see what I was telling you about learning everything we can? This is why we need to learn arithmetic."

Robert had an idea. "I'll get Fabienne. She knows how to do this, and she just sang her last song for the night."

A few minutes later, the barmaid, who had become Big Lou's entertainer, walked into the room Edwin and Robert had rented for the night. "There it is." Robert pointed to the small stack of coins at the edge of the table.

Fabienne approached the table. "How much did you get?"

"I don't know. I've never counted this high." Edwin pushed the money toward the woman.

"Do you mind if I count all of it?" the woman asked.

"Please do," Robert told her, "We want to know how much we have."

Fabienne counted the small pile of coins, made the calculations on paper. "I'll take this dime and go get ten pennies." When she returned, she pushed $1.94 into the eighty percent pile and 49¢ into the twenty percent pile. She counted all the coins in the eighty percent pile and wrote it down, then did the same for the twenty percent pile. "Six hundred and twenty-seven dollars all together." She ciphered again. "You get fifty dollars and sixteen cents. Can you count?"

"Yes, all the way to one hundred," Edwin replied.

Robert echoed, "I can count to one hundred too."

"Then you actually can count forever if you learn just a few words."

"Really?!" Robert felt much smarter.

"Pierre gets twelve dollars and fifty-four cents. Each climber gets six dollars and twenty-seven cents, and the winners share five-hundred-and-one dollars and sixty cents."

"You are very smart! How did you learn to do this?" Robert started counting money. "Half for me and half for Edwin. I already know we each get twenty-five dollars and eight cents. I guess working for Mr. Harrow helped me more than I realized. He taught me how to take his money and return the change. I didn't realize I knew this much!" He smiled broadly and puffed out his chest, but just a little.

As Robert counted their share, Edwin made ten piles of six dollars and twenty-seven cents. "Me too. We sure are lucky we got to work for Mr. Harrow."

A knocking came at their door. Fabienne whispered, "Hide the money. It may be somebody wanting to steal it."

Robert scooped all the piles into the same bag and set it outside on the window ledge. Edwin opened the door. Pierre came in. "Fabienne, why are you here?"

"I was asked to help divide out everybody's share."

"Is it done? I only have a minute before Basil misses me."

Robert brought the bag back inside. "Now, we'll have to count out your share again." He counted out $12.54 before he placed it into Pierre's hand.

"Thank you. See you tomorrow." Pierre quickly exited the room.

"I'll show you how to count forever." Fabienne started counting out stacks of $6.27. "After you get to one hundred, you start at one again, and then when you get to a hundred again, how many hundreds do you have?"

"Two hundred, so you just count using the same numbers for the hundreds?" Edwin slipped his twenty-five dollars and eight cents into his pocket.

Robert inserted his share into his personal moneybag before he continued counting. "So, is it ten hundred and eleven hundred when you get there?"

"You can say it that way, but most people call ten hundred a thousand."

"So then you have one thousand and one... Robert jumped to his feet. His chair crashed against the wall behind him. "What in the Sam Hill is going on here?!"

The other two had just arrived at the same conclusion. "It wasn't out there for one minute. Where did it go?" Fabienne asked.

Robert accused Fabienne. "You knew it was there. None of this was yours, and you could've had somebody waiting to snatch some!"

"How would I have known Pierre was going to come here or that you would put the money out the window?"

"You're right. It must have been Pierre. He knew he was coming here, and he's been staying in one of these rooms. He knows there isn't any place to hide anything in here."

"He kissed me earlier. He didn't feel like an evil man, and besides, he was in here."

"You can't tell anything from a kiss on your hand," Robert replied.

"I mean, he kissed my lips."

Edwin snapped, "What on Earth were you doing that for?"

"It's none of your business if or why I kiss somebody! Let's just figure out how much is missing." Fabienne completed the count. "Four-hundred eight-nine dollars and twenty-five cents."

Robert counted on his fingers. "Three bit-pieces make it four-hundred and ninety dollars. That means we're missing about eleven dollars."

"Whoever grabbed that money had to do it fast. Maybe some fell. I'm going out to look." Robert started toward the door.

"Not without me! You might put it in your pocket and say you didn't find anything."

"You saved my life, Edwin. I would never do that to you, but come on." As the two young men left, Robert locked the door. Fabienne went back to her own room.

"What are you doing?" Pierre asked Robert and Edwin, who were crawling in the dirt beneath their window.

"Ah. Um. Robert dropped his cigar. We're looking for it."

"Right, I dropped it, and of course, it rolled right off into the darkness." Robert eyeballed Pierre suspiciously.

Pierre flipped a silver dollar in the air. "I'd just buy another, but good luck."

"Where did you get that?" Edwin demanded to know.

"You just gave it to me in your room."

You dirty liar. You set us up. Robert decided not to

say anything and try to somehow trick Pierre into confessing later.

"Where is Basil?" Edwin asked.

"In his room, resting up for the climb tomorrow."

"How convenient," Robert remarked.

Pierre's eyebrows raised, his eyes opened wider, and his head cocked back. "Well, as I said, good luck finding your cigar." He walked away. *Strange men!*

Robert went back to searching. "I found a piece of eight!" he whispered.

"I've found a nickel, but it looks really old. I don't think it's one of ours."

"Take it anyway."

Back in their room, Edwin glanced at the table. "The money's been moved!"

"Maybe Fabienne came back in," Robert started counting again.

"Or Basil. Pierre was outside with us." Edwin joined the process. "Twenty-three dollars are gone. It's a lot more this time."

"And the one with the hole is gone. The only people who know how much we had are Fabienne and Pierre. Whichever took the money isn't going to say anything. The winner's pot will have to be what's left, but we better not let it out of our sight for a second."

FIFTY NINE

Robert ate breakfast with the winner's bag inside his shirt, which he had tucked deeply into his trousers. Big Lou served the climbers a hearty breakfast for stamina during the contest. When the sun rose, the folks in Dardanelle migrated to the three-hundred-and-forty-foot-high rock cliff.

"What! Who did that? I never authorized a net!" Big Lou stalked to the closest stake that held the lifesaving device several feet above the ground.

Pierre blocked him. "Nobody can do this. Every single one of them is going to fall. You don't get to kill people."

"It's my game, and I'm taking it down."

Fabienne joined Pierre. "I'll never sing in your tavern again if you do."

Big Lou pushed her aside. "You'll do what I tell you, or I'll throw you back into the gutter, and then what will you do?"

"She can go with me!"

Pierre's accent and frilly shirt did not encourage Lou to perceive the man as a threat.

John Henry stepped in front of Big Lou. "You leave it, or none of us is climbing, and you can just give all these people their money back."

"I'm not the one who took everybody's money! It was them!" Big Lou pointed at Edwin and Robert.

Edwin remembered that Candice Daniels had told him it's how you present yourself when you speak that makes people pay attention. He straightened up his shoulders, stood tall, and spoke in a loud, clear voice. "My good sir, it's of no consequence to you that this net is here, and it's essential for the climbers. You will allow it to remain, or the people here today will spread the word of your behavior far and wide. Therefore, I suggest you leave it."

Big Lou looked at the young man. *He must be the son of a lawyer or something.* "All right, I'll leave it. Gentlemen, come over for inspection."

John Henry, Basil, and the other eight registered climbers stood in a line. Robert tried to determine if any of them was acting as if he had stolen part of the kitty. Big Lou, however, patted them down, examined the chalk bags that hung at the backsides of the men, and then declared. "All clear! You can backtrack even all the way to the ground, but if you fall, you're out. First to the summit wins one hundred dollars! Pick your spots!"

Basil took up a position that looked like it had only a few widely spaced handholds or foot perches.

The crowd badgered him. "Not very smart, are you?"

"You trying to lose?"

"Look. Everybody else is over there on the craggy wall."

"Good night, sweet loser!"

Basil stood where he was.

Big Lou hollered, "GO!"

John Henry started up. Like a lizard, he scurried from one point to the next. The crowd below stood mesmerized, with their eyes riveted on him. His fingers slid into the easy-to-reach crevasses and cracks and grabbed tightly. He raised a leg, draped it over a protuberance, and used it to draw himself up. He dipped his hand into his chalk bag and reached.

Another contestant made his way nearby. He scanned the area around him. Advice was offered from below. "Just above to the right. I think you can…"

Barely fifteen feet up, the drop was quick. He bounced in the net Pierre had blessedly been able to provide with his twelve-dollar share of the betting money. "(^$%(#)#^! Over practically before I got started! Give me my money, Edwin!"

"Sorry you're not the winner." Edwin handed the man a package of coins wrapped in a sheet of paper.

After the man walked away, Fabienne said, "This net won't work once the men get too high."

Above, John Henry slid his thin-soled leather shoe into a crevasse, rotated his knee in, his heel out, and pushed to the right. His fingers gripped a wedge of stone barely half an inch deep. His foot slipped. He dangled from his hands fifty feet up. With his feet, he searched frantically and blindly. He found a bump with one foot and then the other. Secure again, he chalked up. Eight other men still clung to the cliff, barely watched by the gawking spectators who were all watching John Henry.

Edwin, Robert, Pierre, and Fabienne stood apart from the crowd with their eyes focused on the man only thirty feet up. Fabienne asked, "Basil, why are you lying on that ledge? You'll never win like that."

"The others will give out before they make it three-quarters of the way. I won't because I have several places to rest."

"Oh, how very clever of you!"

As if predicted by Basil, a contestant changed his mode to decent. "What are you doing?" screamed a holder of his ticket. "Go up!"

The reply came, "I'm not even halfway, honey. I'm sorry. I don't know if I'll even be able to climb back down with the strength I have left."

"I don't know why I even married you! You always let me down! I should have known better than to bet on you!"

"All right, I'll keep trying."

"You better!"

A nearby climber heard the comment about being able to get down. *That net looks really far away. It might break. The man is an idiot to listen to his wife.* He started down. His supporters yelled for him to keep climbing. Without a wife to persuade him, he continued to the ground, gathered his participant fee from Edwin, and then lay on the safe Earth.

"Coward!" A ticket with the man's name flew

from the purchaser. It gently wafted back and forth as it also made its way to the soil.

Pierre commented to the three beside him, also looking up at Basil, "Two out and thankfully not dead!"

He cares about these people. I don't think Pierre would steal from us. Robert rubbed his neck. "We probably never should have started this betting game. People are going to pressure the climbers to go on when they can't."

Pierre stated his opinion, "They would have done it anyway."

Climber two again informed his wife, "I need to come down, honey."

"Bruce, don't you dare!"

"I'll never make it. I have to!"

"You are the laziest man alive! You'll never see your son again if you quit!"

As Bruce continued on, Basil drew his right foot up to the ledge upon which he had lain and raised himself. Quickly, he was several feet higher with his feet close together, his knees spread wide, and his pelvis held tight to the rock face.

"I'd never be able to flatten out like that." Edwin's thighs hurt just thinking about it.

"He is very flexible," Pierre assured his new friends.

" Ahhhhhhhhhhhhhhhhhhhhhhhhhhhhhhhhhhhhhhh hhhhhhhh!" screamed man four all the way to the net.

All heads turned. The net stretched to only inches

from the ground as it caught the climber who had plummeted from seventy feet up. He lay in the net. Everybody ran over.

"Are you all right?!" Fabienne asked.

The man said nothing.

Fabienne ordered, "Get him to the doctor!"

The man waved her off. A minute later, he informed the crowd, "Just got the wind knocked out of me. I'll be all right."

Pierre looked into heaven and made the sign of the cross. "Thank you, Good Lord!"

Robert had noticed the stretch of the net. "This net won't stop the next one from hitting the ground. We need to get it higher."

"I'm not paying for anything." Big Lou walked away.

He sure is greedy. "I will." Edwin drew out his moneybag.

The owner of the lumber mill called out, "Men, help me bring lumber."

The storeowner added, "I'll bring nails."

Various men in the crowd mobilized.

"I'll get my saws."

"I have hammers."

People dashed away, calling out what they had to contribute.

One hundred and seventy feet up, John Henry stopped moving. *There's nothing I can reach from here.* He looked around to see if he could go down or over and find another path. He saw them working on the net. *Nothing. I'll never make it all the way back down.* "Hurry up and get that net ready! I'll get lower before I drop!"

Twenty minutes after that, the net was secured to the new frame. The mill owner hollered. "That should do it!" He brushed sawdust from his breeches and then held out his hand. "Two dollars for the lumber."

The storeowner requested, "Twenty cents."

Edwin paid up as climber five's own weight became too much for his tired fingers. "I'm letting go!" Not yet as high as the previous man who had fallen, the net worked perfectly.

From much higher than any of the other climbers, John Henry screamed, "Get him out! I'm dropping!"

Sprong! John Henry bounced. He lay unconscious. Contestant two saw the lack of attention of the people below, including his wife, and moved towards the far side of the rock.

Fabienne climbed into the net and placed her fingers on John Henry's neck. "He's still alive."

John Henry revived as he was lowered from the net.

"Where is Bruce?!" called out the woman who had shamed her husband into continuing. "Bruce!" she screamed to no avail.

Bruce did not lie on the ground. Bruce was not visible on the rock. She grabbed the spyglass from Pierre, who had never stopped watching Basil. "He's vanished! The rapture occurred!"

A young boy told his mother, "It's no wonder she's still here."

"Quiet, son. That isn't kind!"

"But right," his sister whispered to her brother.

Nobody thought to look at the out-of-view flat face of the rock. The side that was extremely hard to scale going up and almost impossible going down, but Bruce had finally had enough. Pumped full of adrenaline and anger that his wife would rather see him fall to his death than let him lose, he was quite successfully and rapidly making his way off the mountain to get his son and disappear.

At that point, Basil was over two hundred feet up and much farther to the left than his original point of ascension. This time, he sat with his feet dangling. He waved at the crowd.

Nobody below was able to hear Ross, one of the other two men high on the cliff. "Basil, I might make it to the top before I give out. You won't, going all over the place like that."

"My plan is sure. Do you have a plan, Ross?"

"Of course, I do. Keep going."

Although he had not heard the comment, John Henry realized that everybody's strategy had been the same except for one man. He walked to Robert. "I want a ticket on Basil as the winner."

"You can't buy one now!"

"I needed to win. I only have ten dollars. I'll never get home."

Robert felt bad for the man, but he had to keep the game fair. "Sorry." *He couldn't have stolen the money, he only has ten dollars, but then again, maybe that's an act to throw me off.*

John Henry reached for Robert. Big Lou stepped between them. "You lost fair and square. Don't try roughing up my customers!"

"Lord, help me. I don't have any place to go." John Henry started back toward town. He took a last look at Dardanelle Rock. From his new vantage point, he saw Bruce sneaking his way down the cliff. "That man is escaping his wife. Maybe we can help each other." He circled around to be at the bottom when Bruce arrived.

Frank, the other man on the mountain, trapped himself at two hundred feet. "I'm stuck!"

Basil remembered what he had seen as he had studied the mountain. "There is no way up from where you are. You'd have to go down quite far to get over here where you can go all the way to the top. There is a small ledge just down and to your left. You can go there and rest, then go back down and try to find your way over here to continue. Since I'll have won by then, you could go back to the bottom after you rest."

"Do you know of a place I can rest?" Ross asked.

"You are far from anything. I suggest you try to go as far back down as you can before you give out and drop. Oh, wait! There is a crack you might be able to wedge into. Still, it's pretty far down. It's almost directly below you."

"I'm going to try to get there. Congratulations on winning."

Frank was already on his way to his nearby ledge. "Get down safely."

Below, Bruce's wife was frantic. "I never should

have said such horrible things. Now, God has taken him from me. What will I do? We'll starve. I'll be so lonely. Bruce! Bruce, come back to me! I'm sorry!" She scurried back and forth at the base of the cliff and looked up with Pierre's spyglass.

Fabienne told the woman, "You did act as if you didn't care if he died."

"It's just that I thought he was scared. I thought he could do it if he would believe in himself."

"There is a difference between believing in yourself and being stupid. He's somewhere. You should treat him better in the future. I know how it feels to be considered garbage, and it's not nice. Pierre needs his spyglass." Fabienne held out her hand. She took back the looking tube.

Bruce's wife dropped to her knees and sobbed into her hands. "I'm sorry. God, let him know I love him and need him. Bring him back to me."

Ross tried to find the places he had used coming up. Nothing looked the same. He tried to rest on every foothold that was stable and deep enough to allow his arms and fingers a few minutes of rest. He was tired, tired, tired. *I don't think I'm going to make it. That net won't do me any good if I fall from way up here. Stop talking like that, Ross! Keep trying to get there!* The sandstone he clung to broke loose. He squeezed tighter with his other hand and managed to hold on. *Where is it? Where is it?*

Ross once again attempted to look below him. *Nothing looks like a crack.* He swung his leg to a bump and made good contact. He hung from his right hand and leg, reached down, and slipped his fingertips into a slender depression. Balanced sideways on those three points, he lowered his left leg. *That's deep!* He shifted his weight. His whole toe rested on the perch. He glanced down. *I'm saved!* He brought his other foot to the same ledge. Slowly, he rotated one foot and then the other until he got the sides of the balls of both feet on the narrow two-inch strip of stone. He stood vertically with good grips on large handholds. He leaned his cheek against the cold, hard rock and rested.

Basil recited his path in his mind. He looked up to verify it was as he believed. Since it was, and he was again well-rested, he stood, turned toward the cliff, and then sprung up. Both hands slid into the deep notch two feet higher than he could have reached. He pulled himself up with his arms until his feet found the perches he needed. He stretched far to the left and found a tiny lip of stone, then drew his body hand-over-hand along the ledge as his lower extremities dangled. Six hand-overs and he had made it to the wide vertical crack that provided an easy thirty-foot-rise.

Once back out on the rock face at the top of the fissure, Basil was less than a hundred feet from the top facing an overhang. *You can do this.* He hooked his heel, twisted in his hip, put all his weight on his foot, and reached out into the rock hanging over him. Straight-armed, he drew his stomach in and found another inside foot perch. He twisted the other way, crossed his leg in, and brought his other leg out. *Remember; keep your body close and your arms straight.* Three hundred feet above the hard earth far below, he slowly drew his body along the underside of the ledge. With his life depending on it, he never allowed his bottom to drop away from the rock as he clung to the bumps and holes of the overhang.

At the edge, he reached over to the top where he knew a handhold waited. Without having studied the cliff from below, he never could have seen where to grab. He got his heel on the top and drew himself around the edge.

Far below, the folks clapped and shouted congratulations that Basil could not hear. As he climbed the final twenty feet with the slope beneath him, he let himself truly believe that he could make it to the top.

At the summit, he saluted the observers. As the sun approached the horizon, Basil admired the silver ribbon that was the Arkansas River flowing across the flat land below. After he regained his strength, he would walk the steep but easy trail down the back.

Edwin called out, "Those who bought a Basil ticket meet me at the tavern!"

"But what about Bruce?" Bruce's wife wailed.

"And Frank and Ross?" another person added.

Big Lou could see Ross, who had finally gotten to the crack and had wedged himself in. Bruce and Frank remained unseen. "Probably they're resting somewhere like Ross is. It'll get dark before they can climb down. They'll have to stay where they are until the morning. It's been a long day. I'm going to the tavern. Fabienne will be singing, and I'll have plenty of food to sell, so come on over."

Fabienne followed her employer. She knew she had a Basil ticket, and she had held the tickets of Pierre, Edwin, and Robert since the previous night. She knew their tickets had been bought fair and square before the contest had started. She didn't know if anybody else had bet on the small, slender man. *I'll buy a steamboat ticket and go with Pierre. We'll show up in Little Rock with money. People will treat us decently.*

Pierre hurried off to the backside of Dardanelle Rock with a large canteen of water and a basket dinner for his friend.

As they walked back to the tavern, Edwin and Robert prepared to divide the Dardanelle Rock Climb Betting Game Funds. They knew they had sold only the four tickets. Therefore, they needed to change out a ten-dollar gold piece. Edwin suggested, "Robert, let's ask Big Lou for change." Edwin already had the coin separated out. He quickened his pace, caught up to Big Lou, and drew the money from his pocket. "Would you exchange this into smaller coins? We need to divide the money out to the winners."

"I will, but all my money's locked up back at the tavern. How many people bet on Basil? I wouldn't think it would have been many."

"Only four." Edwin followed the tavern owner toward the kitchen.

"Wait out here." Big Lou shut the door. He

returned with his moneybox, put it on the counter, and opened the lid.

Edwin's face turned red. *You dirty, rotten thief!* "Where did you get that?!" He grabbed a handful of coins, making sure he got the coin with a hole.

Big Lou seized Edwin's hand. "Drop it!" His other hand went for the gun under the counter.

Fabienne screamed, "He'll shoot you! Let it go, Edwin!"

"No! He stole our money! You going to shoot me right here in front of all these people? Where did you get the coin with the hole in it?"

"Somebody must of paid me with it."

Millie, the woman who had bought ten John Henry tickets, spoke up. "I bought betting tickets with a gold coin with a hole. I didn't give it to you, Lou."

Fabienne cupped her hands under Edwin's clenched fist. "Please, drop the money."

Edwin let go of the coins. Fabienne spread the money out on the bar. From time to time, money had disappeared around the town. The locals drew in closer. "That's the coin I gave Edwin." Millie pointed to the coin of contention.

A supporter of Ross called out, "I paid them with a silver dollar that had one flat edge! Is it there?"

Millie scanned the coins. "Oh, my word! There is one!" She picked it up and held it above her head with the flat edge clearly visible. "You better start explaining, Lou!"

He could have gotten away with it if he had

known that some of the money had fallen outside the window, and he had said that he had found it in the street. Unfortunately for Lou, he hadn't had an ounce of control when he had seen Pierre sneak up the stairs, made a guess, and then slipped into the room next to the one he suspected was Pierre's destination.

Lou had figured Robert and Edwin would attempt to hide the money, and he thought that would most likely be outside their window. Lou had quickly made his way across the adjoining room and slid open the window. There it was. He had put one hand against the bag so the whole thing wouldn't fall and then reached inside. He had wrapped his fingers around as much as he could quickly grasp. He drew his hand out as Robert reopened his window. All he could think was to get his hand out of view. He hadn't noticed a piece-of-eight drop.

Now that he had been found out, Lou drew the gun from under the counter and waved it in the air. "I don't have to tell you anything! I can't believe you would believe some strangers over me!" Lou started sweating.

"Things aren't adding up right to believe you," Millie swept the coins towards her hand.

"Touch that money, and I'll shoot you!" Big Lou pointed his pistol at his fellow townswoman.

The front door opened. "It's Bruce!" a person in the kitchen door exclaimed.

All eyes, except one, turned. There stood Bruce, holding his one-year-old child. During the second that everybody was distracted, John Henry rushed in from the kitchen. He snatched the pistol and slammed Big Lou into the rack of liquor behind him. Bottles tumbled off the shelves and smashed on the floor.

Heads swung back in the direction of Lou, now unarmed and missing a tooth. Edwin exhaled the breath he had been holding. "Good work, John Henry!"

"What should we do with Big Lou?" Millie asked.

For the last several years, Big Lou had not treated her kindly, but he had given her a place to live and food to eat. Fabienne pleaded for him. "Give him a chance to prove his story. We owe him at least that."

She hurried to the door. "Bruce, you should go talk with your wife. She's sorry, and she's frantic. She's still at the cliff, praying to God that you're safe."

"She doesn't care about me, and she wants to take my son from me."

"She was just talking tough. She shouldn't have, and now she knows it. Go talk with her," Fabienne encouraged the man to reconcile.

"I'll talk to her, but I'm not promising anything." Bruce retreated out the door, still carrying his child.

Her focus returned to the debate behind her, where John Henry was tying Big Lou to the bar. "How much money did he take, Edwin?"

"Thirty-four dollars all together. Eleven dollars went missing when we put the moneybag outside the window. Twenty-three more disappeared when we were looking for it."

"Take thirty-four dollars and pay the winners."

Big Lou huffed, "You don't have any right to be telling anybody what to do!"

"Anybody want anything different to happen?" John Henry asked.

The folks in the tavern called out, "Take the money. The winners should get all they're due!"

Millie counted out the coins, including the one with the hole and the one with the flattened edge. "Anybody with a Basil ticket, come forward." She dropped the money into Robert's hands.

Fabienne made her way through the crowd and then handed Edwin four tickets.

So that everybody could see them, Edwin held them high and circled. "These are real tickets!"

Robert held out the moneybag. "Madam, here is your bright future."

Fabienne accepted not only the money but also the prediction of better times ahead. "John Henry, why don't you stay here and be our sheriff?"

"Maybe nobody else wants me," he replied.

"What do you say, people of Dardanelle?"

"Please take the job," the townsfolk begged.

"All right, I'll do it. First thing is to find a place to lock up Big Lou until his trial for thievery."

Edwin looked at Robert and then informed John Henry, "We got the money back. We're not pressing charges, but keep him tied up until morning. We'll leave now and be long gone."

Robert opened the door to their room. Fabienne

stepped in. "I'm leaving with Pierre. I've brought your half of the winnings."

Edwin already knew he and Robert were going to stick to their words. "Just give us the coin with the hole and the one with the flat side. You, Pierre, and Basil have the bright future I promised."

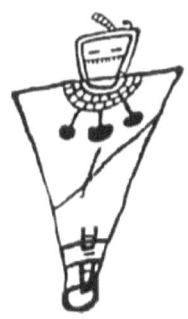

SIXTY

The men on the plateau above the village arrived at the basket with a very fat bear on a long pole. They had decided they would divide the meat, fat, and other parts into nine portions. The bear's hide, however, they would not cut into nine pieces but would instead give the whole thing to one person. What they had not decided was who it would be.

"Do you think it is too heavy for the basket?" Tizhu, one of the Cherokee husbands, asked.

"We should skin it and cut it up like the buffalo." Waya stepped out of his place, supporting the carcass. "I will get what we need." When he was in the lodge, he told his family, "We got a huge bear. I am taking up a tarp, baskets, and tools."

"Do you want help?" Luyu asked.

"There are more than enough of us up there already. Everybody will need to help when we get it down here. We should make more of those smoked sausages."

Sally stated emphatically, "I will do no more cleaning of intestines."

"Those sausages were delicious. I'll help clean them. Do you want to make all our share of meat into sausages?" asked Stephanie.

Ann joked, "Roscoe told me all the women have asked him how he made them. That bear may not have enough intestines.

Stephanie refined her previous statement. "I am not cleaning intestines for anybody but us, and other people in this family need to help clean ours."

"I'll help," Luyu offered.

Helen's stomach turned over. "I can learn how to do that, but I don't know if I can eat anything inside an intestine."

Waya spoke up. "I will help. Helen, you do not need to. I will be back when it is butchered."

"All right, my wonderful husband." Luyu kissed Waya goodbye.

When the men arrived in the village, each family carried away a heavy load of meat and one-ninth of the bear's fat and intestines. The hide was filled with ground salt and rolled up with the head and paws still attached. They tied it onto the ceiling of the community building.

The women stopped working on the nuts. Everyone except the very young children took a section of the intestines into the creek.

"This is much easier." Sally squeezed out the contents and let the water flow through the tube of flesh.

After the intestines had been thoroughly washed,

they pulled the outer flesh from the inner membrane. When the intestine preparations were complete, everybody decided to leave the rest of the bear processing until the next day.

The men arrived home so tired they only cleaned themselves up before going to sleep. The women and children rendered fat. They chopped, mixed, and spiced the meat, then stuffed the mixture into the thin membrane they had harvested from the animal's intestines. They tied the sausages in six-inch-long sections of spiced meat.

It was just before sunrise when the village had turned the entire bear into sausages. They washed and then fell into their beds.

As the women and children slept, the men started the fires. They hung the strings of sausages in the smoke. When the sun sank below the horizon, the village was a cloud of smoke, small fires, and hundreds of pounds of cooking bear meat.

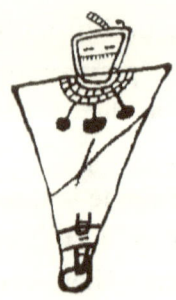

SIXTY ONE

Edwin and Robert rode into the town of Shoal Creek Post Office, the mail depot on the south side of the Arkansas River. Since they were pushing their horses hard trying to get to the man they knew as Doctor Smith, they paid for grain and hay for their animals and then got a room with two beds. They both took a long, hot bath. Robert's back was healing well. So far, the trip hadn't been a problem. Robert had never been out of Little Rock before he went running for his life. At the moment, he was enjoying the adventure.

Edwin was too, but he wanted his parents to know he was all right, especially his mother. The problem was that he barely knew how to write, and Robert didn't know anything about writing. They decided to try. Edwin bought paper, envelopes, and a pencil. He did his best to write what Robert wanted to say to his family. Edwin then wrote a letter to his own parents, asking them to give the news to Mr. Strong and Mrs. Daniels. He thought about it for a long time and then decided he didn't care if other people knew. He wrote a letter to Elizabeth too. He put each in its own envelope and then all of them in a larger envelope to Mr. Strong in Maumelle. They walked back to the post office and paid the fee to send the package. After a good meal, they slept, planning to leave early the next day.

SIXTY TWO

Raymond stayed awake to see if anybody sneaked around during the night. He couldn't see every part of town at the same time, but he made frequent circuits. When morning arrived, he left town again and moved Sergeant to another location. Then, wearing his wool clothes and coat, he wrapped up in his blanket.

As Raymond slept, Edwin and Robert rode eighteen miles through the woodlands. Just before the sun went down, they forded a small stream named Caney Creek.

Justin's condition had improved greatly, so George, Morris, Matt, and Justin had left Horsehead Post Office and traveled to the town of Ozark.

In Rock House Cave, Lola talked with Sebastian at twilight. "Nobody has come to get us. Raymond must be at Harmony. How can we live knowing Raymond will find us? Just like he did when we were riding away from Perryville, he could shoot you before you even knew he is there."

Sebastian knew she was right. He threw a saddle

on his black stallion. "I'm going to Harmony. I'll sneak up on him and shoot him first."

Lola handed him the rifle. "Thank you."

Sebastian slithered through the field around his adopted town. He knew Raymond was there somewhere. He looked for signs of his enemy between the buildings. He observed the short center street of Harmony. He cautiously circled by the light of the half-moon but found no evidence of Raymond.

Raymond circled too. *If I don't see anything by morning, I'll go to Indian Territory.*

All night the two men attempted to find evidence of the other. God protected Sebastian. Both men remained undetected by the other.

The sun rose. The people of town once again left their homes. Raymond felt sure that none of the people he was searching for lived in Harmony. He crawled toward the woods where his horse waited. Sergeant had done nothing for the last few days except eat grass, so Raymond decided to push forward quickly. He urged his horse into a canter.

Sebastian spent the day searching. He felt he needed to eliminate the man who robbed Lola of peace.

When Raymond got to Spadra, he went to look at the mill. It had completely burned down. He gloated. *That will show them not to mess with me.*

He and Sergeant cantered all the way to Horsehead Post Office. The postal stop irritated him. It reminded him that he didn't have anybody who wanted to hear from him.

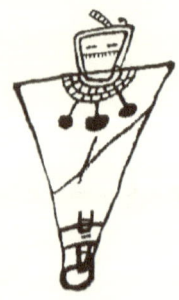

SIXTY THREE

It had been six days since Ppahiska had left Fort Gibson. He stood at the Spring River ford of the Neosho River. "I do not want to go all the way to Leotie's land. We agreed we would not go to the same section of land all the time."

Wakanda replied, "We have to go where they are. The herd may leave soon, and we are already on this side."

The other men waited while their chief and their mystery man decided if they should take what they had and go home or continue north. They did not cross. Blessedly, when they came across the antelope, they also found Wesa.

Not far from the border of Leotie's land, Wesa stalked the herd. They were supposed to hunt in different sections, so many Cherokee villages would get the trade items. He wanted to honor the agreement, but he needed enough food to get his village through the winter. He had to take the prey that was available, and the antelope were where they were. When he saw Ppahiska and his men, he saw a solution and signaled.

The men of Ppahiska's village pulled both sides of the wagon covers up a foot. They hid inside their weak defenses and looked out. Wesa's party got into position and then let loose a barrage of arrows.

The animals stampeded south. The herd was so thick that Ppahiska's men would have been trampled into pulp if they had not been in the wagons. One animal after another went down as the crush of thousands of antelope forced them in front of the men with arrows.

A large stag slammed into the wagon. Chetan tumbled backward into Tatonga. Their nocked arrows released into the air above them. Blessedly, they stuck in the canvas. Antelope in flight hit and cracked wagon bows. Long horns pierced the cloth between the herd and the men. An antelope attempted to jump the high obstacle. It failed to reach the required height. Its horns ripped the cloth, but its body bounced off and tumbled to the ground. A second antelope sprung. It tore completely through the ripped canvas and landed in the wagon. Suddenly up to its knees in buffalo heads and surrounded by people, the animal attempted to impale everything around it. Its horns slashed Mantu.

Enapay remembered the fight of his youth when he had killed a panther. As the horns swung away, he threw his body at the antelope and plunged his knife into its heart. Standing over the dead animal, Enapay asked Mantu, "How bad is it?"

Mantu nocked an arrow. "I am fine. Let us kill antelope while we can."

"Let me see your side," Enapay ordered his friend. Mantu raised his slashed shirt.

"Take the shirt off." Enapay tied the shirt tightly around Mantu's body. He handed him his bow. "Go."

Both men rejoined the slaying. Animal after animal slammed the wagon. Arrows dropped from bows and flew away on random paths. Even so, dead animals piled up. Those that dropped in front of the wagons didn't get trampled into mangled flesh as the rest of the thousands of antelope flowed past.

When the herd had finally passed, the men got out of the wagons to see the results. Antelope blood covered the wagons, the canvas was slashed, and bows were cracked, but otherwise, the wagons were intact. The pulp that surrounded the wagons would have been unidentifiable if they had not already known what it was.

Wakanda walked over and examined Mantu. The wound was not life-threatening. It was, however, long and needed to be sewn closed. Wakanda got his bag and went to work.

Paytah ran to Wesa with Ppahiska's message while the others heaped the salvageable carcasses on top of the buffalo heads. Capa counted the number of hooves in the mangled antelope flesh.

Paytah returned. "Wesa said, 'If we pay the trade items to the village, they will take the trampled bodies and repay us later.' "

Ppahiska waved to acknowledge the agreement. As soon as Wakanda finished stitching Mantu's side, they left the mashed carcasses behind and started toward the village.

The people saw the approaching wagons. A single woman went to the edge of the village. "I am Salali of the Cherokee. I was wondering when the antelope would come onto our land. Do you have the talisman?"

The man who joined her opened the medicine bag around his neck. He drew out a stone embedded with shiny gray cubes of galena. "I am Ppahiska of the Quapaw."

Salali stated what she saw. "You have many antelope." She signaled to her people that it was safe to come out.

"And more were trampled in the stampede," Ppahiska informed the woman.

"The first trade is for the talisman to gather mussels, but this is very many antelope."

Ppahiska was prepared to be fair. After all, he had the rest of the seeds and shells given to then by the soldiers. "There are buffalo heads under them from much further south, but we do have many antelope. We will give you seeds too."

Salali negotiated to get everything owed to her village. "And you must also give us one mussel shell for each antelope."

Ppahiska spoke to Capa. "Count our shells."

Capa went to the wagon and counted them into a basket. "Forty-eight."

Salali thought for a moment. "How many antelope in the wagon? How many trampled in the field?"

Ppahiska told her, "Twelve in the field. Sixty-two in the wagons."

"Give me the talisman, the mussel shells, and the seeds. You can take forty-eight antelope. If you give us the other fourteen, you can take the trampled animals."

Ppahiska would never agree to an unfair trade. "No. You would get fourteen completely usable beasts with a hide. We would get twelve mangled bodies. Offer again."

Salali asked, "Do you want the bodies in the field?"

"I gave them to Wesa's village," Ppahiska replied.

"He is the one who has gone three times to the land of Leotie?"

"I do not know how many times."

"He needs no more. He has already taken many."

"He has less than you think. He did not have wagons to protect them when the herd ran past, and just as you, he has to pull them home on a travois. He has many people in his village. He needs them."

"Since you request not for yourself, you can have the twelve in the field for Wesa. We will each take half of the extra fourteen."

Ppahiska said, "Agreed."

Close by, Wakanda heard the conversation. *Ppahiska learned Colonel Howland's favorite word.*

Capa gave Salali the shells. Instead of looking at the shells, she opened the package of seeds. "This is many seeds. Probably more than five hundred and fifty."

Ppahiska pointed out the other side of the possibilities. "It may be less."

"Either way, it is enough for me. Do you want to count them?"

"No. If it is more, you can have them."

"We will gather the mussels before it gets too cold."

"Good luck," Ppahiska told her, "In three days, one of us will come to the river to get the talisman back."

At the Neosho River crossing, the men in Wesa's hunting party washed antelope pieces. Wesa looked up at Ppahiska, "We took the trampled animals. Did you give the trade items?"

Ppahiska told him, "Yes. We gave Salali seven of the antelope in our wagons for them."

"So many." Wesa then offered, "For those you gave to us, if we can put ours in your wagons and go with you to your village, we will help you skin yours after we finish ours."

Ppahiska again said, "Agreed."

Each of Wesa's men cleaned his own antelope carcasses and extra trampled parts. Then they helped with Ppahiska's antelope until all the carcasses were gutted for the long ride to their villages. The two groups rode together with buffalo and antelope piled high.

Mantu told everybody the story of Enapay courageously facing the slashing horns when he killed the antelope in the wagon. "He truly is 'roars bravely in the face of danger'."

Wesa and his men skinned and cut the carcasses into large parts. Each man in Wesa's hunting party finished his two antelope and then rolled the bones, horns, hooves, bits of mangled meat, and other parts in the hides to later load on the empty travois pulled behind their horses. After each of Wesa's men finished his share, he helped the men of Ppahiska's village.

Before they had all the antelope skinned, the new moon had enshrouded them in deep darkness. Ppahiska told Wesa, "You can stay in our village tonight."

"I accept. This is the last time we will come this way. Leotie's people have almost finished the bridge to their northern land. We have been letting them come over and take trees. It is good that you got it into the treaty that they could cross our land up by my village. It will be much easier for us. Thank you for thinking about us."

The men approached home in a gloom so deep not a single shadow was cast. Mantu detected trouble without vision. "I smell smoke!"

Chetan looked through his spyglass. The blackness of the night and thick billows of smoke concealed everything except the flames that flickered throughout the village. "The village is on fire! Get in the wagons now!" Chetan hollered at the horses, "Forward run!"

Sure that the entire village had burned to the ground, flinging water in every direction, they charged across Five Mile Creek. They found ten intact lodges and more tubes of ground bear than they could count.

The nine men wiped tears caused by the thick smoke, or perhaps the thought that their families were dead.

"I think you already have plenty of meat," Wesa remarked.

Ppahiska only replied, "All of you can sleep in the empty lodge." He hurried to his own.

Every man did the same. After believing they would never again see their wives on this side of death and then finding them alive, their reunions were passionate.

SIXTY FOUR

In the morning, Wesa and his hunters ate bread, eggs, and bear meat sausages as they listened to Wakanda's story.

"These are very good. How did you make them?" Wesa ate another sausage.

Roscoe understood what Wesa had asked. The previous day, he had been asked the same question multiple times. He knew the words. He again passed on the recipe.

Wesa asked, "Do you want to trade for some of them? I want my wife to eat some. Then, she will make more for me."

Capa replied before anybody else could do so. "I see you still have three pottery jars. I will fill one with sausages if you give me the other two empty jars."

Wesa handed Capa one jar, "Thank you. You can take the two empty ones when you bring the full one."

After Wesa's group left, Capa brought up the subject of the amount of antelope. He said to Noah, "Tahatankohana, my family does not need six antelope. We already have enough meat. Wichahpi saw the sewing kit you gave to Zitkala for a wedding present. She wants one. If you have more, I will trade five antelope for a sewing kit."

"Let me ask." Noah called all the people in his family to the side and told them what Capa wanted. "Do you want to have five more antelope to cut up?"

Dustu commented, "We can use the food when we cross to the western sea, but they are not my sewing kits."

Adahy said, "I will help cut them into strips," followed by every other family member, including Ke, confirming that she or he would help.

Chumani stated the same thing she heard the others say, "I will cut one."

Noah told her, "Thank you, Chumani."

Ann said, "Maybe Mantu or Paytah will want to trade. It's all right with me to trade the extra sewing kits we bought."

"Make sure we get the hides," Luyu instructed her grandson.

Noah got several sewing kits, went back to Capa, and handed him one. Noah's family picked up eleven antelope bodies rolled in hides to take to their lodge.

Ppahiska said, "What are you doing? Each family gets six."

Capa said, "I traded five of mine for this sewing kit for Wichahpi."

Mantu overheard. "Do you have another? I know Nahimana would like one."

"I have more. I will trade with you." Tahatankohana handed one to Mantu.

"What about me?" Paytah asked. Noah gave him a sewing kit.

Ppahiska said, "I need all our antelope, but I heard Mikoishe talking about those kits. She will be very unhappy if our family is the only one without one. What about the bear fur? Would you take that, Tahatankohana?"

Capa said, "That belongs to all of us."

Noah turned to Capa. "Open your sewing kit." Capa did so. "I will give to each family either a sewing kit like this one or a set of red, green, blue, yellow, and black thread like these spools."

Enapay, James, and Tatonga went to speak with their families. When they returned, Capa, Mantu, and Paytah had already left with a sewing kit, a second set of the thread, and one antelope.

James and Tatonga took the thread, all six of their carcasses, and gave up their rights to the bear hide. Ppahiska clutched a sewing kit as he negotiated with Noah for the extra thread. Noah said to Ppahiska, "We will give you the thread, but you owe this family one favor in the future."

"Agreed."

Noah gave his chief the six spools of thread. Ppahiska took his prizes to his family, already cutting up their six antelope.

Enapay stated his decision. "We will take the thread for the hide. We also don't need all six antelope."

310

Tatonga said, "I will trade with you. We will talk in my lodge." The two men carried away four of Enapay's antelope.

Eli said, "I'll get the hide. May I tan this one?"

"I don't see why not," his brother-in-law replied.

Tom declared, "It's just like a store but without a building."

SIXTY FIVE

At the end of the same day, George stood beside Frog Creek. He reminded his father, Matt, and Justin what Sebastian had told them back in Harmony. "Sebastian said, 'Always cross a creek or river as soon as you get there if you can.' There is no bridge here, and the water is low."

"I don't think it will be a problem. I don't see any rain, but let's cross anyway." Morris rode into the water. They set up camp and slept west of Frog Creek. Unknown to them, rain drenched the Boston Mountains far to the north.

The following morning, Justin looked at Frog Creek full to the brim and completely impassable. "What happened?"

Matt already sat on his horse. "This happened at Fletcher Creek just before Abraham and his family came. It must have rained way upstream."

George tied on his bedroll. "I think it's a sign that we'll be successful. We never saw Raymond at Horsehead Post Office. He has to be behind us."

Morris mounted up. "Frog Creek should hold him up pretty good."

"Yep." George got on his horse too.

They rode the easy road to Van Buren, where they stopped for the day. They paid for oats, hay, water, a stall for their six animals, and a lockable storage room for their supplies, and then found accommodations for themselves.

SIXTY SIX

South of the Arkansas River, Edwin and Robert had also continued their westward travels. They approached the half-mile-long causeway beyond Point Prairie that had been built over the marsh. Thousands of snow geese ate the plentiful fish that were easy to catch in the shallow waters. A bobwhite called from a little island in the large expanse of wetlands. For a few minutes, they watched a pair of tundra swans and observed beavers making a lodge far out in the deeper water.

Almost across the shallows at the western edge of the marsh, a raccoon washed a fish it had caught. Suddenly, an alligator surged up and gobbled down the raccoon, along with the fish it still held in its paws.

"Did you see that?!" The wooden planks of the causeway were not far above the water. Edwin kicked his heels into his horse. "I don't want any sneaky, hungry alligator coming out of the water and eating me."

Robert stayed tight on Edwin's rear as they galloped across the last several yards of the boardwalk and then onto the stony ground that had once been a riverbed. The sharp rocks poked into the hooves of their horses. After they were far from the water, they got down and walked. The rough terrain hurt their feet too. When they came to a pond surrounded by soft soil with tall, nutritious grass, they decided to stop.

Edwin took off his boots and rubbed his feet. "You know, Robert, it takes a real man to admit he made a mistake and then do everything he can to fix it. This trip hasn't been easy for you, especially being injured and all. I'm really proud of you for doing this. You shouldn't think you're not good enough like you said earlier."

"You really think so?" Robert took off his shoes too.

Edwin pinched his nose shut. "Yes, I do, but I also think we both have awfully smelly feet. Mrs. Daniels would never put up with this! Let's wash our feet and boots in the pond." Edwin stood up and hobbled to the water. "Just because Candy isn't here doesn't mean I should be any less than she wants me to be. She says I'm going to be a great man someday. I think you and I both can be. When you get back to Fletcher Creek, learn everything you can. Elizabeth is learning to play the flute. She sounds like she's making angel music."

"Good idea. Maybe all my family should."

"Yep. I think so anyway." Edwin started in on his feet with a bar of soap.

SIXTY SEVEN

That day, as Sergeant loped along, Raymond felt sick to death of people. He didn't stop in Ozark. Instead, he rode until the high waters of White Oak Creek stopped him. He looked at the obstruction. He hated the water and life. Actually, he hated everything. He let out a stream of profanities.

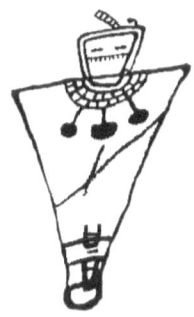

SIXTY EIGHT

On the first of December, an hour after sunup, Robert and Edwin walked into the store at Fort Smith. Edwin asked, "How's the road north of here?"

"It depends on what you want to know. There's nothing up there but Indians. They can be mean or nice. The road is good, but there are creeks that can hold you up. You can get more supplies about every week, depending on how fast you travel. But winter is coming. You won't be able to get to St. Louis before winter."

Edwin thought aloud. "If we get that much, we'll have to walk and have the horses to carry our supplies."

Robert peered through the glass countertop as he spoke. "What's a week north?"

"Fort Gibson, but they have high prices."

Meanwhile, Edwin examined the items on the shelves. "We'll have to pay what they want. Our horses need to be able to keep going. Is there plenty of grass along the road?"

"There's prairie grass as far as you can see."

317

Robert looked up. "So far, we've mostly stayed in towns."

"Do you need some suggestions about what you should get?"

"I'm afraid so." Robert did fear, but only that the man would take advantage of him. He was happy when the supplies looked plentiful, seemed appropriate, and were reasonably priced.

The supplies included two travoises and harnesses. The supply master explained, "A horse can pull fifty percent of its weight all day but can only carry twenty percent. This is more than enough to get you beyond Fort Gibson and all the way to Fort Leavenworth."

At the Arkansas River crossing, Robert paid the fare. He and Edwin rode the ferry to the northern side. They continued up the road until the middle of the day when they were forced to set up camp. The same Boston Mountain rains that had blocked Raymond at White Oak Creek had also made Skin Bayou, the river that lay before Robert and Edwin, impassable. Not far to the east, Raymond sulked as he cooked bacon.

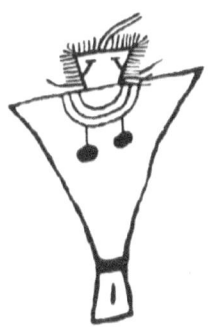

SIXTY NINE

The sun nestled into the mountains. Morris raised his hand to halt them. He looked through their small telescope. "I'll go alone and determine if it's safe for us to join the men ahead."

George told him, "Be careful, Pa. Keep your hand on your gun under your coat."

"I'll wave like this if I want you to come." Morris slid his hand back and forth horizontally in front of them. "If I don't want you to come. I will wave to you like most people would." He put his hand in front of him and drew it toward his body.

Assuring Morris that he understood, Matt stated, "The opposite of what's normal."

"Right." Morris rode toward the strangers. He wasn't even all the way to the men when he vigorously slid his hands from side to side through the air.

Morris hugged the unknown men as George rode toward them. "Who on Earth could they be?"

Matt equally had no clue. "I have no idea who your father would know way out here."

They were about as far away as Morris had been when they realized who they had encountered. They joined the men and hugged them too. Matt reminded Robert, "I told you not to come," then hugged Edwin. "Hello, Edwin. I think you have some explaining to do."

"About what?" Edwin replied.

Robert replied, "I didn't slow you down or get in your way, and we were here first."

Justin changed the direction of the conversation. "I'm glad to see you. How are you?"

"I'm doing well now." He raised his shirt and showed his back.

Edwin figured he was already on Matt's bad side about something unknown. He didn't want to make it worse, especially since he hoped the man would be his father-in-law when the time was right. Therefore, Edwin didn't say anything about Robert's condition. He decided he had better leave it to Robert to explain what had happened in Perryville if he ever said anything.

Robert didn't want any secrets lurking around to bite him. After everybody had hugged everybody and held a cup of hot coffee, he decided to come clean. "I want to tell you how Edwin saved my life."

"Edwin saved your life?" Justin stated, more as an encouragement to tell the story than a question.

Robert told them the story with the help of Edwin.

Matt commented, "I told you, you would slow us down. We wouldn't have gotten to Harmony in time."

320

Edwin ladled food into everybody's plates. "Tell us what happened in Harmony."

While they waited for Skin Bayou to become passable, they shared all the details of their voyages. Matt and Edwin came to an understanding about Elizabeth. Unless they married, Edwin would always be a gentleman and never, ever would anything beyond holding hands or a mild kiss occur, or Edwin would be feeding the worms.

Matt rode back to Fort Smith and booked passage for six people to Maumelle at the end of December. That was, if they arrived back at Fort Smith in time and the weather wasn't already too bad to travel the river. He returned to Skin Bayou. At two different rivers, six men and one man impatiently waited for the waters to recede.

SEVENTY

All the produce grown or gathered around Noah's village had been stored for the cold months ahead. Now, they had time for other tasks.

Ann sewed the Canada goose wings onto an old worn-out doeskin dress Luyu gave her.

Stephanie beaded the moccasins.

Luyu plucked out all the long, stiff guard hairs then trimmed the winter wool of the enormous buffalo fur Chetan's family was to tan for Colonel Howland. Helen carded the large pile of soft down that Luyu cut off as she cropped the hide to a uniform thickness.

The first bull Chetan had shot without permission and the two they had legally acquired with Dustu, Adahy, and Waya had short summer hides. Bethany, Hanataywee, and Ehawee got only a fourth of the down from all three of the summer hides put together. Sally's pile of yellow fur was quite small as well. Other women in the village also cut and gathered buffalo hair.

Many of the men in the village sat in the meeting lodge building carts, looms, or spinning wheels. Except for Luyu and Zitkala, all the newly married women were with child. Zhawe asked Petang. "Why is Zitkala not pregnant?"

Petang informed his childhood friend who had married Dowanhowee and had also moved to the Quapaw village, "Because I do not want her to be."

Zhawe was proud to say his wife was with child. He continued to press the subject. "Why not? Are you doing what Nikiata told us when we were skinning those antelope?"

"That is not something for you to be concerned about."

"I worry that something is wrong. Like your wife threw you out of her bed."

"Stop being nosey. You are worse than a woman."

"So, she did throw you out of her bed?!"

"I am not telling you anything." Petang walked away. He knew what he was doing. He was protecting the life of the woman he loved by doing exactly what Mystery man Nikiata had told him to do. Even though they all said she would have no problem, he agreed with Tatonga. Zitkala was a small person. He didn't want to take a chance. He believed they had plenty of time to have children.

At the request of Zitkala, Petang stopped working on a second loom. Instead, he set to work on a spinning wheel. Noah joined him because he liked Petang and wanted to build something together.

The new, improved basket to the top of the Boston Mountains hung on the rope. Mantu's antelope horn injury healed as he, Paytah, Chetan, and James converted the old basket into a wagon to be used in their village.

That night, while those in Noah's village slept, the snow began falling across Indian Territory. In the cold morning air, Noah and Dustu came into the lodge with their arms full of wood. Noah was warm and dry in the fur hat Roscoe had given him when they had lived at Bacon's Trading Post in Pine Bluff.

Dustu brushed the snow from his head. "We need to make mukluks and hats for the people who don't have any."

Hanataywee teased him. "You mean like you? Come here and let me warm you up, then I will start making you some."

"I will make one for you, my wolf," Luyu told her husband.

"And I'll make some for you and Grams," Stephanie told Tom and Helen.

Helen declined, "I'm sure you would make me wonderful shoes and a very warm hat, but I want to learn. Will you show me how?"

"Of course. I'll make one for Pop to demonstrate how. We'll have a grand time making them together."

"Yes, we will." Helen liked her new granddaughter very much. For over twenty years, she'd had only her husband, Woodrow. Now she felt blessed with family everywhere. She sat with them in the lodge as it got colder outside, and the snow got deeper.

The women, except Sally, started knitting hats

with the brown buffalo yarn. Sally used her yellow yarn. "I'm glad I shot this buffalo. Without her, I would never get warm at night."

"I'm very happy that I married Stephanie. She keeps me nice and snuggly warm." Eli put his arm around his wife.

The conversation made Tahatankohana focus on how much he loved Ann and what he had been thinking since Eli's birthday when he, Stephanie, Eli, and Ann had sat on top of the mountain by Fletcher Creek. He felt he was the man he wanted to be, and that was Noah. When night approached, he asked, "Father, will you help me bring in wood?"

Chetan had noticed that Tahatankohana had been very quiet, and they had more than enough wood in the lodge. He knew something was on his son's mind. "Of course, my son."

Outside, away from everybody, Tahatankohana stalled and shuffled before he finally brought up what he wanted to discuss privately with his father. "Father, you know I love my name, but people change their names when life gives then a new one. I believe life has chosen to give me the name Noah. Noah is who I feel like. I want to be called Noah."

"Your name has always been Noah as much as it has been Tahatankohana. It will not upset me for you to go by Noah. You are still my same son."

"Thank you for understanding, father. I want you to know I love you very much."

"I know you do. I love you very much too, and no

name will ever change that." They gathered the wood and went back inside.

Chetan had told his son the truth. He actually did not mind. Many times, he had heard Ann whisper her love to his son during the nights. To her, he always was Noah. He didn't mind his son wanting to be the man his wife loved.

Bethany asked, "What did you do? Go to the moon to get the wood?"

"Yes," Chetan told her.

Noah explained what had caused the delay, "I want to ask all of you to call me Noah. Noah is who I am."

"I surely will, my husband," Ann told him.

The rest of the family also agreed.

Noah continued, "One more thing. I also want to name my son Christopher."

"You do?" Stephanie stated with surprise.

"Your father told me about his first grandson. I think he should have his name."

Sally set down the mukluk insert of brown buffalo yarn she was knitting and then hugged her brother-in-law. "That would be wonderful!"

Ann said, "I hope we get to meet Christopher soon. I'm ready to be not pregnant."

Noah told her, "But you are so beautiful with our baby in there."

"You don't have an aching back, and you're not the one who can't get comfortable enough to sleep," Ann replied.

"I know, my wife, so I've made you this pillow

with the buffalo hair I took before it was all made into yarn." Noah handed Ann a wide, deep sleeve full of clean, soft buffalo hair. "You can put this under Christopher and lie on your side the way you like."

"You are so thoughtful. I never even saw you making it. I'm tired. I'm going to try it out." Ann went to their sleeping area and tucked the pillow under her belly. "It's perfect!" she called out. She had a good sleep for the first time in many nights.

SEVENTY ONE

Justin led his horse through the gate. "I'm looking forward to seeing Nancy, I mean, Sally. I wasn't nice to her just before they left. I'm glad I'll be able to apologize."

Edwin had discovered that Justin had kissed Sally. It irritated him that he hadn't. Even though Edwin had his eyes on Elizabeth, it got under his skin every time Justin said anything about Sally. Edwin snapped more loudly than he should have, "Would you please stop talking about Sally?"

That was when Justin realized Edwin must also have feelings for her.

Private Ezra Knuckles stood close to the six men who arrived as he shut Fort Gibson's gate for the night. He knew of one Sally. The one who had sat at the officer's table wearing a red dress and ruby necklace. "You mean Sally Williams?"

All six men looked at him. "What do you know about her?" Edwin asked.

"She and her sister made a big stir around here several months ago when some soldiers touched them.

328

Colonel Howland made some of our men carry sacks of rocks for two days and lose some rations too." Ezra barred the gate before he escorted the newcomers to the place where they could set up a tent.

Justin unbuckled a packsaddle. "Nobody should have been touching them."

"I agree. It wasn't me. I'm just telling you what happened. Anyway, the colonel invited them and their family to eat with him. Sally showed up in that red silk dress, wearing that ruby necklace and sat down right across from Lieutenant Jackson. He was livid. He jumped up and accused her of stealing the necklace. She said it was hers. Colonel Howland commanded that she give it to him while he sorted it out, but Sally said it had a kiss for her on it, and she wasn't giving it to anybody."

Edwin smiled. Sally had cared about the kiss he had put there.

Ezra continued the story. "Lieutenant Jackson started for her, but her brother-in-law and the man Sally said was her husband stood between them."

"She's married?!" both Edwin and Justin asked together.

"She said she was married to the old man."

"She married an old man?" The six men asked together as they pulled the travois away from the horses.

"That's what they said. Frankly, I don't believe it."

"So, what happened then?" Matt encouraged the soldier to go on.

"Bring your animals to the stable, so they can get out of the snow. Anyway, the colonel told the lieutenant to sit down. Sally's brother-in-law asked to talk with her in the other room. The colonel didn't want to let them leave, so Sally's sister said she would stay in the room. He let Sally go to the other room, but he ordered them not to leave the building. Her brother-in-law made her give him the necklace. She ran away, crying. He gave the colonel the necklace, and then he, his wife, and the old man left too."

"So, she lost the necklace. Too bad." Morris followed across the courtyard.

"No! Her brother-in-law is a very clever fellow. The next day, he went to the colonel with some legal mumbo jumbo. The colonel thought about it all night and half a day and then decided to give the necklace back to Sally. He told Lieutenant Jackson to write her ownership papers for the necklace and the dress too. Lieutenant Jackson refused to do it, and he actually even argued with the Colonel. Of course, Colonel Howland threw him in the stockade for that. Lieutenant Olson wrote the paper. The necklace and dress are hers now."

"That's wonderful!" Edwin was very pleased that Sally no longer had stolen property but something she legally owned.

"Do you know where they are?" Matt asked.

Ezra wasn't sure if he should tell them what he knew about their location. "They said they were going to the Western Sea."

"If they've gone, then they're safe, and we can go home." George took the saddle off his horse.

"Why wouldn't they be safe?" Ezra asked.

"Why do you care?" Morris asked back.

Ezra asked the same question back. "Why do YOU care?"

Edwin thought he could clear things up. "It's my kiss on the necklace. I can describe it to the colonel or whoever saw it. Then you can tell us where they really are."

"Make your arrangement for your animals, then go set up your tent. I'll come back after I talk to Colonel Howland."

Matt paid for one day's feed and stabling for six horses and two mules. They set up their tent and got all their provisions inside.

Colonel Howland told Private Knuckles to bring the men after they had secured their belongings. Fifteen minutes later, Private Knuckles escorted the six men into the command building. He knocked on the inner door. Through the closed door, Ezra stated, "I have them, Colonel Howland, sir."

A voice on the other side of the door ordered, "Send them in, and come in here as well."

Colonel Howland sat behind his desk, which had a paper laying on it. Normally, the colonel wouldn't get involved in a matter like this, but he thought this involved people who had special importance to him. Standing behind the men who had just arrived at the fort, Ezra pointed his finger at the one the colonel had asked him to identify discretely. The colonel was surprised which one Private Knuckles pointed out. The colonel pointed at the man Ezra had identified as the girl's lover. "Tell me what the necklace looks like," he commanded.

"There are twenty-one rubies in six prong settings. Ten on each side about this big." He put his pointer fingers together with his thumbs on both hands and held them together. "The center stone is about this big." He made a circle with his pointer finger and his thumb. "It's set in a gold swirly setting. Between each stone are long gold swirly beads. The clasp on the back is a loop with a hook on the other side."

"Why is this necklace important to the girl?" The colonel gazed into the eyes of the one barely old enough to be a man, let alone a lover.

Edwin informed the colonel, "Because I put a kiss on the large ruby, in case she ever needs one."

"I doubt she will ever be short of as many kisses as she wants," the colonel stated.

Justin jumped in, "You ought not to talk about her! You don't know her. She's not like that!"

"You love her too, then?" The colonel tried to determine how much these people cared.

"I did once, but I love somebody else now." Justin loved Morris's daughter, Carmen. However, he had been very smitten by the beautiful, intelligent woman for a while.

Robert explained, "Anyway, how anybody feels or felt about Sally is only part of this. We care about all of them. Dr. Smith healed a pig for me so that I could marry my wife, and I'm the one who stupidly told people some information about where they were recently seen."

"Who is Dr. Smith?" the colonel didn't know the name.

Morris entered the conversation. "The man is Noah Swift Hawk, but he called himself Dr. Luke Smith when Robert and Edwin first knew him." Morris pointed to the men from Fletcher Creek. "We knew him as a man named Abraham. He was still pretending to be a doctor."

"He was *pretending* to be a doctor?" the colonel asked because a person who didn't know what he was doing could hurt somebody.

Edwin replied, "No, sir, he really is a doctor." Then explained, "He treated many sick animals in Little Rock and cured a boy who'd had severe pain for years."

Robert reminded the colonel, "And he cured my father-in-law's pig."

Matt added what he knew. "He made me some medicine that cured me of a tapeworm, and he made shoes that are fixing my son's club feet."

"He saved my wife when she had almost drowned, and we also know he properly set a broken ankle and cared for a man with broken ribs," stated Morris.

The colonel maneuvered for still more information. "All right, but we don't know any man who goes by any of those names."

"He's married to a girl named Ann Williams. She's gone by the names Isabelle Smith and Lily. They were traveling with an older man named Roscoe Bacon, who called himself Theodore when he was with us. Then there is Eli Yates, who called himself James Bacon. His wife is Stephanie Williams, actually Yates, because Eli married her. She also goes by Marie. Eli, Stephanie, Eli's father Tom Yates, and his grandmother Helen Yates would have come through here about a month ago with Sally and her Uncle James Williams."

The colonel knew a white man named James. That man had never said his last name. The colonel hadn't seen him since the buffalo hunt. "Why do you want to find them?"

Morris gave the explanation. "An assassin who goes by the name Joe Smith has been sent primarily to find Ann Williams but also Noah Swift Hawk. He is supposed to take them alive to Judge Daniel Hall in Little Rock, but they can be taken dead. From what we know about Joe, he will take them dead. He is also looking for Sebastian and Lola De La Cruz; some people Noah and his family helped. He wants to kill them as well."

The colonel said, "If a judge put out a dead or alive post, a man who kills them is doing nothing wrong."

Robert said, "Except he wants Ann because she insulted him in court and because she married a man who is part Indian, and besides that, Judge Hall didn't do it officially. He illegally got a man out of prison and sent him after the two of them."

Edwin had seen the judge in the Harrows' house. "The judge was going to shoot the two of them in Mr. Harrow's house, except Mrs. Hall stopped him. I saw it myself."

"What did she do that insulted the judge?" Ezra asked.

"Stay out of this, Private," the colonel commanded.

Edwin answered anyway. "She told the judge she was going to fill the world with Noah's babies, and she would be right before God, but he would still be wrong. And she called Judge Hall a horrible person."

Ezra spoke again. "She's just about to fill it with one baby."

The colonel glared at him.

George looked into the eyes of the colonel. "I'm glad she's going to have his baby. If you ever saw them together, you could see how much they love each other. I hope some woman will love me like that one day."

The colonel believed them when they said the judge was not doing things properly. "How close is this Joe Smith?"

Morris replied, "We don't know for sure, but we spent the night with him at Gum Log Creek just south of Dover. We left the next morning. He did not."

"Why didn't you kill him?"

George was appalled that the colonel thought they should have killed the man. "That would have been murder. How could you suggest such a thing?"

"I don't think you should have killed him. I was asking for your reasoning." The colonel instructed the six men, "Please wait just outside of this building. Private, stay here."

The six men walked out of the room. The colonel gave a signal to Ezra. Morris and his party left the building but waited by the door.

Robert stood outside the command building. "It would be great if they can tell us exactly how to get there. I don't want to get there too late. I just couldn't live with myself if something happens to them."

Matt added, "I'm sure we're ahead of Raymond, but that could all be for naught if we wander around up north trying to find their village."

Edwin said, "I also hope they know where they are. Not only so we can tell them to get out of here but to see them again and tell about everything new. I can't wait to see Dr. Smith's face when I tell him Mr. Strong and Mrs. Daniels are getting married."

Ezra went back into the office. "I'm satisfied. They're talking about giving them news of mutual friends, and the man named Tahatankohana called his wife Ann. But they did call the man Raymond and not Joe Smith."

The colonel wrote on the sheet of paper before him. Since Ezra was one of the men who had been to the village, he asked, "Do you want to take a secret, one-soldier trip up there?"

Even though it wasn't a dangerous mission, Ezra was proud Colonel Howland believed he was worthy of sending him on such a special mission, and all by himself, too. "Yes, sir."

"Let's make it an official military trip. Find out if they have any more dynamite. If they do, buy what they have before you leave. Take rations like before and a wagon, so you can bring back the dynamite if they have any. Get what you need and see if you can find a volunteer for a brief fight and a two or three-day stay in the stockade for two weeks double rations. You probably know somebody who wouldn't mind helping. When you find one, send him over."

Ezra brought the men back into the colonel's office.

"I'm assuming you will go back home and not with them," the colonel stated.

"Absolutely going home!" Edwin spoke right up. "I am not breaking my word to Elizabeth." He had told her he would be back in the spring. This way, he would probably even get to see her before spring. The colonel looked at the older men.

Morris responded to the silent question. "Going home. Not moving away."

The colonel handed Private Ezra Knuckles the completed piece of paper that authorized him to take a wagon, four mules, one thousand dollars in silver coins, and rations for seven men for fifteen days. "Private Ezra Knuckles will take you to them and purchase the items we want from them, if they have any. Private Knuckles, don't bring home any buffalo meat this time but look into getting some of those mussels in brine. If the weather permits, leave in the morning."

"Yes, sir," Ezra replied.

"One more thing, Private. Tell Lieutenant Olson to report to me immediately." Robert, Morris, Matt, and Justin turned to follow Ezra out of the room. Edwin and George stood still facing the colonel. The colonel looked up at Edwin and George with a slight smile on his face. "Gentlemen, another moment, please." Those who had started away stopped and turned back. "You go on, Private Knuckles."

"Yes, sir." Ezra went to speak to Lieutenant Olson.

"I think I can hold up this Raymond for a few days. Describe him to Lieutenant Olson when he gets here. He'll draw a picture."

Justin stated the obvious way to identify the man. "He probably still has the remains of a bruised eye and a bruised left jaw."

Nobody denied the name. Just as the colonel had suspected, the man's name was Raymond.

"You fought with him?" the colonel asked.

Matt didn't want the colonel to get the wrong idea. "No, it was somebody else. We appreciate your help, and even though they are blissfully unaware of this situation right now, I'm sure our friends do too."

"James is a friend, and so is Noah's father, Chetan."

"Do you know Noah's real name?" Edwin had wondered about that ever since he had found out that his friend's real name was not Doctor Luke Smith."

"I don't, but I think Private Knuckles does." They heard the door then Lieutenant Olson entered the room.

"Reporting for duty." The lieutenant saluted.

"These men are going to describe Joe Smith. Please draw him and then let these men go to their tent. After they have left, knock on my door."

"Yes, sir." He went to the desk in the outer room, sat, then dug out some paper and a pencil from a drawer. The six men followed the lieutenant without correcting the name.

"First, tell me about the shape of his face."

As Lieutenant Olson worked on the picture of Joe Smith, Private Blanders arrived. The colonel heard the door again. "Come!" he called out.

Ham Blanders walked into the colonel's office. "Reporting for duty as directed by Private Knuckles."

"I thought it might be you. Close the door."

George looked at the drawing. "That's him!"

"I think so too," Morris agreed.

Edwin complimented Lieutenant Olson with another new word he had learned. "That was incredible. I never knew that could be done."

Lieutenant Olsen opened the door. "Much obliged, son. You all go on to your camp." Morris, Matt, Robert, Edwin, George, and Justin walked out. The lieutenant knocked on the colonel's door.

"Bring it in," the colonel directed from behind the closed door.

Lieutenant Olson walked across the room and handed the picture to Colonel Howland.

"They think this is accurate?" the colonel asked.

"Yes, sir."

The colonel dismissed him. "Good work. Don't tell anybody what you were doing. You can go. Close the door on your way out." When the colonel saw Lieutenant Olson walking across the yard toward the barracks, he handed the picture to Ham. "You can go. Don't tell anybody what we discussed."

"Yes, sir." Private Blanders looked forward to a good scuffle. Not only penalty-free, but also coming with extra whiskey, coffee, and sugar. The rest of the extra rations would be nice too.

SEVENTY TWO

The Boston Mountains, not far to the north, forced the air into the coldness high above. Snow fell as Raymond prepared to sleep. He didn't want to be stepped on by the horse he had in the tent with him to protect it from the wind and the snow. He put his packsaddles between him and Sergeant.

For three cold, snowy days, Colonel Howland delayed the start of Ezra's mission in order to protect his man and his mules. Robert didn't like the delay. Each day he asked Ezra to suggest that they move on from Fort Gibson. Ezra did no such thing. He didn't question the colonel's choices. He knew his commander would tell him when it was time to go. However, since Robert knew it was a much better plan to go with Ezra, he waited and fretted.

They all wondered if Raymond was holed up somewhere, coming their way, still in Harmony, or off in some other direction. They were sitting in the barracks talking with the soldiers when they got word that somebody new had arrived at the fort.

"I told you we needed to go," Robert whispered.

Ham stood up. "I'm going to the store. Do not leave these barracks."

Ezra followed Ham out the door. He, however, went to Colonel Howland's office. He knocked. "Private Knuckles with a status report, sir."

"Come in." Ezra stepped into his commanders' office. "Shut the door."

Ezra did so. "He may be here. Shall I pack?"

"Yes. Be ready to leave in the morning if it's snowing or not."

"I have an idea. Issue them uniforms. Let them go and come back as soldiers."

"We don't have seven extra uniforms."

"I've been sizing them up with our men. Send Willcox, Gree, Easton, Coons, Sisco, and Sergeant Anders on a two-week mission that requires civilian clothing."

The colonel thought then spoke. "I'll accomplish our objective. Send Anders to me."

Ezra left to do as instructed.

Sergeant Tim Anders went to the quartermaster to request supplies. He handed the requisition to Sergeant McCormick. "I'll take the buckskins now and come back for the rest in the morning."

With six buckskin outfits, the sergeant went to speak with the men he was ordered to take to check for evidence of skirmishes east of the Seminole tribe on the border between the Creek and Choctaw. "Report at sun up in your buckskins. Turn in your uniforms tonight for cleaning while we're gone."

Sergeant Anders ordered the private assigned to laundry duty, "Tonight, thoroughly clean and completely dry all uniforms turned in. Private Knuckles will be here to get them in the morning."

As he started out the door, yelling came from the store. Hoping for relief from the monotony of life far away from everything, Sergeant Anders and almost every other soldier ran toward the commotion.

The man who had just arrived at Fort Gibson slugged an insulant idiot.

Blood ran from Ham's busted lip. He renewed the newcomer's black eye.

Raymond's rage broke loose. He charged and pounded his fists into the soldier's guts.

Ham flew backward out the door. The man he had purposefully insulted and slugged landed on top of him.

If some stupid soldier thought he was going to push him around, he was wrong. Raymond wanted to knock the man's head off. He slugged the soldier in the face. Blood from Ham's nose flew into the snow.

Ham pushed Raymond off and jumped to his feet.

Sergeant Anders ordered Private Ham Blanders, "Stop this instant!"

Ham's fist had already boxed Raymond's head.

Blood ran from Raymond's ear. He was more than ready to start killing people. He pulled his knife.

The colonel's commanding voice rang out, "Don't do it, or I'll blow your hand off!"

Raymond saw the colonel's stripes. He knew the

man hadn't gotten to that rank without knowing how to shoot. Raymond dropped the knife. "He started it."

"Throw them both into the stockade," Colonel Howland ordered. "Anders, find out what happened, and file a report."

As they walked back to the barracks, one of the soldiers asked his buddy, "Why did he have to stop it?"

At rifle point, Sergeant McCormick marched the two men to their jail cells. Once confined, Anders took the statements of Ham Blanders, Sergeant McCormick, and the man calling himself Joe Smith.

Ezra turned in Ham Blanders' bloody uniform, Colonel Howland's uniform, the uniforms needed by the six men leaving with him in the morning, and his own.

During the night, the snow stopped. At first light, Morris and the rest of his party left the fort. They waited in the extremely cold morning air. Anders walked to the supply office. Private Dennis was on duty. "I need six buffalo hides."

"I need a requisition," the private replied.

"You want me to wake up the colonel?"

"If he didn't authorize it, then he didn't want you to have them."

"He didn't know how cold it was going to be."

Private Dennis repeated his statement. "I need a requisition."

"Fine." Sergeant Anders waited thirty minutes before he knocked in the colonel's door. "Sergeant Anders here."

"Come," the colonel already sat at his table. Sergeant Anders handed him a cup of hot black coffee.

"I need a requisition for six buffalo hides."

"Fill one out, and I'll sign it. Add whatever else you need."

Sergeant Anders went to the desk and got a form. He filled it out. "Coffee too. It's really cold."

The colonel sipped the warming brew brought by Sergeant Anders. "Thank you for bringing me this coffee." He signed the form.

Anders slapped the paper on the store counter. "I've got a requisition for supplies."

Private Dennis got the buffalo hides and coffee. He handed them to Sergeant Anders. "I'm just following orders."

"I know." Sergeant Anders wasn't happy about having to traipse around in the cold. He rode out with his men. *Why can't everybody be like the people in Ppahiska's tribe?*

Ezra arrived at the store with a wagon and four mules. He handed his well-thought-out requisition to Private Dennis. Once all the supplies were loaded, he joined Morris and the others. Justin, Edwin, George, and Robert transferred the supplies from their animals into the wagon. In the very cold air, all six civilians changed into military uniforms and then took the ferry across the Neosho River with Ezra.

SEVENTY THREE

Since they had three sets of animals, the plan was to change animals at the mid-day meal and travel fast. The first two days of Ezra's mission, Colonel Howland held Joe Smith. The third day of Joe Smith repeatedly yelling, "You can't keep me here!" the colonel walked into the stockade and sat Sergeant Anders' report on the table.

"Mr. Joseph Smith, I have other things to do than deal with you, and you did try to kill one of my men. I could have you executed. However, Sergeant Anders' report states the private over there started the fight, but you swung the first blow. Therefore, I'm going to let you tell me directly what happened."

After grilling Joe for hours, the colonel decided he had stalled as long as was anywhere close to realistic. "You may buy whatever supplies you need. If you can't write, I'll get Sergeant McCormick to come over. You can tell him what you need. After Sergeant McCormick has delivered what you purchase to the stable, one of my men will escort you over there. You will pay for stabling and feeding your horse then pack under my man's supervision. He will then escort you out. You are banned from this fort forever."

"What about him?" Joe asked.

"What I do with my soldier is not your concern. Shall I send for Sergeant McCormick or paper?"

"Paper and something to write with." Joe made a long list, including a buffalo hide, a larger tent, warmer clothes, and warmer footwear. He also wrote on the paper. "May I put the clothes on in here?"

The master of supplies went to Joe's cell and handed him the clothes. "Fifteen dollars and thirteen cents. That includes the fee for taking care of your horse. He's a fine horse and a pleasant fellow."

"His name is Sergeant because he's the boss."

Sergeant McCormick laughed. "Be careful about which officers you point that out to." He handed Joe his bag of money. "Count it all and make sure it's all there." He knew it was because he'd had possession of it the whole time.

"It's all here." Joe gave the sergeant the money requested.

"As one fiery, hot-headed man to another hot-head, I'm telling you to get control of yourself. Don't be the puppet of other people. That private got you to do what he wanted because he likes to fight. You ended up in the stockade. Words are only words. People and life can do all kinds of things to you, but you get to choose how to respond. Don't choose to be stupid." Sergeant McCormick turned and left the man to his life.

Not only did they throw me in jail, they also subjected me to an idiotic lecture about being a good boy. On his way out of the fort, Joe asked the man escorting him, "Which way to Quapaw land?"

"Cross the Neosho River on the ferry, take the road north to Spring River, cross back to this side of the Neosho, and then follow Spring River north. When you get to the Boston Mountains, you're there. There are four villages of them up there."

"Any white people living with them?"

"I think the one right beside Spring River has a couple of white women there. Heard one has long, yellow hair."

"Much obliged for the information."

To finalize the message that the man was not getting back into the fort, Colonel Howland had ordered the gate to be shut as soon as Joe was outside. Private Morris did so.

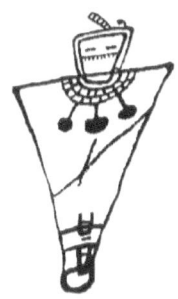

SEVENTY FOUR

Not far to the north, Noah told Ann, "This time last year, I hated the world. I thought I would never see you again. Today, I love everything. You're with me. Our first child will be born soon, and everybody in our family is together. Before this year is over, I want to make Roscoe our relative. Then, everything will be perfect."

Ann liked his idea. "Since this year has only a few days left, we should talk to the rest of the family when we get up. We'll have the ceremony as soon as possible."

Noah said, "I've finished the pipe. I hope everybody else is ready."

"We finished the ceremonial outfit we made with the white leather you earned in Little Rock, and Stephanie told me Eli has finished the knife."

"When we were in Little Rock, we were somebody for a few days, weren't we?"

"Everywhere we go, everybody knows you're special and wonderful. I knew it from the beginning."

"Thank you for thinking so, my wife. I think

you're special and wonderful too." Noah shared that love with his wife as they lay on their soft mattresses.

The family confirmed they were ready to bring Roscoe into the family officially. They decided to have the ceremony the next day if Nikiata had Roscoe's new name. Sally went to speak with him and Mina. First, she asked, "Nikiata, have you found Roscoe's new name?"

"Yes, I have the name," he informed her.

"Mina, tomorrow we want to have the ceremony to make Roscoe our relative. We would like to use your old home. If you are willing, what can we give you for the use of it?"

"You can use it for free. I behaved horribly when you first came here. I owe it to you."

"We can't reduce what we do in making Roscoe our relative. He means too much to us."

"Ann paid for the use with a cut and scar across her neck, and she almost lost their baby. Noah practically killed himself to get his child back from the spirit world. Ann hovered over the spirit world to save her husband and the child and to bring them back. All of us encountered the spirit world. Noah, Ann, you, Wakanda, and Nikiata battled demons. Isn't that a high enough price?"

"If you look at it that way, I guess it is. Thank you." Sally turned back to Nikiata. "I have been told what I am supposed to do and was also told you know what to do during the ceremony."

"I do."

"Thank you for doing this for us. Both of you." Sally went home to let the others know they could use the lodge and that Nikiata did have Roscoe's new name.

Ke became the messenger. He went to each lodge. "We are making Roscoe our relative tomorrow. You are invited to join us at mid-day in Mina's old lodge."

Ann, Stephanie, and Sally prepared together in a perfectly choreographed dance. The five other women in the family joined them. Chumani desired to help. Even though she created as much confusion as a three-year-old could, they encouraged her to do so.

SEVENTY FIVE

On the road south of them, the assassin told himself, *this is all their fault. If they weren't such horrible people, I wouldn't need to rid the world of them. Now, I'm out here where the world is freezing over. I'll teach them not to do this to me. I'll cut their bodies apart a little at a time.* He imagined the pleasure he would get from hearing their screams. *I'll have to keep their heads whole though, so Judge Hall knows I got the right ones.* The man born 'Raymond Pence' no longer thought of himself as that man. After months of hating the woman he had wanted to possess and the man she had chosen instead of him and then hating the two he had been sent to bring in, he had wholly become Joe Smith.

He pulled back on the reins. "Sergeant, maybe I should give you a new name. I don't want to be reminded of those ratbag soldiers down at Fort Gibson. I know it's early, but I've got to get warm. Yes, I know we need a fire, but this is the prairie, and there aren't any trees. At least you have warm fur."

Joe dismounted. *I'll put on all my clothes and get*

under my blanket and buffalo hide. "You think that'll keep me warm enough, horse?" Sergeant looked at his owner silently. "Don't look at me like it's my fault we're out here. I already told you it's their fault!" Joe set up, then shivered in his tent.

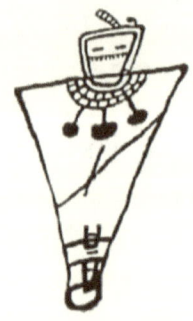

SEVENTY SIX

Chetan prayed over the following day's breakfast. "God in Heaven, we thank you for sending Roscoe into this family. Help us be the best family we can for each other with love and help. Thank you for all the other people in this lodge, including the five on the way."

"What? Mother?" Noah asked for everybody.

Bethany pretended she didn't have any idea what Noah wanted to know. "Yes?"

"Are you pregnant?" Noah asked.

"Our next child should arrive in August."

"Congratulations!" Ann hugged her mother-in-law. The rest of the family added their best wishes. After enjoying mussel chowder and freshly baked sweet bread, they started the preparations. At mid-day, they were ready to adopt Roscoe into the family. Mina's old lodge contained a glorious feast, four grandfather stones, several bowls, and some jars full of various items.

Wakanda wore his bone hairpiece. He hung his bone breastplate over his ceremonial yellow deerskin outfit. He cleansed the lodge with sweetgrass and smudged each person as they came to support Roscoe's adoption.

When everybody was inside, Wakanda sprinkled a tobacco circle in the lodge center, leaving only a small break in the ring. "We give tobacco to Mother Earth, the stone people, the animals, the plants, and all the grandmothers and grandfathers who have gone before us. We ask for your blessings in this space."

Noah and Eli entered the lodge in yellow buckskin pants, shirts, and moccasins, along with Ann, Stephanie, and Sally in yellow buckskin dresses and moccasins. They slowly entered through the opening in the tobacco circle. Wakanda picked up an eagle feather fan lying on a mat on a table and fanned them with the smoke of sweetgrass burning in his smudging bowl.

Once all of them stood inside the circle, Roscoe came into the lodge in his ceremonial white buckskin shirt, intricately beaded around the neck, cuffs, and lower edge, along with white buckskin pants and white moccasins also beaded beautifully with a matching design.

Wakanda asked the five in the circle, "What do you ask of the sacred circle?"

"We ask for this man, Roscoe Bacon, to join with us in the circle of our family."

Wakanda turned. "Roscoe Bacon, these people ask you to become a part of their family. Although they have no obligation by blood, in the same spirit of love they have for a blood relative, they wish to care for you for the rest of their lives."

"I understand that these five people have asked me to join their family."

"For the rest of your life, in the spirit of love, will you care for them as blood relatives, even though they have no right by blood to ask this?"

"I promise to care for each of these people as long as I live as if they are my blood relatives."

"Enter the circle of this family." Wakanda directed Roscoe to enter into the circle through the opening in the tobacco. He then took a handful of tobacco from a bowl and closed the circle.

He picked up one of the grandfather rocks and placed it in the east. "Wanbli, eagle spirit, you have come once to this village. We ask you to come again and bless this joining." Wakanda put the next stone in the south. "Coyote, you trickster who tried to keep this family apart by eating them. Come now and bless this joining." He placed the next grandfather stone in the west. "Mato, grizzly bear, this family will come to you in the west. Bless this joining and protect them now and as they come your direction." He positioned the last stone in the north. "Tatanka, white buffalo, you have sent many of your family to feed this family. Bless them and continue to provide as they travel forward into the future."

Noah withdrew two pouches from the medicine bag around his neck and handed them to the mystery man. Wakanda removed from their pouches the two halves of a new calumet made by Noah. The bowl was made of red pipestone. The eighteen-inch-long stem made from dogwood tree was wrapped with alligator skin, and also elk, bear, and coyote hides. Hanging on ribbons of black, white, yellow, and red was an eagle feather, mallard feather, snow goose feather, and Canada goose feather. Two rows of pearly mussel buttons were attached with ribbons of blue and green.

Wakanda held the bowl in his left hand and the stem in his right, pointing to the east. He sprinkled tobacco on the ground and spoke, "East, bring many days to this new family." He put tobacco in the bowl, then turned and offered tobacco to the south. "South, like spring, let this family be warmth and life to each other."

Once again, tobacco went into the pipe. He turned and offered tobacco to the west. "West, Holy Spirit that lives in the hearts of men, continue to live in the hearts of these six people. Create a strand of seven cords between them and yourself that will never be broken."

He placed tobacco in the bowl, then turned north, and then sprinkled tobacco on the ground. "North, give endurance, strength, truthfulness, and hope to this family as they endure the pain of life."

He added more tobacco to the pipe and the ground, and then touched the pipe to the ground. "Mother Earth, provide for this family abundantly through their whole lives."

Wakanda pointed the stem up and outwards after adding more tobacco to the bowl. "Father Sky, with Mother Earth, give light to the day and warmth to their bodies and lodges."

He added one more pinch of tobacco to the bowl.

"Creator of the universe, Mother Earth, Father Sky, and the four directions, we offer this pipe and this family to you."

Wakanda then lit the pipe and handed it to Noah. Noah spoke. "Roscoe, you are a fine person and a good friend and now my family." Noah smoked the pipe and handed it to his wife.

"Roscoe, if it had not been for your caring heart that first provided a place for Noah and then for all of us, there would be no family but only grief. You have given us the gift of this family. We are your family." She smoked the pipe and passed it to Stephanie.

"Roscoe, provider of warmth, food, love, and compassion. You not only gave a stubborn mule the continued opportunity for redemption, but you did the same for us. I will love you until I draw my last breath." She smoked the pipe and handed it to Eli.

"Healing came to this family because you offered us your home and resources, your cooking and friendship, and finally your heart. I don't take that lightly. A heart freely given is a powerful source of strength. I thank you for yours, and I give you back mine." He smoked the pipe and passed it to Sally.

"Roscoe, you gave us a place to survive safe, warm, and happy. You shared food, knowing you would not have enough for yourself in the end. You also gave healing to my aching heart by sharing your own story. You shared your knowledge of cooking and plants. You even stayed alive for us when death tried to steal you. I love you no less than any person in this family." She smoked the pipe and handed it to Roscoe.

Roscoe took the pipe. "I had words I had planned to say, but your words of love, appreciation, and acceptance have overwhelmed me. You are truly the family I have waited for my entire life. Every time I came close to having a family, something was always lacking. From the time you five first came into my life, you have felt like my family. You made Pine Bluff a home. You have never held back one iota of love from me. I am truly honored to be a part of this family. I will try my entire life to be worthy." He smoked the pipe and handed it to Wakanda.

Wakanda tapped out the tobacco into the waiting bowl and separated the two halves of the pipe. He placed the parts into their pouches and then handed the pipe stem to Roscoe and the bowl to Noah. "Your entire lives, you will each carry a part of the calumet. Together you hold the life of this calumet." Both men put their half into the medicine bags that hung around their necks.

Wakanda called the six to sit on stools inside the circle. He dipped his finger in a clay bowl, painted four blue lines down Noah's nose then four blue marks across his checks. "These blue lines signify a sacred change in your life as you become a new person as one family with Roscoe." He stepped over to Eli and did the same.

He washed his hands in clear water and then took a bowl of red paint to Ann. He put his whole hand into the bowl and wiped the paint across her whole forehead, across her nose and cheek, then the other cheek and last across her chin. When her whole face was red, he stated the symbolism. "You have been reborn as you take on the responsibilities of this new relationship adding Roscoe to your family." He painted Sally and Stephanie the same as Ann and repeated the same words.

He came to Roscoe. He painted his face red and told him, "You have been reborn as you take on the responsibilities of this new relationship to join this family." Then he put down the red paint, washed his hands in the large bowl of water, and retrieved the blue paint. He drew a blue circle around his face. "You are a new person." He painted a blue line across Roscoe's forehead. "You will think and decide, always remembering that you are a part of this family. Everything you do will affect them." He painted a blue line across both cheeks. "As part of this family, you must be willing to fight to protect them." Wakanda dipped his thumb in the blue and pressed it against Roscoe's chin. "Your words will be of love, encouragement, and hope to the people in your new family."

Wakanda put down the paint, picked up his medicine stick, and waved it over Roscoe. "Great Spirit, grant Roscoe the wisdom and willingness to fulfill his duties within this family and community. You are now Huka; you are adopted." He put down the medicine stick and stepped out of the circle.

Chaska beat the drums. The six people in the circle together walked the honor round inside the circle as the guests in the lodge sang the honoring song.

Sally picked up the pitcher and cup from under her stool. She poured ruby chokecherry juice into the cup. She handed it to Roscoe. "A person of different blood has been received as a relative. You will receive security, peace, love, and a home as long as Ann, Eli, Stephanie, Noah, or I live."

Roscoe drank the tart juice.

Ann picked up the bowl and spoon that was under her stool. She fed Roscoe a spoonful of wasna and then gave the bowl of ground cornmeal, bear fat, and sugar mixture to Roscoe. "A person of different blood has been received as a relative. You will receive security, peace, love, and a home as long as Noah, Eli, Stephanie, Sally, or I live."

Stephanie picked up her bowl. She walked to the stick with a burning ember at the end that Nikiata had placed there unobserved. She lit the bowl of sage in her hand then removed an eagle feather from the medicine bag that hung around her neck for the first time. Starting at his feet and rising to his head, she fanned the sage smoke over Roscoe. "A person of different blood has been received as a relative. You will receive security, peace, love, and a home as long as Noah, Eli, Ann, Sally, or I live."

Next, Eli grasped the bowl that held the knife with a handle made from the antler of the elk that Noah and Ann had driven through the front door of the trading post in Pine Bluff. Its blade was a piece of Arkansas whetstone they had picked up after they left Fletcher Creek. Held out across both his palms, he offered it to

Roscoe. "A person of different blood has been received as a relative. You will receive security, peace, love, and a home as long as Ann, Noah, Stephanie, Sally, or I live."

Last, Noah retrieved his bowl. He removed an eagle feather on a red ribbon, which he tied in Roscoe's hair. "A person of different blood has been received as a relative. You will receive security, peace, love, and a home as long as Eli, Ann, Stephanie, Sally, or I live."

Chaska beat the drums. The guests sang the making of a relative song. The drums stopped. Nikiata stood up. "A member of the community wishes to give Roscoe a new name."

"I give this gift for my new name." Roscoe held out a box full of sheets of paper with the information he had documented about plants. However, at the request of Nikiata, Noah, and Wakanda, he did not state what was in the box.

Nikiata stepped into the circle. "I accept the gift. I went to seek the vision of Roscoe's new name. I had no food and only drank water for eleven days.

On the eleventh night, I dreamed I went into a white man's building. The building contained very much knowledge in many books. I looked at book after book. Then, across the room, I saw a very old grandfather sitting cross-legged on the floor. He wore a bone breastplate. He had eagle feathers tied in his long white hair. On his face were many wrinkles. In his leathery hands, he held a long rope. He looked down as he tied prayer knot after prayer knot.

Then, he sat with his eyes closed for a long time. When he had completed all except the last knot, he opened his eyes. He looked directly at me and then across the room. I turned to see what was there.

By the door, Roscoe waited. We left the building together. Outside, I saw the same grandfather beside a horse, holding the reins. Roscoe got on it. Grandfather motioned for me to get on the horse too. I jumped on and landed partially inside the animal. I knew it was not real. That was when I saw a golden thread attached to Roscoe's back. Grandfather said, 'Apenimon'. The thread started to pull Roscoe away. I called out, 'I want to go with you!'

"Grandfather still held the horse's reins. 'You cannot go with him,' he said.

"I woke up. Apenimon means 'worthy of trust'. This name was attached to your soul by the ancestors. For the rest of your life, you must use this name in all ceremonies, but you will not speak this name often. It will be known only to your new family and the people at this ceremony where you have received the name, 'Apenimon'."

Nikiata looped a cord of sweetgrass and cedar fibers around Roscoe's neck. Roscoe was officially a newly named family member of Noah, Ann, Eli, Stephanie, and Sally.

Roscoe spoke, "I wish to give gifts to this community. Will the Ceyapaha present them?"

As planned, Nikiata agreed, "I will."

Together, Noah, Ann, Stephanie, Sally, and Eli

said, "In honor of Apenimon, we also wish to give gifts to this community. Will the Ceyapaha present them?"

Nikiata spoke to everybody in the lodge. "I will. It is time for the Winpeya."

To each family, Roscoe had given two large steel butcher knives, two india rubber canteens, four corked glass jars of wooden matches, and a large iron dutch oven filled with dried, compressed vegetable and potato cubes.

Eli, Noah, Sally, Stephanie, and Ann had given for each person over the age of six, three-inch-wide and three-foot-long strips of cloth of each of the six colors, and a bag of sage, cedar, sweetgrass, and tobacco. To each girl under six, a cloth doll and each boy under six a leather ball, both stuffed with tiny goose feathers. For the village, so all four lookout-posts could use a spyglass at the same time, they had given Ppahiska three more spyglasses. To each female over ten who did not already have one, they gave a sewing kit, and to those who did have one, a package of beads. To each male over ten, who did not already have one, they gave a steel hunting knife in a sheath with a pocket that held a small whetstone. The others received a set of steel fishing hooks and a bundle of fishing line.

After the giveaway, they feasted. The weteca, all the food and drink that remained, Roscoe put into tin coffee pots and lidded cooking pots for every family. Roscoe was officially part of the family.

SEVENTY SEVEN

Joe rubbed his frostbitten toes. *$%@#^&& women! First Lola, then Adeline and Ann Williams too. I don't know why any man wants one! They tempt you, then rip your heart out. They're all whores. I hate women!* He put all his socks and his boots back on. He hobbled to Sergeant, crammed his foot into the stirrup, and tried to rise. His frozen toes couldn't take his weight. He tumbled to the ground. *I need shelter. I won't survive another night out here.* He mounted on the other side, pulling with his hands as well. *Is that smoke?* He pulled out his telescope, verified a thin column to the south, and then commanded his horse. "Run!"

Lathered and breathing hard Sergeant brought Joe to a lone wagon beside the road. "I need help! I'm freezing!" He fell off his horse.

"Help me, Hazel!" The owner of the wagon dashed to the man. "We need to get him to the fire!"

The woman gently lowered Joe's arm to the ground, where they had pulled him close to the fire. "I'll brush down and dry the horse, or it'll freeze too." The woman filled a large cup with coffee, which she handed to her husband. "Fred, honey, try to get this into him. I'll pour the rest into a pot for the horse. That will help it too." She climbed into the wagon to get a towel and pot.

Sergeant drank the warm stimulate while Hazel took off his bridle, riding, and packsaddles and set them aside. Joe barely had enough consciousness to drink, but the fluid triggered his automatic response. He swallowed.

Fred started a pot of coffee before he set to rubbing Joe's hands between his own. Hazel came back and lay beside the half-frozen man. She wrapped her arms around him. "The fire will warm him on that side. I'll warm him on the back. You better check his toes."

"Toes don't look good at all!"

"Don't rub them. The skin is too far gone."

"It'll be a miracle if they don't drop off!" Fred brought Joe's bare feet closer to the fire.

Hazel repositioned to keep her warm body beside Joe. Fred raised the man's head, poured more coffee into his mouth, then went to look over the horse. "He shouldn't have run his horse so hard, but then he would've frozen before he got here, and that galloping did heat up his horse." He wiped the horse down again and then tied him to the wagon with his oxen.

"Don't die." Hazel got more warm coffee into the man.

The man groaned. "It's all Lola's fault!"

Hazel stroked the man's hair. "It's all right. You can tell us after you're good and warm."

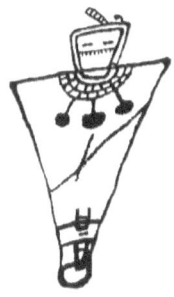

SEVENTY EIGHT

Petang ran into the village. "Soldiers are coming!"

Ppahiska hurried to the lookout. He looked at the people approaching through one of the new spyglasses. One of the men held up a broken arrow. "That's Ezra Knuckles. Let them come." He went back to the village. "Ezra Knuckles is coming with other soldiers. Go to your positions, just in case."

With their rifles, the village men scattered to secure positions. The man who spoke English and knew Ezra very well stood on the village side of Five Mile Creek. James asked, "Why have you come, Ezra?"

"This isn't good. These are friends. Ask one of your family from Harmony to come here."

"They aren't here," James lied.

One of the soldiers with Ezra said, "Then why is Eli walking across the field?"

James wasn't falling for that trick. If he turned to look, that meant he thought it was possible. "None of them are here."

Morris really did see Eli coming across the field, but he knew James was protecting his family. "We're friends here to help, but we understand. We don't mind standing here for a few more minutes."

"They were here, but they left a long time ago."

Eli was close enough. "It's all right, Uncle James. Let them come."

"Come on." James made an unobtrusive stand-down signal to those ready to defend the village.

When the soldiers were on the north side of Five Mile Creek, Eli touched each one as he named them and told where they came from. "Morris from Fletcher Creek. Morris's son George. Matt, also from Fletcher Creek. Matt's son Justin. Edwin from Little Rock, but he may think of Maumelle as his home now. You know Ezra." To the last man, Eli said, "I apologize. I remember you brought your pig, but I don't remember your name."

"Robert. Formerly from Little Rock. Now I have no home."

Eli asked, "Why are you here?"

As agreed, they let Robert talk. Everybody walked to the village, "We're here to warn you about an assassin."

"I was afraid of that. Ann is due to have a baby any day and Stephanie in a few months. This is the worst time possible," replied Eli.

"But, you do have two, maybe three days."

As soon as they got into the village, Noah, Ann, Stephanie, and Roscoe greeted their friends. Ppahiska and Wakanda welcomed Ezra as well as the men they didn't know.

Partly because she wanted to hurt Justin for

choosing Carmen instead of her, but mostly because she wanted to kiss Edwin. Sally gave the young man a big kiss. Edwin kissed her back before he said, "I have a girlfriend. This is her father."

"You put your kiss on the necklace for me. Having it has meant a lot to me, but I wanted a real one. Please, nobody tell Elizabeth. I'm the one who kissed Edwin."

"It's all right. I know what happened. I don't think there is any reason to pass that knowledge on to anybody at home. Do any of you?" Matt looked at the others from Fletcher Creek.

They all assured Sally and Edwin that the kiss would remain a secret.

Robert returned to the issue at hand. "Someone is coming for Ann and Noah." Robert couldn't help himself. He kept looking at the woman with the scars on her face.

Finally, she said, "Yes. I am the one. I am sorry about what I did."

Robert didn't know what to say. "I'm being rude. I'm sorry."

Mina asked Sally because she was standing beside her. "What is rude?"

In Quapaw, Sally said, "Acting badly."

"I was rude to Ann?"

"Not exactly the same. You were hateful. Rude is not close to behaving as badly as you did."

"I was hateful. Tell Robert. I wish I could go back in time and change how I treated Ann."

Sally told Robert what Mina had said. Robert

replied, "Looks like you've learned to speak Quapaw. Tell her I said we all have things we wish we had done differently. I want to tell you about something. First, I want to show you something." He raised up the back of his shirt and turned in a circle.

Matt whispered to Morris, "I'm glad he's telling them and not trying to cover it up."

"Robert, what happened?" Sally asked with much concern.

"I was stabbed and almost died twice because of something I did." Sally translated. Everybody saw his back and focused on Robert. "I guess you should all know."

Sally held up her hand to stop him. "You should have a better translator?"

Robert was afraid for Dr. Smith or Dr. Smith's father to be next to him when he explained what he had done. "James, will you?"

"Sure." James moved next to Robert

Robert decided to tell the story the way Zane had. Every few sentences, Robert paused to let James repeat his words in Quapaw.

"...I left my family in a safe place and tried to come here alone. I slept in a dirty stable. The wound became infected, and I became delirious. As God would have it, my horse took me to Perryville, where Edwin, S.R., and the assassin found me."

Everybody gasped.

"They saved me when the infection in the knife wound was about to kill me. The doctor told them it was hopeless, but they didn't give up. They used whiskey, maggots, and spider webs. Really, I should be dead. The infection was in my brain, I'm sure. Those things never should have saved me. When I regained the ability to know what was happening, I found out the man who had thrown the knife into my back had helped save me.

"At first, I was furious that they had let the man get near me. They had even known from the beginning that he was the one who had tried to kill me. Then, I found out his story. It took me some time, probably even until just now, to really understand and forgive him.

"He didn't want to kill me. At the time, he had felt trapped and didn't know how to get out. In the end, he did find a way to complete the mission to pay for his freedom and for him to be out of it.

"That's why he worked so hard to save me. He didn't want the consequences of what he had started, and he didn't want to be a murderer." Everybody listened intently to the emotions in Robert's voice. "The assassin passed on the name he had when he took the job. It wasn't his real name anyway, and he didn't want the name, so he gave it to Raymond Pence."

Eli stopped the story. "Wait. Raymond from Perryville?"

"Yes. He was with Adeline, a very nice woman who runs the inn in Perryville. Raymond was about to beat her up, but S.R. ran in there, stopped him, and slugged him a few times. Then Zane, that's the assassin's real name, somehow convinced Raymond to sell him his farm and take up the assassination job using the name Joe Smith."

Stephanie interrupted, "The only reason he would do that would be to find Lola and Sebastian. Did Zane or Joe, or whoever he is, tell him where to find them? How would he know? Is everybody at home safe?"

Robert was losing control of the story, and he didn't yet want them to know what he had done. "He told Raymond if he found Ann and Noah, he would find Sebastian and Lola in the process, but then he left a note that Justin found saying to go to Harmony and warn them."

"Why would he say anything about us?" Ann asked.

"Because that's who the assassin was sent to find," Robert replied.

Noah said, "So it must have been Judge Hall who recruited the man out of prison."

"Yes."

Chetan stood up. "How did you find out about this?"

Robert was sure Chetan was going to kill him, but he deserved it. "I told Judge Hall that Russell French saw Sally and Eli by Spadra."

Sally slapped him. "How could you?! We helped you with the pig!"

"I wanted the twenty dollars. I wanted to make a better life for Bertha. I didn't think he would actually be able to find you. I know it was the wrong thing to do, and I wish I had never done it. Not because I almost died, but because of everything it caused."

Stephanie repeated her question, "What happened in Harmony?"

Morris spoke up, "We went there and warned them. Lola and Sebastian went to some cave. Smitty got everybody ready. Earl helped us get out of town without running into Raymond, so we could warn you. We don't know what happened after that."

Sally said, "That Raymond! Ann wanted to shoot him. She should have done it. Just like Noah should have killed Gus."

Robert put his head into his hands and sobbed. "I'm so sorry."

Mina wrapped her arms around Robert and let him cry on her shoulder. "I believe you."

Ann looked at them. She believed both of them really were sorry about what they had done. "I forgive both of you. I believe you've learned what you should learn."

Chetan added, "And you almost died trying to right what you did wrong. You didn't give up, and you didn't let anything stop you. I forgive you too."

Capa said, "How can you just forgive him? Robert did this to all of us. Mantu is wounded. What could he do to help defend us?"

Mantu felt offended that Capa questioned his abilities. "I shot plenty of antelope right when it happened. I can shoot one man now."

Stephanie remembered how anger had almost

destroyed her and her relationship with her family. She didn't want to be filled with anger again. "I forgive you too."

Eli said, "You realize it wasn't just Ann and Noah? It was every person in Harmony, and every person here, and who knows who else? How many people could have died or been injured for your twenty dollars?"

"I know that now. That's why I said I wish I could go back and change what I did." Robert looked at the man he knew as Dr. Smith. The man who had made it possible for him to marry Bertha.

Eli stood up. "Right now, Robert, I'm walking away. We need to start packing. I'm going to get wagon number two."

Noah knew it would be better not to speak his mind. "Eli, I'll come with you, and get wagon one."

Ezra said, "May I walk with you? I have something I want to talk about."

Noah waved him over. "You can get wagon three. We need one more person."

"I'll come too." Roscoe left with them.

"Colonel Howland wants me to buy any dynamite, blasting caps, and fuses you will sell us. That is, if you have any more."

Noah, Roscoe, and Eli made a few minute signals to each other. Noah told Ezra what they had decided. "We'll sell you four more sets for the same price each as the last time you bought some."

Ezra started thinking. He knew the colonel would

want it all, but he didn't have enough gold. "Which mules do you want me to get?"

Roscoe knew which mules were his, but it wouldn't be easy to describe them. "Any six with the patchwork skin."

Noah whistled. A group of horses and mules started in his direction. Noah got Blanco and Chocolate into position. "You start with those two." He pointed toward Beauty and Dollie.

Ezra buckled the harness straps. "I only have one thousand dollars in gold coins. We had no idea you would still have so much. I'm sure the colonel wants it all. Maybe we could give store credit for the last two hundred."

"We can't go to Fort Gibson. We have to go north into Cherokee land."

"Maybe you can trade with people here for other things you need, and then they could use the credits next time they come to Fort Gibson? Also, the first trip here, part of the payment for the dynamite was rations for thirteen men for seven days coming up and four men for seven days going back. We had three-hundred and fifty-seven meals. I brought the same amount this time, but we have only seven men each way. We used one-hundred and five to get here. We need the same to go back. That would leave me rations for one-hundred and forty-seven meals that I can give you."

"I want my friends to have one hundred meals worth of rations to get from Fort Gibson to Fort Smith. Going home, hunt for one meal a day, or eat only two meals per day. That's thirty-five more, plus the other forty-seven. I'll take eighty-two meals worth of rations. I'll see what else we can work out."

When they had the four sets of mules in the harnesses, they returned to the lodge. Eli said, "Roscoe, let's go over to the cave and get the rest of our things."

Roscoe jumped off the wagon he had driven to the lodge. "Coming."

Capa followed, "I'm going to make sure you don't get anything that's not yours."

That comment made Wakanda again wonder what had happened to Capa's thoughts and behaviors. "I don't want an argument to arise, deciding who owns what. I'll come too."

Chetan thought he heard both Capa and Wakanda say they needed to be sure the white men didn't steal. He called out, "Eli! Roscoe! Come here!" They halted. "It will be better if I go with Waya."

Eli got an uncomfortable feeling from Capa all the time. "That's a good idea."

Chetan asked his new father-in-law. "Waya. Will you help me?"

The four Indian men rode to the cave. Everybody else pitched in and helped carry items out of the lodge. Noah and Eli stood in one wagon, Dustu and Adahy in another, and Roscoe and Tom in the third. The women in the lodge explained how everything was marked to show which wagon to take for packing.

As they packed, Justin spoke with Sally. "I'm sorry about the way I did things. I still care about you. I was the first to say I was coming to warn you. I don't want anything bad to ever happen to you."

"But you love Carmen."

Justin didn't see any reason to lie. "Yes. We're more alike."

"I forgive you. I don't mean to be bossy or a know-it-all. I'm sure I would be a horrible wife."

"You will be a wonderful wife for the right man."

"That's what everybody says. It's just that nobody wants to be the right man."

"You are very sweet and beautiful. You'll find him."

"I'm not in one place long enough for anybody to even get to know me, but thank you for saying so."

Ann passed a package to Noah. "Ahhh!" She put her hand to her belly.

"What's wrong?! Is Christopher coming?!" Noah put down the package to get out of the process.

"It's gone now. It's nothing."

"Only bring little things," Noah told her.

Fifteen minutes later, Ann felt the pain again. She whispered to Bethany. "Mama, I think Christopher may be coming."

"Tell me what you feel."

"Pain right here, and I feel like I have to use the chamber pot."

"Let me know as soon as you feel a pain again."

When Chetan, Waya, Capa, and Wakanda returned with the fourth wagon, Ann went to Bethany. "Mama, it's back and much worse."

"You're right. I think my grandson will come today. I'm not surprised. All this fuss put you into labor. Did you tell Noah yet?"

"He knows about the first time but not since. I'm scared something will go wrong."

"Everything will be fine. Luyu and I are here. Go tell your husband."

"Do you think I can wait until the packing is done?"

"Probably."

SEVENTY NINE

Fred and Hazel slept in their blankets under Joe's buffalo fur, with Joe squeezed tightly between them. The man they had saved woke. Joe felt warm. Then he felt bodies. He raised his head ever so slightly and glanced around. *A wagon. A fire. They have wood! What a gift! There's my gun.* He slowly reached for the weapon. Quietly, so as not to wake the people around him, he drew the trigger back. He pointed the barrel at the man's chest and then pulled the trigger. Just as the woman's eyes flew open, Joe shut them for good with a second bullet. *Now, it's all mine.* He rolled the corpses away.

Fred's hand flipped toward the fire. *What's a burned up hand when I'm dead anyway. I'll be dammed if I'm letting him have anything.* Fred clenched a flaming branch. His hand blazed with his mode of revenge. He flung the tree limb onto the wagon canvas. Flames erupted. Fred's eyes went out as the wagon fire raged.

Joe dashed to the wagon. Frantically, he worked at the rope knot that secured Sergeant to the inferno.

After being almost frozen, now, he was much too hot. He jerked the final length of rope from the wagon. "@%^#% people! Don't they know they could have hurt us?!" He kicked Fred's dead body out of the way and grabbed the buffalo fur.

The frantic oxen lowed loudly. They jerked and kicked to no avail. *The fire will cook them. You can't get a beefsteak any fresher. I'll stay here for a few days and eat them. Humm. I should do something about these bodies.* He picked up the woman and chucked her into the flames, then heaved Fred's heavy corpse onto his shoulder. He turned his head away and walked toward the inferno. He dumped Fred beside his wife. The crash sent burning canvas into the sky. Joe knocked a piece off his head and backed away with singed hair.

EIGHTY

In the village, Noah realized they needed another wagon. "James, would you sell me your wagon for credit at Fort Gibson?"

James handed Noah a crate. "Is one hundred and thirty-five dollars too much?"

"That will be fine."

James knew they needed the wagon immediately so the packing could continue. "May I unhitch the team from this wagon and get it?"

"That would be perfect." Noah jumped down and called Ezra over. "James gets a one hundred and thirty-five dollar credit. Come in here, write it, and sign it."

Petang heard them make the deal. "I will talk with my family, but I think I can sell you mine. They are fine young horses. Forty each."

Noah asked, "Ezra, how much credit would you give for my eighty-two meals worth of rations?"

Ezra did the math. "Thirty-seven seventy-two."

"Put the rations in a pile. If Petang trades with me, write him a credit for fifty."

Petang returned. "I know where to catch more. I will sell them."

"Help me carry this," Noah told Petang.

Noah, Eli, and Petang moved the dynamite, caps, and fuses into Ezra's wagons. Ezra separated out what he thought was the correct amount of rations.

Noah attempted to strike a deal. "Petang, I would like to give you thirty dollars, a fifty dollar credit at Fort Gibson, and all the rations Ezra divides out for three female horses. I may want to buy more."

"Let me get Zitkala to look at the rations." Petang waved his wife over as he walked toward her. They talked quietly and then went to Noah. "We will do it if Zitkala thinks we get the right amount of rations, and they are things she wants."

Noah told Ezra, "I'm trading the rations for a horse. Zitkala wants to see what you have."

Wakanda saw Noah at Ezra's wagon. He called him by the proper name for an apprentice mystery man. "Tahatankohana, come to my lodge for a short time."

Noah called out, "Ehawee, Wakanda wants to speak with me. Please translate for Ezra and Zitkala."

Petang, Zitkala, and Ezra traded items with Ehawee's help. Zitkala and Petang carried home twenty-six pounds of cured salted bacon, three unopened pint-sized bottles of molasses, four unopened gallon jugs of cider, and the remainder of the vinegar in the keg. When they came back again, the rest of the family came with them. They took two five-pound sacks of sugar, a ten-pound bag of split peas, and twenty candles. They also took all fourteen unused three-ounce bars of hard soap. Since it was too cold to wash, Ezra was more than happy to give up all the soap. Zitkala also took a ten-pound bag of rice, seven unopened tins of butter, twenty-one compressed cubes of dried vegetables, and twenty-one more of potato. They left the spruce beer, whiskey, green coffee beans, and salt.

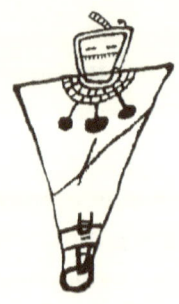

EIGHTY ONE

Nobody was in Wakanda's lodge when the mystery man and Noah entered. The smoke of sage, tobacco, cedar, and sweetgrass filled the lodge. Two mats sat on the floor beside the fire. A blanket lay on the ground beside the mats. Noah could see lumps under the cloth. Wakanda pointed. He instructed his apprentice. "Sit."

Noah sat on the mat and waited for Wakanda to continue. "Tahatankohana, since Chetan and Bethany brought you to find out what you should become, I have known you would be a mystery man. I have trained you. You have trained yourself about many things. You have passed your teacher. I am very proud of you.

"Your heart, mind, and body are good. The good people you touch love you. You have picked a good family. You even knew that you would not find your family here and left to find them. You have helped many people everywhere you went and came home in time to help your own people.

"You are pure. As they must, those who are not

pure hate you. Never forget it is because you do the right thing that these people are against you. Never believe you have done something wrong. It is time for you to be declared a mystery man."

Wakanda drew the blanket back a short distance. He picked up the halves of a calumet. He pointed the pipe stem to the east, south, west, and north. "I tell all the directions to come and bear witness." Wakanda touched the stem to the earth and then raised it up toward the sky. "Mother Earth, Father Sky, and the Living Spirit, come and bear witness." Wakanda joined the bowl to the stem. He put kinnickinnick into the bowl then lit the herbs with a red-hot stick from the fire. "Come and bear witness. The mind of Tahatankohana holds the knowledge of a mystery man. He holds knowledge from the red man, the white man, and the Creator of the universe." Wakanda drew in a lung full of smoke and then handed the pipe to Tahatankohana.

Tahatankohana took the pipe stem close to the bowl and brought the stem around counter-clockwise to make a half-circle arc. "As I continue through life, keep my mind open to receive knowledge." He drew in a puff of smoke. Making the circle complete, he continued to circle the stem until it pointed toward Wakanda.

Wakanda took the pipe. "The powers tested Tahatankohana and tried to destroy his body. First, by the human attack of Roy Butterfield and an attack by the laws of the white man. Then, by fire at the Williams

Farm. Water and air protected him. Water and air were fickle. Later, they tried to freeze him in the Arkansas River. The power of the Great Spirit and the feminine overruled them. On its own, water tried to drown him in the Little Maumelle River, but a four-legged animal joined with him to save each other. Afterward, the spirit of the trickster tried to eliminate him by coyote attack. Humans tried again with poison in the swamps of Arkansas. Many times in many ways, you have survived." Wakanda smoked and passed the pipe over.

"Strengthen my body to be able to do what is needed to serve where you lead me." Tahatankohana smoked the pipe and passed it back through its circular path.

Wakanda took the pipe. "Consider the spirit of Tahatankohana. It has gone into the afterworld twice. That world could not keep him. He returned both times." He inhaled another lungful of pipe smoke and then circled the pipe back.

Tahatankohana received the pipe. "Open me to the Holy Spirit, who is the only true and living spirit." He smoked the pipe.

Wakanda spoke again, "See the heart of Tahatankohana. At risk to himself, his heart cared enough to heal many animals and the boy in Little Rock. His heart opened to the people in Fletcher Creek. He healed them, and he taught them so they can take care of themselves. His heart cared about people he did not know when he saved Sebastian and Lola. He cared for the people in this village, even though we had not treated him or his family well. He gave us back the ability to care for ourselves. See that his heart could only join with others who are the same." He smoked and passed the pipe.

"Open my heart to continue to care and to receive the love that surrounds me." He received the pipe, smoked it, and passed it back.

Wakanda continued, "East, South, West, North, Mother Earth, Father Sky, and Great Spirit, receive Tahatankohana as the mystery man he is." He passed the pipe one last time.

"Mystery man I will be and will do everything I can to perform the duties required." Tahatankohana smoked from the pipe of his birth village and then passed it back to the man who had done the most to make him into the mystery man he was.

Wakanda took the pipe and laid it back in the bowl. He pulled the blanket further back. He then picked up the bone breastplate that had been in his family for more generations than he could remember and put the strap over Tahatankohana's head, so it hung from his neck. He picked up the bone hairpiece and tied it into Tahatankohana's hair with the soft deerskin strap. Wakanda pulled the blanket further back. He revealed a fur of minks with the heads cut off at the necks and then sewn back on so they hung facing out, the bodies sewn together at the sides with the legs dangling on the outside and the tails hanging at the bottom. Wakanda placed the fur over Tahatankohana's shoulders. Last, he picked up a painted box turtle rattle and placed it in Tahatankohana's hand. "You are not to be the mystery man of this village. I am grateful the Great Spirit I now know is the Father, the Son, and the Holy Spirit, gave me the special honor to prepare you as an offering to a much larger world. Go as a mystery man, Tahatankohana. I am very pleased with you."

Tahatankohana felt overwhelmed that Wakanda had honored him and named him as a mystery man at such a young age. He knew when Wakanda passed on his place to Nikiata; it would be a long time in the future. "I am honored that Wakanda, the one who possesses magical power, has been my teacher and has found me worthy."

At that moment, Wakanda wanted to be a strong mystery man, not a man who would miss a friend and felt sad. Wakanda told him, "You are worthy. Wrap up all of these things that are now yours in that blanket and then go." Noah left Wakanda's lodge with the items Wakanda had bestowed on him wrapped in the blanket.

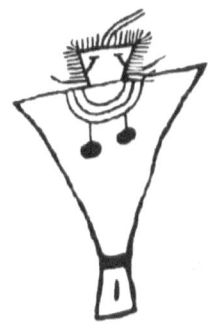

EIGHTY TWO

While Wakanda had confirmed Noah as a mystery man, Capa had watched the transaction between Petang and Ezra. He noticed that some of the rations Ezra separated out for the trade still sat in the wagon. Capa felt very unhappy about the changes in the village and the world. He thought the beer and whiskey might make him feel better. He decided to talk with Ezra. "Ehawee, tell Ezra that they are not going to have enough food going home. I will trade food for the beer and whiskey."

Ehawee explained to Ezra what Capa wanted. Ezra knew the colonel wanted mussels. "Four gallons of mussels in brine for two gallons of beer, the third gallon of beer for twenty-one bear sausages, and a pint of whiskey for ten loaves of freshly-cooked bread."

Ehawee passed on Ezra's answer. Capa picked up two of the jugs of beer. "Bring the others. I'll get the sausage and mussels and tell Wichahpi to have the bread ready in the morning."

Ezra listened to Ehawee and then followed Capa

with the other jug of beer and the whiskey he hadn't previously squirreled into his own sack. He left Capa's lodge carrying two gallons of mussels in brine and a package of bear meat sausages. Capa brought out the other two gallons of mussels.

Noah saw Petang, Zitkala, and Tatonga carrying rations into their lodge. He went to speak with Petang. "I will buy two more female horses with money."

Petang agreed. "I want to thank you for everything you have done for me. I will sell them."

"You're welcome. I enjoyed teaching you to climb the cliff and figuring out how to make the looms and spinning wheels together." Noah counted eighty dollars worth of gold coins onto the table.

As he passed Ezra's wagon, Roscoe noticed the unopened bag of green coffee still sat where Ezra had put the rations he planned to trade. "You didn't want green coffee beans last time. I'll trade for them again."

Ezra remembered seeing walnuts and butternut squash as they had packed the wagons. "Can you get to the walnuts or any of that squash?"

Roscoe offered four cups of shelled nuts and seventeen squash. Ezra agreed. Everything had worked out well. He only gave up things he didn't need. Most importantly, he got the mussels the colonel wanted and the four crates of dynamite with accessories. *Colonel Howland is going to be very pleased.*

Noah secretly packed the blanket with the items Wakanda bestowed upon him into the wagon. *Now, I have to find somebody who wants to finish the hide and buffalo head, and I need to buy a wagon full of hay."* Noah walked back to their lodge, empty of everything except the bedding they would use that night. The fifth wagon was almost full. "I would like to buy the village's wagon and enough hay to fill it. I will give one hundred and fifty dollars to Ppahiska to buy another wagon, then give six dollars to each family for the hay, and pay twenty-five cents more to any person who will help load the hay into the wagon. Last, I will give the village a fifteen dollar Fort Gibson credit voucher for one male and three female sheep."

Ppahiska remembered that he owed this family a favor for the spools of thread they had given him when the village had divided the antelope. He decided to influence the people as that favor. "We don't need the wagon this winter. We can buy another in the spring. Most of the animals will be going with them. We won't need as much hay. Four sheep out of all the sheep we have will not make a difference to us, but it will to Chetan's family. They have done much to help our people, especially us in this village. I think we should do this. Does anybody not want to do this?" Nobody said anything. "Give each family the six dollars and twenty-five cents," Ppahiska instructed Noah.

Noah walked to Ppahiska, counted one hundred and fifty-six dollars into his hand, and then gave each family their six dollars. When he came to Capa, his wife Wichahpi, said, "I will finish tanning the hide and head for the ten-dollar credit."

"Thank you, Wichahpi." Noah counted six dollars into Capa's hand. "Come get them now?"

Capa put the money in his medicine bag and then walked with his wife and their daughter, Awinita, to get the hide, head, and credit voucher. Awinita wanted to stay and play with Chumani, who was only a few months younger. Bethany knew Ann was going to deliver her baby that night, she needed to rest, and there was already too much commotion. "Not tonight."

Forty-nine people went back to the cave with Noah and the wagon he had purchased from the village. By the light of the lanterns, and being very careful not to set anything on fire, they filled the wagon with hay. When they parked the hay wagon with the other five already packed, they were ready to leave.

Noah gave each person who helped a bit piece and then added another dollar to each family for helping pack everything else. Everybody said goodnight.

The men who had come to warn Ann and Noah went to Chetan's lodge to share their more personal news. When they got in the lodge, Bethany and Luyu had supper ready. Ann remained on her bed.

"Aren't you eating?" Noah asked.

"I didn't have just one random pain. The pains are every five minutes."

"You should have told me."

"You had things to do. Sitting with me wasn't necessary."

Noah complained, "You should have told me. You are much more important than anything I was doing."

"My husband, being here at that time wasn't

392

import— Ahhh!" Another pain racked her body. She took hold of Noah's hand. "I do need you here now."

Luyu instructed Chetan. "Go find out if we can use Mina's lodge tonight. Ann doesn't need all these people in here. Everybody else needs to spend the night over there."

"But she's my sister," Sally refused to be dismissed.

Ann stated her wishes, "I want Sally, Stephanie, Noah, Bethany, and Luyu to stay here. If they want to be here, Helen, Hanataywee, and Ehawee too."

"I'll go ask." Chetan left the lodge. He was back in a short minute. He picked up Chumani. "Come on, men." Ke continued to sit. "Ke, you are one of the men."

Ke had wanted to see how a baby was born. "I am? I did not know I was a man yet."

"For this, you are."

Ke followed his father. "Why is Noah not coming?"

"It is his baby."

"I thought it was Ann's baby. How did his baby get in there?"

"I cannot tell you tonight. I will tell you later. Everybody bring wood. We are going to need a lot to warm a lodge as cold inside as it is outside."

Noah told his mother, "I have read that book about midwifery repeatedly. Still, I feel so nervous."

"This child is not just any child. He is your son, but do not worry, Luyu and I are right here. Everything will be fine."

Ann focused on Noah's face as she just about squeezed his hand into a pulp. After hours of labor, Bethany ordered Ann, "Push hard. He's coming."

"Noah!" Ann called out.

"I'm here, my wife."

They heard the cry of Christopher as Bethany held the tiny miracle. "Your mother told me I would be the first to hold you. Now here you are in my arms, and you're perfect." She passed him to Luyu, who wiped the blood away. Luyu gently handed the baby to his father.

Noah kissed the forehead of his son, looked at his small perfect body, and then wrapped him in the blanket that Sally had made for him with her yellow buffalo fur yarn. Noah handed their crying baby to Ann.

Ann worried. "He's crying. He doesn't like me."

Luyu said, "It's just hard to come into this world, and the crying is good.

"Look at his tiny fingers. He's so beautiful." They were about to be thrown into the freezing cold world, and yet Noah was full of joy. "I love you, my wife. I love you too, my son."

They were sure everybody heard Christopher. Ehawee went to tell everybody that he had arrived anyway. She answered everybody's next question. "Yes, he is perfect. You can see him tomorrow before we leave. Ann is resting tonight."

394

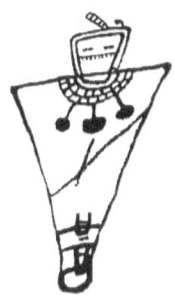

EIGHTY THREE

Morning arrived. Algoma held her grandnephew. "This is a horrible day to have a tiny baby outside."

Chetan agreed. "I know, but we left space in the wagon for Ann and Christopher."

Dowanhowee handed Noah a large winter fur. "We want you to have this to make it warmer for Ann and Christopher."

Tears fell from Ann's eyes. "Thank you. I'm glad we got to know our family."

Noah let all those in James' family hold Christopher because they were relatives. Other people, he allowed to look at his son as he held him.

While everybody looked at the baby, Chaska touched Sally's hand. "Come to my lodge. I have something to give you."

Sally put on her mukluks, hat, coat, and scarf and walked out of the door with Chaska. Edwin and Justin watched her go. In his lodge, Chaska handed Sally a pipe bowl shaped like a buffalo made of a piece of yellow pipestone.

"Chaska, this is beautiful!"

"It is the one you shot that we butchered together. I will keep the pipe stem that goes with it. We will always be bound together. I will never forget you or these days. There is no other woman like you. If things were different, I would have wanted to take the seven steps together, but I will be the village leader someday. I have to marry a Quapaw woman, even though I would rather marry you. So maybe it is good you have to leave. It would be hard to see you and be married to somebody else."

"I respect you for doing what is best for your people, but I am glad to know your heart wanted me. Mine wanted you."

Since Sally was leaving, Chaska allowed himself to do what he had desired for a long time. He took her into his arms. The long, delicious kiss had to end too soon. They knew they should rejoin the others. Sally lovingly carried her treasure across the village. She held out the sculpture for everybody to see.

Justin didn't know why it bothered him that Sally had gone off with Chaska. He loved Carmen, but it got under his skin that another man might be holding or kissing Sally. He decided they had only left to get the tiny statue.

After eating breakfast, Noah and his father went for the animals they were taking. Noah separated out a young, pure white male and female sheep, and a spotted one he thought was already pregnant.

When he got the completely black female, Ppahiska told him, "If you take the black one, I want Chetan's other Fort Gibson credit."

Close by, Chetan gathered their goats. He heard the negotiation. He wouldn't be able to redeem it. If his son wanted the black sheep, he was glad to trade. "I'll tell Ezra to write the transfer of ownership."

Noah tied the string of animals to a wagon. "Edwin, I wish I had been able to talk with you. I hope you understand."

"Robert and I could ride north with you and then circle back to the south from up at the Cherokee crossing," replied Edwin.

Robert reminded them, "There isn't enough food."

"My husband," whispered Ann, "We can feed them for a few days. We have plenty of food, and I would love to have everybody with us for a while. Besides, what if they run into Raymond going south? He would recognize Edwin and then know they were up this way. That would put everybody here in jeopardy. I love these people. I don't want them to be in danger."

Even though Ann had spoken softly, Chetan heard. "We cannot take a chance with the safety of our people. I insist they come with us. Also, with the very cold air, it would not be good for the animals to get wet crossing Five Mile Creek."

Noah answered, "I agree."

Chetan left to talk with the others in the family before he walked to Ezra's wagon. "You need to come north to protect the location of this village, and your horses should not get wet. You can't cross the creek. We'll feed you while you are with us."

As Chetan talked with Ezra, Sally hugged the young women who had been her friends. Except for Mikakh, all of them had husbands. Sally didn't have anybody. Even though she knew why he did it, it hurt her when Chaska acted as if he didn't care that she was leaving.

Two hours after they woke, all the goodbyes were over. Ann and Christopher got in the wagon. Everybody prayed the bedding and furs would keep the bitter cold away.

Sally saw the eyes of Chaska. He held the pipe steam against his heart. She pulled the yellow buffalo carving from her pocket and pressed it to hers. They knew they loved each other.

Seven wagons went north along Spring River. Two miles north of the village, they crossed on the bridge built by the Cherokee. Noah looked behind them and hoped the cold wind pushing the dry snow along the edge of the prairie would fill their tracks quickly.

EIGHTY FOUR

The run-aways wore blanket coats and heavy furs while they prepared the mid-day meal. Christopher stayed cuddled to his mother. Not even his eyes peeked out at Noah, who brought Ann hot food. "Waya and grandmother went ahead. He says they'll kill everybody in a wagon train without even a chance to explain." As they traveled southwest to the village of Leotie, everybody prayed the woman would remember the Cherokee warrior who had recently married Noah's grandmother.

The Cherokee village leader went out into the snow to greet two lone people. "Waya! Why are you here?"

"We need your help."

Noah's grandmother knew Cherokee women preferred to negotiate with other women. Therefore, Luyu informed Leotie, "We have a new baby in our family. It will soon be much too cold for him out here. We will trade to stay in your lodges, have a hot meal tonight, and another in the morning, but we have a large family, many animals, and six wagons."

"What do you trade?"

Packed in the wagons not far away, but unseen, they had the items Roscoe Bacon, the sixty-year-old man they had just adopted into the family, had brought from the trading post he had sold that spring. They also had packages of apple and lime seeds.

Leaving room for Leotie to ask for more, Luyu offered what they had previously decided. "To each family that lets a group of us stay in their lodge, we will give ten steel fishhooks, one fishing line, ten steel needles, and one spool of either white, black, yellow, red, green, or blue thread, and one red flannel shirt. We have three groups of four people, a group with three adults, a seven and a three-year-old, another group of four and a baby, and one group with five people."

"One more shirt per family."

"That is too many."

"I will only allow this if you give two shirts."

"The baby will freeze. I agreed." Luyu acted as if she had been bargained down due to their desperate need for warmth.

Leotie held her head high. "Pull your wagons into a circle, put all your animals in the middle, and then stand in your groups."

"We cannot bring out the mother or baby, but the others will. We will get them."

"I will talk to my people." The village leader left them to bring in the wagons and tend to their animals.

Even though they were short eight blankets for

their horses and four for their sheep, with their thick winter coats and the wagons blocking most of the wind, Waya thought the animals could make it through the night outside. The family divided as planned and waited.

Leotie returned. "More than six families are willing to help. Do you want to divide up more?"

Luyu explained, "Some of us speak only English, some only Quapaw or Cherokee, but some speak both. We cannot divide more and have a translator in each group." Luyu didn't mention that all the women would have a protector.

"I would let some of you stay in my lodge, but I want to let other families have what you are trading."

Waya remembered the story about what had happened that fall. Salali was not this woman, but she had let them take many stomped antelope when their Quapaw chief had asked not for himself but for others. He spoke up. "Because you arranged this for us, we will give you a set of what we give to the families we stay with and one more set without the shirts to divide between the other families that were willing to help us and one package of apple seeds for the whole village."

"That will make more peace in the village. Bring the woman and baby. I will take them to their lodge first." Noah got Ann and their son wrapped in a large buffalo fur and then carried the rest of their bedding.

EIGHTY FIVE

A night colder than all the previous nights settled over Joe and his horse. "Why did that stupid man do that? We could have had everything we need." Joe rubbed his numb fingers together. "When I get there, I'll kill everybody and use their lodges until the weather warms up. I'll take their heads to Little Rock in the spring." Sergeant grazed beside his owner, who was once again shivering inside a few blankets and a buffalo hide.

EIGHTY SIX

A few miles northwest, Noah, Ann, and all the people traveling with them sat in warm lodges eating hot food. After a warm, restful sleep and then a hot breakfast, they thanked their hospitable hosts, loaded up, and continued south. When the mid-day break was over, the family said goodbye to the men who had traveled hundreds of miles to warn them. Assuming they would be south of the man sent to bring the heads of Ann and Noah to Judge Daniel Hall in Little Rock, the men traveled towards the Fort Gibson Road.

Partway across the land, Robert pointed. "What's that?"

Ezra pulled out his spyglass. "It looks like a horse beside a tent. Get your rifles ready."

They already knew they were loaded. They double-checked their weapons anyway. Several yards from the tent, Ezra called out. "Hello in the camp." They heard nothing. He called out again, "Friends here. Can we join the camp?" Still, no reply. "Wait here."

The tethered horse paid him no attention as it

munched grass. Ezra stood beside the tent. "You all right in there?" No answer. "Friend here." He looked in. A man lay on his stomach. *It's strange for a man to be sleeping that soundly so long before sundown.* "Sir!" he called out loudly. "Friends here. Are you all right?" He pushed on the man's foot with his own. The man didn't move. "Sir, are you all right?" Ezra pushed harder on the boot then realized the answer to his question. The man in the tent was not all right. He was dead. "Come over."

George, a person who paid attention to things, stroked the horse's neck. "I know this horse."

They pulled the man out of the tent and rolled him over. "He's Joe Smith!" exclaimed Ezra.

"What happened?" wondered Justin.

Morris pushed around the blankets with his boot. "As cold as it's been, a person alone probably would have frozen."

Matt emptied the tent. "Joe, actually Raymond, is a stupid man. You can't change your identity and keep anything from your previous life. Like that horse and the initials, R.P. carved into this saddlebag."

Edwin held his hand above his eyes and peered into the distance. "We need to tell Noah he doesn't have to leave."

Morris nixed the plan. "This man may be done for, but Judge Hall is not. When he finds out this attempt failed, he'll try again. They need to be long gone before the next killer is sent after them."

Justin remembered Lola's fear. "We should at least

tell Lola the man who kidnapped and beat her is gone."

Matt tapped his vest pocket. "We have tickets for the steamboat to Little Rock. We don't have time to go to Harmony."

"You can send a letter," Ezra suggested.

Morris agreed, "Good idea. I'll write it, so she knows it's real."

They were all dressed in army uniforms. However, since Private Ezra Knuckles was the only real soldier, he gave the orders. "We need to inventory these supplies." He opened the saddlebag. "I wonder where he got all this frozen meat. You can take any that's left after we get to the fort."

Robert asked, "What about the horse?"

Ezra thought about it. *The army doesn't have any claim to it.* "The six of you can take it. We need to bury the man." Ezra started to remove Joe's boots. "He doesn't need these."

Edwin didn't want to create another of whatever had been in Lucy's parlor, looking like the shade of Roy Butterfield. "Stop! Leave all his clothes on him. Let him rest in peace, or go to Hell, but don't make a ghost."

All of them had heard Edwin's story. They believed something had been in Lucy's parlor and decided they didn't want to leave another of whatever that had been beside the road. They pushed Joe Smith into his grave in every stitch of clothes he had on his body.

At the edge of the vast prairie, with the money

from Joe's saddlebag, all his supplies, the tent, Sergeant, the horse's riding saddle, packsaddle, blanket, and bridle, they left Raymond Pence, also known as the assassin Joe Smith, in the place he had met his maker.

Acknowledgments
* Though I live not where I love
Cover
Hristo Argirov Kovatliev
Chapter Heading
Rennet Stowe, Native American petroglyphs, flicker, digital image, modified, taken July 16, 2010.

Follow Me Online
https://www.ChanceandChoicesAdventures.com

Did you like this story?
Please write a review!
https://www.amazon.com/Stone-Cold-Chance-Choices-Adventures/dp/194585815X/

Chance and Choices Adventures
by Lisa Gay
Pray for Justice
Choose Your Consequences
No Remorse
Means of Escape
Torn Hearts
Xida People
Stone Cold
Goodbye Hideout
Along the Way
The Western Sea
Sally's Sketchbook

Books by The Traveler
Provence: a land of lavender and olives